IN THE

An Elemental Assassin Book

JENNIFER ESTEP

Venom in the Veins

Print book ISBN: 978-0-9861885-6-5
eBook ISBN: 978-0-9861885-5-8

Cover Art © 2018 by Tony Mauro
Interior Formatting by Author E.M.S.

Fonts: *CCAltogether Ooky* and *CCAltogether Ooky Capitals* by Active Images, used under Standard License; *Times New Roman* by Monotype Typography, used under Desktop License; *Trajan Pro* by Carol Twombly/Adobe Systems Inc., used under EULA.

Published in the United States of America

THE ELEMENTAL ASSASSIN SERIES
FEATURING GIN BLANCO

Books
Spider's Bite
Web of Lies
Venom
Tangled Threads
Spider's Revenge
By a Thread
Widow's Web
Deadly Sting
Heart of Venom
The Spider
Poison Promise
Black Widow
Spider's Trap
Bitter Bite
Unraveled
Snared
Venom in the Veins

E-novellas
Thread of Death
Parlor Tricks (from the Carniepunk anthology)
Kiss of Venom
Unwanted
Nice Guys Bite

Venom in the Veins

AN ELEMENTAL ASSASSIN BOOK

JENNIFER ESTEP

To all the fans of the Elemental Assassin series who wanted more stories, this one is for you.

To my mom, my grandma, and Andre—for everything.

✭ 1 ✭

"Tonight is going to be *awesome*."

I looked over at Finnegan Lane, my foster brother. "Really? Why is that?"

He grinned. "Because we're eating at the most expensive restaurant in Ashland, and I'm not paying for it."

I rolled my eyes. "Only you would judge the quality of a meal by how much it impacts your wallet."

Finn's grin widened. "What can I say? I'm a total food connoisseur that way."

In keeping with his so-called connoisseur status, he grabbed a roll out of the bread basket in the center of a table, slathered it with honey butter, and shoved the whole thing into his mouth. Finn sighed with happiness as he chewed and swallowed. Then he grabbed another roll and slathered even more butter onto it than he had on the first one. He was probably wishing the butter was melted so he could dunk his entire roll into it.

Being a fine Southern gentleman, Finnegan Lane considered butter a dipping sauce, rather than a mere garnish, and he felt the exact same way about ranch dressing, honey mustard, sour cream, and even mayonnaise on occasion. And I agreed with his assessment one hundred percent, being a fine Southern lady myself.

We were dining at Underwood's, the city's most expensive and highfalutin restaurant, the sort of fancy, froufrou place that frowned on treating butter and other common condiments as dipping sauces. Their loss.

Pristine white linens covered our table, along with gleaming crystal wineglasses, polished silverware, and the sterling-silver bread basket that Finn was rapidly emptying. Everything from the linens to the glasses to the butter knives was either patterned, etched, or stamped with a small fork, the restaurant's rune and a symbol for all the good food it served.

Our table was situated in the back corner, right next to the floor-to-ceiling windows that offered sweeping views of the Ashland skyline. Down below, the lights burned bright and steady in the surrounding shops and restaurants, inviting people to step inside and get out of the cold, snowy evening. The combined glow of the lights stretched across the Aneirin River, making the water shimmer like a silver ribbon as it curled through the downtown area. In the distance, I could just make out the white gleam of the *Delta Queen* riverboat casino, anchored at its usual dock.

I admired the view for another moment before staring back out at the restaurant. It was just after six o'clock, and Underwood's was filling up for the evening. Some diners were already cutting into their grilled steaks and charred chickens, but most folks were clustered around the bar, squeezing in one last business meeting over drinks before either heading home for the day or getting their party started for the night.

Finn and I were here on business too, waiting for Stuart

Mosley, Finn's boss and the president of First Trust bank.

I checked my watch. "What did you say Mosley was doing? It's not like him to be even a few minutes late."

Finn finished chewing and swallowing his second roll. "He's overseeing a few final details for the charity auction tomorrow night. You know, the one with all of Mab's stuff." He paused. "At least, the stuff that wasn't destroyed during the Briartop robbery last summer."

I made a face. "Oh. That."

Mab Monroe had been the Fire elemental who'd run the Ashland underworld for years before I killed her for murdering my family. After her death, Mab's massive art collection had gone to the Briartop museum to be displayed, but a group of giant robbers had crashed the exhibit's opening-night gala, destroying much of the art. Of course, I'd stopped the robbers, but not before they'd killed and injured several innocent people during their attempted heist.

What was left of the art had been put into storage, and various legal wranglings had gone on for the last several months, until the Briartop board of directors had finally decided to auction off everything for charity. The money raised would go to the robbery victims and their families, as well as helping to pay for repairs and new security measures at Briartop. Something that was desperately needed, since the museum kept getting knocked over like it was a common convenience store rather than a prestigious art institution.

"Mosley's on the museum board, right?" I asked.

Finn reached for a third roll. "Yep. The charity auction was his idea, and he's the one who's overseeing everything, including cataloging and storing the art and arranging for the rest of Mab's things to be safeguarded until the auction."

All the talk of the Fire elemental made my hands start itching and burning, and I stared down at the marks branded into my palms, each one a small circle surrounded by eight thin rays. Spider runes, the symbol for patience.

Even now, all these years later, every time I looked at the scars, I still half expected the runes to be as red, raw, and blistered as the night Mab had burned them into my skin with her cruel magic. The marks might have faded to their current pale silver, but my memories were as hot and fresh as the rolls Finn kept gobbling down.

My hands reflexively curled into fists, hiding the scars, but I forced them open again. A silverstone ring stamped with my spider rune glinted on my right index finger, and I twisted it around several times. Then I raised my hand, grabbed the spider rune pendant hanging around my neck, and ran it back and forth on its silverstone chain. Focusing on the solid, tangible feel of the other runes—my spider runes *now*—helped me to ignore the lingering phantom pain in my palms and all the horrible memories that came along with it.

"I hope the boss man gets here soon," Finn said. "I'm *starving.*"

He reached for the fourth and final roll in the basket, but I smacked his hand away.

"Leave one for Mosley. This dinner was his idea, after all. And as you so eloquently pointed out, you're not the one paying for it. He is. The man should actually get some food for his money."

Finn's green eyes narrowed, and he rubbed his thumb over the hilt of his butter knife like he was thinking about brandishing it at me.

I grinned. "You really want to get into a knife fight with *me?* Go ahead, sugar. You just go right ahead."

His gaze dropped to the long sleeves of my black pantsuit jacket and the two knives that he knew I had tucked away there—silverstone blades that were a lot stronger and sharper than the pitiful little one he was holding.

He sighed and put down his knife. "You're no fun."

My grin widened. "So you keep telling me."

A waiter came over to our table. "Ms. Blanco?" he asked. "Ms. Gin Blanco?"

I tensed. "Yeah, that's me."

The waiter bowed and held out a bottle of champagne. "Compliments of the gentleman to your right."

I looked over at the table in question to find a man with dark brown hair, blue eyes, and tan skin staring at me. Liam Carter, one of Ashland's many criminal bosses, respectfully raised his own glass of champagne to me, as did the two giants sitting with him. I tipped my head, politely acknowledging his presence and his gift, even though I was sighing on the inside.

Even here, in a nice, quiet restaurant, on an evening when I just wanted to relax, I couldn't escape being myself, Gin Blanco, the Spider, Ashland's most feared assassin and the supposed queen of the underworld.

The waiter expertly popped open the champagne, poured glasses for Finn and me, and left our table. I didn't really want any champagne, but it would have been exceedingly rude to ignore the gift, so I lifted my glass to Carter in a silent toast of appreciation and respect and drank a generous portion of the cold, sparkling liquid. He returned the gesture, then started talking to his two associates again.

I took another, much smaller sip of champagne, just to be polite, but the fizzy bubbles created an intense ticklish sensation in my head. I set my glass aside and raised my hand to my face, so that no one would notice me twitching my nose from side to side to alleviate the pressure. Owen Grayson, my significant other, teasingly called it my sour carrots face, like I was a rabbit who had bitten into something she didn't like.

Champagne almost always made me feel this way, and a couple of mouthfuls was all it took to trigger a violent sneezing fit, something I couldn't afford in front of Carter or the other bosses dining here. They would think I was a lightweight who couldn't hold her liquor, which would totally ruin my badass reputation.

Finn sipped his own drink and sighed with appreciation. "What do you have going on with Liam Carter that would prompt him to send you champagne?"

I shrugged. "I'm helping him negotiate a peace treaty with one of his rivals. He's also been coming to the Pork Pit a lot lately. Supposedly, he just *loves* my cooking, but I think he's really there to flirt with Silvio. But so far, Silvio has been resisting his advances. Apparently, Silvio's coffee date over the holidays didn't go so well, and he's a little gun-shy now."

Silvio Sanchez was my personal assistant and even more reticent and cautious with his feelings than I was with mine.

Finn eyed Liam Carter's navy suit and gave an approving nod. "Well, he certainly has good taste in champagne and clothes. Those are two definite points in his favor. Silvio could do a lot worse."

I snorted. "Let me guess. You would judge a man's dating potential by how expensive his tie is."

"If I were interested in guys? Absolutely. Clothes don't make the man, but they certainly can help." Finn reached up and infinitesimally adjusted his own silver tie, which was already perfectly straight, before smoothing down his gray suit jacket. "Then again, there are those of us who are just naturally beautiful."

He winked at me, then patted his coif of walnut-brown hair. Once he was sure it was still perfectly in place, he grabbed his butter knife again and started turning it back and forth, like it was a mirror that he was trying to line up with his face.

"If you start admiring your reflection in that, I'm going to take that knife away and cut you with it," I warned. "Knives are for eating. Or stabbing people. Nothing else."

Finn grinned and opened his mouth to respond, but his gaze flicked past me, and he waved at someone across the room. "Ix-nay on the ill-kay talk. Mosley's here."

I looked in that direction. Stuart Mosley pointed us out to the hostess by the entrance and headed over to us, winding his way around the other tables and nodding at the folks he knew.

Mosley was a dwarf, around five feet tall, with wavy silver hair, hazel eyes, and a hooked nose that made him look like he'd been punched in the face more than once. Like Finn and most of the other men in the restaurant, Mosley was wearing an expensive suit, although his was a dark, anonymous navy instead of my brother's more stylish and flashy pewter-gray.

He reached our table. "My apologies," he rumbled. "I had to handle a few last-minute details for the charity auction tomorrow night."

I nodded back at him. "Finn told me as much. Please sit. We were just looking over the menu."

Mosley settled himself at the table, and the waiter came over and took our drink orders. Scotch for Finn and Mosley and a gin on the rocks with a twist of lime for me. Gin for

Gin, as was my tradition. A few minutes later, the waiter returned with our drinks and took our dinner orders.

Mosley downed his Scotch in one long gulp and signaled for another, which the waiter quickly deposited on the table. Then he sighed and shook his head. "I swear, this event is going to be the death of me. I just spent the last hour debating whether we should have white roses or orchids at the auction site tomorrow night. An hour! As if I care about the *flowers*."

I hid a smile. Stuart Mosley might be one of the most influential men in Ashland, but he'd never struck me as a society schmoozer. From the tidbits Finn had told me over the past few weeks, the other board members were driving the dwarf plumb crazy with their increasingly elaborate and expensive ideas for the auction.

"This was supposed to be a low-key event, but they've turned it into a damn *circus*," Mosley kept grumbling. "If it were up to me, I'd have the auction in the middle of a field somewhere. But no, we had to have food and flowers and music and a *venue*." He spat out the last word like it was a curse.

"And just when I think everything is finally *settled*, someone wants to change the flowers at the last minute. I thought that white orchids were perfectly fine, but no, apparently, I'm wrong, and white roses will be far more *elegant*." He spat out that word as well, as though he had heard it so often that he wanted to permanently remove it from everyone's vocabulary.

"Well, look on the bright side—it will all be over with tomorrow night," Finn said, trying to be cheerful.

Mosley massaged his temples. "Trust me, I am well aware of that, and I am counting down the hours."

After a few seconds, he sighed, dropped his hands, and

steepled his fingers together. "But the two of you didn't come here tonight to hear me complain. You came to talk about Fletcher."

Finn and I both sat up a little straighter. Fletcher Lane was Finn's late father and my assassin mentor, so he'd meant the world to both of us. He'd also been friends with Mosley, who seemed to know all about Fletcher's tendency to help people who couldn't help themselves, especially as the assassin the Tin Man.

"Anything you could tell us might be useful," I said. "Anything at all, no matter how small or insignificant it seems. Especially when it comes to Fletcher and the Circle."

The Circle was a secret society that was responsible for much of the crime and corruption in Ashland. Mab Monroe had been heavily involved in the group, and so had my mother, Eira Snow. Something that had come as quite a shock to me, since I'd thought that Mab had killed my mother and my older sister, Annabella, because of a long-standing family feud between the Monroes and the Snows. But the truth was that the other members of the Circle had ordered Mab to murder my family—something they were going to pay for dearly.

Ever since I'd found out about my mother's involvement with the shadowy group a couple of months ago, I had been tracking down every single scrap of information on the Circle and its members that I could find. My search had eventually led me to several safety-deposit boxes that Fletcher had entrusted to Mosley to watch over at First Trust bank.

"Well, I know that you've seen all those photos Fletcher left behind in his boxes," Mosley said. "And by now, I imagine that you've identified everyone in the pictures. The folks who are still alive, anyway."

Finn and I both nodded.

"But other than that, I don't think I can be of any help," he continued. "Fletcher never told me much about the Circle. Just that the people in those photos were some of the members, that they were all extremely dangerous, and that I should be careful if I ever had any dealings with them. All I ever really knew was that Fletcher was keeping an eye on those folks. I asked him about the Circle, of course, more than once. But for some reason, he just didn't want to talk about it. He always seemed…sad and a bit…regretful whenever I brought it up."

Frustration surged through me, but I wasn't surprised. Fletcher had loved keeping secrets, and he would have been especially careful with one of this magnitude. I doubted he would have told Mosley anything about the Circle if he hadn't had to rent those safety-deposit boxes from the dwarf in order to keep the information safe.

Still, I wondered at Mosley's assessment of Fletcher's emotions. Why would the old man be sad about the Circle? Much less regretful? This puzzle still had a lot of missing pieces, so I decided to focus on one of the few leads I had.

"What about Mason?" I asked. "Did Fletcher ever mention anyone by that name to you? Anyone at all?"

I held my breath, hoping, hoping, hoping that I might finally get an answer about who Mason really was, other than the mysterious leader of the Circle and the man who was ultimately responsible for my mother's murder.

Mosley drummed his fingers on the table, thinking. But after a moment, his fingers stilled, and he shook his head. "Not that I recall. There are a lot of Masons in this town. I've done business with several folks with that name, but no one sticks out or seems like they could be the person you're searching for. I'm sorry, Gin."

My breath escaped in a loud, disappointed rush, but I forced myself to smile at him. "It's not your fault. Sometimes I think Fletcher was far too sneaky for his own good."

"Ain't that the truth." Mosley smiled back at me, but sadness tinged his expression. "Ain't that the truth."

The waiter returned with our food, and we dug into our meals. My black-pepper-crusted steak was perfectly cooked and seasoned, while my potatoes au gratin were baked to a delicious, crunchy golden-brown and loaded with gruyere cheese, sour cream, chives, and bacon. It was hard to beat a gourmet steak-and-potatoes meal, especially at Underwood's, where it was always done right.

While we ate, Mosley regaled Finn and me with all sorts of tales about Fletcher, from the silly to the serious. The two of them had been far better friends than I'd realized, and they'd done everything together from fishing to facing off against various bad guys.

Fletcher's death would always be a cold sting in my heart, and I would always feel guilty that I hadn't been able to save him from being murdered, but it was nice to reminisce about the old man and how much we had all loved him. It eased the ache of his loss, at least for tonight.

We were eating dessert—caramel-apple cheesecake topped with vanilla-bean whipped cream, warm caramel sauce, and dried apple chips—when Mosley snapped his fingers.

"You know what? I do remember something else, an old book that Fletcher left with me. I think he was going to put it in a safety-deposit box." His cheerful expression faded away. "But he never got the chance to tell me what to do with it before he died."

Hope sparked in my chest.

Finn leaned forward, his eyes bright with excitement, as eager as I was. "Where's the book?" he asked. "Do you know what's inside it?"

Mosley shook his head. "Nope. I respected Fletcher's privacy, so I never looked through it. All I know is that the book is in my new house, buried in a box somewhere. I'm almost done putting stuff away from my move, and I'm down to my last few boxes. I should be able to find it in a day or two—"

His phone rang, cutting him off. Mosley picked up the device and grimaced as he stared at the number on the screen. "If this damn auction doesn't kill me first," he muttered.

"Problems?" I asked in a wry tone.

"Unless I miss my guess, there's been some new crisis with the *flowers*." His lips curled in disgust, and he shook his head. "I would ignore it, but she'll probably just keep right on calling until I answer. Please excuse me."

"Of course," I murmured. "Take your time."

He flashed me a grateful smile, then got to his feet and swiped his finger across the screen. "This is Mosley."

He started talking into his phone and slowly wandered away from our table.

And that's when I realized that we were being watched.

A woman sitting alone at the end of the bar swiveled around on her stool, her dark gaze sweeping back and forth across our table, watching Finn and me.

Finn didn't notice her, so I scraped up the last bite of my cheesecake, ate it, and set my fork and plate aside, acting perfectly normal. All the while, though, I stared at her out of the corner of my eye so she wouldn't realize that I'd spotted her.

She was quite lovely, with long, wavy brown hair, dark eyes, and bronze skin, and her little red cocktail dress hugged her body in all the right places. The bright scarlet made her stand out against the backdrop of dark suits, and more than one person eyed her with obvious interest.

A guy decided to try his luck, and he swaggered over and started chatting her up. But the woman ignored his attempt at suave charm and leaned to the side. Her gaze focused on Finn and me for another moment, then skittered away to someone else.

Stuart Mosley.

Even though that guy was standing right in front of her, still talking, the woman was squarely focused on the dwarf, who was now pacing back and forth along the wall, growling into his phone.

My eyes narrowed. Why was she interested in Mosley?

My spider rune scars started itching and burning again, almost as if they were trying to warn me about this potential new threat. Or perhaps that was just my own always-simmering paranoia immediately boiling up to red-alert levels.

The guy asked her something, probably offering to buy her a drink, but the woman shook her head, grabbed her red clutch off the bar, got to her feet, and walked away from him. She headed toward the dining area and started skirting around the tables, her gaze still fixed on Mosley.

I elbowed Finn in the side, making him drop his last bite of cheesecake onto his gray silk tie. He gasped in horror, tossed his fork aside, and dabbed his napkin at his tie. He managed to wipe off the cheesecake, but a big blotchy spot remained behind from the caramel sauce.

"This tie is a Fiona Fine original that Bria gave me for Christmas," he muttered, shooting me a dirty look. "It is my very favorite tie, and now it has a *stain* on it, a stain that will probably *never* come out."

"Don't worry. I'll buy you a new one." I discreetly tilted my head in the woman's direction. "Focus, Finn, focus. You ever seen her before?"

He finally quit glaring at me and shifted his attention to the other woman. After a moment, he perked right back up again. "No, and that's a shame. Because *yowza!* Remember what I said about clothes helping to make a man? Well, that dress is doing the same thing for her."

"She's not a bank client?"

He studied her a little more closely, then shook his head. "Nope. I've never seen her at the bank."

The woman left the maze of tables behind and made a beeline straight for Mosley. She also popped open her red clutch and reached for something inside.

I dropped my hand below the tabletop and palmed a knife. I started to surge to my feet to cut her off from Mosley, but Finn touched my arm, stopping me.

"Wait, Gin," he murmured. "Wait. Relax. She's not going to do anything to him in the middle of the restaurant. Besides, Mosley can take care of himself. Let it play out."

I stayed seated, although my fingers tightened around my knife. The feel of the spider rune stamped into the hilt pressing against the larger, matching scar in my palm steadied me and helped me rein in some of my worry.

Finn was right. Whoever she was, the woman wasn't going to hurt Mosley in front of all these witnesses. Not even the most brazen assassin would do something that stupid.

Mosley finished his call, and the woman sidled up to

him. She favored him with a wide, dazzling smile, showing off the fangs in her mouth that marked her as a vampire, and then leaned forward, giving him an up-close and personal look at her impressive cleavage. I tensed when she pulled her hand out of her purse, still half expecting her to come up with a weapon...but she only drew out a gold tube of lipstick.

The woman uncapped the tube and ran the red lipstick over her pouty mouth, giving Mosley her best come-hither look and letting him know that she was available for whatever he wanted.

"See?" Finn leaned back in his chair. "She's just trying to pick him up. She probably wants someone to pay for her drinks and dinner. Quit being so paranoid, Gin."

He might be right, but if that was the case, then why hadn't she let the other guy at the bar do that? That man had been right in front of her and more than eager to buy what she was selling, but she'd ignored him in favor of walking all the way across the restaurant to try her luck with Mosley instead.

I shook my head. "I still don't like it."

"Well, you're in luck, because neither does Mosley," Finn replied.

Sure enough, the dwarf politely shook his head, turning down whatever the woman had proposed. He started to walk around her, but she moved in front of him, blocking his path. She tried again, but Mosley shook his head, the same as before. This time, he did move around her, heading toward Finn and me.

Mosley had his back to the woman, so he didn't see her dark eyes narrow, her red lips pinch together, or her manicured fingers curl around her lipstick tube like she wanted to bean him in the back of the head with it.

But I did.

I had never seen her before, but in that moment, I realized something important: she wasn't the kind of woman who took no for an answer. Whatever she wanted from Mosley, she was determined to get it.

Finn had been wrong before. I wasn't paranoid, and tonight wasn't going to be awesome.

It was going to be dangerous.

osley returned to our table, sat down, and tossed his phone aside. He let out a long, loud sigh and massaged his temples again.

"The death of me," he muttered. "These people are *literally* going to be the death of me."

He downed what was left of his Scotch, then grabbed his fork to eat the rest of his cheesecake. I discreetly tucked my knife back up my sleeve so that he wouldn't see it.

"Who was that woman you were talking to?" Finn asked in a casual voice, fishing for information. "Someone involved in the auction coming over to say hi?"

Mosley shook his head. "Nope. I've never seen her before. She said her name was Vera. She wanted to buy me a drink, but I told her that I was happy with my current companions."

Finn opened his mouth, probably to ask more questions about the alluring Vera, but I elbowed him in the side again. He shot me another dirty look, but he kept quiet. There was no use worrying Mosley with my suspicions, especially since nothing had happened.

Yet.

I pulled my own phone out of my purse, pretending that I was checking my messages, while I discreetly watched Vera.

She stared at Mosley for a few more seconds, still silently fuming, then whipped around on her red stilettos and stalked back over to the bar. She signaled the bartender and handed over her credit card. Five minutes later, she strutted out of the restaurant without a backward glance.

I frowned. I'd expected her to put up much more of a fight. Maybe send a drink to Mosley or even come over to our table and try to flirt with him again. Not just walk away. A cold finger of unease crept down my spine, but once again, I kept my suspicions to myself.

Mosley finished his dessert and pushed his plate away just as his phone beeped with a new text. He stared at the screen and sighed for the third time. "I hate to cut this short, but duty calls. As do floral arrangements."

"Of course," I said. "Good luck with the auction."

He harrumphed. "At this point, I just want the whole bloody event to be *finished*. I will be quite happy if I never have to debate the costs, merits, pollen counts, and elegance factors of orchids, roses, or any other flowers ever again."

Mosley signaled for the check, and the waiter handed him a black leather folder. The dwarf started to reach for his wallet, but his phone beeped again, and he passed the folder over to Finn.

"Here, Finn. Take care of this, will you? I've got to answer these crazy people."

"But—"

He started to protest, but Mosley had already picked up his phone, pushed his chair back, and walked away from the table. Finn stared at the folder in his hand, then over at his boss, but the dwarf was focused on his call and completely ignored him.

I snickered at my brother's forlorn expression. "What were you saying about how awesome it was going to be not paying for dinner?"

Finn stabbed the folder at me. "Don't push your luck, sister. Dad taught me how to kill people too, remember? I can still murder you with my dessert fork."

I just snickered again.

Ten minutes and several hundred dollars on Finn's credit card later, we left Underwood's, rode the elevator down to the ground floor, and stepped out onto the sidewalk. It was after eight o'clock now, and so frigid that the snow flurries had hardened into pellets of ice that stung my cheeks with their sharp, cold intensity.

Mosley had finished his call and followed us outside. Now he tilted his face into the wind and drew in a deep, appreciative breath. "Ahhh. There's nothing quite like a brisk walk to aid in the digestion. Isn't that right, Finn?"

He clapped Finn on the shoulder, but my brother pulled his gray cashmere scarf even higher up on his neck.

"Yeah. Brisk. Right." Finn's response was far less enthusiastic, although his sour mood had more to do with paying for dinner than the chilly weather.

"Did you check on the Barnes account before you left the office?" Mosley asked. "I meant to mention it earlier, but I got distracted with all the floral crises."

Finn nodded. "Of course. I even called to let him know that we had discovered the accounting error…"

While the two of them talked a final bit of bank business,

I tucked my purse under my arm and zipped up my black fleece jacket. Not because I was cold like Finn but because the motions let me discreetly study my surroundings.

Expensive sedans and SUVs lined both sides of the street on this block and the two beyond, a clear sign of the crowd inside Underwood's, but the other businesses had already closed for the night. The rest of the area was deserted, except for the lone valet shivering in his red parka and sitting on his stool behind the wooden podium at the restaurant entrance. No cars cruised by, and the only sounds were the faint whistle of the winter wind and the resulting spatter of ice against the sidewalk.

The peace and quiet should have reassured me, but it didn't. Even though I didn't spot anyone lurking around, I still felt like we were being watched again.

Finn and Mosley finished their conversation, oblivious to my subtle surveillance and increasing concern. The valet started to get up off his stool, but Mosley waved him off.

"Don't bother," he said. "My car's only two blocks down. It won't kill me to walk that far."

He tipped the valet anyway, then turned back to Finn and me. "I'll start looking for that old book of Fletcher's first thing in the morning. As soon as I find it, I'll give you a call. It might take me a few days, though. At least until the auction is over and the items have been shipped out to the buyers."

I would have happily gone over to Mosley's house right this second and torn his things apart searching for the book, but I made myself nod politely instead. The book had been buried in a box somewhere for years. It would keep for a few more days. "Thank you for that and for a lovely dinner—"

Finn snorted, reminding me that he had paid for dinner, but I ignored him.

"And thank you especially for all the stories about Fletcher," I finished. "It was nice to talk about him, to remember him."

Mosley smiled back at me. "Yes, yes, it was nice."

On an impulse, I stepped forward and hugged him. Mosley seemed surprised by my gesture, but after a moment, he hugged me back. Despite the fact that he was more than three hundred years old, he was still quite strong, even for a dwarf, and he easily squeezed the air out of my lungs.

Just when I thought he was going to crack my ribs, Mosley finally let me go. I discreetly sucked down breath after breath, while he clapped Finn on the shoulder again, making my brother stagger back.

"Well, then," the dwarf rumbled, still smiling. "I'll let you two get on with your usual shenanigans. Good night."

Finn regained his balance and murmured his good night, and I managed to wheeze out mine as well. Mosley waved at us, then walked away. My brother pulled his keys out of his coat pocket, and the two of us crossed the street to his silver Aston Martin.

Finn unlocked the car, opened the driver's-side door, and slid inside the vehicle. I had started to do the same on the passenger's side when I spotted a faint movement off in the distance.

My head snapped up, and I looked around again. I didn't see anyone except Mosley, still heading toward his car, and the only other thing stirring in the night was a cloud of snow drifting out of a dark doorway that the dwarf had just walked past.

My eyes narrowed. No, not snow—smoke.

A small red glow burned in the inky shadows, and a giant wearing a black leather jacket and a black knit toboggan stepped out of the doorway and onto the sidewalk. The giant sucked in a little more of his cigarette, then flicked it away. The butt hit a nearby car and bounced off, shooting off a few hot sparks that the cold wind quickly snuffed out.

The valet was sitting on his stool, with his head down, texting on his phone, so he didn't notice the offending cigarette. Even if he had, I doubted the valet would have called out and confronted the seven-foot-tall giant. That was a good way to wind up with some broken bones.

The giant blew the last of the cigarette smoke out of his nostrils like a dragon from some old Bellonan fairy tale, then stuffed his hands into his jacket pockets and ambled along the sidewalk, going in the same direction as Mosley.

Maybe it was the hard, flat expression on the giant's face, his anonymous black clothes, or the way he glanced up and down the street, making sure that the area was still deserted, but somehow I didn't think that littering was going to be the only crime he committed tonight.

Mosley was growling into his phone again, so he didn't notice the other man. The dwarf stopped at the corner long enough to glance around and make sure no cars were coming down the street, then crossed over to the next block. The giant did the same, then followed him. Several of the streetlights were busted out on that block and the one beyond, bathing the entire area in shadows.

It was the perfect spot for a mugging—or worse.

"Um, Gin? Are you getting in the car?" Finn leaned over the console and looked up at me. "Or are you just going to stand there with the door open and let the snow swirl around inside and ruin my leather seats?"

I tossed my purse down onto the passenger's seat, then unzipped my jacket, shrugged out of it, and put it in the car as well. "Drive around and pick me up at the far end of the street."

He frowned. "What? Why?"

"I'm going to take a walk. Make sure Mosley gets to his car okay."

"Is this about that Vera woman again?" Finn sighed. "I told you that you were just being paranoid—"

I shut the car door, cutting him off. Maybe he was right. Maybe I was being paranoid. After all, Vera didn't seem to be hanging around on the street anywhere, but I'd learned a long time ago that it was better to be paranoid than not, especially in this town.

The loud *smack* of the car door slamming shut echoed down the street, causing the giant to stop and look over his shoulder. I ducked down and scooted forward behind the car parked in front of Finn's Aston Martin so the giant wouldn't see me.

Finn peered at me through the windshield, an incredulous expression on his face. He clearly thought I had lost my mind. I made a shooing motion with my hand. He rolled his eyes, but he cranked the engine, steered his car away from the curb, and zoomed down the street.

Finn took the first right at the end of the block, and the rumble of his car quickly faded away. The giant stayed where he was on the sidewalk, staring in that direction. But Finn must have made another turn and disappeared from his line of sight, because after a moment, the giant relaxed and headed after Mosley again.

I followed him.

I crept along the sidewalk on the opposite side of the street, moving parallel to the giant. I stayed low so that he wouldn't spot my head over the tops of the cars and tracked him through the windshields and the gaps between vehicles. I also palmed one of my silverstone knives. I didn't know for sure that the giant was up to no good, but I was going to be prepared in case he was.

The giant looked around again, as if double-checking to make sure no one else was around, then quickened his pace, heading straight toward Mosley, who was still talking on his phone. Mosley stopped at another corner, glanced around for traffic, crossed the street, and stepped onto the next block.

The giant also stopped at the corner to check for traffic. While his head was turned in the opposite direction, I hurried around one of the cars and sprinted across the pavement so that I was now on the same side of the street as the two men. But instead of stepping out onto the sidewalk behind Mosley and the giant, I stayed in the street, still creeping from car to car and keeping the vehicles between us, so that the giant wouldn't look back and spot me on the sidewalk behind him.

Mosley walked about halfway down the block and stopped at his car, a very nice black Audi. He was still talking on his phone, and he paced back and forth on the sidewalk, clearly wanting to end his call before he got into his vehicle.

"The auction is tomorrow night...too late to change anything else...doesn't matter about the flowers anyway..." Snippets of his conversation echoed down the street, although the gusts of wind and ice quickly drowned out his words and blew them away.

Since Mosley had stopped, the giant slowed his pace as well, pausing to light another cigarette, as though he was just out for a late-night smoke and stroll. All the while, though, he inched closer and closer to Mosley.

The dwarf finally noticed the giant, and he nodded,

politely acknowledging the other man's presence. The giant nodded back, keeping up a friendly façade as he ambled along, still smoking. But the giant didn't move past Mosley, and he didn't turn around and wander back in the opposite direction. That alone told me that he was up to no good. Although if he was going to mug Mosley, he should go ahead and do it now, while the dwarf was distracted by his call.

So what was the giant waiting for? And what did he want with Mosley? I didn't know, but I was going to find out. I tightened my grip on my knife. One way or another.

While Mosley talked and the giant smoked, I moved from car to car, creeping closer and closer to them. Neither one of them spotted me, so I left the street, skirted around the back of an SUV, and crouched down next to the sidewalk. Then I peered around the side of the vehicle and drew in a breath, getting ready to leap out and take the giant by surprise from behind.

"We've talked this thing to *death*," Mosley growled. "There's nothing else left to say. I'll see you tomorrow night. Good night." He tapped the screen, ending the call. "And good riddance."

Mosley shoved his phone into his pants pocket and drew out his car keys, grumbling to himself, although I couldn't hear what he was saying. He shook his head, as if trying to clear away his frustration, then lifted his key fob to unlock his car—

The passenger's-side door opened.

Mosley stopped cold, shocked by the unexpected movement, which gave the giant plenty of time to flick his cigarette away and come up behind him.

A woman climbed out of Mosley's car, shut the door, and stepped onto the sidewalk in front of him. Long, wavy brown hair, dark eyes, red stilettos, and a slinky red dress now covered by a black coat.

Vera might have left the restaurant after Mosley had turned her down, but she hadn't given up on him—not at all.

Instead, she had come out here and broken into his car to lie in wait for him. And this time, she'd brought along some giant backup to make sure that she got exactly what she wanted from the dwarf.

✲ 3 ✲

Mosley quickly shook off his shock. His eyes narrowed, and he backed up and angled himself to the side so that he could see Vera and the giant at the same time.

"Who are you?" he asked. "And what are you doing in my car?"

Vera stepped forward. "You really should have let me pick you up in the restaurant. The evening would have been a whole lot more pleasant for you. For a little while, anyway." She shook her head. "But you just had to be difficult, so now we're going to have to do things the hard way. Isn't that right, Eddie?"

The giant cracked his knuckles. "Yep."

Mosley glanced at Eddie for a second, before focusing on Vera again. "What do you want? My phone? Wallet? Car?"

She let out a low, mocking laugh. "Please. If I'd wanted your phone or wallet, I would have pickpocketed them at the restaurant. And, as you can see, I didn't need your keys to get into your car. Although it is a very nice car, and it'll be a sweet little bonus for us for a job well done. Won't it, hon?"

Eddie cracked his knuckles again. "Don't you know it."

Mosley's mouth hardened into a tight, thin line, and he slid his keys back into his pocket. He flexed his fingers a few times, even as his gaze moved from Vera to Eddie and back again, as if he was warming up and debating which one of them to tackle first. I admired his brawler instincts, but he didn't have to worry about his attackers.

Because the Spider was here, and I was more than happy to take care of such things for my friends.

Vera must have realized that Mosley wasn't going to go quietly, because she grabbed something from her red clutch, then tossed her purse down onto the sidewalk. She flicked her wrist, snapping open a black metal baton, like the kind a cop might use to subdue a suspect.

"Now, why don't you be a dear and get in the car?" she asked. "The three of us are going for a ride."

Mosley stared at the baton in her hand. He didn't make a move toward her, but his body tensed, and his hands clenched into fists, as if he was still thinking about resisting.

"Do you really think this is the first time I've been threatened by a couple of punks?" he said.

Vera twirled her baton around in her hand with expert ease. "Nope. But it's going to be the last time unless you do exactly what I say. Now, be a good boy, and hand your keys over to Eddie. Right now. Before I crack open your skull and let you bleed out all over the sidewalk."

Mosley kept staring at her, still debating his options.

Eddie must have grown tired of waiting, because he stepped up, grabbed Mosley's arm, and tried to force him forward, but the dwarf dug his heels into the sidewalk and stayed put. Eddie's dark eyes narrowed, and he tightened his grip and tried to shove Mosley forward again. But Mosley was strong, just like the giant was, and he held firm in his stance, determined not to be moved.

Vera kept twirling her baton around, watching the two men seesaw from side to side, pushing and pulling against each other. All three of them held their positions, each one debating who would lash out first and break the tense stalemate.

I was waiting for something too, or, rather, someone— Finn, who should have been here by now.

Impatience filled me. How long did it take to drive around a couple of blocks—

A pair of headlights popped on at the far end of the block, and Mosley, Eddie, and Vera all winced and threw their hands up against the bright, harsh, unexpected glare.

Finn zoomed his car in their direction, wrenching the wheel and hitting the brakes so that the vehicle stopped sideways in the middle of the street. Mosley, Eddie, and Vera all instinctively backed away from the car, even though they were still standing safely on the sidewalk.

And that was my cue.

I surged to my feet, hurried around the side of the SUV that I was hiding behind, and sprinted forward, heading straight for the giant, since he was the closest.

Eddie must have heard the slap of my boots against the pavement, and he spotted me running toward him. He cursed and shoved Mosley away. The move took the dwarf by surprise, and he lost his balance, staggered forward, and smacked face-first into the brick wall of the nearest storefront. Mosley let out a low groan and put a hand up against the wall for support, clearly dazed.

Eddie turned toward me and fumbled under his coat, drawing a gun out of the waistband of his jeans. I ran up to him and slashed down and out with my knife. Eddie jerked his arm back at the last second, so that my blade slammed into his gun instead of his wrist, but the blow was still hard enough to make the weapon slip through his fingers and clatter to the pavement.

I stepped forward and kicked the weapon away, sending it skittering down the sidewalk behind me, well out of Eddie's reach. I whirled back around to the giant, but he recovered faster than I expected. Before I could lift my knife and attack him again, Eddie darted forward, reached out, and locked his hand around my throat, trying to choke me to death.

"You think you can cut me up? No fucking way!" he yelled.

I whipped up my knife to stab him in the chest, but once again, he was faster, and he bent down, grabbed hold of my leg, and hoisted me up and off my feet all in one smooth motion. Eddie lifted my entire body high over his head, supporting me with both hands, like I was a gym weight that he was easily bench-pressing. Then the giant growled and stepped forward, heading toward the curb.

Uh-oh. This was going to *hurt*.

I barely had time to grab hold of my Stone magic and harden my skin into an impenetrable shell before he bellowed out an angry roar and slammed me down onto the hood of Mosley's car.

SMACK!

My hips and legs crashed into the hood, severely denting it, while my head and elbows snapped back against the windshield, cracking the glass in three separate places.

Despite the protective shell of my Stone magic, it was still a brutal, bone-bruising blow, and hot, sharp needles of pain exploded in my body, stabbing into my head, my spine, and all the way down my arms and legs. My brain sloshed around like warm gelatin inside my skull, and my knife slipped from my twitching fingers and clattered to the street. I felt like a cartoon character who had been shoved out of an airplane without a parachute, had slammed into the ground at warp speed, and then had an anvil dropped on her for good measure.

SPLAT!

"How do you like that?" Eddie growled. "Not so tough now, are you?"

He lunged forward to grab me again, but I shook off my daze, brought my foot up, and kicked him in the face. His nose made a loud, satisfying *crunch* under my boot, and he yelped and staggered away.

"Probably about as much as you liked that." My words slurred together, telling me that I probably had a concussion.

Finn threw his car into gear, opened the door, and surged to his feet, waving at me. "Gin! Move! Now!"

Out of the corner of my eye, I saw Vera running toward me, her metal baton held high overhead. So I threw myself to the left, rolling off the opposite side of the car. I hit the pavement, which was even harder than the car hood, and more hot needles of pain stabbed through my body. That second hard landing also made my brain slosh around again. I lost my grip on my Stone magic, and my skin reverted back to its normal, vulnerable texture. I let out a low groan that was quickly drowned out by another, louder sound.

Crack!

Vera slammed her metal baton into the windshield right where my head had been, shattering and spraying glass everywhere. The sharp shards rained down on me, slicing into my head and hands and making me hiss with even more pain, but it was better than the alternative. If not for Finn's warning, Vera would have split my skull open like a ripe melon.

Finn cursed and dove back into his own car, probably reaching for the gun he kept in the glove box. Eddie must have realized what he was doing, because the giant ran straight at Finn, his hands held out in front of him like he was going to slam the car door shut and crush my brother between it and the metal frame.

Vera snapped up her baton again and came around the car after me, but I reached down, grabbed a handful of broken glass off the street, surged to my feet, and tossed it straight into her face. She screamed in surprise and turned to the side, throwing her arm up to shield her face from the flying shards.

I scooped up my knife off the ground and headed after Eddie, determined to cut him off before he got to Finn. I could have thrown my knife at the giant, but he was so big and strong that a blade in his back probably wouldn't slow him down, much less kill him outright. So I aimed lower. This time, I reached for my Ice magic and sent a spray of daggers shooting out at the giant's legs. A couple of Ice daggers punched into his left calf, making him yelp. His leg buckled, and he pitched forward, severely off-balance.

Finn's head snapped up at the giant's yelp, and he finally realized the danger. He quit fumbling for his gun and leaped out of the way just as Eddie barreled into the car door, slamming it shut. The giant's head banged into the driver's-side mirror, hard enough to crack the glass. His legs flew out from under him, and he dropped to the ground.

CRACK!

To add injury to injury, Eddie's skull snapped back against the asphalt with a loud, sickening impact, and blood immediately started pooling under his head. The giant didn't so much as twitch after that, and I knew he was dead from the massive head trauma he had just suffered.

Finn whirled around and flashed me a thumbs-up, telling me he was okay. I nodded back at him—

"Enough!" Vera hissed. "That's enough!"

Eddie might be dead, but she was not.

I whirled around, expecting to see Vera raising her baton to try to bash me again, but she had another, better plan in mind. She sprinted back across the sidewalk to where Mosley was still slumped against the storefront wall. She grabbed the dwarf, spun him around, and laid her baton across his throat, using him as a human shield.

Finn and I raced forward, leaving the street and hurrying back up onto the sidewalk.

"Stop! Stay back!" Vera hissed again. "Or I'll crush his windpipe!"

She dug her baton into Mosley's throat. He winced at the hard length of metal digging into his skin, but he remained calm and still, even as he blinked away the rest of his daze.

"Who are you?" I said. "Who sent you? What do you want with Mosley?"

Vera opened her mouth to say something, then thought better of it and pressed her red lips together. Her dark gaze flicked up and down the street, as if she was afraid that someone else was here and watching her.

"Nobody sent me," she finally snarled. "This is *my* territory. Mine and Eddie's. All I wanted was to pick up a rich sugar daddy for the night. Have some drinks, a nice dinner, and then roll the guy for everything he had on him.

But you two just had to come along and play hero, didn't you? You ruined our plan. You ruined everything!"

She stared at Eddie lying in the street. So much blood had pooled under his cracked skull that it almost looked like his head was resting on a glossy scarlet pillow. Vera sucked in a ragged breath, and tears gleamed in her eyes. But she wasn't ready to give up yet, and she backed up a couple of steps, dragging Mosley along with her. She wet her lips, her gaze darting around again, this time looking for a way out. But there wasn't one, and we all knew it. Still, I tried to reason with her.

"It's not too late," I said. "Just let him go, and tell us who you're working for."

She wet her lips again, and for a moment, I thought she was actually considering it. Then her gaze dropped to Eddie's body again. Rage and grief burned in her dark eyes, and I knew this could only end one way now.

Finn realized it too, and he shifted his stance, getting ready to charge Vera right along with me. We had to get to her before she made good on her threat and crushed Mosley's windpipe with that baton.

Mosley saw the shift in Finn and me, and his hands curled into fists. I wondered how many times he'd been in a similar situation. Probably quite a few, given the stories he'd told over dinner about his adventures with Fletcher. Either way, I knew I could count on him to strike when the moment was right.

Finn grinned, although there was a hard, dangerous edge to his expression. He didn't like people threatening our friends any more than I did. "You know, boss, while we're all just standing around, there's something that I've been meaning to ask you." He paused a moment for dramatic effect, even as his grin sharpened. "How about a raise?

What do you say? Think you could give me a little pay bump? You know, for going above and beyond the call of duty?"

Vera's pretty features twisted into a wild, angry expression, and she dug the baton a little deeper into Mosley's neck, grinding the metal into his skin like it was a saw. "What are you talking about? You need to back off. Now!"

"I don't know," Mosley replied in a hoarse but steady voice, never showing the slightest sign of fear, even as he played along with Finn. "Given everything that's happened at the bank over the past few months, a raise might be out of the question right now."

"Really?" Finn countered. "Are you sure you don't want to rethink your position? Especially given what a valuable employee I am?"

"What are you two babbling about? Shut up!" Vera snapped. "Shut up and step back! Now! Right now—"

She was so angry and distracted by their inane banter that she lowered the baton a fraction of an inch from Mosley's throat, but that was all the opening he needed. With one hand, he grabbed the end of the baton, yanking it out of Vera's grip. With the other hand, he latched onto her wrist, wrenching her arm down and back at an awkward angle.

Crack!

The sound of Vera's arm breaking seemed as loud as a gunshot in the cold, quiet night. She screamed, but she still wasn't ready to give up, and she lashed out with her good arm, swiping her nails at Mosley's face like she wanted to scratch his eyes out. Mosley stepped back, avoiding her attack, then whirled right back around and slammed the metal baton into her head.

I didn't know if he meant to do it, if his survival instinct took over, or if he just got lucky, but he hit her square on the temple, and given his dwarven strength, that one blow was more than enough to crack open her skull. Vera's scream abruptly cut off, and blood spurted everywhere, just like it had with Eddie. Her eyes rolled up in the back of her head, and she dropped to the ground, dead before she even hit the sidewalk.

Finn and I both rushed over to Mosley, who loomed over Vera, the baton still clutched in his hand.

"Boss!" Finn said. "Are you all right?"

Mosley reached up and slowly wiped something off his face. He stared down blankly at the wet, red smears—Vera's blood—glistening on his fingertips. He blinked, and a shudder rippled through his body. Instinct and luck, then, instead of actual intent.

Another horrified shudder rippled through the dwarf's body, this one so violent that it jarred the baton out of his hand. The metal rod *clanged* to the sidewalk right beside Vera, letting out a series of sharp, ringing notes before it finally rolled to a stop.

"Boss?" Finn asked again, in a much gentler voice.

Mosley kept staring at the blood on his fingertips. A third shudder rippled through his body, and he dropped his hand to his side and focused on Vera lying at his feet.

"Better than her," he rasped in a low voice. "Better than her."

❊ 4 ❊

espite the screech of Finn stopping his car and the yells and screams of the fight, no sirens sounded in the distance.

Of course, we were a couple of blocks away from Underwood's, but if the valet stationed outside the restaurant had heard the commotion echoing down the street, he hadn't called the cops. No surprise there. Most folks in Ashland knew that summoning the po-po was a crapshoot at best. You might get an honest officer who was truly dedicated to protecting and serving...or you might get a corrupt official who could barely be bothered to do his job. At least, not without a substantial bribe to properly motivate him.

If it had just been Finn and me, I would have loaded Vera and Eddie into the trunk of Finn's car, driven away, and called Sophia Deveraux to help us dispose of the bodies. But Mosley had been the target, and he was a public figure with a reputation and a business to think about. If Vera and Eddie had been working for someone, I didn't want that person to try to blackmail Mosley about their deaths later on or cook up some other scheme against him. That meant covering our asses and getting the cops involved—at least, the cops I knew I could trust.

Besides, I wanted to know every little thing about Vera and Eddie, and police databases were always a good place to start drilling down into folks. I wanted to know if this was a simple mugging, like Vera claimed, or if someone was targeting Mosley for a more sinister reason.

Finn looked at me, as if he was thinking the same things. "Time to call Bria?"

"Yep."

Luckily for me, Detective Bria Coolidge, my baby sister, was one of the good cops. Finn pulled out his phone and dialed her, since she was also his lady love. He talked to her in a low voice for a few moments before putting his phone away and giving me a thumbs-up, telling me that Bria was on her way. Then Finn got into his car, cranked the engine, and drove it into a nearby alley so he wouldn't have to explain why Eddie's blood was smeared all over the driver's-side mirror and why the vehicle was sitting in the middle of a double homicide.

Mosley kept staring down at Vera with a dull, blank expression. The adrenaline of the fight was wearing off, and the sickening shock of killing her was quickly setting in, even though it had been self-defense.

I grabbed his arm and gently steered him away from her body. We stopped at the corner, and I scanned this block and the one up ahead, wondering if someone else might be lurking in a shadowy doorway, watching us—

An engine rumbled to life, and a car barreled out of an alley across the street from us. At first, I thought it was Finn, driving back out here for some reason. Then I realized that this car was black, not silver like his. The car's headlights hit Mosley and me, illuminating us like we were a couple of deer about to get mowed down on some dark country road. For a second, I thought that was exactly what was going to happen, since the car was picking up speed and heading straight at us.

I reached for my Stone magic and stepped forward, ready to tackle Mosley and shove him out of the way—

At the last second, the car swung away from us and made a sharp left turn onto the main street, causing its tires to squeal in protest. I squinted, trying to get my night vision back after the headlights' searing glare, but the windows were tinted, so I couldn't see who was inside. The driver gunned the engine, and the car zipped away. A few seconds later, the driver made another sharp left, and the vehicle vanished from sight.

I bit back a curse. I hadn't even gotten a look at the license plate, so I had no way of tracking down the vehicle. Whoever was inside was long gone, so I focused on Mosley.

"Are you okay?" I asked.

But he didn't seem to have noticed the suspicious car or how close it had come to running us over. Instead, he was staring at Vera's body again, his face twisted into a sad, miserable expression.

After a moment, Mosley shook his head, as if to clear away his dark thoughts, and looked at me. "Yes. I'm fine, thanks to you and Finn."

I hesitated, not wanting to cause him any more pain, but if this hadn't been a random attack—and that speeding car definitely made me think it wasn't random—then we needed to figure out who might have been behind it. "I know this has been traumatic…"

"But you want to know if this was a simple mugging or

something else. And if it was something else, then who might have sicced those two on me and why." Mosley finished my thoughts, then gave me a grim smile. "Like I told Vera, this isn't the first time someone's threatened me. I imagine it won't be the last."

"I wouldn't ask you this right now if I didn't think it was important."

"I know," he said. "And I shouldn't be so upset. You heard about my adventures with Fletcher over dinner, so you know Vera isn't the first person I've killed in self-defense. But being in this area, seeing her lying on the sidewalk, realizing how young she is...it reminds me of Joanna. And it's a damn waste of a life, just like Joanna's was."

Joanna, Mosley's beloved great-granddaughter, had been abducted and murdered by the Dollmaker serial killer about two years ago. She'd gone out to dinner with friends at Underwood's one night and had never come back home.

Mosley fell silent, lost in his own dark thoughts again, and I remained quiet, giving him the time he needed to start processing this. After a minute, he roused himself out of his memories and looked at me again.

"I've never seen this woman or that giant before tonight," he said. "They aren't bank clients."

"Then who are they? And why did they target you?"

He shrugged. "Given what Vera said to me in the restaurant, I thought she was looking for someone to pick up her tab. Or that she was a professional working girl trying to turn dinner into a longer, more lucrative date. Maybe she thought I looked like an old, rich, easy mark."

"Why would she think that?"

He tapped his hooked nose. "I'm not the most attractive man around, Gin. Tonight wasn't the first time I've been propositioned like that. Although I pissed her off when I turned her down. I was annoyed by all the phone calls about the auction, and I wasn't as nice about it as I could have been." He shrugged. "Maybe that's why she was waiting out here. Maybe I made her so angry that she wanted to get something out of me, one way or another."

"Maybe."

Mosley frowned at the doubtful note in my voice. "But you don't think it was random."

No, I didn't. Oh, I could believe that Vera had targeted Mosley in the restaurant because she thought he looked like a rich, easy mark. But how had she known which car was his? I supposed that Eddie could have been lurking outside and spotted the dwarf parking his vehicle and heading into the restaurant. Maybe the giant had snapped Mosley's photo and sent it to Vera as a heads-up for a potential victim.

But that still didn't explain who was in the other car that had zoomed away after Vera and Eddie were dead. Sure, it could have been someone who'd seen the fight and didn't want to stick around and get involved or even someone who'd had a few too many drinks at Underwood's to drive home safely. But if that were the case, the car would have plowed straight into Mosley and me, not veered away smoothly at the last second.

No, I didn't think any of this was random. Not at all. But Mosley was upset enough, and I didn't want to worry him any more, so I didn't share my suspicions.

Instead, I shrugged. "You know me and how I always go straight to the worst-case scenario. But let's assume it wasn't random. Anyone with a particular grudge against you? Anyone make any recent threats? Anyone you think could be behind this?"

Mosley stuck his hands in his pants pockets and slowly rocked back and forth on his feet, thinking. "Well, lots of folks were extremely upset by the recent robbery attempt at the bank. I got several threats about that, but now that everyone's items have been returned and security has been dramatically increased, most of the hubbub has died down. Honestly, I've spent so much time working on the auction the last few weeks that I haven't paid attention to much else."

He fell silent, although he kept rocking back and forth, lost in his own thoughts again. I thought about pressing him further and trying to jog his memory, but I decided against it. Mosley had already been through enough tonight, and the only thing that mattered right now was that he was okay.

I scanned the street again, wondering if that mysterious car might careen back around, but it didn't reappear, and everything remained quiet. So my gaze flicked over to Vera sprawled on the sidewalk and then Eddie slumped out in the street. Their arms and legs stuck out at awkward angles, like they were puppets whose strings had been suddenly severed, and blood had pooled underneath both of their heads, like their skulls were eggs that had been cracked open and were oozing everywhere. These Humpty-Dumptys had had great falls, and they were never, ever getting put back together again.

By all appearances, this looked like a simple mugging, but I couldn't shake the feeling that something else— something *more*—was going on. Then again, Finn claimed that I saw plots, especially Circle plots, everywhere I went and in everything that happened to me and my friends these days. He wasn't wrong about that.

But I wasn't usually wrong about these sorts of things either.

And the longer I stared at the two bodies, the more certain I was that this was just the beginning of a whole new wave of trouble for Mosley—and for me too.

Finn returned from parking his car just as a siren wailed in the distance. Blue and white lights flashed at the far end of the street, growing brighter and closer. A few moments later, a navy sedan pulled over to the curb, right behind Mosley's car with its dented hood and busted windshield.

The driver's-side door opened, and a woman with blue eyes and blond hair that peeked out from underneath her blue toboggan got out. A giant who was roughly seven feet tall, with a broad, strong body, dark eyes, a shaved head, and ebony skin, climbed out of the passenger's side. Detective Bria Coolidge, my baby sister, and Xavier, her partner on the force.

Bria and Xavier looked at the giant lying on the street before moving over and examining the woman sprawled across the sidewalk. Then the two cops walked over to where Finn and I were standing with Mosley at the corner.

"Thanks for coming," I said.

Bria flashed me a warm smile. "Anytime. You know that." Then she turned her attention to the dwarf. "Mr. Mosley. Nice to see you again, although I wish the circumstances were better. Can you tell me what happened?"

She went into full-fledged detective mode, pulling a pen and a small notepad out of the back pocket of her jeans. Meanwhile, Xavier drew his phone out of his black leather jacket and took photos of the crime scene, documenting everything, from the two bodies to the blood and broken glass to Mosley's battered car.

Bria carefully listened and wrote down everything
Mosley told her, then went over and conferred in quiet
tones with Xavier, who pulled on a pair of black crime-
scene gloves and scooped Vera's red clutch off the
sidewalk. He popped it open, plucked her driver's license
out of the bag, and showed it to Bria, who nodded, as if
she'd been expecting the information all along. Curious.

She also pulled on a pair of crime-scene gloves, and
Xavier crouched down and rolled Eddie over onto his side so
she could dig his wallet out of his back pocket. She showed
Xavier the dead giant's driver's license, and he nodded back
to her the same way she had to him. Very curious indeed.

Eventually, Bria and Xavier finished documenting
everything, and she crooked her finger at me, since Finn
was talking to Mosley about bank business, trying to
distract him from staring at Vera's body again.

I walked over to the cops. "You got something?"

"Actually, yes." Bria gestured at the two bodies. "Meet
Vera and Eddie Jones, a married pair of professional
muggers. Both of them have extensive rap sheets that
include solicitation, assault, battery...you get the picture.
Tonight isn't the first time the two of them have pulled a
scam like this. Vera's the bait. She lures the victim out of a
restaurant or bar and into a shadowy alley, where hubby
Eddie is waiting, then—"

"*Bam!*" Xavier smacked his fist into his hand. "Eddie
comes up behind the guy and knocks him out, and then the
two of them roll the poor sap for everything he has on
him—wallet, phone, jewelry."

"So you know them?" I asked.

They both nodded.

"We've busted them a couple of times now, but we've
never been able to make anything stick, since none of the

victims has been willing to testify." Xavier grinned. "What with those guys being so happily married and all."

"Right," I drawled. "So you think this was random?"

Bria shrugged. "Well, Vera and Eddie usually stick to Southtown, since folks flock to that area when they're looking to have a good time on the sly. It's just easier pickings over there. This is the first time I know of that they've strayed out of that area. Although we have gotten several reports of muggings in this neighborhood over the past few weeks. The owner of Underwood's spoke to our captain about it a couple of days ago. He wanted to know why his very generous donation to the police department's annual fund-raiser wasn't resulting in this sort of crime being kept away from his restaurant."

"Donation?" I snorted. "Heh. You mean he wanted to know why he wasn't getting anything for his bribe money."

She shrugged again. "Something like that. But you think Mosley was specifically targeted, don't you?"

"Why would you say that?"

Bria pointed at me and made a little circle with her index finger. "Because I can see the wheels turning in your mind and the worry written all over your face. But who would have a reason to go after Mosley? Some angry bank client?"

"I don't know. But you don't get to be as powerful, wealthy, and influential as he is without making some serious enemies." I started pacing back and forth on the sidewalk. "And if this was just a mugging, then why didn't Eddie bash Mosley on the head as soon as he reached his car? Why didn't Eddie just go ahead and kill him? If you only want what's in a guy's wallet, or maybe even his car, then you're not going to be too concerned about what shape you leave him in. It's a simple smash, grab, and go."

"That's how it usually goes down with Vera and Eddie's

victims," Xavier said. "They've already put a couple of guys in the hospital with broken bones this year, and it's still January."

I kept pacing. "So why didn't they follow that same script tonight? Because they didn't—not at all. Eddie didn't lay a hand on Mosley until *after* Vera got out of the car and confronted him. It's like the giant was waiting for her to double-check and make sure they had the right guy before he did anything. Even then, Eddie just grabbed Mosley's arm like he was going to force the dwarf into his own car instead of really hurting him. This seems more like an attempted kidnapping than a mugging to me."

"Maybe they did want to take Mosley someplace more private," Bria suggested. "Given all the wealthy folks who eat at Underwood's, maybe they saw this as an opportunity for a bigger score. Maybe they wanted more than his car and wallet and planned to take Mosley back to his house and see what was worth stealing there. Maybe they heard about the recent robbery attempt at First Trust and decided to try something similar. Or maybe they were hoping to get banking information out of him, whether it was Mosley's personal info or some other accounts."

All her theories made sense, and any one of those scenarios could have been the muggers' motives, but I couldn't shake this bad, bad feeling in the pit of my stomach. "But what about the other car? The one that pulled out of the alley after we took down Vera and Eddie?"

Xavier looked at Bria. "Maybe Vera and Eddie added somebody to their crew. A lookout or someone more familiar with this neighborhood. Plus, if they were going to take Mosley's car somewhere, either back to his house or over to a chop shop, then they would need someone to pick them up and drive them away afterward."

That made sense too, but it still didn't ease my concern. I rubbed my aching head. "I don't know. I just don't know what to think right now."

"Don't worry." Bria laid a gentle, understanding hand on my arm. "Xavier and I will look into it. We'll find out if Vera and Eddie were the ones working this neighborhood and if they were a solo act or reporting to someone else."

"You can count on it," Xavier added.

"Thank you for that." I paused. "And for not saying that I'm paranoid like Finn always does."

Bria and Xavier exchanged a knowing look, their lips stretching into amused grins.

"Well, you *are* totally paranoid," Bria said. "But that's one of the things we love about you, Gin."

"So you love me because I see crazy Circle conspiracies everywhere." I sighed. "Great. Just great."

Bria laughed, slung her arm around my shoulder, and hugged me. Then she stepped back, and her grin faded into a far more serious expression. "You might be paranoid, but you've also been right way too many times for me to doubt you now."

"Me too," Xavier chimed in. "Trust us, Gin. We'll help you get to the bottom of this. If someone is after Mosley, we'll find out who they are and what they want."

The love, trust, dedication, and determination shining in their eyes made a lump of emotion swell up in my throat. I nodded and hugged Bria tight, before doing the same to Xavier.

"All right, all right," Xavier rumbled. "That's enough of that. We're tough-as-nails cops, remember? Hugging completely ruins our street cred. Besides, we've got work to do."

I hugged him again anyway, then stepped back. "Right. I'll leave you to it."

Xavier winked at me, and then he and Bria went back over to look through Vera's clutch and Eddie's pockets a second time for any clues they might have missed.

I stayed where I was, my gaze flicking over everything again. Vera's and Eddie's still, crumpled forms, the pools of blood oozing out from underneath their bodies, the shattered windshield glass glittering like sharp diamonds all over the sidewalk and street.

Nothing out of the ordinary for Ashland. It was all perfectly in keeping with a mugging gone right and the victim fighting back and winning against his attackers.

Still, the more I studied the scene, the more worried I became. Someone had wanted *something* from Mosley, and they had sent Vera and Eddie to get it, probably by any means necessary. Kidnapping, torture, murder. Those weren't out of the ordinary for Ashland either. Not at all.

I just wondered what Stuart Mosley had that was so important—and how long it would be before his enemy tried to take it from him again.

✵ 5 ✵

ria and Xavier finished their preliminary examination and called in the crime scene. About ten minutes later, a couple of patrol cars arrived, lighting up the entire block with their flashing blue and white lights. Bria and Xavier directed the other cops as they cordoned off the area and started collecting evidence, including Mosley's beat-up car.

Given my nocturnal activities and my reputation as the Spider, more than a few of the cops eyed me, their emotions ranging from curiosity to wariness to open hostility. Time for us to go. Finn led Mosley and me through an alley and over to the parking garage where he'd stashed his own car, and away we went.

Thirty minutes later, I was sitting in a cherry-red chair in an old-fashioned Southern beauty salon. Glossy magazines were stacked more than a foot high on the table next to my right elbow, while a plastic pink tub full of tubes of lipstick and bottles of nail polish perched on the table to my left. More tubs bristling with combs, brushes, rollers, scissors, and other teasing, curling, and cutting implements lined a long counter that took up most of a nearby wall.

The air smelled like the chemicals used in the perms, hair dyes, and other beauty treatments, along with a sweet, soothing hint of vanilla. Normally, I found the mix of strong and soft scents comforting, but tonight they made my stomach roil. The memory of the Dollmaker serial killer dyeing my dark brown hair a bright platinum blond to try to turn me into his dream woman was still a little too fresh in my mind for me to relax in the salon like normal.

"He threw you around like you were a piñata, didn't he, darling?" a light, feminine voice murmured.

I looked over at Jolene "Jo-Jo" Deveraux, who was sitting right next to me, staring at me with her clear, almost colorless eyes, and evaluating my many cuts, bumps, and bruises. For a moment, I was so lost in my memories that I thought she was talking about Bruce Porter, the Dollmaker. But then I realized that she was referring to Eddie, the giant mugger.

Of course she was. New week, new bad guy pummeling me to a bloody pulp. Nothing out of the ordinary for the Spider, right down to all the emotional wounds that the battles left behind on my black heart. Although Bruce Porter and his sadistic ritual of kidnapping women, painting their mouths with blood-red lipstick, and then beating them to death had wounded me far deeper than most.

A couple of weeks had passed since I'd faced down Porter, but sometimes it felt like it had happened just an hour ago. During the day, I could focus on all my other problems to keep the flashbacks at bay, but that wasn't the case at night. More often than not, I woke up screaming from the memory of Porter chasing me through the cold, snowy woods, determined to murder me the same way he had so many other women.

In the end, I'd managed to kill Porter, but he'd still left

behind a horrible scar on my heart, one that wouldn't heal for a long, long time—if ever.

I shook my head to clear away the unwanted memories and focused on Jo-Jo again. It was after nine o'clock now, and the dwarf was ready for bed, in her long white fleece housecoat patterned with tiny pink roses. Her middle-aged face was free of its usual understated makeup, and her white-blond hair was wrapped in pink sponge rollers. I'd never understood how Jo-Jo managed to sleep in those rollers, especially every single night. They always dug into my scalp and gave me a terrible headache whenever I used them. But she was the beauty expert, not me.

"*Piñata* is a bit generous," Finn chirped from a nearby couch. "After all, a piñata puts up some resistance when you whack it. Gin was more like a rag doll tonight."

"You're not helping," I muttered.

"I'm sitting here providing the color commentary. That's all the helping that I need to do," he said in a smug voice. "Besides, *I* wasn't the one who got body-slammed into a car. That was all *you*, Gin."

"Come outside with me, and I can fix that."

Finn ignored my threat, licked his thumb, and turned another page in the beauty magazine he was reading. I glared at him, but he kept right on ignoring me, although Mosley let out an amused chuckle.

The dwarf was sitting in the corner, idly rubbing his wing tip across the back of Rosco, Jo-Jo's basset hound, who was curled up in his wicker basket. Rosco's eyes were closed, but his paws twitched, and little grunts of pleasure rumbled out of his mouth, telling everyone how much he was thoroughly enjoying his back rub.

"Well, no matter what happened, let me get to work on you," Jo-Jo said.

A milky-white glow sparked to life in her eyes, as well as on her palm, and she leaned forward and started moving her hand up and down in front of my body.

In addition to using her Air elemental magic to smooth out her salon clients' wrinkles and keep their skin looking young and firm, Jo-Jo also used her power to heal me whenever I tangled with a dangerous enemy. She had already worked her magic on Mosley, who'd had some ugly bruises on his throat from Vera's baton, and now it was my turn. Finn, of course, had escaped the entire incident unscathed. Lucky son of a gun.

The invisible pins and needles of Jo-Jo's magic stabbed into my body from head to toe as she grabbed hold of the oxygen in the air, circulated the healing molecules through my wounds, and then used those same molecules to stitch my cuts together, reduce the swelling, and fade out my many bruises. I gritted my teeth against the uncomfortable prickling sensation of her Air magic, which was the complete opposite of my own cold, hard Ice and Stone powers.

A few minutes later, Jo-Jo dropped her hand, the milky-white glow snuffed out of her eyes, and all those annoying pins and needles finally quit stabbing into my body.

"There you go, darling," she said. "Good as new."

"Thanks to you."

Jo-Jo winked at me. "Customer service is my specialty."

Finn tossed his magazine down onto the couch and got to his feet. "Good. Now that everyone's healed, I can drop Gin at her place, and then the boss man and I can go to my apartment."

Mosley frowned. "What do you mean?"

"I mean you're coming home with me tonight," Finn said.

The dwarf was so surprised that he stopped petting Rosco, who let out a plaintive whine.

But Mosley ignored the basset hound, stood up, crossed his arms over his chest, and gave my brother a stubborn look. "I might be an old man, but I am still perfectly capable of taking care of myself. I don't need a babysitter."

"Well, at the very least, you need a chauffeur, since you don't even have a car right now," Finn countered. "Or do you not remember the cops getting ready to tow it away?"

Mosley glowered at him, but Finnegan Lane was impervious to angry looks, even from his boss, and he kept right on talking, the way he always did.

"You have no idea how much it pained me to see all the dents in that beautiful, beautiful piece of machinery. Not to mention the broken windshield." Finn clutched his fist over his heart for emphasis. "We're talking deep, sharp, stabbing *physical pain*."

"It pained *you*?" I sniped. "*I* was the one who got body-slammed into the hood and windshield, as you so eloquently put it."

Finn waved his hand, dismissing my words. "And that's just another Tuesday night for you, Gin. We're talking about Stuart here. Quit trying to hog the limelight."

Hog the limelight? My fingers twitched, and my left eye joined in with the annoyed chorus. At that moment, I was very, very tempted to show him what deep, sharp, stabbing physical pain *really* felt like, courtesy of one of my knives.

Mosley jutted out his chin, still being stubborn. "I can take a cab home."

Finn raised his eyebrows. "You mean home to that rustic mansion that's way up on that ridge all by itself? Where more muggers could already be lying in wait for you? Where no one would hear you scream as you were tortured for days on end? Much less find your mutilated body after the fact? Think again, mister."

Other than the occasional quip, Finn hadn't said much while Mosley and I had been getting healed, but apparently he'd come to the same conclusion I had—that tonight's attempted mugging was far more than what it seemed to be. More than that, I could see the tension in his shoulders and hear the worry in his voice. Finn had already lost his dad, and he didn't want to lose the other father figure he had in Mosley.

The dwarf stabbed his finger at Finn, almost poking him in the chest. "*You* don't order me around. In case you've forgotten, *I'm* the boss. Not to mention old enough to be your grandfather several times over. I've already forgotten more dangerous situations than you've ever even been in."

"Oh, I doubt that, given Gin's propensity for getting herself into trouble with the worst of the worst," Finn drawled. "Do you know how many times she's almost died in the past sixteen months or so?"

"Hey!" I said. "When did this become about me?"

But it wasn't about me—not really—and the two of them didn't even look at me. They were still too busy glaring at each other, and it seemed their argument was going to keep right on going, since both of them were far too mule-headed to give in. I rolled my eyes, got up from my chair, and stepped between them, looking at Mosley.

"We spent a lot of time talking about Fletcher at dinner and the adventures the two of you had. So think about the old man," I said in a soft voice. "What would he want you to do? Both as the Tin Man and as your friend."

Mosley glared at me for a moment before his expression slowly softened into one of grudging acceptance. "He would want me to stay with Finn until we figure out if there's anything else going on here."

"Good. Then it's settled."

He opened his mouth like he was going to argue, but I held up my hand, stopping him.

"Then it's settled," I repeated in a firm voice. "And I don't want to hear another word about it."

After a moment, he nodded and gave me a sheepish grin. "Yes, ma'am."

"Excellent!" Finn clapped his hand on his boss's shoulder. "What do you say, roomie? Ready to go home, eat junk food, and talk about cute girls until the sun comes up?"

Mosley winced, and his lips curled up with equal amounts of fear and horror at the thought of all that male bonding. Now he was the one who was feeling deep, sharp, stabbing physical pain. Couldn't blame him for that.

The three of us thanked Jo-Jo again for her healing services, then left the salon.

Finn dropped me off at Fletcher's house, my house now, and steered his car around in the driveway to head back to his apartment in the city. Mosley stared at me through the passenger's-side window with that pained expression on his face again, like he was hoping I would stop the vehicle and save him from the impending Finnegan Lane slumber party. I grinned and waved good night to them.

Once they were gone, I turned around in a slow circle, studying everything from the dark woods in the distance to the flat yard in front of the house to the rocky ridge that dropped away at the far edge of the grass. I also reached out with my Stone magic, listening to the emotional vibrations that rippled through the gravel driveway beneath my feet, the brick and other stone that made up the house, and the rocks hidden in the snow-dusted grass and the woods beyond.

But the only sounds that echoed back to me were the high, piercing whistle of the wind sweeping over the ridge, the gentle *plop-plop-plop* of snow falling from the tree branches, and the rustle of a few small animals through the dead leaves, burrowing deeper into their shelters for the night. No one had been near the house since I'd left for dinner earlier. Good. I had no desire to deal with any more attackers tonight.

So I walked over to the porch, unlocked the front door, and stepped inside the house. I had just toed off my boots when my phone buzzed. I pulled it out of my purse and stared at the screen. The text was from Silvio Sanchez.

I sighed. Of course. My personal assistant had an annoying habit of tracking my phone and contacting me the second I got home to make sure I was okay. I swiped the screen so I could read the message.

Muggers? Really? What happened to a nice, quiet dinner with friends?

I thought about not responding, but if I didn't, he would just keep texting until I did. So I sent him a brief and deliberately vague message.

I'm fine. See you tomorrow at the PP.

I waited several seconds, wondering if he would text me back, but for once, Silvio restrained himself, and my phone stayed silent. A minute passed, then two, then three. I grinned. The vampire was probably pacing back and forth, glaring at his phone, and cursing my stubbornness in not immediately calling and telling him all the juicy details.

Silvio worried over me worse than a mama duck over her baby, and this was my subtle way of reminding him that I was perfectly capable of taking care of myself. Plus, I liked annoying him a little bit.

But Silvio had also become part of my family, so I didn't leave him hanging for too long. Besides, I wanted to know more about the muggers, and Silvio was great at finding out people's dirty little secrets. So I texted him again.

Muggers were a married couple. Vera and Eddie Jones. Please find out what you can about them. Mosley was the target. See what enemies he might have as well.

Less than thirty seconds later, my phone buzzed with a new message.

Finally! Thank you. Getting started right now. ☺

I sighed again and shook my head, although I was still grinning. Silvio was dedicated to the extreme, and no doubt he would have a full, thorough, and lengthy report for me first thing in the morning. But I had my own resources right here at home, and I decided to utilize them. Besides, I was too restless to watch TV or go to bed yet.

Not when Mosley might still be in danger.

I locked the front door behind me and headed into Fletcher's office, my office now, and flipped on the lights. An old, battered desk, some wooden bookcases, several metal filing cabinets. It looked like your typical home office, but it was really a treasure trove of information, far more valuable than any stash of diamonds or gold, since it helped keep me prepared and alive.

Fletcher had spent years meticulously compiling information on criminals in Ashland and beyond, especially those heavy hitters who might be a threat to him as the Tin Man, back when he was actively working as an assassin.

And it was a tradition he'd continued, even after I'd taken over the family business as the Spider. So this was the perfect place to start looking for information on Vera and Eddie Jones.

But I wasn't holding out much hope that I would find anything. The two muggers had seemed competent enough, but neither one of them had had any powerful elemental magic or other special, deadly skills that would have put them on Fletcher's radar. Over the past few months, Silvio had been helping me update the old man's information, but I didn't recall any mention of anyone fitting Vera's and Eddie's descriptions. Still, I wanted to check the files anyway, just for my own peace of mind.

I grabbed the relevant files, sat down at the desk, and got to work. Truth be told, it was a nice way to unwind after the earlier fight. Oh, I didn't enjoy going through the documents and photos nearly as much as Silvio did, but seeing Fletcher's handwriting and scribbled notes made me feel like he wasn't completely gone, like he was still here guiding me, in whatever small way he could.

I didn't find anything in the files about Vera or Eddie. No surprise there, since muggers were a dime a dozen in Ashland. But I wasn't ready to give up, so I poured myself a glass of gin, then toasted the picture of Fletcher that was perched on the corner of the desk. I sipped my drink, relishing the cool slide of the liquid down my throat before it transformed into that slow, sweet burn in the pit of my stomach. More gin for Gin. I'd definitely earned an extra round or two tonight.

While I enjoyed my drink, I stared at Fletcher's photo. Seeing the old man's walnut-brown hair, green eyes, and tan, wrinkled features as he looked out over the scenic landscape of Bone Mountain always comforted me. But the longer I stared at his face, especially his sly, knowing grin, the more I wondered what he would have done in this situation.

At the beauty salon, I had told Mosley to think about what Fletcher would have wanted him to do, and I decided to apply the same logic to myself. And I realized that I should be thinking not about what Fletcher would have wanted me to do but rather what the old man might have *already* done himself.

So I finished my gin, went back over to the filing cabinets, and started searching through the folders for one specific name.

Stuart Mosley.

And sure enough, I found a folder with the dwarf's name scribbled on the tab, neatly filed away in its proper place. Now that I was staring at it, I vaguely remembered Silvio mentioning the file to me when he had gone through this drawer, although neither one of us had looked at it at the time.

The file hadn't surprised me then, and it didn't now either. Fletcher's enemies as the Tin Man weren't the only folks he'd kept tabs on. He'd also tracked those who might be a threat to the people he loved. Like Deirdre Shaw, Finn's Ice elemental bitch of a mother. Or Harley Grimes, the Fire elemental who'd kidnapped and tortured Sophia Deveraux, Jo-Jo's younger sister.

Given how powerful, dangerous, and influential the Circle was, it made perfect sense that Fletcher would have kept a file on Mosley too. It would have been his way of protecting and watching out for his friend, especially since he'd given Mosley the treacherous task of safeguarding those safety-deposit boxes full of information on the evil group.

I took the file over to the desk and sat back down. Then I poured myself some more gin, opened the folder, and started reading.

Most of it was pretty standard stuff. Various loans, real estate, and other business deals that Mosley had made, who had profited and been hurt by them, some threats he'd received, and all the people who might want to take their anger against him to the next, deadly level. Several pages also dealt with the murder of Joanna Mosley and Fletcher's search for information on who might have killed her. I set those pages aside to add to my own file on Bruce Porter, the Dollmaker.

I was almost to the end of the file when I came across a photo of a beautiful woman with long black hair, green eyes, and perfect skin. In the picture, the woman was wearing an emerald-green evening gown and smiling wide as she clinked her champagne glass against Mosley's, as though the two of them were best friends. Fletcher had scribbled a note on the bottom of the photo—*AE?*—but for once, I knew exactly what he meant, since I recognized the woman.

AE were the woman's initials, and her name was Amelia Eaton.

I was so surprised that I lost my grip on my glass, and it thumped down to the desk, sloshing gin onto the wood. I reared back in my chair, blinking and blinking, wondering if I'd looked at the photo or read the initials wrong.

But I hadn't.

Amelia Eaton was a name I hadn't heard in years, but looking at her smiling face brought back all sorts of memories—none of them good.

I forced my shock aside and peered at the bottom of the photo again, then flipped it over to look at the back, wondering if Fletcher might have scribbled down any other notes, but he hadn't. I also sorted through all the information in the file again, but her name and face didn't appear anywhere but in this one picture.

So what had Amelia and Mosley been celebrating? I didn't know, but the photo looked like it had been taken at a party quite some time ago, given the fancy but outdated gown she was wearing. And Amelia seemed perfectly happy with Mosley, given the way she was beaming at him. So why had Fletcher included this picture in the file? What potential threat had he seen in her?

The more I thought about it, the more puzzled I became. Because I knew with absolute certainty that Amelia hadn't sent those two muggers after Mosley. She simply *couldn't* have.

Amelia Eaton had been dead for years—and I was the one who'd killed her.

✤ 6 ✤

I studied the photo for several more minutes, but I didn't glean any clues from it.

Amelia and Mosley were the only people in the shot, holding their champagne flutes and standing in front of an enormous fireplace. Bookcases flanked the fireplace, indicating that they were in some sort of study or library, but the knowledge didn't narrow down the location. The picture could have been taken at any party at any mansion at any time before I'd killed Amelia.

By this point, it was creeping up on midnight, and I was out of information and ideas, so I downed the rest of my gin, wiped up what I'd spilled on the desk, and slid Mosley's file back into the appropriate drawer. Then I turned off the lights and left the office.

I took the photo with me, though. Maybe Silvio would see something in it that I'd missed. Or maybe Mosley could tell me when and where it had been taken and what he and Amelia had been discussing that had made her so happy.

I took a long, hot shower to help myself relax, then put on my pajamas and went to bed. I fell asleep almost immediately and drifted along in a calm, empty, soothing blackness. But eventually, a memory bubbled up to the surface of my mind, and the blackness vanished, replaced by swirling shadows that slowly morphed into shapes, lights, colors, and sound...

"I don't like this," Fletcher muttered. "I don't like this at all."

"Relax," I said. "We've been studying our target for weeks. We know everything there is to know about her. What could possibly go wrong?"

The old man sighed. "Now you've done it. You've jinxed *us, Gin, plain and simple."*

I grinned at his grumbling. "And here I thought that you didn't believe in jinxes. You always tell me that people, especially assassins, make their own luck."

He huffed. "And I've also told you time and time again that Lady Luck is a fickle bitch. You might make your own luck with all your planning and preparation, but never forget that she can screw you over at any moment. Just because she can. Just because she feels like it. Just because wants to see you squirm. *"*

Still grinning, I raised my binoculars to my eyes and looked out over the landscape.

Earlier this afternoon, Fletcher and I had left the humble confines of the Pork Pit behind for the grand expanse of the Eaton Estate. We'd parked his old white van on the side of the road and stuck a plastic bag in the window to make it seem as though we'd had engine trouble. Then we'd grabbed our black duffel bags full of supplies and hiked three miles through the woods, avoiding the giant guards and skirting around the fences that ringed much of the estate.

Now we were safely ensconced in a thick patch of pines,

hidden back in the shadows. A sandy shore started at the edge of the trees and ran down to the man-made lake that one of the Eatons had added to the estate a few generations ago. The evergreen trees, white sand, and blue water created a picture-perfect scene, made even more so by the sun streaking the sky with its orange-sherbet rays as it slowly sank behind the forested ridges on the far side of the lake.

I scanned the shoreline, but I didn't spot anyone walking along the water. No surprise there, given the dozens of Private Property, No Trespassing *signs posted in the forest and along the surrounding roads. The Eatons didn't take too kindly to folks traipsing onto their land, not even for something as innocent as a summer swim. Once I was sure that Fletcher and I were alone, I turned my attention toward the estate's crown jewel: the Eaton family mansion.*

Well, calling it a mansion *was a bit of an understatement. The Eaton ancestral home was a mammoth chateau-style structure made of sleek gray granite that soared five stories tall. Picture windows and balconies covered much of the structure, which was perched on top of a wide, flat hill to take advantage of the views of the lake and the forested valley below. Despite its massive size, the mansion still maintained a delicate, elegant air, with its intricate carved stonework, carefully crafted crenellations, and steep gabled roofs.*

I dropped my gaze from the upper levels and focused on the enormous stone terrace that jutted out from the back. Small round tables covered with emerald-green linens lined one side of the area, along with an impressive buffet and several towers of champagne glasses. White twinkle lights lined many of the tables and were strung up like electrified spiderwebs on the mansion's windows. A wooden parquet dance floor took up another section, and a string quartet was tucked away in the back corner. No one was dancing yet, but the soft strains of classical music floated through the air, punctuated by sharp trills of laughter.

Guests dressed in lightweight summer suits and cocktail frocks milled around on the terrace. A faint breeze offered a bit of relief from the evening August heat and made the women's skirts billow out, like they were colorful butterflies twitching their wings and fluttering from one group to the next. Waiters wearing white shirts and pants with emerald-green bow ties and tuxedo vests circulated through the cliques, offering champagne to everyone.

But the most notable things were the roses.

Dozens of crystal vases boasting perfect white roses perched on all the tables, including the buffet ones, and even more vases were lined up along the low stone wall at the edge of the terrace. Strands of roses wound through many of the glasses in the champagne towers, and white rose petals had been scattered all over the dance floor. The breeze made the silky petals twirl through the air, adding to the dreamy, romantic scene.

My nose twitched, and I had to hold back a sneeze. Normally, I found roses to be a pleasant enough scent, but so many of them covered the terrace that they gave off an overpowering and sickeningly sweet stench, one that I could smell all the way over here in the trees. Or perhaps I thought the aroma was foul because I knew what dark, rotten things lurked underneath the glitz and glamour.

I lowered my binoculars, stuffed them into my duffel bag, and turned to Fletcher. "How do I look?"

After our hike through the woods, I'd shucked off my usual black assassin clothes and changed into a blue sundress with spaghetti straps and a flowing skirt that fell to my knees. The silky fabric skimmed my body, highlighting my curves without weighing me down. Jo-Jo had dyed my hair a bright, coppery red and curled it into loose waves. Silver shadow coated my eyes, which had been tinted a dark brown thanks to a pair of contacts, while an innocent pink gloss covered my lips. A small diamond solitaire on a thin silver chain rested against my throat.

All put together, the dress, red hair, brown contacts, makeup, and jewelry formed the perfect disguise. I looked like a completely different person from my usual low-key self. No one would ever connect this young woman with Gin Blanco, college student and barbecue waitress.

But I wasn't here as Gin tonight. No, tonight the Spider had come out to play.

The only things that didn't go with my party-girl outfit were my shoes, which were unfashionably flat, sturdy, black leather sandals with straps that wound up past my ankles. But if I truly had jinxed us like Fletcher claimed and things went wrong, I would be leaving the party in a hurry, and I would definitely prefer function over fashion in my footwear then.

Fletcher's green gaze sharpened, and he gave me a critical once-over. "You look good. Real good. Just like you belong with all those rich folks. You got your knives?"

I held up my black purse. "Locked and loaded, just like always."

In addition to the knife in my bag, I had two more strapped to my thighs underneath my sundress. But I shouldn't need more than one blade to do this job.

The old man nodded and looked back over at the terrace through his own binoculars. After a few seconds, he sighed, lowered the lenses, and ran a hand through his dark brown hair, which had more than a little gray in it.

"I still don't like this, but you're right. There's nothing out of the ordinary about the party. So I guess you should go join the fun." He winked at me. "But don't worry. I'll be here watching out for you."

I grinned back at him. "I wouldn't have it any other way."

I left our observation spot behind and melted into the surrounding woods. I took a long, winding route through the trees and came out in one of the paved lots where the guests' cars were being parked, as though I'd left my vehicle behind and was making my way across the grounds with everyone else.

I fell in step behind an older couple, chatting them up, and walked right on past the bored-looking vampire guards who were manning the wide, arching trellis covered with twinkle lights that marked the party entrance. The guards were supposed to be checking invitations, and I had a fake one in my purse, but the men weren't taking their jobs seriously, and they didn't give me a second glance.

Fletcher had been wrong. I hadn't jinxed us, and this job was going to be smooth sailing.

I said good-bye to the old couple, then grabbed a glass of champagne from a passing waiter and wandered around, as though I was admiring the views of the lake and the woods. In reality, I was scanning the crowd, searching for my target. And I quickly spotted her, holding court less than thirty feet away.

Amelia Eaton, the current owner of the Eaton Estate.

Amelia was a beautiful woman, with long black hair that had been wound up in an elaborate braided bun. Her eyes were a light, bright green, and her skin was as pale, smooth, and flawless as marble. Unlike the other women with their simpler frocks, she was wearing a floor-length, sequined, emerald-green ball gown that looked like it had cost more than some of the diamonds the other people were sporting, including my own. And her jewelry was even more impressive. Even from this distance, my Stone magic let me easily hear the proud murmurs of the square emeralds that made up the choker around her neck. Each jewel was practically shouting about how large, pretty, and expensive it was.

Amelia was standing in the center of the terrace, a glass of champagne in her hand, surrounded by a flock of fawning admirers, all of whom laughed at some joke she made. She threw her head back and laughed too, her red lips parting to reveal the pearl-white fangs in her mouth. I couldn't hear her words, but her light, sly tone carried on the breeze, and everyone was paying complete, rapt attention to her. She was the belle of the ball, the perfect picture of society grace, beauty, and elegance.

But there was nothing pretty, prim, or proper about her bloodlust.

Amelia Eaton was a vampire, but instead of drinking regular old bagged blood, or even nipping a few pints from the necks of willing donors like many rich vamps did, she preferred to be a little more old-fashioned when it came to getting her required nourishment. Amelia liked to hunt down her dinner, snap its neck, and drink its blood.

And her prey of choice was other humans.

Rumor had it that her vampire ancestors had built their estate in the middle of all this forested land so that they could still have their modern creature comforts while they were chasing down their dinner way out here in the woods. Supposedly, the bones of the family's victims, from the first Eaton to the current generation of Amelia, littered the surrounding forest like dry, brittle leaves. I believed it, given what Fletcher and I had uncovered during our investigation.

Working at the Eaton Estate paid great, but it was also extremely hazardous to your health, since Amelia often used the staff as her own personal wine list, draining every single drop of blood out of anyone unlucky enough to catch her eye. And as if that wasn't bad enough, she also enjoyed snacking on other parts of them. Fingers, toes, internal organs.

But Taylor Samson hadn't known about any of that. He was just a poor engineering student, trying to save enough money from his summer job as a groundskeeper at the swanky estate to return to college in the fall.

Now he wasn't going anywhere ever again.

Taylor had disappeared at the beginning of the summer, three weeks after he'd started working at the estate. His mother, Tricia, had panicked when she couldn't reach her son, a panic that had ended in sickening heartbreak when his body was found a week later by a couple of hikers who'd gotten lost in the woods and had wandered onto the estate by accident.

Of course, Amelia was responsible for Taylor's brutal murder, given the gruesome puncture wounds that marred his mangled body, but she had more than enough money and influence to get the cops to turn a blind eye to what she'd done. The police had barely investigated, much less charged her with anything, and they'd quickly declared that Taylor had gone too far into the woods and had been mauled to death by a bear. Case closed. So Amelia had had her cake—or, rather, Taylor—and literally eaten him too.

But Taylor's mother had heard whispers about the assassin the Tin Man, someone who could help when the law utterly failed, as it so often did in Ashland, and she had reached out to Fletcher through his various back channels. Now here I was, all dolled up and ready to get revenge—

justice—*for Taylor Samson and all the other people Amelia had snacked on just because she preferred to eat organic and enjoyed the thrill of the chase. Just because her family had power and prestige and she knew that she could thumb her nose at everyone and actually get away with being a fucking* cannibal, *just like her ancestors before her.*

Well, not anymore. She was the one who was going to die tonight.

I sipped my champagne, wrinkling my nose to keep from sneezing at the fizzy bubbles, and plotted the best way to get close to Amelia. She was still in the middle of her fawning sycophants, and I couldn't have gotten through them even if I'd barreled into the group like a football linebacker blitzing a quarterback. So I waited, smiling blandly at everyone who caught my eye and walking around the terrace in circles, as though I were searching for someone.

Five minutes later, Amelia emptied her champagne glass and handed it off to a waiter. Then she turned on her green stilettos and sashayed over to the buffet tables, as though she was going to get something to eat that wasn't a terrified college kid.

Time for the Spider to strike.

I exchanged my own half-empty glass of champagne for a fresh, full one. Then I sidled toward Amelia, sliding past the groups of people that stood between us, calculating how long it would take me to reach her.

In five…four…three…two…one…

I accidentally-on-purpose rammed my shoulder into Amelia's and deliberately sloshed my glass of champagne all over the front of her fancy gown.

"Whoopsie!" I chirped in a loud, bright voice that said that I wasn't sorry at all. "I didn't see you standing there."

"You idiot!" Amelia hissed, staring down at the rapidly spreading stains. "You've ruined my dress!"

I frowned, as though I was terribly concerned, and bent forward so that I could get a better look at the damage. Then I straightened back up and airily waved my hand, making my puny diamond solitaire ring glint weakly in the setting sun.

"Oh, I thought you were actually serious *there for a second. But you're just wearing a knockoff. No real damage done, right?" I chirped in that same bright voice again, as though I didn't have any sort of brain in my head.*

People gasped and backed up, since most of them were well acquainted with Amelia's legendary temper. Eyes wide, they looked back and forth between the two of us, wondering how she was going to react to my casual insults.

Amelia opened her mouth, probably to cuss me out, but I started toying with my necklace, deliberately sliding the small diamond solitaire back and forth on its silver chain to catch her attention, the way you might dangle a toy mouse in front of a cat. Her gaze locked onto my neck, just like I wanted it to, and a slow, knowing smile curved her blood-red lips.

"You're absolutely right," she purred in a soft, silky tone. "There's no real harm done. I'm sorry I snapped at you. Why don't you let me get you a drink to make up for it? Something from my private wine cellar?"

I shrugged and shoved my empty glass at the closest waiter. "Sure. Whatever."

Amelia's smile tightened at my bored, dismissive tone, as though she was grinding her teeth to keep from lunging forward and burying her fangs in my throat in front of her guests. "Follow me."

It wasn't a request, and people fell back even more as

Amelia turned on her heels again and swept past them. A couple of vampire guards came up behind me, not so subtly directing me after her. Some of the other partygoers shook their heads and gave me sad, sympathetic looks as I walked by, realizing that they would never see me again—alive, anyway. Amelia might not have been charged with Taylor Samson's murder, but his death had sparked plenty of ugly rumors about what she really did here.

The only person who wasn't leaving here alive tonight was Amelia, but of course I couldn't tell anyone that. So I plastered a happy, ditzy smile on my face and trailed after the vampire like a bunny walking straight into a hunter's snare.

"Wait a second. Did you say private wine cellar? That would be awesome! Although I hope you have something down there that's better than that cheap champagne the waiters are serving. It's already lost all of its bubbles." I pouted as though this was the worst thing in the world.

One of the guards behind me snorted, as if choking back a laugh. No doubt he thought I didn't realize what I'd gotten myself into and that I should be worrying about far more dangerous things than flat champagne. But this was the scheme Fletcher and I had rehearsed, and I was following our script to the letter.

Amelia thought she was in control, but she was the one who was snared in my web. She just didn't know it yet. But she would soon enough, and then she would die screaming for her arrogance.

I followed her into the mansion. I glanced around and sighed, as though I was utterly bored, although I was really trying to keep from gawking at the fine furnishings. Gilded silver mirrors, dark mahogany tables, stained-glass lamps. And that was just what I could see in this one foyer.

The guards shut a pair of glass double doors behind us, muting the sounds of the party outside, and I pushed my awe away and focused on my target again.

Amelia glanced over her shoulder and crooked her finger at me. *"This way."*

"Sure," I chirped again, still playing the part of the clueless partygoer.

She walked through the foyer, opened a door, and headed down a flight of steps, as though she really was taking me to the wine cellar. The soft murmur of the party faded away, replaced by the sharp snap-snap-snap-snap of her stilettos striking the stone. Each stab of her heels banged as loudly as a nail being driven into a coffin—her coffin.

We reached the bottom of the steps, and Amelia led me to the far end of a long hallway. With its thick stone walls and cool, drafty air, the area had far more in common with a dungeon than a wine cellar. We were deep underground now, and I knew Amelia had brought me down here so that the people upstairs at the party wouldn't hear my screams.

She just didn't realize that no one would hear her screams either.

Amelia opened a door and stepped into a room with thick black plastic covering the floor from wall to wall, as though this area was being remodeled, despite the tables, chairs, and other furniture still in here. I recognized the setup for what it really was: a murder room.

Blood was a bitch to scrub out of stone, and why go to all that effort when you could line the floor with plastic instead? Plus, I could hear the walls wailing with the panicked cries of all the other people who'd been brought to this room, only to leave it dead, drained of blood, missing body parts, and rolled in plastic, like they were just one more piece of garbage to be disposed of.

Amelia faced me, her smile growing wider and slowly revealing her gleaming white fangs. "It's a good thing you've already ruined my dress," she purred again. "I won't mind getting your blood on it nearly so much now."

My eyes widened, and my mouth fell open, as if I was just now understanding what was really going on. "Oh, I'm sorry, but you have the wrong idea. I'm not into having all the blood forcibly removed from my body. So sorry to disappoint. I'll just be going now. Ta-ta, sugar."

I turned to leave, only to find the two guards blocking my path. The vampires grinned at me, but the fangs in their mouths didn't worry me at all.

"In case you haven't realized it by now, you're not leaving this room alive," Amelia crowed behind me.

"Funny," I drawled. "I was just going to say the same thing about all of you."

The two guards headed toward me to restrain me, but I whipped my knife out of my purse, tossed the bag aside, and charged at them. I went low, ducking the first guard's awkward arm tackle and slicing my knife across his stomach. He screamed and staggered back, his blood spraying all over the black plastic on the floor.

The second guard stopped short, shocked by what had happened to his buddy, but I was already moving in his direction. I sliced my knife across his gut as well. He joined his screaming pal on the floor, and I whipped back around to take out Amelia.

But she wasn't as surprised as her guards, and she had already grabbed something from a nearby table that I hadn't noticed before.

A stun gun.

She pulled the trigger before I could even think about throwing my knife at her, and two probes shot out from the end of the barrel and streaked through the air toward me. I lurched to the side and reached for my Stone magic, trying to harden my skin so that the probes would harmlessly bounce off my body, but I wasn't fast enough. The two probes stabbed into my chest like needles, and a jolting shock of electricity hit me a second later.

I gritted my teeth against the hot, searing pain roaring through my body and clutched my knife even tighter, trying to hold on to it and stagger over to Amelia so I could at least stab her to death before I passed out. But the electricity was too great and just kept cascading through me in wave after hot, jolting, shocking wave.

White spots exploded like fireworks in my field of vision, and every single nerve ending in my body felt like it was on fire. My teeth rattled together like dominos, and blood filled my mouth as I accidentally bit my own tongue. My knife slipped from my fingers and thumped to the black plastic. My knees buckled, and I joined the weapon on the floor a second later, my arms, legs, and chest twitching in time to the agonizing bursts of energy.

All the while, Amelia kept her finger on the trigger, pumping more electricity into my body. She walked over to me, bent down, and smiled, her fangs flashing in her mouth again. "Is your blood boiling yet, you arrogant little bitch? I hope so. Because I like my dinner warm..."

Thankfully, I didn't hear any more of her taunts. The electricity jolted over me again, stronger than before, and I finally blacked out from the hot, searing pain...

I woke up thrashing around in my bed, still feeling that electricity charging through my body, burning me up from the inside out. Several seconds passed before I realized that I was safe at home. I let out a ragged gasp and flopped back against the pillows, trying to catch my breath as the last remnants of the nightmare slowly faded away.

Well, at least I hadn't dreamed about the Dollmaker chasing me through the woods again. That was just about the only good thing I could say about remembering my confrontation with Amelia.

Moonlight slipped in through the white lace curtains, bathing my bedroom in a soft, silvery glow, and I focused on the hulking shapes of my nightstand, dresser, and other furniture, letting the familiar sights ground me.

My heart finally slowed, and I thought back to that night. I'd forgotten how vicious Amelia had been, and her hitting me with that stun gun hadn't been the worst thing she'd done to me. I could easily picture her sending those two muggers after Mosley with orders to bring him to her so she could torture whatever information she wanted out of him before she drank his blood, snacked on his liver, and chewed on his bones, just for fun.

But Amelia was dead, and her cruelty along with her. So who was targeting Mosley? And why?

I thought back over everything that had happened tonight, and I kept returning to Amelia Eaton.

I couldn't shake the feeling that Fletcher had once again left me a clue from beyond the grave and that if I didn't figure out exactly what it meant, Stuart Mosley would be the one to pay the ultimate price.

❋ 7 ❋

iven my nightmarish memory, I tossed and turned for a few hours. When I finally did go back to sleep, I woke up much later than usual, and I had to throw on my clothes and hustle to the Pork Pit, my barbecue restaurant in downtown Ashland.

Despite my hurry, I still parked my car several blocks away from the restaurant, got out, and stepped into the flow of human traffic on the sidewalks. As I headed toward my destination, I glanced around, making sure that no one was watching or following me.

Mosley might have been the target of last night's attack, but I had plenty of enemies of my own, including Hugh Tucker, the vampire who was the Circle's number one enforcer. Fletcher had said that it was always better to be on your toes, and I was taking his advice to heart, especially these days, when I could never be sure who was working for the Circle or when or where they might strike next.

But no one paid any attention to me, and I made it to the Pork Pit unscathed. I performed my usual checks on the storefront door and windows to make sure no one had carved an elemental rune bomb into them overnight in an attempt to freeze, fry, or otherwise magic me to death when I opened the restaurant this morning.

But everything was clean, so I unlocked the front door and stepped inside.

Two familiar figures stood at one of the stoves along the back wall. One was a dwarf with pale skin, black eyes, and glossy black hair shot through with neon-blue streaks. Her hair matched the bright blue work apron patterned with tiny black skulls that covered her blue T-shirt and black jeans. She was humming a soft, cheery tune, and the impressive muscles in her arm bunched and flexed as she stirred a spoon around in a large metal vat on the stovetop.

A much leaner, middle-aged vampire with bronze skin and gray eyes and hair hovered at the Goth dwarf's right elbow. A plain blue work apron covered his impeccable gray shirt, tie, and pants, and he was holding a small tablet, as though he'd been recording the cooking session.

Sophia Deveraux, my head cook, and Silvio Sanchez, my personal assistant, both turned around at the sound of the bell over the front door chiming my arrival.

"Ah, there you are," Silvio said. "It's not like you to be late. I was just getting ready to call and make sure you were okay."

Of course he had been. Sometimes I thought the vampire was far more concerned for my safety than he was for his own. Still, I appreciated the fact that he looked out for me, and I gave him and Sophia a sheepish shrug.

"Sorry. I overslept."

I shut and locked the front door behind me, then walked by the blue and pink vinyl booths that lined the windows and headed past the tables and chairs in the middle of the floor. I unzipped my jacket and hung it on a rack in the corner close to the cash register, grabbed a blue work apron, and tied it on over my clothes. When I was properly attired, I stepped around the counter and went over to the stove, where Sophia and Silvio were still standing.

"What's going on here?" I asked.

"Sophia was showing me how to make Fletcher's secret barbecue sauce," Silvio said. "It's a fascinating process, especially since she didn't measure anything."

He gave her a chiding look, and Sophia snorted in response.

"Don't need to measure," she rasped in her broken voice. "Been making it for years. Could do it in my sleep."

"Yes, but cooking is a science," Silvio protested. "Proper measurements really are the key to any great recipe…"

He started expounding on the merits of precisely measuring ingredients, as well as correct cooking temperatures, timers, and thermometers, but it was a totally one-sided conversation, since Sophia started humming again as she added a final bit of brown sugar to her brew. I drew in a deep breath, enjoying the rich scents of cumin, black pepper, and other spices that seasoned the air from the simmering sauce.

"Well, I think it smells fantastic, just like always," I said.

Sophia winked at me, then turned off the heat, dipped a wooden spoon into the sauce, and held it out to Silvio. The vampire set his tablet down on the counter, leaned forward, and tasted the sauce.

"It *is* good," he admitted. "And it tastes the same as always. Even though you didn't measure *anything*."

"Mmm-hmm." A knowing, triumphant note colored Sophia's response.

Silvio's lips puckered, and he gave her a sour look. Sophia arched her eyebrows, daring him to keep challenging her cooking methods, but he knew when he was beaten, and he respectfully tipped his head to her. Then he untied his apron, hung it on one of the hooks on the wall, grabbed his gray suit jacket from the coat rack, and shrugged back into it.

Silvio stepped around the counter, sat down on his usual stool, and grabbed his tablet, transforming back into my assistant. "Since you need to open the restaurant in a few minutes, let's skip the morning briefing and go immediately to recapping your dinner with Stuart Mosley last night."

I groaned. "Can't that wait a few more minutes? I just got here. I need to prep for lunch."

"You can talk and chop vegetables at the same time," he said in a dry tone. "I have faith in you, Gin."

I rolled my eyes, but I also knew when I was beaten, so I started slicing up tomatoes and lettuce while I told Silvio everything that had happened, including Vera Jones propositioning Mosley inside Underwood's and then her and Eddie's attack on the dwarf outside the restaurant. Silvio nodded the whole time, absorbing my words and typing notes on his tablet keyboard. He typed in a final few thoughts, then looked up at me.

"I reached out to my contacts last night. I'm still waiting for some of them to get back to me, but from what I've been able to find out so far, your two muggers are definitely small-time. No known gang or criminal affiliations."

Disappointing but not surprising, given what Bria and Xavier had told me about Vera and Eddie. Since it looked like the muggers were going to be a dead end, literally, I moved on to the other thread I had to follow. "What about Mosley? Does he have any enemies who might have been behind the attempted mugging, kidnapping, or whatever that was?"

Silvio shook his head. "No one who jumps out at me. Mosley is rock-solid, from the bank's finances to his own personal conduct. No debts, no scandals, and no bad habits, like drinking or gambling. He's a tough but fair boss, and everyone who works for Mosley respects him, as do the people who conduct business with him. The only recent trouble he's had was when Deirdre Shaw tried to rob First Trust bank, but Mosley has made substantial reparations and assurances to his customers, and he's been exceedingly generous to the families of the bank guards who were killed." An admiring note crept into Silvio's voice. "Another bank, another businessman might have gone under because of the robbery attempt and the subsequent fallout but not Mosley. He excels at crisis management as much as he does everything else."

Again, disappointing but not surprising, given everything Finn had told me about how tirelessly the dwarf had worked to undo the damage Deirdre Shaw had done to his bank and its reputation. Stuart Mosley was a stand-up guy all the way around.

I'd already struck out twice, but I had one more at bat. So I pulled that photo of Mosley and Amelia Eaton out of the back pocket of my jeans and slid it across the counter to Silvio, who leaned over and studied it.

"What's this?" he asked.

"I found it in Fletcher's office last night, in a file he had on Mosley. You came across the file a few weeks ago when we were cleaning out the cabinets. Remember?"

Silvio's eyebrows shot up in surprise. "I remember seeing a folder with Mosley's name on it, but I didn't actually look inside it. I didn't think there would be anything important in it. I still can't believe that Fletcher kept a file on Mosley, like he was just another one of Ashland's criminals. I thought they were friends."

"Fletcher kept files on everyone, *especially* his friends." I tapped my finger on his tablet. "Are you telling me that you've never typed down a few notes about my strengths and weaknesses? My knives, fighting skills, and elemental magic? You know, just in case I ever went hard-core evil, and you had to figure out some way to stop me?"

That was exactly the kind of worst-case scenario that I could imagine Silvio preparing for, since he prided himself on being ready for anything. He fidgeted on his stool, not meeting my gaze, although a telltale blush stained his cheeks, as though I'd just revealed one of his deepest, darkest secrets. So he *did* have a file on me. Interesting. I wondered what it said.

Silvio cleared his throat, pointedly changing the subject. "But I still don't understand why you think this photo is relevant now. This is Amelia Eaton, right? From what from I remember, she died years ago."

"Yeah. I know."

He picked up on the cold, flat tone in my voice. His eyebrows crept up a little higher in his face, and understanding filled his gray eyes. "Oh. You killed her, didn't you?"

"Yeah." My gaze dropped back down to the photo on the counter. "So why did Fletcher keep this picture of her and Mosley? He had to have some reason, and I want to know what it is before I ask Mosley about the photo."

"Don't worry," Silvio said. "I'll look into it, and I'll find out everything I can. Trust me."

"I do trust you. Believe me, I do."

He flashed me a smile, pulled the photo closer, and

studied it again, searching the background for clues like I had last night. After a few moments, he started typing on his keyboard again, and I remembered one more thing that I wanted to mention to him.

"On a personal note, it might interest you to know that Liam Carter was also at Underwood's last night. He sent a bottle of champagne over to me. Nice guy, for a crime boss. When are you going to go out with him?"

Silvio's fingers froze on his keyboard. He didn't look at me, but his left eye started twitching. "My love life—or lack thereof—is not up for discussion this morning. Or any morning, for that matter."

"Oh, I think it would make for a *fine* discussion. Why, we should add it to the morning briefing just to make sure that we discuss it *every single day.*"

Silvio remained steadfastly silent, but his eye kept twitching and that telltale blush flooded his face again. I laughed and went back to chopping vegetables, realizing that I'd teased him enough for one day.

While Silvio texted and emailed his sources, still looking into Vera and Eddie Jones, Stuart Mosley, and Amelia Eaton, the rest of the waitstaff showed up, including Catalina Vasquez, Silvio's niece. Everyone got to work, refilling ketchup bottles, rolling straws and silverware into napkins, wiping down tables, and the like. At eleven o'clock sharp, I opened the front door to my first customers.

For the next few hours, I cooked, cleaned, and cashed out folks until the lunch rush finally died down. Around two o'clock, the bell over the front door chimed, signaling the arrival of a new customer.

Owen Grayson stepped inside, shrugged out of his black overcoat, and hung it on the rack by the door. Even though I'd just seen him yesterday afternoon when he'd come to the Pork Pit for a late lunch, I still drank in the sight of him. With his black hair, rugged features, and broad shoulders, Owen was the epitome of tall, dark, and handsome, and I wasn't the only woman who admired him as he strode across the restaurant. But he only had eyes for me, and I for him.

Owen stepped around the counter, and I wrapped my arms around his neck and gave him a long, lingering kiss. His hands dropped to my waist, pulling me closer, and he leaned down and rested his forehead against mine. For a moment, all the noise, clatter, and commotion of the restaurant faded away, and we were the only two people in the room. I focused on the warmth of his skin touching mine, the soft brush of his breath against my face, the faint hint of his metallic scent tickling my nose. We stood there for the better part of a minute, holding on to each other and soaking in the love, care, and comfort that flowed between us.

Owen kissed me again, then drew back. His violet gaze focused on my face, and concern creased his own features. Just like Bria, he could see my worry. "Rough night?"

"Rougher than I would have liked."

Owen had been hanging out with his younger sister, Eva, last night, so he'd missed the dinner with Mosley, but I'd called him this morning when I'd been racing around the house getting ready and told him what was going on. I had insisted that I was fine, but it still warmed my heart that he'd come to the restaurant to check on me. His consideration was just one of the many things I loved about him.

"Have you figured out who was behind the attack yet?" he asked.

I jerked my thumb over my shoulder at Silvio, who was still typing away. "Not yet, but we're working on it."

Owen grinned. "I would expect nothing less from the mighty Spider."

Silvio pointedly cleared his throat.

"And her trusty assistant, the great Silvio," he added.

The vampire huffed. "You make it sound like we're some sort of cheesy magic act. I feel like I should be wearing a black cape and a top hat and waving around a wand."

"Aren't we?" I asked. "You're trying to find out who might want Mosley dead. That's not too different from pulling a rabbit out of a hat, especially given all the crime in Ashland."

"Well, if we're a magic act, then I should get to saw you in half," Silvio quipped.

"That's a bit homicidal."

"Says the assassin," he shot right back at me.

Silvio gave me a triumphant look, knowing that I didn't have a comeback for that particular zinger. Owen snickered at our bantering, then stepped around the counter and sat down on a stool next to the vampire.

Owen ordered a barbecue chicken platter with sourdough rolls, coleslaw, baked beans, onion rings, and a sweet iced tea, while Silvio requested some of the cherry-almond cookies I'd baked this morning, along with his third coffee refill. Sometimes I thought the vampire could subsist on sugar and caffeine alone.

Sophia helped me fix their food, and the four of us chatted back and forth while the dwarf and I got everything ready and slid their plates across the counter.

Owen tucked into his meal and sighed with pleasure. "The chicken and the baked beans are fantastic today. I swear the barbecue sauce gets better every time I eat here."

"Of course it tastes great," I crowed. "Because *I* make it."

Sophia jabbed her elbow into my side hard enough to make me wince. "*I* made the sauce today, remember?"

"I certainly do now," I wheezed, and massaged my aching ribs.

Like all dwarves, Sophia was exceptionally strong, but she didn't know her own strength sometimes, especially when she was trying to teach me a lesson.

"Well, my thanks go to the cook." Owen winked at the Goth dwarf, who smiled back at him.

Now that credit had been given where credit was due, Sophia went over to the ovens to slide in another tray of her sourdough rolls. Owen and Silvio dug into their food, while I moved around the restaurant, refilling drinks for the other diners, clearing away their dirty dishes, and wiping down the tables after they'd paid up and left.

I had just cashed out the final group of diners and told the waitstaff to take a break in the back when the bell over the front door chimed, and two more customers stepped into the restaurant: Mallory and Lorelei Parker.

Mallory was a three-hundred-plus-year-old dwarf with a fluffy cloud of snow-white hair, while Lorelei, her great-granddaughter many times over, was around my age, thirty-one or so, with black hair, blue eyes, and pretty features. The two of them shrugged out of their coats and hung them on the rack by the door.

Given how empty the restaurant was, I thought they might slide into a booth so they would be more comfortable, but Mallory marched straight over to the counter, and Lorelei followed her.

Mallory's quick, precise movements made the stacks of diamond rings on her fingers flash, along with the impressive diamond choker around her neck. No matter how big or small the occasion, I'd never seen her without a plethora of jewels.

Lorelei was also wearing diamonds, although hers were far more subdued, limited to a single ring with a rose-and-thorn pattern, her personal rune, the symbol for how deadly beauty could be.

The two of them slid onto stools beside Silvio. Mallory gestured at me with a sharp, impatient wave, and I walked over to her and Lorelei, who gave me a far more polite and normal nod of greeting.

"Ladies," I drawled. "What can I do for you today?"

"I want to hire you," Mallory pronounced in her twangy, hillbilly voice, going straight past niceties and getting down to business.

Not what I'd expected her to say, but she was my friend, so I decided to play along. "Okay. For what?"

"For what you do best, Gin." Mallory leaned forward and stabbed her finger at me. "I want you to find whomever is behind that attack on Stuart Mosley and kill them."

✳ 8 ✳

Again, not what I had expected her to say, but there was no missing the anger and determination glinting in the dwarf's blue eyes.

"Finn called and told me all about it this morning," Mallory continued in that same sharp voice.

I frowned. Finn had called and left me a message while I was oversleeping, saying that everything was quiet and he was going to stick to Mosley like glue all day. He hadn't mentioned anything about looping in Mallory.

"Finn called you about Mosley?" I asked. "Why?"

Mallory ducked her head, but not before I noticed the pink blush staining her wrinkled cheeks. "Finn thought I would want to know, since Stuart and I are old friends."

Lorelei snorted. "If by *old friends* you really mean *old friends with benefits*, then yes, you could say that. One might even say that the two of you are the very *best* of friends."

Mallory's blush brightened, and she waved her hand, making her diamond rings sparkle again. "In my day, it wasn't polite to talk about a lady's relationship with a gentleman."

Lorelei snorted again, amused by her grandmother's old-fashioned sensibilities.

"And how did you and Mosley become such good friends?" I asked.

"Stuart and I knew each other growing up, although we lost touch over the years. A couple of months ago, we ran into each other during that cocktail party at First Trust bank." Mallory's blush brightened even more. "Things just…progressed from there."

I had seen the two of them talking during the bank's doomed party, right before Rodrigo Santos and his men had tried to rob the guests, and I remembered how friendly they had seemed. Good for them for finding each other again after all these years.

"Lorelei and I just came from the bank," Mallory continued. "Did you know that stupid, stubborn fool actually went to work today? As if he wasn't almost killed last night!"

"Actually, the bank is probably the safest place for Mosley to be," Lorelei pointed out in a calm, reasonable voice, as if she'd already said this more than once. "It is one of the most secure buildings in Ashland, and the bank guards and employees are all exceedingly loyal to Mosley. Nobody's getting to him there."

"Well, I don't like it." Mallory shook her head. "I just don't like it."

"Now you sound like Gin," Silvio murmured.

"Yep," Owen chimed in. "As paranoid as paranoid can be."

"Hey!" I leaned over the counter and lightly punched my significant other on the shoulder. "Have we forgotten about Hugh Tucker and the Circle? Not to mention the underworld bosses who want me dead. I have very good reasons for my paranoia."

"I know." Owen grinned. "But you get all cute and sexy when you get worked up about it."

He winked at me. I rolled my eyes and punched him on the shoulder again, but I was smiling the whole time.

A few more folks trickled into the restaurant, and I went over and took their orders. Mallory and Lorelei decided to eat as well, since we hadn't finished our conversation.

Ten minutes later, Sophia handed me several plates, and I served the other customers, along with my friends—grilled cheese with a side salad for Mallory and a buttermilk fried chicken platter with sourdough rolls, mashed potatoes, and mac and cheese for Lorelei.

I checked on the other customers, making sure everyone had what they needed, then came back over to the counter, where Mallory and Lorelei were still sitting with Silvio and Owen.

Lorelei must have been hungry, because she'd already polished off one piece of the golden-brown, crunchy fried chicken, but Mallory just moved her salad from one side of the bowl to the other, and she hadn't even touched her grilled cheese. She was still worrying about Mosley.

Since Lorelei was eating and Mallory was brooding, I decided to do some more work. So I put some mayonnaise in a large bowl, then added white vinegar, sugar, salt, and a generous dash of black pepper to make the tart, tangy dressing for the rest of the day's coleslaw. I grabbed a whisk and started blending the ingredients together.

Mallory finally sighed and put down her fork without taking a single bite of her salad. "It would be one thing if Stuart was going to work at the bank where it's safe all day. But he's not. Oh, no. He's on his way over to the Eaton Estate right now to make sure everything's ready for that charity auction tonight."

Shock jolted through me. The whisk slipped from my hand, hit the side of the metal bowl with a loud *clang*, and dropped down into the coleslaw dressing. "What did you say?"

"That Stuart is going ahead with the auction tonight," Mallory repeated. "Didn't Finn tell you?"

"No, not that. Where did you say it was being held?"

"The Eaton Estate." She frowned. "Why?"

I thought back to my conversation with Mosley at Underwood's last night. He'd said something about having to find a venue, but he'd never mentioned exactly *where* the auction was being held, and I hadn't asked. But the Eaton Estate? That couldn't be a coincidence…could it?

I looked over at Silvio, whose thoughtful expression told me that he was thinking the same thing. I nodded, and he reached down, pulled the photo I'd given him out of his briefcase on the floor, and slid it over to where Mallory and Lorelei could see it. Owen leaned forward so he could study the photo too.

"Amelia Eaton," Mallory said. "I haven't thought about her in years. Where did you get this?"

"I found it last night in a file in Fletcher's office."

The two women looked at me, understanding filling their faces. They both knew about Fletcher's propensity for keeping track of criminals, as well as the people he had helped as the Tin Man. People like Lorelei, whom Fletcher had rescued from her abusive father.

Lorelei pointed at Amelia's smiling face. "Wait a second. Isn't she dead?"

"Most definitely," I muttered.

Mallory and Lorelei stared at me. So did Owen.

"You and Fletcher?" he asked in a soft voice.

"Yeah."

Nobody said anything, but Owen reached across the counter and squeezed my hand in a silent show of support.

Silvio cleared his throat. "I was just looking into Ms. Eaton, but my information is preliminary at best. Do you happen to know when or where this photo might have been taken?"

He directed his question at Mallory, who picked up the photo so she could get a closer look at it. After several seconds, she set it back down on the counter again.

"I can't tell when, but this looks like it was taken at the Eaton Estate. See all those fancy little letter *E*s carved into the fireplace?" She tapped her finger on that part of the photo. "From what I remember, the main library at the estate has a fireplace that looks like this one."

I peered at the photo. Despite how carefully I'd studied it last night, I hadn't noticed the letters before, but now that Mallory was pointing them out, I could see that several small *E*s were carved into the marble right above the fireplace mantel. She was right. This photo had most likely been taken at the estate.

"What about Amelia Eaton?" I asked. "Do you know anything about her?"

Mallory's blue gaze grew dark and distant as she thought back. "Not much. Like I said, I haven't thought about her in years. To me, she was just another snooty socialite from an old-money Ashland family. Of course, there were all those nasty rumors floating around about her actually eating people instead of just drinking their blood like regular vampires do. But the rumors always seemed to die down after Amelia made a few generous charity donations."

"I'm guessing those weren't just rumors," Owen said. "Not if Gin and Fletcher were involved."

The image of Amelia looming over me, her fangs

glinting like knives in her mouth as she plotted the best way to fillet me, filled my mind. *I like my dinner warm.* Her voice echoed in my ears.

My fingers clenched into fists, and I had to shake my head to clear away the memories. "Unfortunately not."

"Well, other than that, I don't remember anything about her," Mallory said. "I'm sorry, Gin."

I shrugged. "It's not your fault."

We all fell silent again, each of us staring at the photo and trying to figure out what it meant—if it meant anything at all. Amelia Eaton was as dead as dead could be, so there was no way she had sent those two muggers after Mosley. But Mosley having the auction at the Eaton Estate made all sorts of little warning bells chime in my mind.

Mallory noticed my tense expression. "You're really worried about Stuart, aren't you?"

I let out a breath. "Yeah. Fletcher knew that Amelia was dead, so he kept this photo for some other reason. I want to know what it is."

"Does that mean you'll look into this for me? Find out who went after my Stuart and why?"

Her voice took on a soft, almost pleading note, especially when she said *my Stuart.* Lorelei might have jokingly called them *old friends with benefits,* but it was obvious that Mallory cared very deeply about Mosley. I couldn't say no to her, just like I couldn't say no to anyone who asked for my help.

"I'll do you one better," I said. "I'll go to the auction tonight and keep an eye on things. Just in case someone is up to no good. How's that?"

Gratitude shimmered in Mallory's blue gaze, and she held her arms out to me. I leaned across the counter and hugged her.

"Thank you, Gin," she whispered in my ear. "This means the world to me."

"No thanks necessary. It's what I do, remember?" I murmured back to her.

Mallory hugged me even tighter, making me wince. Like Mosley, she was still quite strong, despite her advanced years, and I had to bite my tongue to keep from telling the dwarf that her gratitude was slowly cracking my ribs.

Finally, Mallory drew back. She cleared her throat and blinked her eyes, as though holding back tears. Lorelei noticed her grandmother's emotion, and she started chattering on about how good lunch had been, trying to distract the older woman. Lorelei kept up a steady stream of conversation as she and Mallory slid off their stools, paid for their meals, and shrugged into their coats.

We all made promises to meet up and keep an eye on Mosley at the auction. Now that we were going out later, Owen had to get back to work and wrap up a few things. So he kissed me good-bye, grabbed his own coat, and left the restaurant with Mallory and Lorelei. That left me alone at the counter with Silvio.

My assistant waited until the three of them had disappeared out of sight of the storefront windows before turning around on his stool and facing me. "There you go again, throwing yourself headlong into possible danger just because someone asks you to."

I sighed. "I know. But Mallory and Lorelei are my friends. So is Mosley, and I'm not going to let anyone hurt them."

Silvio's gray gaze softened. "I know. And I'm going to do everything I can to help you keep Mosley safe. And yourself too."

"Thank you."

He nodded and picked up his tablet to get back to work, while I returned to my cooking.

By this point, the whisk had sunk below the surface of the creamy coleslaw dressing all the way down to the very bottom of the bowl.

I couldn't help but think it was an omen of things to come—and that I was like the whisk, slowly drowning in a mayonnaise sea of trouble.

✿ 9 ✿

The afternoon passed quietly at the restaurant, and Sophia and Catalina took over for me around five o'clock so I could go home, shower, and get dressed for the auction. Once I was ready, I drove over to Owen's mansion.

I found him in the downstairs living room, standing still while Eva, his younger sister, skillfully twisted his black tie into the perfect bow. I leaned against the doorway and watched them.

Owen looked gorgeous in his classic black tuxedo, but Eva was dressed for a night at home in a blue Ashland Community College sweatshirt, sweatpants, and thick socks. Her black hair was pulled back into a messy ponytail, and her blue gaze was fixed on Owen's bow tie.

"I don't know why you can't do this yourself," she said. "I've shown you how to do it a dozen times now. It's the easiest thing *ever*."

"Maybe for you," Owen said. "Besides, maybe I just like having you do it for me."

"Making your baby sister into your fashion slave?" Eva rolled her eyes at his teasing. "Whatever, bro."

"Looks like you guys started the party without me," I called out.

Eva finished with Owen's bow tie, and they both looked at me. Owen let out a low wolf whistle of appreciation, while Eva clapped her hands.

"You look amazing, Gin!" she squealed.

I smoothed down my dress, which Finn had insisted that I buy when he'd dragged me out shopping to the Posh boutique a few weeks ago. The dress was a beautiful royal-blue crushed velvet and featured a sweetheart neckline that plunged down, highlighting what cleavage I had, while cap sleeves made of sheer black fabric covered my shoulders. The tiny black crystals on the sleeves were arranged to look like small webs, while a larger spiderlike pattern marked the center of the bodice, making me look like, well, the spider in the center of her own web. My silverstone spider rune pendant hung around my neck to further emphasize who and what I was, while my spider rune ring glinted on my finger like usual.

My dark brown hair hung loose and simple around my shoulders, although I'd gone dramatic with my makeup. Dark, smoky shadow and liner covered my eyes, while deep plum lipstick completed my diva look.

I fiddled with one of my sleeves, then the other, straightening them both the tiniest bit. "You don't think it's too much?"

Eva grinned. "Absolutely not."

She made Owen stand next to me so she could take pictures of us with her phone, like we were two kids about to go to the prom.

Owen leaned over and murmured in my ear. "You look

so good in that dress that I'm tempted to skip the auction and stay here."

"And Mallory would kill us both if I didn't keep my promise to watch out for Mosley."

"Trust me, it would be worth it, and I would die a very happy man."

I reached up and straightened his bow tie before sliding my hands down his muscled chest. "Well, the auction won't last all night. We'll talk more about your suggestion later. In much greater detail."

His violet eyes warmed, and his lips curved up into a teasing, devilish grin that made my heart skip a beat. "I'll take you up on that."

I grinned back at him. "I'm counting on it."

"Ewww!" Eva crinkled her nose. "You guys realize that I can totally hear you making your sexy-time plans, right? Now, quit lusting after each other and look this way again."

Owen and I laughed and turned back to the camera.

Eva finished taking photos, then went into the kitchen to put out some snacks for her study date with Violet Fox, her best friend, along with Catalina Vasquez and Elissa Daniels. Owen and I got into his car and headed over to the Eaton Estate.

Owen drove past the Ashland Botanical Gardens, then steered his car through the estate's open main gate and up a long, steep driveway. We crested the top of the hill, and a giant wearing a green suit jacket pointed us toward a parking area that was already bristling with cars.

Owen handed his keys off to a valet, then came over, opened my door, and helped me out of the car. He offered me his arm, and the two of us fell in step with the people streaming out of the lot and walking along a winding path. The trees fell away, and the Eaton mansion loomed up before us.

It looked exactly the same as I remembered it, five stories of gray granite dotted with windows and balconies and topped with steep, sloping roofs. This wasn't the first time I had returned to the scene of one of my many crimes, but for some reason, the sight of the mansion made me uneasy. Maybe because I hadn't been able to identify the threat to Mosley yet—or figure out how it was possibly connected to the woman I'd killed all those years ago.

At the far end of the path, several giant guards were stationed around a white trellis covered with twinkle lights, directing people into the auction. Owen handed our invitation to one of the guards, who checked it and waved us on through.

We walked through the trellis entrance and stepped onto the gray stone terrace that stretched out from the back of the mansion. At first glance, it seemed like your typical Ashland society shindig. People, lights, music, food. But the longer I looked around, the more uneasy I became. My arm slipped out of Owen's, and I moved forward, my gaze darting from one thing to the next. It took me a few seconds, but I finally realized why I felt so uncomfortable.

The terrace was decorated *exactly* the same way it had been the night I'd killed Amelia Eaton.

Tables covered with emerald-green linens. An impressive buffet. Towers of champagne glasses. White twinkle lights everywhere. A dance floor. A string quartet. It was a common party setup and one that I'd seen dozens of times before. But everything was *exactly* the same, right down to the waiters with their emerald-green bow ties and tuxedo vests and the classical music that trilled through the air.

I blinked and blinked, but my vision remained sharp and clear, and nothing changed. It was like I'd stepped back in time—or was still trapped in my nightmarish memory. I almost expected to see Amelia holding court in the center of the terrace like she had back then. My gaze even snapped over to the spot where I'd first seen her, but of course she wasn't there.

Dead—Amelia Eaton was *dead*. I knew this with absolute *certainty*. But I couldn't shake this intense feeling of déjà vu, and I kept scanning the area, still searching for her.

"Gin?" Owen asked. "Is something wrong? You have a really weird look on your face."

"Just a bad memory." I shook my head and took his arm again. "C'mon. Let's find Finn and Mosley."

We moved across the crowded terrace, and I finally noticed some differences between back then and right now. Instead of a hot summer night, this was a cold winter's eve, and space heaters lined the area, blasting out some much-needed warmth. The charity auction was also a far more formal affair than Amelia's cocktail party had been, and the men wore tuxedos, while the women sported evening gowns and sequined wraps, although the flimsy fabrics provided little protection against the chilly breeze.

The feel of that cold wind and the glitter of the gowns, as well as the solid, comforting strength of Owen's arm linked through my own, slowly helped me relax. I almost chalked up the decorations to coincidence.

Until I noticed the white roses.

They were *everywhere*—perched in the vases on the tables, wound through the towers of champagne glasses, even twined through the white lights that had been strung up along the stone wall at the back of the terrace. White rose petals had also been scattered over the wooden dance floor, and they gusted up into the air like fragrant flakes of snow. I caught one of the petals in my fingertips and brought it up to my nose. Even the overpowering, sickeningly sweet stench was the same, with that same hint of foul rot lurking underneath.

Another wave of déjà vu washed over me, even stronger than before, and my earlier worry bubbled right back up again. I rubbed the silky petal between my fingers, thinking about all the calls Mosley had gotten about the flowers last night. Whomever he'd been talking with had thought that the roses were extremely important, and my paranoid self couldn't help but think that person had wanted the flowers to further recreate Amelia's final party. But who? And why? What was the point of all this?

"Gin?" Owen asked again. "What's wrong?"

"I'm just wondering who ordered the roses."

He gave me a strange look, clearly not understanding what I was talking about, but I didn't feel like explaining, so I flicked the rose petal away, and we walked on.

Many of the partygoers were standing along the stone wall, and Owen and I went over there to see what had attracted everyone's attention.

The lake was frozen.

A solid sheet of elemental Ice covered the man-made lake in the shallow valley below, and it gleamed like a silver mirror that had been laid over the water. Several men and women in brightly colored sequined costumes skated on the Ice, doing elaborate spins, twirls, and jumps, much to the delight of the *oohing* and *aahing* crowd. Several Ice elementals wearing green bow ties and tuxedo vests stood on a wooden platform down by the lakeshore, their eyes glowing as they concentrated their magic on the water, keeping it frozen solid for the skaters.

"No wonder Mosley was complaining about the auction budget getting out of control," I said. "Hiring those Ice elementals to keep the lake frozen would have cost a fortune all by itself, not to mention paying the skaters to perform."

"But can you really put a price on such a grand spectacle?" Owen asked.

I snorted. "That sounds like something Finn would say."

"Yep," he agreed. "And it's probably the exact justification that whoever planned the auction used to waste all this money."

Owen and I turned away from the ice-skating spectacle and looked back over the terrace again. I finally spotted Finn waving at us, and we walked over to him and Bria.

Every man here had on a black tuxedo, but Finn wore his better than most, and his walnut-brown hair gleamed under the lights. Bria looked absolutely stunning in a tight silver-sequined gown with long sleeves. Her blond hair was sleeked back into a high bun, and her simple, understated makeup brought out her blue eyes.

More than one person gave her an admiring glance, although Finn possessively cupped her elbow, shooting *drop-dead-she's-mine* looks at any man who even thought about approaching and trying to steal her away from him.

"Finally," Finn said. "I thought you two were *never* going to get here. Now I can take a break and let someone else worry about assassins lurking around every corner."

He grabbed two champagne flutes from a passing waiter, then bowed low to Bria before presenting her with one of the glasses. Finn winked at my sister and clinked his flute against hers. "As well as focus on my lady love."

Bria arched her eyebrows, but she stood on her tiptoes and whispered something into his ear. Finn blinked rapidly, as if he was having trouble processing her words, but the wide smile that creased his face told me what Bria had suggested to him. Sexy times, as Eva had so succinctly described them earlier.

"And where is the man of the hour?" I asked.

Finn gestured with his glass. Stuart Mosley was standing a few feet away with Mallory and Lorelei Parker. Mosley was also wearing a tuxedo, while Mallory looked elegant in a pale blue gown, and Lorelei was the epitome of glamour in a slinky black-sequined dress.

Mosley had his arm threaded through Mallory's, and it was easy to tell from their adoring glances at each other that they were far more than just old friends with benefits. They made a lovely couple, and I wasn't going to let anyone ruin their happiness tonight.

I turned back to Finn. "I thought you were going to stick to Mosley like glue. Not let him wander around by himself."

"He's not by himself. Mallory and Lorelei are with him."

I gave him a look.

Finn rolled his eyes. "Oh, relax, Gin." He gestured around with his glass again. "See the giant guards roaming around? They all work at the bank, which means they're all Mosley's men. Trust me. He's perfectly safe here."

He was right. More than two dozen giant guards wearing tuxedos were patrolling the terrace, ready to deal with drunken debutantes, boisterous businessmen, and any other potential dangers. Maybe it was how weirdly similar everything was to the night I'd killed Amelia, but I still couldn't shake the feeling that something was very wrong here.

I looked at Bria. "Anything new on Vera and Eddie Jones? Did either one of them have any underworld connections?"

She shook her head. "Nope. Other than their rap sheets, Xavier and I haven't found anything suspicious on them so far. Neither has Silvio, from the updates he's been texting me."

I wasn't surprised, but frustration still surged through me. The answer was probably right under my nose, so close and obvious that I just couldn't see it. That was the way these things *always* went.

But even more worrisome, I felt like I *knew* the answer to my questions—who had hired the muggers, who was targeting Mosley, and why this party seemed identical to Amelia's bash.

I couldn't shake the nagging feeling that I was forgetting something extremely important, something I should have remembered the second I'd found that photo of Mosley and Amelia in Fletcher's file. Once again, I racked my brain, but I couldn't quite grab hold of the memories that were buried in the muck of my mind.

But I wasn't ready to give up, so I looked at Finn again. "Did anything out of the ordinary happen today? Anyone suspicious come by the bank? Any threats at all?"

He shook his head. "Nope. We worked all morning and through lunch reviewing several accounts, then came over here this afternoon to oversee the auction setup. We've been here ever since."

"So you actually haven't been beset by deadly assassins at every turn," Owen drawled.

Finn took a sip from his glass, then made a face. "Not unless you think that drinking flat champagne qualifies as mortal danger. But with this cheap swill, that may very well be the case."

Although I hope you have something down there that's better than that cheap champagne the waiters are serving. It's already lost all of its bubbles.

The sound of my own voice whispered in my mind as I thought about that snide remark I'd made to Amelia. On impulse, I grabbed Finn's glass out of his hand and took a drink.

"Hey!" he protested.

I ignored him and swished the liquid around in my mouth, really *tasting* it. I couldn't be certain, since it had been so long ago, but it seemed just like the champagne that had been served that night, right down to how flat it was. This was rapidly going from weird to downright creepy.

The few bubbles in the champagne still tickled my sinuses, and I had to swallow and wrinkle my nose to keep from sneezing. Finn, Bria, and Owen all stared at me with puzzled expressions, so I handed the glass off to a passing waiter and forced myself to smile at them.

"Sorry. I was thirsty."

They all kept staring at me, clearly wondering what was going on, but luckily for me, Mosley walked over to us, along with Mallory and Lorelei. Mosley grabbed Bria's hand and bowed to her, before doing the same to me.

"Bria, Gin," he rumbled. "You both look wonderful. I hope that Finn and Owen realize how lucky they are."

"Don't I know it." Owen wrapped his arm around my waist and hugged me close.

I reached up and tweaked his bow tie. "And I know it too."

He grinned. "I wouldn't have it any other way."

I grinned back at him for a second, then tipped my head to Mosley. "And you're looking quite dashing yourself. Especially given what happened last night."

Mosley harrumphed and waved his hand. "I've already moved past that nasty incident, and you should too, Gin. Despite what you might think, I highly doubt that anyone is after me."

Mallory elbowed him in the side. "And Gin is the professional here, not you, Stuey. If you won't listen to me, then you should at least listen to her."

Stuey? I mouthed to Lorelei. She grinned and shrugged back at me.

"Well, I'll be a lot better once this whole circus is over with," Mosley grumbled. "Seriously, what did we need with ice-skaters? What do they have to do with the auction? But that's what the board members wanted. One of them, anyway."

"Just one of them?" Bria asked.

He sighed. "Yes, the proverbial thorn in my side."

Mallory patted his arm in understanding. "Don't feel bad, Stuey. That woman would drive anyone plumb crazy with all of her demands."

"Who?" I asked.

Mosley had started to answer me when a series of whispers rippled through the crowd, indicating that someone particularly rich, powerful, scandalous, or all three had arrived.

The crowd parted as a woman strode across the terrace toward us. She was stunningly beautiful, with long black hair wound up into an elaborate braided bun, green eyes, and flawless skin. Her sequined emerald-green evening gown clung to her body like a second skin, while a slit up the side accentuated her long, lean legs.

She strutted over to us with all the confidence of a supermodel working the catwalk, knowing that everyone was watching her and her alone. Her smooth, sinuous movements were the epitome of grace, beauty, and elegance, but they also reminded me of the way a panther might stalk its prey for the night.

My eyes widened, and my gaze darted from one thing to the next. Her hair, eyes, skin, dress, even the way she moved. Just like the party decorations and the white roses, everything about her was eerily, sickeningly familiar.

The woman walking toward me looked *exactly* like Amelia Eaton.

❋ 10 ❋

The woman stopped right in front of me, put her hand on her hip, and struck a pose, as if inviting everyone to admire her. No, not inviting admiration, *demanding* it.

I kept staring at her, but her features were the same as before. Black hair, green eyes, perfect skin. I even spotted the pearly flash of fangs in her mouth that marked her as a vampire.

It was like Amelia Eaton had stepped right out of my worst nightmares and back into the real world to haunt me. The edges of my vision blurred, my heart hammered in my chest, and the champagne I'd drunk roiled around in my stomach, threatening to come back up.

Dead, I reminded myself. Amelia was *dead*, and I was the one who'd made her that way.

The cold, hard knowledge comforted me. Slowly, my vision cleared, my heart slowed, and the champagne stayed down in my stomach, where it belonged. I drew in a deep breath and let it out to further steady myself, although it took me another moment to shake off the last of my shock.

When I was calm, I studied her again, much more

carefully this time, and I finally started to notice the subtle differences between this woman and the one I'd killed.

She looked to be in her mid-twenties, which made her younger than Amelia had been when she died. This woman was also a bit taller, with a strong, muscled body that still had plenty of curves in all the right places. Her nose was a touch longer, her cheekbones a bit higher, her eyes a lighter, brighter green. Still, the resemblance was uncanny. This woman wasn't Amelia Eaton, but she was the next closest thing: her daughter.

Amelia's daughter. Of course. How could I have forgotten about *her*?

Those memories buried in the muck of my mind immediately broke free and flooded my thoughts, each one bringing a fresh wave of pain with it—along with more than a little guilt, shame, and self-loathing.

I hadn't forgotten about Amelia's daughter. Not really. It had just never occurred to me that she could be connected to the attack on Mosley, especially since I was the one who'd killed her mother. But even more than that, I hadn't wanted to think about what *I* had done to *her*, especially since it was the same cruel, heartless, unforgivable thing that had been done to me once upon a time.

She must have sensed my surprise, because she stared right back at me, her gaze flicking over me from top to bottom. Her mouth puckered in thought, but after a few seconds, she dismissed me as unimportant and turned to Mosley.

"Stuart," she said in a cool voice. "So lovely to see you."

She stepped forward and air-kissed both of his cheeks. Mosley didn't move away, but he didn't return the gesture either.

"Everyone," he said. "This is Alanna Eaton. She's on the Briartop board of directors and has been very…involved in planning the auction."

Alanna.

The name slammed into my heart like a knife, even as screams echoed in my ears—her screams. But no one else seemed to notice my misery, so I shoved my memories back down into the muck of my mind. There would be plenty of time later to drag them out into the light, examine them, and catalog my many, many failings.

Given Mosley's hesitation in describing her, Alanna must be the person who'd been causing him so many headaches over the past few weeks. That meant she was most likely responsible for the ice-skaters on the frozen lake and the other decorations—the same kind of decorations that had been strung up here the night I killed her mother. Seemed as if I wasn't the only one who was obsessed with the past.

"Alanna," Mosley said, "I want to thank you again for all your help. Everything turned out beautifully."

"Oh, no. Thank *you*, Stuart. I'm so glad you decided to take me up on my suggestion to hold the auction at my family's home."

Alanna smiled, but the expression didn't even come close to reaching her eyes, and her tone was anything but warm, despite her seemingly kind words. She reminded me of a marble statue—sleek and beautiful but utterly cold to the core.

"After all," she continued, "I don't get to visit the family homestead *nearly* as much as I would like, given all the weddings, parties, and picnics that you book here year-round."

She said *weddings, parties,* and *picnics* like she really

meant *invasions*, *epidemics*, and *plagues*. Mosley winced, as though she'd just sliced open his guts with her verbal daggers.

Everyone knew that the Eaton Estate could be rented out for weddings, anniversary dinners, and the like—for a hefty fee, of course. Among the society folks, having an event here was a status symbol that told everyone how much money you had. But the way Alanna was talking made it seem like Mosley was renting out the estate against her wishes. But how could he do that? Alanna owned the estate…didn't she?

She looked at Mosley a moment longer, then plucked one of the white roses out of a vase on the table next to her. She brought the flower up to her nose and inhaled deeply, enjoying the scent, before tucking it behind her right ear. "I think the roses are the perfect finishing touch, don't you?"

Mosley cleared his throat. "Yes. Just like you said they would be on the phone last night. I'm glad we were able to add them at the last minute."

"Mmm." Once again, her tone was anything but warm, despite his compliment.

So Alanna was the one who'd been repeatedly calling Mosley last night. She seemed like the kind of person who would incessantly quibble over the smallest detail until she got her way, but I wondered if she'd had an ulterior motive. All those calls would have also been an excellent way to track Mosley, especially if she'd ordered a couple of hired hands to kidnap the dwarf and bring him to her. That would make her smart and devious, as well as demanding. A dangerous combination.

Mosley cleared his throat again. "Let me introduce you."

He made the introductions. Alanna inclined her head to

everyone in turn, although she didn't step forward and air-kiss anyone else's cheeks.

"And let me introduce my companions as well." Alanna snapped her fingers, and a man separated himself from the crowd and strode over to us. He was a couple of inches over six feet tall, with spiky blond hair, hazel eyes, and a muscled body. "This is Terrence Phelps, my head of security."

Phelps smiled, showing off his fangs. So he was a vampire like his boss.

"And now let me introduce my date," Alanna purred, her voice taking on a note of sly satisfaction. "Darling! Over here!"

She fluttered her hand, and another man broke free of the crowd and strode toward us. His black tuxedo highlighted his tall, strong body, and his black hair and eyes gleamed under the lights, as did the neatly trimmed black goatee that clung to his chin. He had one of those ageless faces, although I knew he was in his fifties, roughly the same age my mother would have been, if she had lived.

If this man hadn't been involved in her murder.

Cold shock doused me from head to toe, like I was a figure skater who'd been unfortunate enough to crack open a hole in the elemental Ice and plunge into the chilly lake water below. I blinked and blinked, wondering if my mind was playing tricks on me the way it had with Alanna.

But it wasn't.

He was *here*. At the auction. Walking toward me as though he weren't my own personal nemesis.

The man reached Alanna, and she gazed up at him a moment before turning her attention back to the rest of us.

"Everyone, this is my date for the evening," she purred again, that same sly, satisfied note in her voice. "Hugh Tucker."

That cold shock intensified, like I had ice running through my veins instead of blood. My fingers, my toes, even the tip of my nose. Everything felt frozen right now, especially my heart, which somehow kept beating, despite the frigid fist that squeezed it tight.

I just stood there, staring dumbfounded at the vampire. Even with my rampant paranoia about the Circle and their many plots, I'd never expected to see *him* here. Hugh Tucker kept to the shadows, where he could better carry out the Circle's deadly schemes. This was the first time he had crawled out into the light of such a public event since Deirdre Shaw's death.

So why was he here? Why the charity auction? And what did he have going on with Alanna?

The questions shattered my shock and swirled around in my mind like the white rose petals fluttering through the air. The flowers weren't the only things here that were rotten.

Owen and Finn both tensed, as stunned and wary as I was. So did Mosley, Mallory, and Lorelei. But Bria had a far more unexpected—and violent—reaction. My baby sister darted forward and slapped Hugh Tucker across the face as hard as she could.

The solid, satisfying *crack* of her hand against his cheek echoed across the terrace, even louder than the classical music. Everyone stopped their conversations to stare at us. The society folks knew a juicy bit of intrigue when they saw it.

"That was for my mother, you son of a bitch!" Bria hissed.

Her blue eyes glittered with rage, and her fingers twitched, like she was thinking about slapping him again. My sister didn't often lose her temper, but when she did, watch out. And I knew exactly what she was pissed about: Tucker's failure to stop our mother's murder, despite his claims that he'd loved her.

Terrence Phelps stepped up beside Tucker, as if to protect the other vampire from any more slaps, but Alanna made no move to intervene. Instead, she stood off to the side, an amused expression on her face. It was the first bit of real emotion she'd shown this whole time.

Several giant guards headed in our direction, but Mosley waved off his men, silently telling them that he had the situation under control. He also looked over at the orchestra members and made a circular motion with his finger, asking them to start playing again. After a few more seconds of shocked silence, music floated through the air again, and people slowly returned to their conversations, although all eyes were still focused on us.

Tucker remained calm in the face of Bria's anger. He lifted his hand to his cheek, massaging away the red, lingering sting of the slap, then smiled at her, showing off his white fangs.

"Lovely Bria. You are the spitting image of your mother," he murmured. "And even more important, you have Eira's fighting spirit, just like your equally lovely sister does."

He'd meant it as a compliment, but rage stained Bria's cheeks a dark pink. She lunged forward like she was going to slap him again, but Finn grabbed her arm, and she let him stop her.

"You're just lucky that I can't shoot you in front of all these witnesses!" she hissed again.

Tucker's smile widened, revealing even more of his sharp, pointed fangs. "What can I say? I have always been exceptionally lucky that way."

"Oh, yes," I said in a dry tone. "Cockroaches always find a way to survive."

Tucker turned his toothy smile to me. "Oh, be nice, Gin. Don't insult the cockroaches like that."

Mosley crossed his arms over his chest. "I should have you removed, Tucker."

"Oh, but you won't do that, Stuart," Alanna said. "You wouldn't want to cause any more of a scene than your friends already have. After all, that might impact the success of the auction, and we just can't have that. All those poor widows and orphans affected by the Briartop robbery deserve every single penny that we can raise for them."

She didn't care about all those poor widows and orphans. Not one little bit. She was just twisting the situation around to her advantage. But as much as I hated to admit it, she was right about the drama distracting people. Everyone was still staring at us with open curiosity, and several people were on their phones, probably texting the gossip to their friends.

"Why did you bring him here?" Mosley growled.

Alanna's eyes glittered with triumph, and a thin, satisfied smile curved her red lips. "Because this is *my* family's home, and I have the right to bring whomever I want here. Despite your feelings to the contrary."

Mosley's lips pinched into a tight line, but he didn't respond to her taunt.

Alanna snapped her fingers again. "Phelps, be a dear and fetch me a drink."

Phelps nodded, then walked over to a waiter.

"Come now, Hugh, darling," she said. "Let's have a drink. All this boring conversation is making me terribly thirsty."

Tucker's nostrils flared a bit, and a spark of annoyance flashed in his black eyes, as if he didn't like being called her *darling*. But the emotion vanished as quickly as it had appeared, and he held his arm out, playing the part of the perfect gentleman to her elegant lady.

Alanna threaded her arm through his. She gave Mosley one more satisfied smirk, and then the two of them strode away into the still-curious crowd.

11

Alanna Eaton glided away like a shark swimming through the shallows, searching for her dinner for the night, with Hugh Tucker right by her side.

Owen, Finn, Bria, Mosley, Mallory, Lorelei, and I watched them move from one person to the next, Alanna exchanging air kisses and cooing pleasantries to everyone, while Tucker stood silently by her side.

Phelps handed Alanna a glass of champagne, but he didn't even look at Tucker, much less offer to get the other man a drink, which told me that he was loyal only to Alanna. It made me even more curious about what she was doing here with Tucker. He certainly wasn't her date, despite her claims.

Finn was the first one to shake off his surprise and speak up. "Hugh Tucker out in the open for everyone to see. This can't be good."

"No, no, it can't be." I looked at Mosley. "There's something I need to show you."

I had been hoping to pull him aside and do this privately, but I wanted answers right now. So I grabbed my phone out of my black clutch and called up that photo of him with Amelia Eaton, since Silvio had scanned and emailed the picture to me earlier. I passed the phone over to Mosley, and he held it out where the others could see it.

"Where did you get this?" he asked.

"Fletcher had it."

With everything that had been going on, I hadn't had a chance to tell Finn about the photo, and he gave me a sharp look, realizing that I'd found it in the old man's files. I shrugged back at him.

"I'm guessing this photo has something to do with why Alanna hates you so much," I said.

Mosley sighed and handed the phone back to me. "Alanna's never been fond of me, but I can't really blame her for it."

"Why not?"

He sighed again, longer and deeper this time. "Amelia didn't manage the Eaton family fortune very well. She always spent far too much money, a mistake that she compounded by making several bad investments. Eventually, those investments wiped out her cash reserves. Long story short, the estate was mortgaged to the hilt. That photo was taken after I agreed to extend Amelia yet another loan. But she never got the chance to repay it, since she died soon after that." He paused a moment, as if what he was going to say next made him uncomfortable. "After her death, the bank took possession of the property."

"Wait a minute," Owen said. "First Trust bank—*you*—actually own the Eaton Estate?"

Mosley nodded. "Yes, I own the estate. I rent it out for various events to pay for the taxes, upkeep, and the like. The remainder of the money goes into a trust fund for Alanna. She was only fifteen when her mother died. I thought it was the least I could do for her, since Amelia left her with nothing."

Mallory patted his arm. "That's a lot more than most folks would have done for that girl. You have nothing to be ashamed of, Stuey. Nothing at all. It was just business. You didn't make Amelia spend her money and put the estate up as collateral. She made those choices all on her own."

He flashed her a grateful smile. Mallory leaned in a little closer to him, and Mosley curled his arm around her waist.

"It must be a very sizable trust fund," Lorelei murmured. "Given that Fiona Fine designer gown that Alanna is wearing."

"And her hoity-toity attitude," Bria chimed in.

We all looked over at Alanna again, who was still air-kissing her way through the crowd, with Phelps and Tucker trailing along behind her.

"How did I not know this?" I glanced at Finn. "Why didn't you tell me that Mosley owned the estate?"

"Because I thought you knew. It's pretty common knowledge." Finn shook his head. "Then again, you pay exactly zero attention to anything that doesn't involve you killing people."

He didn't know how ironic his words were. Because this *had* involved me killing someone—Alanna's mother. Which, in turn, had led to Alanna harboring a deep-seated grudge against Mosley for taking control of the Eaton Estate. Her mother had died, and she'd lost her family's home. I would have despised him for that too. Those were certainly two of the reasons I hated Tucker, his boss, Mason, and the rest of the Circle. I'd lost the exact same things Alanna had lost, and I was just as angry about them as she still was, even all these years later.

But in this case, Alanna's anger was misplaced, since *I* was the one who'd killed her mother.

That had been the first domino to fall in this long chain of events, and now here we all were. I wondered if Alanna realized that I was the one responsible for her mother's death. Thanks to my disguise back then, I didn't look anything like I had the night I killed Amelia. So far, Alanna hadn't paid much attention to me, but that could just be an act to get me to lower my guard so she could strike out at me later. No way to know for sure.

Given Alanna's obvious disdain for Mosley, there was no doubt in my mind that she was the one who'd sent those two muggers after him. And I was betting that she'd been the person driving the car that had almost mowed down Mosley and me after the muggers died.

But why? Alanna had had years to get her revenge on Mosley. So why target him now? What had changed in her world?

The obvious answer was Hugh Tucker.

He never did anything by accident, and he'd come here for a reason, even if I couldn't see exactly what it was. But it must be something big, something important, something to do with Circle business, for him to show his face at a party that my friends and I were attending. So what was he using Alanna for? Or was she using him? All the questions made my head pound.

"I need a drink," I muttered.

"You're not the only one," Bria said.

We kept watching Alanna, Phelps, and Tucker. Alanna was talking with someone, not paying the slightest bit of attention to us, while Phelps took her empty champagne glass and trotted off to get a fresh one. But Tucker looked over his shoulder at me.

After a few seconds of silent scrutiny, he grinned, held his hand up to his head, and snapped off a salute to me. The arrogant, mocking motion increased my worry that much more. Finn was right. Hugh Tucker out in the open like this only meant one thing.

Trouble—and lots of it.

A series of bells chimed, signaling the end of the cocktail hour and ice-skating extravaganza and the beginning of the auction. Owen offered me his arm again, and we followed our friends across the terrace, through some open doors, and into the mansion.

If the outside of the Eaton mansion resembled a grand chateau, then the inside was an impressive museum. All the antique furniture was polished to a high gloss, as were the stained-glass and other windows. Paintings of the mansion, grounds, lake, and surrounding forest adorned the walls, all of them housed in gleaming gold frames that featured vines and other scrollwork. Still more vines, flowers, and animals were carved into the gray stone walls next to the paintings, making it seem as though the flora and fauna were admiring the picturesque landscapes.

Owen and I kept walking until we reached the grand ballroom in the center of the mansion. The ballroom was just as beautiful as everything else, and sparks of opalescent white shimmered through the gray marble floor, making it seem as though we were standing on a bed of diamonds. The sparkling marble continued up the walls before spreading out across the ceiling, which soared a hundred feet overhead. An enormous chandelier hung in the middle, with its sprays of crystals tapering down to a sharp point, as though it were an oversize arrow that was about to break loose from the ceiling, drop down, and skewer a target on the floor below.

A table was set up by the ballroom entrance, and everyone had to get in line to receive a numbered placard in order to bid on the auction items. Up ahead, I spotted Alanna, still on Tucker's arm, letting him squire her around, with Phelps trailing along behind them.

Owen tracked my gaze. "What do you think they're up to?"

"Nothing good. Come on. Let's check on Mosley. I want to make sure he's protected, just in case Alanna decides to sic Tucker on him."

Owen and I got our placards, then headed over to our friends, who had already gone through the line. Mosley and Mallory were shaking hands and thanking everyone for coming, but they weren't alone. Two giants I recognized as security guards from First Trust bank hovered nearby. Looked like Mosley had taken steps to keep Mallory and himself safe. So Owen and I walked over to Finn, Bria, and Lorelei, who were sipping champagne and staring at Alanna and her two companions.

"So that's the big, bad Hugh Tucker in the flesh," Lorelei murmured. *"Hello, honey. He's handsome, for an older guy. I can see why your mama would have been attracted to him."*

Bria and I both shot her angry looks, and Lorelei held up her hands in mock surrender.

"I'm just saying," she said.

I started to look over at Tucker again, but Bria stepped in front of me, blocking my view.

"Forget about him," she said. "He knows that I can't shoot him and you can't go after him with your knives in front of all these people. He's probably just here to try to rattle you. Don't give him the satisfaction of getting under your skin."

I raised my eyebrows. "Says the woman who just bitch-slapped him in public."

A guilty blush stained Bria's cheeks, and her hand crept up to the silverstone pendant around her neck—a primrose, the symbol for beauty. She fiddled with the necklace for a few moments before letting it drop back down into place.

"I shouldn't have done that. It's just... I've been thinking a lot about what you told me. About him being in love with Mom but not doing enough to try to save her from Mab and the Circle. Seeing him here and realizing that he's alive and Mom isn't, and that Annabella is dead too... I just...lost it."

The pain shimmering in her eyes punched me in the gut. Sometimes I forgot that Bria had suffered just as much as I had and that she still felt the loss of our mother and sister as deeply as I did. I reached out and hugged her tight.

"Believe me, I know the feeling," I whispered in her ear before letting go.

Even now, the spider rune scars in my palms itched and burned, and I wanted nothing more than to grab the knife out of my purse, storm across the ballroom, and bury the blade in Tucker's black, black heart. But I couldn't do that.

Besides, I had Mosley to think about too. Whatever Alanna wanted, whether it was revenge against him for taking control of her family's estate or something else, she'd enlisted Tucker to help her get it. I needed to figure out what she was up to—and how it tied into the Circle—before Mosley or anyone else got hurt.

"Oh, you two need to quit being party poopers," Finn said. "Alanna and Tucker aren't stupid. They aren't going to do anything to Mosley, us, or anyone else here. This is just their opening salvo, shooting across the bow of our boat, so to speak, and letting everyone know that they're coming for us. So until something actually happens, we might as well relax and have a good time. We can't let them sink our battleship that easily."

Cheesy metaphors aside, Bria and Finn were both right. If nothing else, Tucker wanted to rattle my cage, and I wasn't going to let him realize how much it bothered me that he was here. So I forced myself to nod at Finn.

"Excellent!" he chirped. "Let's mosey around and see if anything in the auction strikes my fancy."

Lorelei snorted. "I don't think Mab had any paintings of dogs playing poker."

Finn sniffed. "Please. My tastes are *much* more refined than that. For instance, I'm particularly fond of cats playing poker."

Lorelei laughed and promised to catch up with us later, then went over to check on Mallory. Finn and Bria set off around the ballroom, and Owen and I fell in step behind them.

Two sections of chairs took up the center of the floor, arranged in front of a wooden podium topped with a microphone. After the viewing hour was over, everyone would be seated, and the auction would begin.

We moved over to the red velvet ropes that had been strung up around the perimeter to separate the crowd from the auction items lining the walls. Most of the smaller objects were housed in glass display cases, including rings, necklaces, and other baubles that Mab had worn, along with statues, carvings, vases, and other objects d'art. Far more of Mab's things had survived than I'd expected, given the destruction that Clementine Barker and her giants had caused at the Briartop museum.

Mosley had also arranged to add the contents of Mab's mansion to the auction, and large sections of the ballroom were devoted to chairs, lamps, desks, and other furniture. Each item was adorned with a large white identification tag that also featured the minimum starting bid.

Owen let out a low whistle. "Fifteen thousand dollars for an end table? Seriously? That thing is so tiny and flimsy-looking that I'd be afraid to put so much as a book on it."

Finn stared at the table with a dreamy expression. "That would look fantastic in my apartment."

Bria nudged him with her elbow. "Well, then, you should *totally* buy it."

Finn ignored her sarcasm. "I *totally* should. After all, it's for a good cause, right?"

I snorted. "Please. The snob in you just wants to be able to say that you have Mab Monroe's fifteen-thousand-dollar table in your apartment."

He grinned. "Absolutely."

We strolled on to the far side of the ballroom, which narrowed to a long corridor with several rooms branching off it. Finn stopped to talk to one of his bank clients, and Bria stayed with him, while Owen went to get a drink. I wanted to see the rest of Mab's things, so I walked down the hallway, going from one room to the next until I reached the main library at the end.

The library was beautiful, with picture windows, mahogany furniture, and rugs with black-and-white paisley patterns. Two large overstuffed armchairs and a low table crouched in front of a fireplace that was flanked by floor-to-ceiling bookshelves. I eyed the small *E*s carved into the stone above the mantel. Mallory was right. That photo of Mosley and Amelia had definitely been taken in here.

Lorelei was in the library, staring at a freestanding bookcase that was positioned behind the red velvet rope. Tears gleamed in her eyes, and she dabbed them away with her fingertips to keep from ruining her makeup. I glanced around, wondering if someone might have said something to upset her, but no one else was in here.

"Lorelei?" I asked. "What's wrong?"

She pointed a shaking finger at the case. Books lined the shelves, along with crystal paperweights and other knickknacks. At first, I didn't see what she was gesturing at, but then I noticed a photo in a silver frame that was propped up on a book with a pretty royal-blue cover and shiny silver-foil-trimmed pages.

I expected to see Mab in the picture, but it showed another girl, one with the same black hair and blue eyes as Lorelei. The girl was wearing a white frilly dress and lace gloves and smiling shyly at the camera, as if she was surprised that someone wanted to take her picture. I'd seen photos of her before, so I recognized her.

"That's my mama," Lorelei whispered. "This photo must have been taken at one of those cotillion balls that she and Mab both went to when they were young."

Lily Rose was Lorelei's mother and Mallory's beloved great-granddaughter. She'd been beaten to death by her abusive husband years ago, despite Fletcher's best efforts to save her, and I knew that Lorelei loved and missed her mother as much as Bria and I did ours.

I didn't want to intrude on her grief, so while she wiped away the rest of her tears, I read the white identification card propped up on one of the shelves. *A collection of books and photos from the estate of Mab Monroe. Minimum starting bid: $10,000.*

"That photo is *mine*," Lorelei said in a fierce voice, regaining her composure. "I don't care how much it costs me."

I reached out and squeezed her hand, telling her that I understood.

"There's something in here you should see too, Gin."

Lorelei led me over to a bookcase standing on the opposite side of the library. This case was a twin to the first one, right down to a framed photo also propped up on a royal-blue book with silver-foil-trimmed pages. And just like with Lily Rose, I recognized the three people in the photo instantly.

Mab Monroe with her coppery hair and dark eyes stood on one side. Mab stared into the camera with a bored expression, but the two people beside her looked stiff and tense, as if they didn't want to be anywhere near the Fire elemental, much less have their picture taken with her.

One of them was a beautiful woman with sleek blond hair and blue eyes, while the other was a handsome man with dark brown hair and gray eyes.

Eira Snow and her husband, Tristan.

✳ 12 ✳

For the second time tonight, cold shock flooded my body, drowning out everything else.

I'd never expected Mab to have a photo of my parents, or for that photo to be displayed here. After a moment, my body jerked forward, and my feet moved of their own accord. I stepped right up next to the red velvet rope and leaned forward, staring at the picture, my gaze flicking back and forth over it, trying to see every last little detail at once.

Mallory had given me some photos of my mother a few months ago, all of them taken at cotillion balls that Eira had attended with Lily Rose, Mab, and other society girls. I had grown used to seeing my mother's face again, but Mallory hadn't had any photos of my father, and I hadn't seen any pictures of him since Mab destroyed my family's home and everything in it.

Tristan, my father, had died when I was about five years old, shortly after Bria was born, so my memories of him were few, faint, and dim. But I still recognized his dark brown hair and especially his gray eyes, since they were the same ones that I saw every time I looked in the mirror.

"You have your father's coloring," Lorelei said, looking from me to the photo and back again. "And your mama's features."

I nodded, still too stunned to say anything. My gaze dropped to the identification card on one of the shelves, but it was the same as the card on the other bookcase. *A collection of books and photos from the estate of Mab Monroe. Minimum starting bid: $10,000.*

And the collection was going to be *mine*. Just like Lorelei, I didn't care how much I had to pay for it. I wanted that photo of my father, not just for myself but for Bria too. It would mean even more to her, since she'd never known him at all.

"Why didn't Mosley tell me that a photo of my parents was part of the auction?" I whispered.

Lorelei shook her head. "He probably didn't realize it was them. He didn't tell me about the photo of my mama either."

She must have seen the play of emotions across my face, as well as the tears suddenly stinging my eyes. She didn't want to intrude on my grief either, and she laid her hand on my shoulder. "I'll see you back in the ballroom."

I nodded. Lorelei gently squeezed my shoulder, then left the library.

I stared at the photo for the better part of a minute, especially my father's face, studying and imprinting it on my mind. Then, with shaking hands, I pulled my phone out of my purse and snapped several shots of the picture. No one was going to keep me from bidding on and winning this picture, but I wanted to have a copy of it with me right now. I also texted the images to Bria.

I had just slid my phone back into my purse when heels clattered out in the corridor, warning me that someone was coming. Probably Lorelei, checking to make sure I was okay.

I cleared my throat, blinked back the last of my tears, and looked over my shoulder. "I'm okay. You didn't have to come back—"

The words died on my lips. Lorelei wasn't standing in the doorway.

Alanna was.

Her red lips puckered, as though I had annoyed her just by being in here, but she strutted over to me anyway. We stood there, side by side, in front of the bookcase.

I stared at Alanna out of the corner of my eye, looking past her uncanny resemblance to her mother and sizing her up the way I would any potential enemy. I didn't sense any elemental magic emanating off her, but I was betting that she drank giant or dwarven blood on a regular basis, given the ripple of muscles in her arms. Her smooth, gliding gait indicated that she was fast as well as strong, and I had no idea what other vampiric abilities she might have. Everything about her whispered of power, danger, and death.

I wondered if Alanna shared her mama's cannibalistic appetite for warm blood, flesh, and bones. Probably. Fletcher had told me that hunting humans for their dinner was a tradition that had been passed down from one generation of the Eatons to the next.

All of that made Alanna extremely dangerous in her own right, but most worrisome was the fact that she didn't seem afraid of me. Not one little bit. Tucker had to have told her that I was the Spider and that I always carried several knives, but she didn't seem bothered by the fact that I was within arm's reach. Or perhaps she realized that I couldn't attack her in such a public setting any more than she could go after Mosley.

A few other people wandered into the library, but they stayed on the opposite side, looking at the auction items over there, so I studied Alanna again.

Her green gaze focused on the picture of my parents, along with the blue book it was perched on. Her red lips puckered again, as though she'd bitten into something sour. I wondered if she recognized Eira and Tristan as my parents. No way to tell.

"Interesting photo," she murmured. "I didn't realize how much of Ashland society Mab had chronicled over the years until I was curating the collection."

"You put the items together for the auction?"

She nodded. "I have degrees in art and history, so I suggested the minimum bids. Under Stuart's close supervision, of course. He's been in charge of the auction every single step of the way, from packing up what was left of the art at Briartop, to storing it at his bank, to bringing it over here and setting it up tonight. He's been very…thorough."

Her red lips puckered for a third time, as if Mosley's attention to detail had been particularly vexing, although I couldn't imagine why. Perhaps Alanna didn't appreciate being micromanaged.

"I didn't get to examine the items nearly as much as I wanted to in order to suggest the proper bids, and I didn't get to look at some of them at all, like these books." She waved her hand at the case. "Stuart thinks the auction items are all just old books and furniture. He has no appreciation for the artistry, the craftsmanship, that goes into such things. He didn't let me study them the way I wanted to, the way I *needed* to."

I got the impression that there was far more to her words than I was understanding, but I had no idea why she would be so focused on a case full of books. Or perhaps it was just the principle of not being able to do exactly what she wanted, when she wanted.

"What about the party decorations?" I asked. "Were those your idea too?"

"Of course. My mother used to throw such grand parties here. One year, for the holidays, she hired elementals to freeze the lake so she could teach me how to ice-skate. I wanted to recreate that to remember her, to honor her." Her eyes darkened with memories, as if she was thinking about her dead mother the same way I had thought about mine countless times.

Guilt twisted my stomach, but I kept fishing for information. "Well, the decorations are lovely. I particularly enjoyed the white roses. They have such a sweet, intoxicating scent, almost like perfume. Seeing them brought back so many memories."

I watched her carefully, wondering how she would react to my pointed words, but not a flicker of emotion marred her perfect features. I might as well have been talking to a statue for all the reaction she showed. If Alanna knew that I'd killed her mother, she was hiding it extremely well.

"Mmm." She made a noncommittal sound, then pivoted on her stilettos, putting a bit of distance between us. "Are you planning to bid on this lot? It's one of my personal favorites."

"Why, yes. I'm a bit of a bibliophile. Tell me, is that a first edition of *The Adventures of Huckleberry Finn* on the shelf? I'm a sucker for Southern literature."

"You have quite the sharp gaze, don't you, Ms. Blanco?"

I smiled. "That's not the only thing that's sharp on me. Didn't your new beau, Hugh, tell you that?"

She returned my smile, baring her fangs a bit. "He might have mentioned something to that effect."

"I just bet he did."

Her smile widened, revealing even more of her fangs. I kept my gaze steady on hers, not backing down for a second.

"I don't know what game you're playing with Tucker, and I really don't care."

She arched an eyebrow. "But?"

"But if you go after Mosley again, it *will* be the last thing you ever do. Trust me on that." I let the coldness seep into my wintry gray eyes, telling her exactly how serious I was.

Alanna arched her eyebrow a little higher at my threat, then laughed right in my face.

Her loud, hearty chuckles echoed from one side of the library to the other and back again, attracting the attention of the other people, but I had a feeling that was exactly what she wanted. My hands curled into tight fists, and I had to dig my nails into the spider rune scars in my palms to keep from bitch-slapping her like Bria had done to Tucker.

Alanna finally stopped laughing, although amusement still crinkled her face. "Oh, Ms. Blanco," she purred. "This conversation has been *so* entertaining. I've heard so much about you from Hugh, but it was nice to finally set eyes on you myself."

The way she said that and the hard edge to her toothy smile made me think she knew all about my killing her mother. I frowned. But Fletcher had given me that assignment. How could Tucker have possibly known about it?

"I only wish that I could spend more time with you," Alanna continued. "Perhaps our paths will cross again someday."

"Oh, I'm sure I'll see you again real soon, sugar. Especially if you don't take my warning to heart."

"Warning?" She let out another laugh. "Why, I thought that was a joke. A sad, pitiful, pathetic little joke."

Before I could say that I never joked about killing people, she leaned forward, staring at me with sudden intensity.

"But let me give you a warning in return, Gin. No one keeps me from getting what I want. Whether it's something as simple as a nice, fresh, bloody *steak*..." Her voice trailed off, and her smile widened, revealing even more of her fangs. "Or something a bit more complicated. Something that I can really sink my *teeth* into, so to speak."

The sudden hunger in her eyes told me that she was talking about a far more gruesome, human cut of meat—me.

I opened my mouth to snap back at her thinly veiled cannibalistic reference, but Alanna pivoted on her stilettos again, pointedly turned her back to me, and glided out of the library.

Once again, I had to dig my nails into my palms to keep from charging after her, but I couldn't stop the worry swirling through my stomach.

On the surface, our conversation had been polite enough, at least until our mutual threats at the end. Still, for some reason, I felt a cold sting in my heart, like I'd been bitten by a viper and was helplessly waiting for its deadly poison to kick in and finish me off.

Another series of bells rang out, signaling that the auction was about to start, so I left the library and returned to the ballroom.

People were taking their seats, while a man wearing a tuxedo and holding a wooden gavel was standing at the podium, talking to a woman in a glittering gold gown. Several giants moved around them, rolling glass display cases and carts full of furniture into a line. It was almost like watching the behind-the-scenes action of some bizarre Ashland game show.

Finn was standing along the wall, talking to Mosley, who kept checking his silver pocket watch, clearly wanting to get on with things. Bria was a few feet away from them, staring at her phone and blinking and blinking, as if she couldn't believe what she was seeing on the screen. She must be looking at the images I'd sent her of our parents' picture.

I waved my hand at her. Bria noticed the motion and looked at me. Tears gleamed in her eyes, and she smiled and clutched her phone to her heart, as happy to see our parents' faces as I had been. Bria nodded at me, then hurried over to Finn to show him.

I looked out over the seats. Alanna and Tucker were sitting in the front row in the left section. Tucker said something, and Alanna gave a nonchalant shrug in response. Tucker's eyes narrowed, and he opened his mouth as if to say something else, but Alanna turned away from him and starting whispering to Terrence Phelps, who was sitting on her other side. Tucker leaned back in his chair and crossed his arms over his chest with a stone-faced expression, clearly not happy about being ignored.

Alanna's blatant dismissal of him only made me more curious about what they were doing here together. It obviously wasn't a love match. So what was it? And how did it involve Mosley? Or the mysterious Mason and the rest of the Circle?

I spotted Owen waving at me from the back row in the right section, so I went over and sat down next to him.

"Is everything okay?" he asked. "Where were you?"

"Having a little chat in the library with my new friend Alanna."

Worry darkened his eyes. "What happened?"

"Lots of vague threats and innuendos, for the most part."

I recapped my conversation with Alanna, along with finding that photo of my parents. Owen started to ask me another question, but the auctioneer banged his gavel on the podium, and the ballroom slowly hushed. The auctioneer beamed at the crowd a moment, then launched into his spiel.

"Good evening, ladies and gentlemen. As you know, we are gathered here to bid on items from the estate of Mab Monroe, a prominent Ashland citizen."

I snorted at his benign description, as did several other people. Prominent Ashland citizen? Please. More like homicidal Fire elemental bitch. But I supposed that was the nicest, blandest thing anyone could say about Mab.

The auctioneer's smile dimmed a bit at the lackluster response, but he cranked it right back up to full strength again. "Anyway, you all have your placards to bid on whatever strikes your fancy. Please don't be shy—or cheap. Proceeds from tonight's auction will benefit the victims of the Briartop robbery, along with their families."

The auctioneer nodded at the woman in the gold dress. She rolled a glass display case forward where everyone could see it, then stood off to the side and made elaborate, sweeping hand gestures at the ruby necklace inside, as if her movements would somehow make it even more beautiful.

The auctioneer cleared his throat. "And the first item up for bid is…"

One by one, piece by piece, lot by lot, Mab's things were sold to the highest bidders. The proceedings were far more civilized than I'd expected. Most folks had already picked out what they wanted during the preview hour, and given the hundreds of items up for bid, there was plenty of loot to go around. The only really tense moment came when two women got into a bidding war over a collection of antique crystal candy dishes. But the price finally got too rich for one woman, and the other triumphed, after bidding more than fifty thousand dollars.

I shook my head. Fifty grand for some flimsy old dishes? That was even worse than Finn lusting after that fifteen-thousand-dollar table. Then again, I didn't collect things. At least, not things that were so easily breakable. Those dishes looked like they would crack apart if you put anything heavier than a couple of marshmallows in them. And given how many people wanted me dead, odds were that I wouldn't even get home with those dishes before they got smashed to bits, either by my hand or by someone else's.

Lorelei and Mallory were sitting across the aisle, a couple of rows up from Owen and me. Lorelei was perched on the edge of her seat, tapping her placard against her leg.

The lot with the bookcase and the photo of Lily Rose came up for bid. The auctioneer had barely gotten out the request for ten thousand dollars before Lorelei stabbed her placard up into the air.

"Okay," the auctioneer said, taken aback by her enthusiasm. "I have ten thousand, ten thousand. Will anyone give me eleven? Eleven thousand?"

Lorelei got into a bidding war with someone else, but she eventually purchased the photo, along with the bookcase, for thirty thousand dollars. A relative bargain, considering that she probably would have paid three million for that picture of her mother. Beaming, she hugged Mallory, then got up and went over to the table at the ballroom entrance to make arrangements to pay for her items.

The next lot was the second bookcase with the photo of my parents. And just like Lorelei, I perched on the edge of my seat and whipped up my placard even before the auctioneer finished his spiel.

He blinked. "Well, it looks like the books are going to be some of our most popular items tonight. Must be a lot of readers in this crowd. I have ten thousand, ten thousand. Will anyone give me eleven?"

"Eleven thousand dollars," a familiar voice called out.

I looked up at the front row of seats. Alanna glanced back over her shoulder and smiled at me. I might not know what she was doing with Tucker, but I recognized this game. She knew that I wanted this lot, and she was going to do everything in her power to take it away from me. Just because it amused her.

My fingers squeezed around my placard so tightly that the wooden handle creaked in protest. I forced myself to loosen my grip and smile back at her. Never let 'em see you sweat.

"Twelve thousand," I called out.

"Thirteen," Alanna countered.

"Fourteen."

"Fifteen."

And on and on it went. Everyone's heads swiveled back and forth as they looked from me to Alanna and back again, as though they were watching a tennis match. A hush fell over the crowd, and the only sounds were our voices ringing out over and over again.

Finally, I'd had enough, and I decided to end the bidding. "One hundred thousand dollars."

Murmurs rippled through the ballroom. It was a lot of dough to pay for some old books and furniture, as Alanna had called them.

She turned around in her seat and studied me, her green gaze locking with my gray one. She even opened her mouth, like she was going to top my bid, but Tucker laid a hand on her shoulder, as if he was warning her against it. Her lips pressed together into a tight line, and annoyance filled her face as she glared at him. She didn't like Tucker telling her what to do, but she acceded to his wishes and tilted her head, telling me that I had won.

For now.

"And sold! For one hundred thousand dollars!" The auctioneer banged his gavel on the podium, officially sealing the deal.

Polite applause broke out. Owen grinned and hugged me close.

"I'm so happy for you," he whispered. "I know how much that photo means to you."

I kissed his cheek, then got up, went over to the table, and gave the auction official my bank account information. Even though I wanted to march over to the bookcase right now and grab that picture of my parents off the shelf, I had to wait until tomorrow to collect my things, along with everyone else. Finn had told me that the auction items were going to be stored at the estate tonight under heavy guard until all the payments went through. So I arranged to come back tomorrow afternoon and then returned to my seat next to Owen.

The auction continued for another two hours. Finally, all of Mab's possessions were sold, and people got to their feet and began to leave. I wasn't surprised when Alanna strutted down the aisle and stopped right in front of me. Phelps stood behind her, glued to her side the same way he'd been most of the night, but Tucker hung back, watching us.

"Why, Gin," Alanna said. "Looks like you're an even bigger lover of books than I am."

"Reading truly is one of life's greatest pleasures."

"Well, then, I hope you enjoy your new collection for as long as you can." She tipped her head at me. "Ms. Blanco."

I returned the gesture. "Ms. Eaton."

She swept past me and headed toward the exit, with Phelps trailing along behind her. I looked for Tucker, but the sneaky vampire had already left. Sometimes I thought that he must have been a magician in another life, the way he could seemingly appear and disappear at will.

"Why do I get the feeling that was about a lot more than just some old books?" Owen asked.

"Because it is." I shook my head. "I just don't know exactly *what* else it's about. Alanna has plenty of reasons to hate Mosley, and me too, if she knows I killed her mother. But I can't figure out how Tucker fits into it."

Owen frowned, obviously worried, so I grabbed the lapels of his tuxedo jacket, stood on my tiptoes, and pressed a quick, reassuring kiss to his lips.

"But don't worry. I can handle Alanna Eaton. Up close and personal with the point of my knife, if I have to."

He grinned and kissed me back. "That's the Gin I know and love."

"Yes, it is." I grinned back at him. "Yes, it is."

✲ 13 ✲

I glanced around the ballroom in case Alanna, Phelps, or Tucker might have doubled back, but it looked like they had left. So Owen and I headed over to Finn and Bria.

Mosley stood a few feet away, shaking a final round of hands. The same two giant guards I'd noticed earlier were still shadowing the dwarf, eyeing everyone who approached him. Mallory was standing by Mosley's side, with Lorelei nearby, checking her phone.

I turned to Finn and opened my mouth, but he held up his hand, cutting me off.

"I know what you're going to say, but I've already taken care of everything," he said. "Mosley wants to camp out here at the estate tonight to keep an eye on the auction items and make sure no one tries to help themselves to something that they didn't buy. I'm bunking with him in one of the guest suites upstairs, and a dozen giant guards will be here too. This place is going to be wrapped up tighter than an Andvarian vault. Don't worry, Gin. Nobody's getting to the boss man on my watch."

I opened my mouth again to protest that Hugh Tucker

was a dangerous enemy who was capable of anything, but then I noticed the hard set of Finn's jaw and the way he kept tapping his fingers against his leg. Tucker showing up here had worried him too, a lot more than he had let on, and I knew that he would do everything in his power to protect Mosley.

"And I'm going to follow Mallory and Lorelei home to make sure they get there safely," Bria added. "Plus, Xavier and I will be on call tonight in case Finn needs us here. We've got this, Gin."

I nodded at them. "You're right. You two have totally got this."

Finn and Bria both blinked in surprise, as if they'd expected me to put up a fight about letting them handle things, but I wasn't worried. Finn's guns and shooting prowess and Bria's Ice magic made each of them strong and powerful in their own right, and I trusted them implicitly, especially when it came to something as important as protecting our friends.

"That's it?" Finn asked, an incredulous note creeping into his voice. "You're not going to insist on staying here tonight? Or forcing Mosley to hide in some anonymous safe house?"

I shook my head. "Nope. You're right. This is the safest place for Mosley. Even Hugh Tucker isn't going to be stupid enough to launch a full-scale assault on the night of such a public event."

Bria's eyes narrowed in suspicion. "So what are you going to do?"

I shrugged. "I'm going to go back to Owen's house."

They both kept staring at me with those disbelieving looks. Even Owen was frowning, wondering what I was up to. But for once, I didn't have any ulterior motives.

"What?" I said. "Even the Spider needs to sleep sometime."

Owen and I left Finn and Bria to their protection details and waved good-bye to Mosley, Mallory, and Lorelei. Then we exited the ballroom, got into Owen's car, and drove back to his mansion.

Along the way, I called Silvio and filled him in on everything that happened. He promised to start digging into Alanna to see what connections she might have to Tucker and the Circle. I had just hung up with him when Owen parked his car in the mansion's driveway.

Eva, Violet, Catalina, and Elissa were in the downstairs living room, talking, laughing, eating, and ostensibly studying for their community college classes, although the TV was turned up a little too loud for that. Owen and I told the girls good night before heading to his bedroom.

Owen closed the door behind us, while I went over to one of the windows, pushed the curtain back, and peered outside. My gaze roamed over the backyard and the woods beyond, but nothing moved or stirred in the shadows.

"See anything?" he asked, loosening his bow tie and shrugging out of his tuxedo jacket.

"Nope."

"That's a good thing, right?"

I sighed and let the curtain drop back down into place. "For now. But Alanna is out there somewhere, plotting her next move against Mosley, and most likely me too. I know she is. And Tucker is probably right there by her side, giving her pointers on all my weaknesses."

"You think too much, and you worry even more," Owen

rumbled, draping his jacket and tie over the back of a chair. "Finn won't let anything happen to Mosley."

I sighed again. "I know. And you're right. Finn would take a bullet for Mosley. I just hope he doesn't have to."

"But that's not the only thing that's bothering you, is it?"

I sighed for a third time. He knew me too well. But Owen had a way of drawing me out and making me actually want to talk about my feelings, including my intense guilt and shame. "It's Alanna and what I did to her."

"You mean killing her mother." He said the words without a hint of reproach, but more guilt twisted my stomach.

"For starters," I muttered.

"But that was one of your jobs as the Spider, right? From what you've told me, you and Fletcher didn't go after innocent people."

"No, we didn't, and Amelia Eaton was one of the worst of the worst. But things shouldn't have gone down like they did."

He frowned. "What do you mean? What was different about this job compared to your other ones as the Spider?"

I told him all of it. That first nightmarish memory I'd had of sneaking onto the Eaton Estate and confronting Amelia, as well all as the other memories that had bubbled back up in my mind tonight when I'd first seen Alanna. All the horrible things that had happened after Amelia had captured me and finally, the one thing that I had done to Alanna that was so terrible, so heartless, and so totally unforgivable.

When I finished, Owen winced, realizing why I was so upset, but he immediately came over and put his hands on my arms, squeezing gently and letting me know that he was here for me and that he loved me no matter what.

"Oh, Gin," he said. "I'm so sorry."

"You shouldn't feel sorry for me. You should feel sorry for Alanna."

"I do feel sorry for her," he said. "She got dealt a shitty hand as a kid, losing her mother and her home. But I feel sorry for you too. You're right. Things shouldn't have gone down like they did, but you didn't have a choice. You couldn't let Amelia keep hurting people."

Tears stung my eyes, but I managed to blink them back. "Deep down, I know that. But it doesn't take away my guilt and shame, and it certainly doesn't absolve me of anything. I've done a lot of bad things, but what I did to Alanna…it's one of the worst things I've *ever* done to anyone, which is why I tried to forget all about it. What I did to her…it was the one thing I never wanted to do to *anyone*."

This time, I couldn't stop the tears from streaking down my face. "And now it's coming back to haunt me and, even worse, Mosley too. All of this started because I killed Amelia. I don't care about myself, but Mosley doesn't deserve this. If Alanna murders him, that'll be on *me*. And I'll never forgive myself if that happens."

Owen reached up, cupped my face in his hand, and gently wiped away my tears, his violet gaze steady on mine. "Don't you dare think like that. You are *not* responsible for Alanna going after Mosley. She made her own choice to do that, despite the fact that he has been nothing but good to her all these years. And if she keeps going after him, then she'll suffer the consequences, and rightly so, whether it's you or Finn or someone else who takes her down."

"But I *do* feel responsible for her. Maybe if I hadn't

done what I did back then, she wouldn't be going after Mosley right now."

He shook his head. "And maybe things would be worse. Maybe Amelia would still be alive and killing people."

"I don't know," I whispered. "I just don't know."

Owen pulled me into his embrace, and I looped my arms around his waist and leaned my head on his chest, soaking up his love, strength, and support and letting it comfort me, steady me. We stayed like that for the better part of a minute. I hugged him tight, then dropped my arms and stepped back.

I didn't want to think about what I'd done to Alanna any more tonight, and I really did want to get some rest like I'd told Finn and Bria. I had a feeling that I was going to need it before this was all said and done. So I went over to the bed, sat down, and toed off my black stilettos. This time, my sigh was one of genuine relief rather than sick confusion.

"That bad?" Owen teased, trying to lighten the mood.

I groaned and wiggled my toes into the plush carpet. "I would like to go back in time and kill the person who invented high heels. They're nothing but torture devices."

"Well, maybe I can help with that."

He knelt down on the floor in front of me, picked up my foot, and began kneading my tight, tense muscles. I groaned again, this time with pleasure. He grinned and moved on to my other foot. Back and forth he worked, massaging first one foot, then the other, easing out all the aches and pains there, as well as comforting the far more serious ones in my head and heart.

"How does that feel?" he asked.

"You missed your calling, Grayson. You should have been a masseur."

He grinned again and kept working on my feet.

Eventually, the discomfort faded away, replaced by a slow, simmering heat. I leaned forward, reached down, and ran my hands through Owen's thick hair, enjoying the feel of the silky black strands sliding through my fingers and massaging his scalp the way he was massaging my feet. This time, he groaned with pleasure and leaned forward to give me easier access.

Owen's hands left my feet and slid up my legs, stroking, caressing, and stopping to knead the tight, tense muscles. My fingers drifted lower, slowly trailing down the sides of his face and neck before digging into the strong muscles of his broad shoulders. Neither one of us spoke. We didn't need to. We both knew exactly what we wanted now—each other.

Owen rose onto his knees, his hands gliding to my knees and then farther up my thighs. Our gazes locked together, gray on violet, even as our hands kept moving, moving, moving, sliding every which way. Owen's right hand eased up my thigh, higher and higher, one slow inch at a time, until he cupped my warm, wet heat. He rubbed his fingers back and forth against the silken barrier of my panties, deliberately teasing me. I groaned again, grabbed his head in my hands, and crushed my lips to his.

The simmering heat between us immediately ignited into a raging fire.

In an instant, we had both surged to our feet and were fumbling at each other's clothes. Owen hooked his fingers inside my panties and slid them down. I stepped out of them, kicked them aside, and then pulled his shirt open, making several buttons fly off and *ping-ping-ping* against the lamp on the nightstand. Owen grabbed his wallet out of his back pocket, pulled a condom out of it, and tossed the black leather aside. I reached for his belt while he tore the foil packet open with his teeth. I took my little white pills, but we always used extra protection.

I unbuckled his belt, then unzipped his pants. Owen leaned forward, kissing my neck, even as his hand darted down between us, crept up my thigh, and found my center again. The soft, sure stroke of his fingers made hot pleasure shoot through my body like an arrow hitting its target. I stopped and sucked in a ragged breath, my fingers still clenched around his zipper.

"Don't distract me," I murmured.

"But it's so much fun." Owen grinned and stroked me again.

I let out a low groan and yanked his zipper down, along with his pants and his black boxers. Owen stepped out of his clothes, covered himself with the condom, and picked me up. Our mouths crashed together, our tongues licking against each other. I wrapped my legs around his waist, and Owen walked forward and laid me down on the bed.

We kissed again, hard and deep, and then Owen drew back. His gaze locked with mine, and he thrust into me with a quick, hard motion. We both moaned at how good it felt.

I kissed him again, then ran my hands over his shoulders, enjoying the quick bunch and flex of his muscles. He pulled back, then thrust into me again. I wrapped my legs tighter around his waist, drawing him even deeper inside me.

Our rhythm became quicker, faster, harder, until the bed moaned, creaked, and rattled from the force of our passion.

More and more of those hot arrows of pleasure shot through me, morphing into one continuous wave of heat, until Owen was all that I could see, hear, taste, smell, feel.

Just when I thought we couldn't go any higher together, he thrust into me a final time, and the world exploded. The passion, the pressure, the pleasure cascaded through my body, wave after wave of it, each one searing my nerve endings with its exquisite electricity.

Bull's-eye, baby.

Owen went over the edge with me too, and we both fell completely silent again, breathing hard, our bodies locked together, foreheads touching, just enjoying the emotions surging through us, between us, binding us together.

Tonight, tomorrow, always.

❋ 14 ❋

Eventually, Owen and I stripped off the rest of our clothes, took a long, hot, satisfying shower together, then snuggled together in bed and fell asleep. For a long time, everything was calm and peaceful, but eventually, the peace fell away, shattered to shards by another horrible dream, memory, nightmare from my past...

I woke up tied to a chair.

I blinked and blinked, staring at the ropes that lashed my wrists to the wooden chair. My ankles were also tied down, and my flat sandals were gone, leaving my feet bare. My toes were blue with cold, and I dug them into the black plastic on the floor, trying to warm them up—

The sight of that black plastic made the rest of the night come rushing back to me, and I remembered where I was: Amelia Eaton's so-called wine cellar.

My head snapped up, and my gaze darted from left to right and back again. Stone walls, expensive furniture, the chilly feel of being underground. The murder room was exactly the same as when Amelia had knocked me out with that stun gun, right down to the black plastic on the floor that was just waiting to soak up my blood.

I was alone, and I held my breath and tilted my head to the side, wondering if I might hear someone talking beyond the closed door twenty feet in front of me.

Silence—nothing but cold, dead silence.

Amelia must have summoned a couple of uninjured vampire guards to tie me down and haul away the two men I'd killed. I wondered if she had taken a couple of bites out of the dead men before she'd ordered them to be whisked away. Probably. My stomach turned over at the thought.

I had no idea what time it was or if the party was still going on. But I had no doubt that as soon as the event was finished and her guests had left, Amelia would come down here and deal with me.

I needed to get out of here before that happened.

I shifted in the chair, but the two knives strapped to my thighs were gone. I looked around again, searching for them, but I didn't see the weapons anywhere. My purse and sandals weren't in here either.

The loss of my shoes puzzled me. With all those leather straps, there was no way the sandals had just fallen off my feet. The guards must have deliberately stripped them off, although I couldn't imagine why. Either way, they were gone.

Besides, I had more pressing matters to think about— like getting out of these ropes. I struggled and strained against my bonds, but the ropes were so tight that I couldn't move or loosen them at all, not even a fraction of an inch.

I was looking around the room for something to help me cut through the ropes when footsteps tap-tap-tapped on the floor outside, growing louder and closer with each stride. A few seconds later, the door swung open, and Amelia stepped into the room, followed by four vampire guards.

Amelia had unwound her hair from its braided bun, and her black locks now hung loose around her shoulders. The emerald-green gown that I'd spilled champagne on was gone, and she was now sporting knee-high black boots and tight black pants topped by a blood-red jacket with gleaming gold buttons running down the front. The outfit reminded me of something an Englishman might wear when hunting foxes. A wave of disgust washed over me. She had actually dressed up for this, and I knew exactly what she was going to hunt tonight.

Me.

"Cut her loose, and bring her outside," Amelia ordered.

She smiled at me, showing off her razor-sharp fangs, then slowly licked her lips, like I was a juicy steak that she was about to sink her teeth into—literally.

Another, stronger wave of disgust washed over me, and hot, sour bile rose in my throat. She was planning to make me her nightcap, just like she had so many other poor, unfortunate souls. I wondered if she would only drink my blood or if she would go the extra step of tearing into my body with her fangs, ripping out my organs, and slurping them down like oysters. Probably both, knowing my bad luck.

Fletcher had been right. I had totally jinxed myself earlier by saying that nothing could possibly go wrong. Everything was going wrong, and I didn't know how to escape the gruesome fate that was staring me in the eyes.

More bile rose in my throat, and I almost vomited. But I drew in a deep breath and slowly let it out, forcing down my fear, anger, disgust, and panic. This was exactly what Fletcher had trained me for—how to make the best of a dangerous situation, escape, and live to fight another day. Even when that situation involved a bona fide vampire cannibal.

Amelia wanting to chew on my bones was bad—very, very bad—but at least she was ordering her men to cut me free. Even better, they were taking me out of the murder room, back upstairs, and outside.

By now, Fletcher would have realized that things had gone wrong. The old man was probably hiding in the woods, waiting for a chance to storm inside and rescue me. But I was going to meet him halfway. Once I was outside, all I had to do was fight my way through the guards and make it to the woods. Fletcher would be waiting there, and together we could escape.

So I didn't protest or struggle as one of the vampires stepped forward, pulled a switchblade out of his pocket, and sliced through my ropes. He grabbed one of my arms, while another vamp latched onto my other one. Together they lifted me up and out of the chair and shepherded me out of the room.

We walked along the hallway and back up the stairs to the ground floor. It was past midnight now, according to one of the antique clocks on the wall, and the party was obviously over, since I didn't hear a whisper of sound except for Amelia's boots stabbing into the floor. The marble let out a small, plaintive wail every time her stilettos slammed into it, as though her boots were a substitute for her fangs, slicing into the stones over and over again. The marble had long ago absorbed the fearful cries and pleas of everyone who had made this same forced walk before me.

I pushed the stones' wails out of my mind and peered into every room and looked out every window we passed, searching for any sign of Fletcher. I didn't see the old man anywhere, but he would never *abandon me. No doubt he was watching and waiting for the right moment to help me escape, just like I would have if he'd been captured.*

The vampires forced me out a door and back onto the terrace. Just like I'd thought, the party was long over. Everyone was gone, and all of the food, tables, and champagne towers had been removed. The only things that remained were the white rose petals scattered over the stone.

My nose twitched, and I had to hold back a sneeze at their stench, which seemed even fouler and more rotten than before. Or perhaps that was just because I knew the grisly death that was lurking here—and that it might claim me as its next victim before the night was through.

The guards strong-armed me over to the low wall that marked the edge of the terrace. Down below, the man-made lake shimmered like liquid silver, and I could see the reflection of the full moon rippling in the water like a giant eye that kept blinking at me.

The two vampires released my arms and stepped back so that they were standing in a line with the third man who had been trailing along behind us. The fourth and final vampire stayed inside the mansion for a minute, then pushed a small metal cart out onto the terrace, like the kind you might use at a cocktail party. At first, I thought he was going to make Amelia a drink before she tried to kill me, but then I realized exactly what was on the cart.

A metal glove.

Well, calling it a glove was a bit generous, since it didn't contain any fabric. The metal frame looked more like a brace that you might wear if you'd broken your arm and were waiting for it to heal. I frowned. What was that for? Somehow I didn't think I wanted to find out.

Amelia pulled on the metal glove and secured the device to her right arm using a couple of black fabric bands that were attached to it. Then she raised her hand and waggled her fingers at me.

And that's when I saw the claws.

A long, sharp, curved claw tipped each metal finger on the glove. The way the claws glinted in the moonlight told me that they were probably made of silverstone, which meant that they would be tough, durable, and razor-sharp.

Worry knotted my stomach. Well, now I knew exactly how Amelia butchered her victims. It wasn't enough that the vampire had fangs. She had to have claws too.

Amelia circled me, her green gaze slowly moving up and down my body, as though she were in the grocery store, trying to pick out which cut of meat she wanted for dinner. My hands curled into fists. She wasn't going to snap my neck and suck out all of my blood, and she certainly wasn't going to cut me to shreds with her claws. No way, no how. Not as long as I still had breath left in my body to fight her.

After the better part of a minute, Amelia stopped her circling and faced me again. "Who hired you to kill me? Which one of my dear friends was it?"

Confusion filled me. As far as I knew, Taylor Samson's grieving mother had asked Fletcher to kill Amelia, so why would she think that one of her friends was behind this? Who else had a reason to want her dead?

I didn't know, so I kept my mouth shut. That was almost always the best policy when you were stuck in a dangerous situation where you didn't really know what was going on or who all the players in the game were—

Amelia must not have liked my silence, because she swiped out at me with her hand, like a cat casually batting at a mouse. I jerked my head back, but her claws still raked across my left cheek, making me hiss with pain.

Blood trickled down my face and neck, and several drops fell off my chin and spattered onto my bare feet. I flinched at their surprising warmth.

Amelia held her metal glove out in front of her, studying the scarlet gleam of my blood on her talons. Then she brought her index finger up to her mouth and carefully licked my blood off that claw.

"Mmm. I sense some elemental magic in you. Tasty."

My stomach roiled, but I forced my fear away and focused on the sting of the wounds in my face, using the pain to fuel my own anger and my own will to survive.

Amelia snapped her fingers, like I was a dog she was ordering to perform a certain trick. The sound of her metal claws clanking together made me shudder.

"What's the matter, girl?" she purred. "Cat got your tongue?"

I shrugged, still not speaking.

Her eyes narrowed to slits. "Oh, yes. I could see my dear friends hiring some little fresh-faced ingenue like you to take me out. They don't approve of my activities out here, although that certainly doesn't stop them from using my services to hide their own dirty laundry. Hypocrites." She sniffed at the indignity of it all. "As if anyone actually cares about the pool boys and gardeners that my guards and I snack on from time to time."

Rage roared through me at her casual dismissal of all the innocent people she'd murdered, just to appease her own sick, twisted appetites. The victims' families certainly cared about their dead loved ones.

Fletcher had shown me the crime-scene photos of Taylor Samson's body. Calling it a bloody, tattered mess was a *kindness. The college kid looked like he'd been chewed up and spit out by a wild animal. I'd seen a lot of dead people, and I'd killed my fair share of folks, but what Amelia had done to that young man was one of the most depraved forms of cruelty I'd ever had the misfortune to see.*

She eyed me another moment, then waved her hand when she realized that I wasn't going to talk. "It doesn't matter anyway. You're not going to live long enough to report back to your bosses, whoever they are."

I still didn't say anything, and anger sparked like matches in her eyes. That was all the warning I had before she lashed out at me again. I managed to twist to the side and avoid the full force of the blow, but those talons still sliced across my shoulder, drawing more blood.

I ground my teeth together to keep from screaming, although I couldn't stop myself from letting out another loud hiss of pain. Once again, Amelia smirked at me, then raised her hand and slowly, deliberately licked my blood off each and every one of her claws.

She watched me closely the whole time, and I realized that she didn't want to kill me. Not yet. No, right now, she was trying to scare me so badly that I would start weeping, spill my guts about who had hired me, throw myself at her feet, and beg her not to kill me. Well, that wasn't going to happen—not now, not ever—and it was pissing her off. Too damn bad.

Once she realized that I still wasn't going to talk, Amelia lapped up a final bit of my blood from her thumb, then stabbed her clawed index finger toward the woods in the distance. "I'll give you a sporting chance, just like I give everyone. Start running. Get away, and you live."

She stopped, waiting for me to ask the inevitable question.

"And if I don't get away?" I asked, although the answer was painfully obvious.

She tapped each of her fingers against her thumb, making those horrible metal claws clank-clank-clank-clank together again. *"Then I'll have a nice little midnight snack."*

It wasn't much of a chance or a choice, especially since the four vampire guards pulled out their guns, indicating that I could either start running or die right here on the terrace.

I had opened my mouth to tell Amelia and her henchmen exactly what I thought of them when I spotted a glint of metal in the woods. The glint flashed again and again, like three sly winks, and my heart lifted. It was a signal from Fletcher, letting me know he was here.

"Well, girl?" Amelia purred. *"What do you say? Aren't I being generous, giving you a chance to get away?"*

I bared my teeth at her. *"Nah. You just want to hunt me down like an animal. That's why you took my sandals away. So you could hobble me and make me easier to run to ground. After all, that's what you do out here on your fancy, secluded estate. Well, guess what? I'm not going to play your sick little game."*

An amused smile curved her lips, and she gestured at the four guards with guns. *"And what makes you think that you have any choice?"*

Behind her, a shadow moved in the woods, and I saw the dull gleam of a gun barrel at the edge of the trees.

My smile widened. *"Because I brought backup, bitch."*

She frowned, and then her eyes widened as she realized that I wasn't bluffing and that I hadn't come here alone. She opened her mouth to shout a warning to her men, but it was already too late

Crack!

From his vantage point in the woods, Fletcher fired his rifle and took down one of the guards. The other three men ducked for cover behind the stone wall, as did Amelia.

"Kill them!" she roared. "Kill them all!"

But apparently, she didn't want to stick around to actually see me meet my demise, because she turned and sprinted across the terrace, running away from the fight. So she was a coward, in addition to being a cannibal.

Crack!

Fletcher fired another shot, and a second vampire toppled to the ground, screaming and clutching at the hole in his shoulder. In the distance, I could hear the old man yelling at me.

"Go! Go, Gin, go!"

He didn't have to tell me twice. We wouldn't get another chance at taking down Amelia, and I wanted to end her for all the innocent people she'd killed and for the way she had wanted to carve me up too. So I whirled around and darted across the terrace after her.

I'd only taken a few steps when I was suddenly, painfully reminded that I didn't have any shoes on. Small bits of dirt and grime stabbed into my feet, making curses spew out of my lips. I took another step forward and slipped on those stupid rose petals that still covered the terrace. At the very last second, I managed to windmill my arms and right myself.

I couldn't chase after Amelia if I had to stop every other step, so I reached for my Stone magic and sent it down, down, down, until it had covered my feet and ankles, making them as hard and heavy as concrete blocks and impervious to all the debris that littered the terrace. Once that was done, I concentrated on tracking down Amelia.

The vampire was quick, but that was to be expected,

given all the blood she drank. Still, I could hear her clattering down the steps at the far end of the terrace, and I rushed after her.

The steps wound down the hill to the lake. I leaped off the last step and sprinted forward onto the sandy shore. My head snapped left and right, and I forced myself to stop so that I could figure out which direction she'd gone.

The hill above me blocked out most of the light from the mansion, and what little illumination there was quickly dissolved into deep, dark shadows. I glanced around again, but nothing moved in the inky pools, and I couldn't hear anything over my own ragged breathing and the rapid thump of my heart roaring in my ears.

Where had she gone? If I lost her, we wouldn't get another chance to get close to her again, which meant that there would be no justice for Taylor Samson and all the other people she'd killed—

I spotted a glimmer of metal out of the corner of my eye. That was all the warning I had before Amelia leaped out from behind the stone steps and swiped out at me with her claws.

I jerked back, trying to get out of the way, but the sand sucked at my feet, and I wasn't quick enough. Her silverstone claws zipped across my left forearm, cutting deep into my muscles. I screamed, staggered away from her, and reached for my Stone magic, using it to harden my skin into an impenetrable shell. Otherwise, she'd cut me to ribbons with those damn claws.

I whirled back around to find Amelia licking my blood off her talons again.

"Mmm-mmm-mmm! You have more power than I realized," she purred. "I'm going to have to savor you for as long as possible."

Before I could move out of the way, Amelia lunged forward, slammed her body into mine, and drove me down to the ground.

We landed on a piece of driftwood, and the log splintered under our bodies. My head hit a rock buried in the sand underneath, and white stars flashed in front of my eyes. I lost my grip on my Stone magic, and my skin reverted back to its normal texture and vulnerability.

Amelia snarled and dug her claws into my hair, opening up several stinging wounds in my scalp, but she wasn't trying to cut me this time. Instead, she yanked my head up and tilted it to the side. I realized what she was up to, and I barely managed to send my Stone magic rushing out into my neck, hardening the skin there, before her fangs snapped against my throat.

Thunk.

Thunk-thunk.

Thunk-thunk-thunk.

Her fangs might be razor-sharp, but they couldn't do any real damage against my magic-hardened skin. It was like she was trying to use a couple of dull nails to chip into a solid block of concrete. She growled and tried again but with the same useless result as before.

"You think that a little bit of Stone magic is going to protect you from me?" Amelia snarled. "Think again."

She let go of my hair and positioned herself on top of me. This time, instead of trying to drive her fangs into my neck, she wrapped her hands around my throat.

And then she started squeezing.

Amelia and I were about the same size, but drinking blood gave many vampires enhanced strength, which meant that she was far stronger than I was.

Desperate, I pounded at her with my fists and even tried

to buck her off, but Amelia just grinned and tightened her grip on my neck, cutting off my oxygen. White stars began to flash in front of my eyes again. My skin might be hard as a rock, but I still needed air, and she was taking that away from me one slow, agonizing breath at a time...

I woke up with a snarl, my body tense, my legs twitching, and my hands fisted in the sheets, as though I were still fighting Amelia. My chest felt tight, and my breath came in short, ragged gasps.

Beside me, Owen murmured something incoherent into his pillow, reminding me when and where I was. The weight on my chest was his arm, which he had protectively curled around me, almost as if he were trying to shield me from my memories. If only it was that easy.

I lay still and silent until the last, lingering traces of my nightmare slowly vanished. Owen murmured something else, then rolled away from me, flung his arm up over his head, and started snoring, almost as if he knew that his job protecting me was done for the night. I let out a long, slow breath. At least I hadn't woken him up with my nightmare this time.

But I couldn't go back to sleep, not with my mind still churning, so I slipped out of bed, threw on a fleece robe, and left the bedroom.

Eva, Violet, Catalina, and Elissa were still in the downstairs living room, but they were sprawled across the sofas, fast asleep, with books and highlighters strewn all around them. I quietly moved around the room, turning off the TV and laying blankets across the girls to keep them warm. None of them stirred, so I flipped off the lights and tiptoed out of the room.

I spent the next hour doing circuit after circuit of the mansion, moving from window to window and peering out into the dark night beyond. A beautiful silver frost crusted the landscape, and the grass and trees glinted with sharp needles of ice. It was too cold to snow tonight—but it was never too cold for potential assassins to strike.

And I had a feeling that Alanna Eaton was coming for me.

As I did my laps around the mansion, I thought about everything that had happened at the auction, but I didn't come up with any new answers or insights about what Alanna wanted from Mosley or how Tucker, Mason, and the Circle fit into everything.

Once again, I wondered if Alanna knew that I was the one who'd killed her mother or if she hated me simply because I'd kept her from getting her hands on Mosley during that attempted mugging. No way to know for sure.

She *should* hate me. I hated myself for what I'd done to her, and I hated myself even more for trying so hard to forget about it, and mostly succeeding, until tonight.

I stared out the window again, but the night was as cold and still as before, so I let the curtain drop back into place and returned to Owen's bedroom. He was still snoring softly, so I slipped into bed and curled up against him, trying to let the warmth of his body drive away the chill that had sunk into my bones and the cold sting of the past that continually throbbed in my heart.

❋ 15 ❋

It took a while, but I finally managed to go back to sleep. I woke up the next morning, got dressed, took a shower, and kissed Owen good-bye before we both went our separate ways for the day.

I made it to the Pork Pit a little before ten o'clock. After checking to make sure that no one had booby-trapped the restaurant overnight, I went inside and got started on the day's cooking, including making a vat of Fletcher's secret barbecue sauce. I didn't measure the ingredients, but it turned out perfect, just like always. Take that, Sophia.

Silvio showed up around ten thirty, which would have been early for anyone else but was half an hour late for him. I took one look at his tired face and whipped up a tall mug of hot chocolate, laced with sweet raspberry syrup and topped with whipped marshmallow cream, more raspberry syrup, graham cracker crumbs, and shaved dark chocolate. I also put half a dozen chocolate chip cookies that I'd just taken out of the oven on a plate for him.

Neither one of us spoke as Silvio shrugged out of his winter gear, hung it all up, and sat down at his usual stool at the counter. He fired up his tablet and hooked his keyboard to it, while I passed him the hot chocolate and cookies. He downed the whole mug and ate half the cookies before finally looking at me, as if he needed some caffeine-fueled courage to face me this morning.

"I'm afraid I don't have good news."

I sighed. "I figured as much. Otherwise, you would have started talking the second you stepped inside, instead of fortifying yourself with chocolate first. Tell me how bad it is."

Silvio shrugged. "Well, it's not *bad*, exactly. As far as Ashland standards go, it's been rather restrained...so far."

"What do you mean by *restrained*?"

"It's complicated." He held out his mug. "I need some more sugar before I get into it, and so do you. Trust me."

I refilled his hot chocolate, then made one for myself, sat down on my stool behind the cash register, and leaned my elbows on the counter. "All right. Now that we're both properly fortified, tell me what you found out about Alanna."

Silvio drank half of his hot chocolate before turning his tablet around so I could see it. "Alanna Eaton. Age twenty-six. Born in Ashland, although she really grew up in several different boarding schools all over the world. New York, London, Paris, Geneva."

Pictures of Alanna through the years flashed by on the screen, each one showing her wearing a different school uniform in a different location.

"From what I can tell, Alanna only came home to Ashland on school holidays and for summer break," he continued. "Her mother visited her at school quite often, though, and they took lots of vacations together to places like Bigtime, Cypress Mountain, Cloudburst Falls, and

Snowline Ridge. From all accounts, the two of them were quite close."

Another photo appeared, this time showing a teenage Alanna with her arms wrapped around Amelia's waist, both of them smiling. With their black hair, green eyes, and strikingly similar features, the two of them looked more like sisters than mother and daughter.

Silvio cleared his throat. "Alanna was devastated by her mother's death."

Despite everything that was going on and the danger to Mosley, I didn't regret going after Amelia, and I certainly didn't regret killing the vampire cannibal. It had been her or me, and I'd chosen me, simple as that. Still, the longer I stared at the photo of her and Alanna and their happy faces, the more guilt and shame knifed through my stomach.

Like I'd told Owen last night, it shouldn't have gone down the way it had. I should have done things differently. I should have been smarter, stronger, better. At the very least, I should have spared Alanna the same sort of pain that had been inflicted on me when my mother was murdered.

"Things get much more interesting after Amelia's death," Silvio said, breaking into my thoughts. "That's when Amelia's money problems come to light, and that's when Stuart Mosley gets involved."

"How bad were her money problems?"

He shook his head. "She was flat-busted broke, as you might say. I'm still digging into her finances, but I don't know how she managed to live the way she did for so long. We're talking excessive, over-the-top, frivolous spending and some truly terrible investments, not to mention the constant upkeep of the mansion and grounds. The estate was a serious money pit, even more so than her bad spending habits. I would say that Amelia's mismanagement of the Eaton family fortune is on par with Deirdre Shaw losing so much of the Circle's money."

"And how does Mosley fit into this?"

Silvio hit another button on his keyboard, and a shot of the Eaton mansion popped up on the screen. "Mosley gave Amelia loan after loan. Every single time, she put the estate up as collateral. The weird thing is that she had *some* sort of income, although I haven't been able to track down the source of it yet. But she would get these big deposits every month, usually fifty thousand dollars or more a pop. She'd use that money to pay back just enough of her current loan to get Mosley to extend her another one until…"

"Until I killed her, and she wasn't around to pay back any more loans." I finished his thought.

Silvio nodded. "Exactly. Mosley didn't have a choice. He had to foreclose on the estate and take possession of it in order to recoup his money. And he's done amazingly well with it. Renting out the estate more than pays for its upkeep, gives him a nice return on his investment, and puts a very generous sum into the trust fund he set up for Alanna. He still contributes to her trust fund every single month, just like clockwork, although Alanna actually took control of the money when she turned twenty-one."

"I'm sensing a *but* in there."

"But…Alanna apparently isn't very happy with the arrangement, despite how generous Mosley has been to her." Silvio shook his head again. "If it wasn't for Mosley, Alanna would have been either put into foster care or living on the streets after her mother's death, since she didn't have any other relatives to take her in. But Mosley made sure that she was able to stay at her current boarding school until she was eighteen and then go on to college. She should be grateful that he was so kind to her instead of hounding him the way she has."

"What do you mean? How has she been hounding him?"

Silvio pointed at the photo still on his tablet screen. "Ever since she turned twenty-one, Alanna has been trying to buy the Eaton Estate from Mosley."

"So she wants her family's home back. I can understand that." I could more than understand it. I had gone to great lengths to purchase the property the Snow family home had stood on, although I had never done anything with the land.

"Yes, but it's the *way* she's gone about it," he replied. "Her mother literally left her with nothing, and Alanna's never held a job in her life, unless you count being on this museum board or that charity board. She doesn't have *any* money except for what's in that trust fund that Mosley created for her and what she's made by investing it herself."

"Ah," I said, finally catching on. "So she's basically trying to buy back the estate from Mosley with his own money."

He nodded. "Exactly. Not only that, but the estate is easily worth more than twenty-five million dollars. Alanna is rich, but she's not *that* rich. So Mosley has rightly refused her offers."

"So how is she hounding him?"

Silvio hit some more buttons on his keyboard, and document after document flashed by on the screen. They all looked like legal papers.

"Alanna and her lawyers have used every legal trick and loophole in the book to try to wrest the estate away from Mosley, from contesting the bank's initial foreclosure to debating her mother's mental competency to take out such a massive loan to even trying to get the estate declared a historic landmark." An admiring light filled the vampire's eyes. "She's exhausted all of her legal options, but her continued doggedness is quite impressive."

A thought occurred to me. "What happens to the estate if Mosley dies?"

"I'm still trying to figure that out," Silvio said. "From what I can tell, and from facts stated in Mosley's various legal battles with Alanna, the estate would remain the property of First Trust bank, although who would actually control the bank and its assets is a mystery. The only way to know for sure would be to ask Mosley directly or get my hands on a copy of his will. But I can tell you one thing, Alanna does *not* get the estate if Mosley dies. I'm certain of that."

I sipped my hot chocolate, trying to put the puzzle pieces together in my mind. If Alanna didn't inherit the estate outright after Mosley's death, then why set up that mugging the other night? Why try to kidnap him or whatever her goal had been?

Sure, torturing and killing the dwarf for all the wrongs she thought he had done to her would be fun, but it wouldn't get her what she really wanted. Plus, it would cut off that nice monthly cash flow to her trust fund, further dooming her chances of eventually raising enough money to buy back the estate.

Silvio drained the rest of his hot chocolate, then set his mug aside. "One of my sources at the courthouse did tell me a juicy rumor about Alanna, though."

"What's that?"

"That she's about to make a new offer to buy the estate. Only this time, instead of using her trust fund, she has an outside investor, someone with enough money to actually buy the estate outright from the bank."

My eyebrows shot up. "And who might that be?"

He shrugged. "My source didn't know the investor's name, but she thought she saw him at the courthouse with Alanna the other day. She said the guy had a black goatee."

"Tucker," I muttered. "Hugh Tucker is Alanna's investor."

Silvio nodded. "That's my guess, and that would explain why he was at the auction with her."

I frowned, thinking back to how Alanna had ignored Tucker last night. If he really was her investor, Alanna should have been kissing his ass to make sure that he went through with the deal, instead of treating him like an annoyance. Silvio had given me some big pieces to the puzzle, but I still felt like several parts were missing.

"Maybe Tucker's just the front man," I said, thinking out loud. "Maybe the mysterious Mason is the one who's really backing Alanna."

Silvio looked at me. "You think that Alanna is involved with Mason and the Circle?"

I shrugged. "Tucker was at the auction for some reason. Something more important than a real estate deal, no matter how significant it might be."

"Why would they do that, though? What's in it for them? From everything we know about the Circle, they like to keep an extremely low profile, especially Mason, whoever he really is. Buying the Eaton Estate would *not* be low profile. Not at all. As soon as word got out, the media would be all over the story."

"I know," I said. "And I agree that it's out of character for them. But Tucker—or Mason—must want something, something he thinks that only Alanna can give the Circle."

"But how does it all connect back to Mosley?" Silvio asked.

I shook my head. "I don't know."

I had a sinking feeling that my friend's life depended on me figuring it out—before it was too late.

Silvio promised to keep digging into Alanna, whatever deal she might have cooking with Tucker and the Circle, and how Mosley might be involved in it. He moved over to a booth in the corner so he would have more room to work.

I had called Finn when I got up this morning, and he'd told me the night had gone by quietly and that he and Mosley would be at the estate all day, overseeing the pickup of the auction items. But with this new information swimming around in my head, my worry shot right back up to red-alert levels. So I pulled out my phone and texted Finn to make sure that everything was still okay. My phone beeped back a minute later with a new message.

All quiet on the western front. ☺

Heh. Looked like I wasn't the only literature lover in the family.

By this point, the rest of the waitstaff had shown up, including Sophia and Catalina, and I had to put my phone aside and start cooking, cleaning, and waiting on customers. My worry lingered, though. And I knew that it would until this thing was finished—one way or another.

But the lunch rush came and went with no problems, and even the criminals ate their food, paid up, and left without bothering anyone.

Bria stopped by around noon to grab a to-go order for her and Xavier. She leaned against the counter while I rang up her food. "I found out an interesting tidbit about our two muggers."

"What's that?" I asked, punching buttons on the cash register.

"When they weren't out mugging, conning, and threatening people, Vera Jones moonlighted as a housekeeper at the Eaton Estate, while her hubby, Eddie, worked as one of the gardeners."

I looked up at her. "So that's their connection to Alanna."

Bria nodded. "Yep. Xavier and I are still investigating, but as far as we can tell, Alanna has an agreement with Mosley that lets her visit the estate on a regular basis to make sure that the art, antiques, and everything else are being kept up to snuff. So she's familiar with the estate staff, including our two muggers. Xavier and I will check into the rest of the staff, to see who else might be working for her."

I nodded.

"But updating you isn't the only reason I came by." Bria straightened up. "I didn't get a chance to say it last night, but I wanted to thank you for sending me that photo of Mom and Dad and for buying it at the auction. I didn't even remember what Dad looked like. Not really."

Tears gleamed in her eyes, and she had to stop talking and clear the emotion out of her throat. Yeah, me too. I grabbed her hand.

"I didn't remember what he looked like either," I whispered. "But now we both know, and we'll never forget him again."

Bria nodded and squeezed my hand. I squeezed back, then leaned across the counter and hugged her.

After several seconds, we broke apart. My sister promised to call me if she found out anything else, then paid for her food and left.

I checked on the customers, but everyone had what they needed, so I got to work on another, much bigger order, a barbecue buffet for Finn, Mosley, and everyone else at the Eaton Estate.

I was already going over to the estate to pick up my auction items, and I had suggested bringing lunch when I called Finn this morning. He had enthusiastically agreed. No surprise there. Finnegan Lane could eat barbecue every day of the week and twice on Sundays. But he knew as well as I did that the workers would welcome a good, hot, hearty meal, and you didn't get much heartier than Pork Pit barbecue.

Sophia helped me pack up several large cardboard boxes of food. Then I left the restaurant in her, Catalina's, and Silvio's capable hands and headed over to the estate.

I steered my old white van into the line of cars creeping up the hill. Instead of driving into one of the paved lots like they had last night, today all the vehicles turned into the driveway that circled around an impressive fountain that continuously spewed water in front of the mansion.

I parked my van, got out, and flagged down two giants I recognized as guards from First Trust bank. I showed them the food in the back of my vehicle, and they happily agreed to help me carry it inside. Looked like Finn wasn't the only one around here who loved barbecue.

We took the food to the grand ballroom, which was a beehive of activity. Last night's glitzy, glamorous crowd had been replaced by workers sporting dark coveralls, thick gloves, and sturdy boots. Giants and dwarves carried lamps, mirrors, and more from their spots along the walls and over to Finn, who was holding a clipboard and standing in the middle of the ballroom, right where the podium had been last night. It was gone, along with the rows of chairs.

Each worker stopped in front of Finn so that he could examine their items, check the white tags on them to see who had bought them and where they were going, and mark them off his list.

Mosley was standing next to him, marking items off the list on his own clipboard. He looked far happier and much more relaxed than he had last night, and he was actually humming as he ticked off items one by one.

From there, the workers hauled the items over to a packing station, where they were either securely covered in thick, padded plastic, nestled in boxes, or both. Once the items were properly packaged, the workers took them outside so they could be loaded into the appropriate vehicles and transported to their new owners.

A dwarf walked by me, casually holding Finn's fifteen-thousand-dollar end table under his arm like it was a rolled-up newspaper. My brother had actually bought the table, and he'd even managed to get it for the minimum bid, which was a steal, according to him.

Most of the society folks had sent their assistants and drivers to fetch their items, but not Lorelei and Mallory Parker. The two of them were watching a couple of giants carefully load Lorelei's bookcase onto a large cart so they could roll it outside to whatever vehicle was going to transport it to her mansion. Several cardboard boxes that I assumed contained the books that had been in the case were already sitting on the cart. Lorelei had already grabbed the photo of Lily Rose that had been perched on the shelf. The silver picture frame rested in the crook of her left elbow, along with the blue book it had been propped up on.

I was going to find my bookcase and do the exact same thing with that photo of my parents.

Mallory spotted me and waved. I waved back at her. The

men finished loading everything onto the cart and pushed it toward the ballroom exit, with Lorelei and Mallory following them.

Finn caught sight of me, leaned over, and said something to Mosley. The dwarf looked at me, the two giants behind me, and the boxes in our hands, then pointed to an empty table along the wall, close to the packing station. I nodded back at him and headed in that direction.

The two giants helped me carry the food over there. I unpacked everything, including plates, cups, utensils, and napkins, then rigged up some burners to reheat the food. Large metal tins full of barbecue beef, chicken, and pork. Plastic tubs filled with Fletcher's secret barbecue sauce for those who wanted extra. Bowls brimming with baked beans and coleslaw. And what seemed like an entire mountain of Sophia's sourdough rolls.

I'd also brought along several gallons of sweet iced tea, along with a couple of blackberry cobblers. For a final touch, I set out a tub of vanilla-bean ice cream so that folks could top off their cobbler in the proper sweet, creamy style.

When I finished, I flashed Mosley a thumbs-up, telling him everything was ready.

"All right, folks!" he called out. "Let's take a break and get some lunch!"

He didn't have to tell them twice. The workers left their stations and made a beeline for the food table. So did all of the assistants and drivers milling around, waiting to pick up their bosses' items. Nobody passed up a free lunch.

I made sure that everyone had what they needed, then walked over to Finn and Mosley, who were comparing their lists. "How's it going?"

Mosley's smile was far more genuine today than it had been last night. "We've already shipped out more than half the items. We should be able to wrap things up here in a few more hours. And then this whole thing will finally be *over*."

I didn't know about that, given what I'd learned about Alanna, but I didn't want to ruin his good mood, so I smiled back at him.

One of the workers came over to talk to Mosley, and the two of them drifted away.

I looked at Finn. "And how are things really going?"

He shrugged, but worry tightened his face. "Well, they were fine until about thirty minutes ago. That's when *she* showed up, right before you did."

He jerked his head toward one of the ballroom exits. At first, I didn't understand what had upset him, but then Alanna strolled into view.

She was wearing an emerald-green pantsuit and heels that highlighted her lean, strong figure. She was talking on her phone and pacing back and forth in the hallway outside the ballroom, moving in and out of my line of sight.

My hands curled into fists. "What is she doing here?"

"Supposedly, helping to oversee the packing of the auction items like the other Briartop board members Mosley roped into this," Finn said. "I was going to text and let you know that she was here when you arrived with the food."

The two of us watched as Alanna kept talking and pacing.

"She hasn't made a move on Mosley?" I asked. "No threats against him at all?"

Finn shook his head. "Not so much as a single catty remark. She breezed into the ballroom, air-kissed Mosley, and then pulled out her phone and stalked over there. She's been talking ever since."

"I wonder if she's chatting with her new investor," I muttered.

He frowned. "What investor?"

I filled him in on everything Silvio had told me about Alanna's repeated attempts to reclaim her family estate. The worry lines around Finn's mouth deepened, and I could almost see the wheels turning in his mind.

"But if Alanna doesn't inherit the estate after Mosley's death, then why target him at all?" he asked, voicing the same thought I'd had earlier. "And what do Hugh Tucker and the Circle have to do with this?"

I shook my head. "I don't know, but we need to keep an eye on Mosley until we figure things out. He's safe enough here with his men around, but where is he going after this? Back to your apartment?"

"No, I'm dropping him off at Mallory's. I already coordinated everything with Lorelei. He's going to spend the night with them. I also convinced a couple of the bank guards to bunk at the mansion. I asked him to stay with me again or go to one of Dad's safe houses, but he refused. He insisted on going to the Parkers' mansion and helping them unpack those books that Lorelei bought, but that's just an excuse. I think he's worried that Alanna might try to hurt Mallory to get back at him."

I would have preferred that Mosley go to an anonymous safe house where no one could find him, but I couldn't fault him for wanting to protect Mallory. Besides, Lorelei was a powerful elemental who could make Ice guns with her magic. I'd seen her use the weapons before, so I knew how dangerous she was. I also knew that she would die before she let anything happen to Mallory or Mosley. It wasn't ideal, but Mosley staying at the Parker mansion was still a solid option.

Finn nudged me with his shoulder. "I've got things under control here. So why don't you go get your own bookcase? The workers haven't gotten to it yet, so it's still sitting in the library, along with that photo of your parents."

"Are you sure? I feel like I should stay and keep an eye on Mosley, especially since she's here."

I looked over at Alanna again, but she was still talking on her phone. I wondered what she was up to. She certainly hadn't come here to help with the moving and packing.

"Don't worry, Gin. I'll watch out for the boss man, make sure that he steers clear of Alanna and gets over to the Parker mansion safe and sound." Finn nudged me again. "Now, go. I'll call you if anything changes."

He walked over to Mosley and the other worker, and the three of them got in line to get some food. Alanna stayed where she was, still talking on her phone. I went over to the far side of the ballroom and headed down the corridor toward the library, itching to get my hands on that photo of my parents.

I stepped into the library, which looked a bit empty now that Lorelei's bookcase had been removed. But my case was still sitting in the same spot, and I ducked under the red velvet rope and snatched the photo of my parents off the shelf. I was in such a hurry that I almost knocked the blue book sitting underneath the picture down to the floor, although I managed to reach out and shove it farther back onto the shelf. Then I let out a breath and slowly held the picture up where I could see it.

I stared at my mother for a few seconds, but I was used to seeing her face again, thanks to the photos Mallory had given me, so I turned my attention to my father. With his dark brown hair and gray eyes, Tristan was much handsomer than I remembered, despite the tension that filled his face.

I thought back, trying to use this picture to sharpen my own vague, hazy memories of my father, but it didn't work. Try as I might, I couldn't remember his smile or his laugh.

Sadness rippled through me, dimming some of my joy and excitement. I'd always thought that it was highly ironic—and more than a little disheartening—how I could clearly remember so many of the horrible things that had happened to me but so few of the good ones.

Or maybe that was simply because the bad had outweighed the good for so much of my life.

But this photo was a good memory of my father. Well, technically, it was the *only* memory I had of him, but I'd take what I could get. I would have to give the picture to Silvio and see if he could scan it and crop Mab out of it completely so that only my parents remained—

"Ah, Ms. Blanco. How lovely to see you again," a cool, familiar voice called out.

Startled, I whirled around to find Alanna staring at me. I had been so wrapped up in my thoughts that I hadn't heard her walk down the corridor or step into the library, despite her high heels. I clutched the picture a little tighter in my left hand and casually dropped my right arm down to my side, ready to palm the knife hidden up my sleeve at the first sign of trouble.

"Ms. Eaton. So lovely to see you again as well." A bald-faced lie, but I was going to match her fake politeness for fake politeness, as was the way of Southern women when engaging in verbal warfare.

Alanna glided forward, once again moving with that eerie, sinuous, catlike grace. It was like she didn't have any bones in her entire body, just muscles and tendons that would bend, move, and stretch her limbs however she wanted. I almost expected her head to swivel all the way around on her neck, like a monster from some horror movie.

She glanced at the photo in my hand, and her lips flattened out into a thin, unhappy line. The same sour expression had curdled her face when she'd seen me staring at the picture last night.

I wondered why it bothered her. Maybe it wasn't the picture that upset her as much as the fact that I'd outbid her for the lot. Or maybe Tucker had told her that the photo featured my parents. Maybe she just didn't want me to have this reminder of them when her own mother was dead.

That familiar mix of guilt and shame twisted my stomach, but I forced it away. Fletcher had always said that emotion would get you killed quicker than anything else as an assassin. Maybe it was hypocritical or just plain selfish of me, but I wasn't going to simply lie down and die so that Alanna could avenge her mother. I had been given a job as the Spider, and I had completed my mission. My only regret was the collateral damage I'd done to Alanna along the way.

Once again, I wondered if she knew that I had killed her mother, and once again, there was no way to know.

At least, not until she tried to kill me.

Something that was probably going to happen very, very soon, unless I missed my guess. But I'd never been one to back down from a fight, so I decided to try to wind her up.

"Tell me," I said, "did you ever get that nice, bloody *steak* you were talking about last night?"

"Not yet," she murmured. "But I have high hopes that I'll be dining on it and much more in the near future."

Her green gaze focused on my throat, and she touched her tongue to the tip of one of her fangs, like she was testing if it would be sharp enough to tear into my neck. I held back a shudder at the thought of her eating me like a filet mignon.

After a few seconds, she lifted her gaze to my face. "Here to collect your new treasures?"

"Of course." I gestured at the bookcase. "I can't wait to get everything home and see all the first editions and other surprises."

"I would have thought you would have sent your assistant to fetch everything." She gave a delicate sniff, as if she thought it was terribly inappropriate that I'd come myself.

"Oh, I'm very hands-on," I drawled. "Always have been. I don't like to delegate, especially not when it comes to the hard, dirty work."

"Mmm."

We both knew that I wasn't talking about picking up the bookcase anymore. Alanna stared at me, and I looked right back at her. Yet again, I wondered if she knew what I'd done to her mother, but she was so calm that I couldn't tell. No emotion sparked in her gaze. No anger, no rage, no hate. It was like staring at a blank wall. That was how unnervingly empty her face was.

But as the old saying went, still waters ran deep, and I was betting that Alanna had a whole host of feelings about me—and that none of them were good. Even if she didn't realize that I'd killed her mother, Tucker had to have told her about my being the Spider. Plus, I had stopped her from getting her hands on Mosley the other night. If she was anything like her mother, Alanna would happily kill me for that perceived slight alone.

Footsteps thumped along the corridor, and a couple of giant movers stepped into the library. I stared at Alanna a moment longer, letting her know that I wasn't afraid of her, then waved over the two men, the same ones who'd helped me bring the food inside earlier.

"Well, it looks like my movers are here. It would be rude to keep them waiting. So nice to see you again, Ms. Eaton."

"And you too, Ms. Blanco." Alanna tipped her head at me, then pivoted on her stilettos and glided out of the library.

I watched her go, once again getting the feeling that I was the mouse and she was the cat, just waiting for the right time to leap out of the shadows and finally, fully eviscerate me.

✵ 16 ✵

I stared at the doorway for several seconds, wondering if Alanna might linger outside in the corridor to spy on me, but she pulled her phone out of her pocket and started texting as she walked away. So I turned my attention back to the task at hand.

Under my watchful eye, the two giants carefully pulled the books, crystal paperweights, and other knickknacks off the shelves, covered them with padded plastic, and gently nestled them together in several cardboard boxes. The boxes were then placed on a large cart, along with the bookcase itself. The only thing that didn't get packed up was the photo of my parents, which I was still holding. I wasn't letting it out of my sight, not even to box it up for the drive home, and I cradled the silver frame up against my chest as I followed the movers out of the library.

Most folks were still eating, but Finn had already gone back to work, although he had his clipboard in one hand and a sourdough roll stuffed with barbecue chicken in the other. The two giants rolled the cart over to my brother, who ticked the lot off his list and directed them to the plastic-wrapping station so the bookcase could be cushioned for the ride to my house.

I glanced around the ballroom, but I didn't see Alanna anywhere. Finn noticed my searching gaze. He downed the rest of his makeshift sandwich, licked the barbecue sauce off his fingers, and came over to me.

"She left," he murmured. "I saw her follow you into the library, so I sent the movers back there to check on you. I don't know what you said to her, but she looked pissed, and she stormed out of here without saying a word to anyone."

"Are you sure she's gone? Maybe it was just an act so she could sneak back and get close to Mosley." I looked over at the dwarf, who was chowing down on cobbler and ice cream.

Finn shook his head. "Nope. I followed her outside. She got into her car and drove away. Trust me. She's gone."

I should have been relieved that Alanna had left, but cold worry trickled down my spine instead. If she had still been here, Finn could have kept an eye on her. Now I didn't know where she had gone or what she might be up to.

Finn promised to update me if anything unusual or suspicious happened, as well as pack up any leftover food from lunch, which meant there was nothing more for me to do here. The giants had finished wrapping up my bookcase, so I said good-bye to my brother and followed the movers outside.

I pointed out my white van, and the giants carefully loaded the bookcase into the back and tied it down with bungee cords so it wouldn't slide around. They stacked the boxes of books and knickknacks all around the case, then shut the back doors.

I tipped them both generously for helping me with the food and the bookcase, got into the driver's seat, and locked the doors. I laid the photo of my parents in the passenger's seat, then cranked the engine and left the estate.

I cruised slowly down the hill, careful of the cargo in the back and trying to jostle it as little as possible. My puttering pace gave me plenty of time to admire the botanical gardens on the opposite side of the road.

Since it was the dead of winter, the trees had shed their leaves for the season long ago. Perhaps it was my own whimsy or all the books in the van, but the bare branches looked like spiky brown fingers of ink bleeding up into the blank gray page of the sky. The gusting breeze tangled the branches, making it seem like all those gnarled fingers were clawing at the clouds, desperately trying to pull the puffy masses down to their level.

Despite the cold wind and bleak winter colors, it was still a pretty drive, and I was in no particular hurry to get home. I rounded a curve, going even slower than before so the boxes of books wouldn't move around. I was definitely keeping that first edition of *The Adventures of Huckleberry Finn*, but I'd probably end up donating most of the other volumes to one of the local libraries. Maybe the librarians could auction off some of the first editions to raise money for their literacy programs. That would certainly do more good for the community than Mab ever had.

A few minutes later, I stopped at an intersection. No cars were coming, so I took a longer look at the botanical gardens, once again admiring the dance of the branches against the sky. I was quite familiar with this intersection, and through the trees, I could just make out the beginnings of the gardens' enormous hedge maze. The scene of another one of my many crimes.

The low growl of an engine sounded, drawing my attention. The noise increased, and a black sedan appeared in the distance, racing toward the intersection from the opposite direction, going far faster than the speed limit.

That was the first sign that something was wrong.

The second was the sharp squeal of tires behind me.

My gaze snapped over to the driver's-side mirror. Another black sedan was zooming up behind me, also going far faster than it should have been.

That worry and unease that I'd been feeling at the estate earlier morphed into hard knots of cold certainty in my stomach. I knew what was coming next. Sure enough, both sedans wrenched to the side, blocking the road in front of and behind me, trapping my van in the middle.

I was being ambushed.

Three giants with guns poured out of the car in front of me. I didn't recognize any of them, although I spotted one familiar vampire in the mix. Spiky blond hair, hazel eyes, muscled body. Terrence Phelps, Alanna's head of security.

Phelps climbed out of the driver's side of the sedan. He shouted an order, then waved his hand. I barely had time to put the van into park, turn off the engine, and grab hold of my Stone magic before he and his giants raised their weapons and started shooting at me.

Crack!

Crack! Crack!

Crack! Crack! Crack!

Bullets blasted against the windshield, making me curse and hunker down. Shards of glass hit my Stone-hardened skin and rattled off, adding to the chaos and confusion. One bullet punched all the way through the engine block and the glove compartment before slamming into the photo of my parents that I'd propped up in the passenger's seat. The glass shattered, and the silver frame dropped to the floor and busted open, although I couldn't tell how damaged the photo itself might be.

White-hot rage scorched through my body. Oh, those gun-toting bastards were going to pay for *that*.

But first, I had to quit being a sitting duck and get out of the van. I raised myself up just enough so that I could look into the driver's-side mirror, expecting the two female giants racing toward the back of the vehicle to start shooting as well. But instead of a gun, one of them was carrying a crowbar. I frowned. What was she going to do with that—

Screech!

The giant rammed her crowbar between the two back doors, trying to pop them open and making the van rock from side to side. Smart to come at me from both directions at once, but my attackers were still in for a very rude awakening. It took more than a few giants and guns to rattle me. They'd picked the wrong person to ambush, and I was going to turn the tables and kill every last one of them.

Except for Terrence Phelps. I had some questions for the vampire about his boss. Then he could join the rest of his soon-to-be-roadkill friends.

Bullets kept blasting against the windshield, and many of them punched through the glass and *ping-ping-pinged* around inside the van, throwing hot sparks everywhere. I palmed one of my knives, unbuckled my seat belt, and slid down into the open space between the two front seats.

Crack!

Crack! Crack!

Crack! Crack! Crack!

The gunfire continued at a steady clip, so I crawled

toward the back doors. I kept to the side of the van as much as possible, maneuvering around the bookcase in the middle and climbing across the tops of the boxes of books and knickknacks.

Smack!

A bullet punched into a box beside my elbow, and paper shreds sprayed everywhere like confetti. My eyes narrowed. If those bastards had ruined my first edition of *Huck Finn*…well, they were going to wish they hadn't.

A few seconds later, I was at the back of the van, crouching right next to the doors. The vehicle didn't have any rear windows, but I could still hear the steady *screech-screech-screech* of the crowbar tearing into the seam between the doors.

The two giants back here probably thought that Phelps and the others had either already killed me or at least had me pinned down in the front. If I was still alive, no doubt they would stick their own guns inside the vehicle, shoot me in the back, and finish the job. They wouldn't be expecting me to come at them from this angle. My knife still in my hand, I waited, just waited, for the doors to open and for my enemies to show themselves—

SCREECH!

The loud, ear-splitting burst of noise made me wince. One of the back doors finally wrenched open, and the giant with the crowbar stuck her head inside.

"I see a lot of boxes. What are we looking for again?" she called out over the continued *cracks* of gunfire.

Wait a second. Were they trying to kill me or rob me? Probably both, given my bad luck.

I pushed the thought aside and surged forward, throwing myself out of the van and onto the other woman. The giant screamed in surprise and tumbled backward, losing her grip on her crowbar and landing awkwardly on the pavement. She broke my fall perfectly, and even better, her head snapped back against the asphalt, stunning her. While she was still dazed, I rammed my knife into her heart, making her scream again, then yanked the blade free.

Crack!

The second giant snatched up her friend's crowbar from the road, stepped forward, and slammed it into my back. I grunted at the hard, bruising impact, but thanks to my Stone-hardened skin, the blow didn't do much more than piss me off even more than I already was.

I rolled off the dying woman and came up in a low crouch on the pavement. The second giant stared at me, her face paling as she realized just how much trouble she was in.

I got to my feet and stalked toward her. She brandished her crowbar, backing up all the while, but I kept coming. Her gaze dropped to the bloody knife in my hand, and panic sparked in her dark eyes. The giant started swinging the crowbar in wide, reckless arcs, as if that would keep me from killing her. All the while, she kept backing up, not bothering to look behind her.

The giant took another step back, and her black boot caught on the edge of the pavement. The sudden, unexpected tilt threw her off-balance, and she stumbled backward and landed on her ass in the dirt and grass on the side of the road. The crowbar slipped from her grip and clattered against the asphalt, and she lurched forward, trying to grab the weapon, but I stepped up and kicked it away from her, sending it skittering end over end down the road.

Before the giant could get to her feet, I reached down, dug my hand into her hair, and pulled her head up just enough so that I could bury my knife in her neck. She screamed and flailed her arms, trying to throw me off. I held on and twisted the blade in deeper, until her screams subsided, and her body sagged as the fight, blood, and life leaked out of her.

"You should have watched your step," I hissed, and ripped my knife free of her neck.

She let out a dying gasp of agreement, pitched forward, and did a face-plant onto the ground, already closer to dead than alive—

Click. Click. Click.

The distinctive sounds of fresh magazines being jammed into guns rang out. I whirled around. Three giants stood in front of me, their guns pointed at my chest, with Phelps lurking behind them. They must have realized that I'd gotten out of the van and had come back here to finish me off.

"Assassin bitch," one of the giants growled. "You killed Diana and Penny!"

All three giants raised their guns a little higher, taking better aim at me. There was no way I could close the distance between us and attack before they pulled the triggers, so I reached for even more of my Stone magic to protect myself against the bullets that were coming my way—

Crack!

Crack!

Crack!

I tensed, expecting bullets to slam into my body, but the three giants dropped to the ground instead, all of them killed by headshots. Judging by the sounds, the gunfire had come from the woods behind me.

My heart lifted. Finn must be here. He was the only person I knew of who could shoot like that. He must have heard the gunfire up at the estate, realized that I was being ambushed, and raced down here to help me.

Phelps cursed, lifted his own gun, and started firing at me. But he was backpedaling the whole time, and all of his bullets went wide. I reached for my Ice magic, snapped up my hand, and flung a spray of daggers out at him. But Phelps ducked behind the van, and my Ice daggers hit the side of the vehicle and broke apart into jagged chunks.

I paused for a moment, expecting the vampire to lean around the side of the vehicle and fire at me again, but footsteps smacked on the pavement instead. Too late, I realized what he was doing.

I cursed and charged forward, crossing the asphalt and rounding the side of the van, but Phelps had already retreated all the way back to his sedan. He threw himself into the driver's seat, shut the door, slammed the car into reverse, hit the gas, and screeched down the road. Fifty feet later, he yanked the wheel hard, and the sedan lurched to the side. Phelps threw the car back into gear, turned the wheel again, and zoomed off. A few seconds later, he was gone.

"Dammit!" I snarled. "Dammit!"

If my van hadn't already been shot to shit, I would have lashed out and kicked one of the tires. But since they were just about the only part of the vehicle that wasn't riddled with bullets, I decided not to abuse them.

Footsteps scuffed behind me, and a low, happy whistle trilled out, as though someone was pleased about a job well done. I turned around.

"Hey, Finn. Thanks for the assist—"

The words died on my lips. A familiar figure stood on the road in front of me, but it wasn't Finn. No, this was a tall, lean man with black hair and eyes and a neatly trimmed goatee. One who had his gun aimed straight at my heart.

Hugh Tucker.

17

I tightened my grip on my knife and kept hold of my Stone magic in case Tucker decided to shoot me.

He squinted down the gunsight at me, as if he was seriously considering it. But after several tense seconds, he slowly lowered the weapon to his side, although he kept his finger curled around the trigger, ready to snap up the gun and fire it if I took so much as a single step toward him. Given his amazing vampiric speed, he could easily empty the rest of his magazine into me before I got within striking distance with my knife or even had a chance to fling a spray of Ice daggers out at him. So I held my position.

For now.

"What's up, Hugh?" I drawled, trying to hide my surprise. "You know, I'm starting to think you have a little crush on me, the way you keep popping up wherever I go."

Tucker didn't bat an eye at my insult. He didn't react at all, except to keep staring at me. Alanna Eaton might be hard to read, but Hugh Tucker was a master of the inscrutable expression. If he ever got tired of being a Circle henchman, he could always take up professional poker. I imagined he would be just as good at cards as he was at killing people.

Frustration surged through me, along with more than a little annoyance, but I ignored the emotions. I could be just as calm, cold, and remote as he was. We stood there in the middle of the road, staring each other down, with blood, bodies, and bullet casings littering the pavement all around us.

Finally, Tucker's black gaze flicked to the two giants I'd stabbed to death, as well as the three he'd shot. He shook his head. "Alanna really should have sent more people after you. I told her at least ten, but she didn't listen to me. Then again, she *never* listens to me. That's going to be her downfall."

Of course, I had realized that the giants worked for Alanna, since Phelps had been leading them, but I wondered why Tucker was so casually confirming it—and what this had to do with the Circle.

"And why would Alanna send men to kill me?" I asked, fishing for information. "I haven't done anything to her."

At least, not recently.

Tucker didn't answer me, and we continued our face-off.

"What's this all about?" I asked, trying again. "What did these giants want?"

He flashed me a sly, knowing grin. "You know I can't make it *that* easy for you, Gin. Besides, I'm looking forward to watching you figure it out for yourself."

My eyes narrowed. "Is Alanna some new rival of yours in the Circle? Is this some lame attempt to get me to kill her? If so, you can forget it. I'm sick and tired of doing your dirty work. If you want Alanna dead, then go kill her your own damn self."

I didn't know much about Circle politics, but from what

little I'd gleaned from Tucker, it was a no-holds-barred game with deadly consequences for the losers.

Like Damian Rivera.

With his massive family fortune, Rivera had been one of the Circle's main cash cows, but he'd also knowingly employed Bruce Porter, the Dollmaker serial killer, as his right-hand man. The Circle was all about maintaining its anonymity, and the members hadn't wanted the attention that having a serial killer in the ranks would invite, especially given Bria and Xavier's investigation into the Dollmaker. So they'd sent Tucker to tell Rivera to deal with Porter—or else. But Rivera had ignored Tucker's warning, and insulted him to boot, so Tucker had killed Rivera and framed Porter for his boss's murder.

I had gotten involved because Porter had kidnapped Elissa Daniels, but Tucker had been pulling my strings from behind the scenes the whole time, eventually manipulating me into a position where I'd had to kill Porter in order to survive. So I couldn't help but wonder if Tucker was doing the same thing again right now. Pointing me at Alanna because she'd done something to piss him off or was some sort of threat to him within the Circle.

Tucker shrugged. "I don't care about Alanna. Not in the slightest. She's the one who volunteered for this little mission. As she rightly should have, since the situation is entirely her fault. She never should have let things get this far, this out of hand."

"And what mission would that be?"

His black eyes glittered with a cold, hard light. "Let's just say that Alanna thinks she can do my job better than me, so I've decided to let her try. I'm especially looking forward to watching her suffer the consequences when she fails."

He smiled, baring his fangs, and I knew that he was equating the consequences of Alanna failing with my killing her. But what had she done that required Tucker's attention? What mission could she possibly be on for the Circle? And most important, why had Tucker helped me by killing her men?

Given how many times he had tried to murder me in the past few months, he should have stayed hidden in the woods and hoped Alanna's giants did the job for him. But he'd drawn his gun and shot them instead. Why? My head pounded with all the unanswered questions. Once again, Tucker was playing some game that I didn't understand.

"Well, I don't care about whatever feud you have with Alanna," I snapped. "Do us both a favor, and leave me out of your petty power struggles."

Tucker shrugged again. "I'm not the one who dragged you into this. You have Stuart Mosley to thank for that. You got in Alanna's way when you saved him from her muggers the other night. Now she's coming for you too." He paused. "Then again, I suppose that's only to be expected, since you killed her mother."

Shock jolted through me, and I had to work very hard to keep my face blank. At the auction last night, Alanna had said that Tucker had told her all about me, and I'd wondered if that included my role in her mother's death. But I had dismissed the thought, since no one else had known about that particular assignment except Fletcher and me. At least, I'd thought no one else had known. The old man was dead, and I certainly hadn't blabbed about it to anyone other than my friends. So how had Tucker found out that I was the one who'd murdered Amelia Eaton all those years ago?

And the way he so casually dropped the knowledge made me think he had known about it for quite some time, which was even more worrisome. Had the Circle been involved with Amelia? Or had they somehow been keeping tabs on Fletcher the same way he had on them? More and more questions crowded into my mind, but I didn't have any answers.

Some of my surprise must have shown, because Tucker arched an eyebrow. "Don't blame me," he murmured. "I didn't tell her. Apparently, Alanna figured it out all on her own when she saw you save Mosley the other night. Despite her arrogance, she can be clever on occasion."

So Alanna had been there watching the whole time from her car, just like I'd thought. My knives, my fighting style, the way I walked, talked, moved. No doubt those things were ingrained in her brain, just like all the horrible little details of my mother's murder were ingrained in mine. She had recognized me, and she'd put two and two together about her mother's death.

Tucker might not have told Alanna that I'd killed her mother, but I wondered if he'd confirmed her suspicions after the mugging. But how had he known for sure that I was involved? Had he known about all the terrible things Amelia Eaton did on her estate? And why would he tell Alanna anything about me if he hated her so much? To further pit her against me in hopes that one of us would kill the other? But if that was the case, then why had Tucker helped me now by killing her giants?

Every word he said only added to my anger and confusion, not to mention the migraine pounding like a sledgehammer inside my skull. I just didn't know anything anymore, especially when it came to Hugh Tucker and his twisted motivations.

I opened my mouth to demand some fucking *answers*, even though I knew he would never give them to me, not even if I sliced him to pieces with my knife. But I never got the chance.

Tucker aimed his gun at me again and started backing up, heading toward the trees. Unlike the giant I'd killed earlier, he never missed a step and smoothly transitioned from the asphalt onto the grass. Even if he had stumbled, his vampiric speed would have let him recover his balance long before I had a chance to get close to him.

Tucker stopped at the edge of the trees, raised his gun to his forehead, and snapped off a mocking salute with it. "See you soon, Genevieve."

Then he turned and disappeared into the woods, leaving me standing alone in the middle of the road, still surrounded by all the blood, bodies, and bullet casings.

This road wasn't a busy thoroughfare, but it was only a matter of time before somebody came driving along, and I needed to be gone before that happened. So as soon as Tucker vanished, I hurried over, knelt down, and rifled through the pockets of the dead giants. I was still wearing my winter gloves, so I didn't have to worry about leaving fingerprints behind.

The dead men and women were carrying wallets and IDs, but I didn't recognize any of the names or faces, so I moved on to their phones. The devices were all burners and locked with passwords, rendering them useless, so I tossed them aside in disgust and kept searching. A pack of gum, some lip balm, crumpled tissues, a couple of quarters. I didn't find anything interesting in any of the giants' pockets, much less a bona fide clue that would tell me why they—and Alanna—had targeted me.

Why here? Why now? If Alanna knew that I'd killed her mother, I would expect her to try to kidnap me, so she could torture me for an extended period of time. So she could make her revenge last as long as possible. Not send some anonymous minions to simply gun me down.

I let the last man flop back down to the ground and got to my feet. Then I turned around in a slow circle, studying where the dead giants had landed and searching for anything I might have overlooked. And I found something: the crowbar one of the women had used to force her way into the back of my van.

I see a lot of boxes. What are we looking for again? The woman's voice whispered in my mind.

My gaze flicked over to the vehicle. Thanks to the giant and her crowbar, the right rear door was barely clinging to the rest of the frame, and the opening gave me a clear view of the bookcase tied down in the van, surrounded by boxes of books—books that had belonged to Mab Monroe.

My eyes narrowed. Hmm. Maybe this wasn't about me. At least, not entirely. Maybe it was more about what was in my van.

If she wanted me dead, Alanna could have attacked when we were alone in the library at the estate. But she had waited until *after* I had taken possession of my auction items before she'd sicced Phelps and the giants on me.

Alanna wanted something of Mab's.

It was the only explanation that made sense. And the only reason for Tucker to be involved was if that item had something to do with the Circle. After all, Mab had been a member of the evil group too. Maybe she had set something aside for a rainy day, some damning piece of evidence or blackmail that she thought would keep her safe from Mason and from being killed the same way she had killed my mother.

The more I thought about it, the more certain I was that I was right.

Finding this mystery item must be the mission Alanna had signed up for, the one she thought she could do better than Tucker. But her arrogance had pissed him off, and instead of letting her men take me out and recover the item, he'd helped me instead. Once again, Tucker was playing both sides against the middle, probably hoping that I'd kill Alanna for him the same way I had killed Bruce Porter.

I didn't care about Tucker's twisted reasoning or whatever power struggle he might be having with Alanna. If there was something in one of those boxes that could hurt the Circle, then I was determined to find it.

But first, I had to get out of here.

By now, Terrence Phelps had called Alanna and told her that her plan had failed, and she could already be sending more men to the area. So I left the dead giants where they had fallen, along with the second black sedan, which was still idling and blocking the road.

I hurried over to the back of my van, reached inside the door console, and pulled out some extra bungee cords before crawling inside the vehicle. I wasn't nearly as strong as the giant who had forced her way into the van, but I managed to yank the broken door shut a few inches. Then I threaded the bungee cords through the interior door handle and secured them to the exposed metal framework inside the van, closing the door as much as possible. My crude web would keep the door from falling off and stop any boxes from sliding out of the back.

Once the back door was secure, I climbed up to the front of the van, shoved the broken glass out of the driver's seat, and sat down in it. The windshield had completely shattered, with all the bullets that had punched into and through it, but I didn't mind. At least I had a clear view.

Now came the real moment of truth. I'd turned the van off to fight the giants, but their hail of bullets might have completely destroyed the engine. If the engine was done for, then so was I, since there was no way I could move all those boxes of books by myself, much less the actual bookcase.

Only one way to find out.

I reached down and turned the key, which was still in the ignition. I held my breath, hoping, hoping, hoping that it would start…

Vvv…vvv…vroom-vroom…

The engine sputtered and wheezed for several seconds, as though it were coughing up all the bullets lodged in it, but it finally turned over. The low grumbling drowned out the relieved sigh that escaped my lips. I threw the van into gear, looked around to make sure that no traffic was coming, and hit the gas, zooming away from the scene of my latest crime.

Luckily, I didn't pass any cars around the botanical gardens, but given the engine's continued coughing, I didn't know how far my van would make it before it gave up completely. Besides, I couldn't exactly drive around indefinitely in a bullet-ridden van with no windshield. Most of the cops might be as corrupt as the day was long, but even they would pull me over if they caught sight of my vehicle in this condition—if only to see what kind of bribe I'd offer to get out of trouble.

So I thought about the closest, safest place to where I was and steered in that direction, sticking to the back roads, where I was less likely to run into any other cars.

For once, my luck held, and I made it over to a shipping

yard owned by Lorelei Parker without passing another vehicle. Lorelei was in the process of expanding the shipping yard, which she used for her various smuggling operations, and I drove around a couple of rolls of metal fencing that hadn't been erected yet.

A few minutes later, I parked the van behind one of the hundreds of metal containers that lined the area like oversize building blocks. This part of the yard butted up against the Aneirin River, and the ground dropped away to a steep bank that plummeted down to the dark water. That was going to come in handy later, since I had no desire to explain to anyone why my van now looked like a piece of metal Swiss cheese.

I turned off the engine and leaned forward, listening and peering out the empty windshield. In the distance, heavy machinery rumbled back and forth as containers were moved around the yard, but the sounds didn't draw any closer, and I didn't see any workers in this section.

It didn't seem like anyone had spotted me, so I pulled out my phone, called Silvio, and told him what was going on. He was still at the Pork Pit, but he promised to come pick me up, as well as call around and see who else could help us.

While I waited for him, I reached down and grabbed the photo of my parents, which had fallen to the floorboard when the shooting started. A bullet had hit the corner of the silver frame, shattering it as well as the glass, but the photo itself was still in one piece. I let out a relieved breath, carefully slid the photo out of what was left of the ruined frame, and put it on the dashboard for safekeeping.

Next, I crawled into the back of the van, undid my web of bungee cords, and kicked the broken door open again. Then I hefted the boxes of books out of the van and set them down on the ground a safe distance away. The giant movers had made it look easy, but the books were heavy, and I was sweating by the time I plopped the last box down on the ground.

My phone rang just as I was trying to figure out how—or if—I could move the bookcase by myself. Yeah, that wasn't happening, so I pulled my phone out of my pocket. "You here?"

"Your chariot awaits," Silvio's dry voice sounded in my ear.

An engine rumbled in the distance, and several seconds later, a black van steered around the containers and stopped a few feet away. Silvio got out and walked over to me.

"Where did you get that on such short notice?" I asked.

He spun his silver key ring around on his finger, then held up the attached key chain, which was shaped like a spider rune, just like his tie pin was. "It's mine. After I had to come down to Bullet Pointe to help you, I thought a larger vehicle might come in handy in case of emergency." His gray gaze flicked from one cardboard box to another. "Although I never expected said emergency to involve books."

I shook my head. I didn't know whether to admire or be frightened by his planning, but it was one of the things that made him such a great assistant. "Well, I'm glad it's here. Help me load these."

Given the blood he drank, Silvio was much stronger than I was, and he easily stuffed the boxes into the back of his van, along with the heavy bookcase, which he wrangled all by himself. While he was busy with that, I grabbed the photo of my parents out of my van and slid it into the top of one of the boxes.

"Mosley should give his men a bonus," Silvio said in an admiring voice as he secured the bookcase with bungee cords in the back of his van. "They did a great job cushioning this. I don't think any bullets made it through all those layers of padded plastic."

"Yeah," I muttered. "Too bad they didn't do the same thing to my van. Now, come on. Help me push."

I looked around again to make sure that we were still alone, then put my van in neutral and went around to the back.

"On three," I told Silvio. "One…two…three!"

Together we pushed the vehicle forward. Well, really, Silvio did most of the pushing. But together we forced the van to the edge of the shipping yard and then shoved it over the side of the steep bank. After that, sweet, sweet gravity took over.

SPLASH!

The van careened down the bank and actually went airborne for a few seconds before it plunged into the river below. All of those bullet holes let the water rush right in, and the vehicle quickly sank below the murky surface. Silvio went back to start his own vehicle so we could leave, but I stayed by the river for a couple of minutes, making sure my van was completely submerged.

The water was particularly deep here, and with any luck, the strong current would slowly push the van on down the river. The vehicle was registered in one of my many aliases—Carmen Cole, an oldie but a goodie—so even if the cops did eventually fish it out of the water, no one would be able to trace it back to me.

I waited until all the air bubbles had popped away and the surface of the water rippled and flowed like normal before getting into Silvio's van.

At least, I tried to get into the van. I got as far as opening the passenger's door before he scurried around the front of the vehicle and held up a finger, telling me to wait.

He skirted around me, reached into the door console, and pulled out a roll of black plastic, which he then draped all over the passenger's seat, as well as the surrounding floorboard. It reminded me of that black plastic floor in Amelia Eaton's murder room.

"What are you doing?" I asked.

"Have you looked in a mirror lately?" Silvio asked. "Oh, wait, no, you haven't, because the giants shot them both off your van. Well, let me clue you in to one small fact: you are covered in blood." Despite the fact that he was a vampire and had to drink blood to survive, his nostrils still flared in disgust. "You absolutely *reek* of it."

"So? How is that unusual?"

"It's not unusual. But you are *not* smearing it all over my brand-new van."

"Wait a second. This is a brand-new van? Like brand-new brand-new?" I leaned in closer and drew in a deep breath. Oh, yeah. It still had that new-car smell.

"Yes," Silvio said in a prim, proud tone. "It is brand-new brand-new. I just bought it last week, and I've put a grand total of one hundred and thirteen miles on it so far. Emergency or not, that's much too early to dirty it up with bloodstains."

I rolled my eyes. "Are you going to wipe off my grimy face too, Mom?"

"If I thought it would do any good." His nostrils flared again. "It's even in your *hair*. How did you get blood in your hair?"

"Well, I stabbed this one giant in the neck—"

Silvio snapped up his hand, cutting me off. "That was a rhetorical question, Gin. Totally a rhetorical question."

✽ 18 ✽

After using up the better part of his roll of black plastic, Silvio finally let me slide into his precious new van.

He stabbed his finger at me. "And don't you *dare* touch anything."

I made a big show of tucking my hands into my armpits like I was a little kid. "Yes, Mom. I'll be good. I promise."

Silvio harrumphed, but he was smiling as he shut the door. Then he went around the van, got into the driver's seat, cranked the engine, and away we went.

Twenty minutes later, he steered the van up the gravel driveway to my house and parked in his usual spot. But instead of immediately getting out, we both stayed in the vehicle, peering out the windshield in case my enemies had beaten us back here. I didn't see anyone lurking in the woods, and the stones only muttered about the cold, windy weather like usual. Alanna wasn't here. Neither was Tucker. Apparently, they both knew better than to take on the Spider in her home web.

"It's clear," I said. "Let's get this stuff unloaded."

"I'll unload everything," Silvio countered. "You go take a shower."

I rolled my eyes. "It's just a little bit of blood. Besides, you're a vampire. You're supposed to like that sort of thing."

His gray eyes narrowed, and he stared me down, clearly disagreeing with my assessment. I sighed, but I gave in and followed his orders. By the time I had showered, washed the offensive blood out of my hair, and changed my clothes, Silvio had brought all the boxes into the den, along with the bookcase.

And he wasn't alone.

Owen was here too, carefully rapping on one side of the bookcase, searching for secret compartments. Silvio was doing the same thing on the other side.

Thunk. Thunk-thunk. Thunk.

They both tapped all around the case, but no hollow sounds rang out, and no panels, drawers, or slots popped open.

Owen shook his head. "Nothing. No hiding spots at all. This thing is solid wood from top to bottom—"

He caught sight of me standing in the doorway. He stopped rapping, came over, and hugged me tight. I stepped into his embrace and buried my face in his neck, letting his rich, metallic scent sink deep down into my lungs.

"Silvio told me what happened." Owen drew back and cupped my face in his hands, his violet gaze searching my gray one. "How are you?"

I stood on my tiptoes, wrapped my arms around his neck, and kissed him deep and hard. Owen pulled me closer and kissed me back. I didn't know how long we would have stood there if Silvio hadn't cleared his throat, reminding me that we needed to find whatever Alanna was after before she attacked us again.

I kissed Owen again, then drew back. "Better now that you're here. Ready for another treasure hunt?"

He winked at me. "Always."

Silvio cleared his throat again. "Well, now that we've eliminated the bookcase, we can move on to the rest of the items."

He looked out over the cardboard boxes littering the den. His face brightened, and he rubbed his hands together in anticipation. "I do love a good puzzle."

His enthusiasm was as strange to me as that blood in my hair had been to him.

"You are officially the oddest assistant ever," I said. "Most people try to get out of work, you know. Not dive right into more."

Silvio sniffed. "Well, *I* have a higher standard than most people. I never slack off or shirk my duties. That's what makes me a superior assistant."

I couldn't argue with that. Owen grinned. Yeah, me too.

We all tore into a box and pulled out everything inside. I started with the one that contained the photo of my parents. I laid the picture on the corner of the coffee table, then moved on to the other objects inside. A glass bowl, a fancy fountain pen, other small knickknacks. This box contained the pretty decorations that had adorned the bookcase shelves. Nothing out of the ordinary, but I still studied each piece carefully.

And I found something odd: a blue crystal paperweight that pulsed with elemental magic.

The paperweight was shaped like a small dome with a flat bottom, so it would sit upright. It was about the size of an egg, but it felt much heavier than that. I frowned and held it up to the lights, studying the deep blue color and smooth, sparkling facets. And I realized that it wasn't made of crystal. No, it was a sapphire—a very large and expensive sapphire, judging from the way the gemstone kept trilling about its own flashing beauty.

But I was far more interested in the magic emanating from the jewel. It felt cold and hard, like my own Stone power. My frown deepened. Someone had coated the sapphire with Stone magic. But who? And why?

It certainly hadn't been Mab, since she'd had Fire magic. As an elemental, she would have been able to sense the Stone power just like I had, and it would have felt as wrong to her as Jo-Jo's Air magic always felt to me. The sapphire practically pulsed with Stone magic, which would have made it a constant annoyance to the Fire elemental, like an alarm that screeched every time she walked by it. So why was it in with Mab's things? And even more important, what was all that magic on the sapphire supposed to do?

"Did you find something?" Owen asked, noticing me staring at the paperweight.

"I don't know." I got up and set the sapphire on the fireplace mantel right next to the framed drawing of my mother's snowflake rune so I wouldn't lose track of it. "I'll go back to it later. Let's keep searching."

Mine had been the only box full of knickknacks, and I quickly repacked everything and set it aside. Then I tore into the box of books that was closest to me.

Most of the books were fancy, expensive, leather-bound collector's editions, the kind that folks bought for their home libraries and stuck on the shelves without actually reading them. I doubted that Mab had ever even touched any of the volumes, given how absolutely pristine they were.

At least, they would have been pristine if not for all the bullets stuck in them, like metal bookmarks holding people's reading places. Fresh anger surged through me. I didn't care about ruining my clothes or even getting blood in my hair, but I never, *ever* cracked the spine of any book I read, even if it was just a paperback. All these beautiful books ruined. I should kill Alanna for this alone.

I pushed my anger aside and concentrated on the books. I went through each volume slowly and carefully, searching for dog-eared pages, loose pieces of paper tucked inside, highlighted passages, and any notes that might have been scribbled in the margins. I even checked the front and back covers, along with the spines, in case a letter might be hidden inside the flaps.

Nothing—I found nothing. No marked sections, no notes, and no other indication that anyone had ever even opened the books.

Disappointed, I finished with the first box and moved on to a second one. Beside me, Owen and Silvio did the same.

But the books in my second box were the same as the ones in the first. Frustrated, I threw down my first edition of *Huck Finn*, which now had a nice, gaping hole right in the center of the front cover. The bullet was still lodged deep in the pages, and it winked at me like a metallic mocking eye.

Owen noticed my disgusted look. He reached over, picked up the book, and stared at the bullet embedded inside. "You know what? I kind of like it. This book has character now." He waggled it at me. "*Bullets and books.* That could be your new motto."

"You'd have to add *blood* to that," Silvio quipped.

I snorted, took the book from Owen, and set it aside, but I was smiling as I dove into the next box. He always knew what to say to make me feel better.

Owen, Silvio, and I worked as fast as we could for the next hour, well aware that trouble could come knocking on my door at any moment. By now, Alanna had to be plotting her next move against me. She might not realize that I'd come home yet or that I had Mab's things here, but it was only a matter of time before she did. I didn't know how or when she would respond, but one thing was for sure, it wouldn't be pleasant.

Still, the hour passed quietly, and we managed to go through all the boxes and books without any interruptions or attacks.

Silvio shook his head and set his last volume aside. "I'm sorry, Gin, but I don't see anything special in these books. Sure, some of them are first editions and worth several thousand dollars. At least, the ones that aren't riddled with bullet holes. But I'm not seeing anything that anyone would kill for, not even the most devoted bibliophile."

I sighed. "I know. Me neither."

A loud knock sounded at the front of the house, followed by the sound of a key turning in the lock and the door opening.

"Gin?" Finn's voice rang out.

"In the den!"

Footsteps clomped in this direction, and Finn appeared in the doorway. His green eyes widened, and he let out a low whistle.

"What happened? It looks like a library exploded in here." He frowned. "Along with an ammunition factory. Are those bullet holes in the covers?"

I'd been so busy going through the books that I hadn't called Finn and told him what was going on. So I quickly filled him in about the ambush on the road outside the botanical gardens.

"Where's Mosley?" I asked. "Is he okay?"

"He's fine. The auction is finally finished, and we

shipped out the last of the items about an hour ago. I dropped Mosley and a couple of the bank guards off at the Parker mansion like we planned, then came over here," Finn said. "Don't worry. Lorelei's there too. She knows to keep an eye out for Alanna."

I nodded, got up, and put the ruined copy of *Huck Finn* that I'd been double-checking on the fireplace mantel next to that strange sapphire paperweight. Then I looked out over the mess that Owen, Silvio, and I had made in the den. Books covered every available surface, from the flagstones in front of the fireplace to the coffee table in the center of the room to every single one of the couch cushions. Finn was right. It did look like a library had exploded in here.

Still, I wouldn't have minded the enormous mess if I'd found what I'd been searching for…whatever that might be.

"Alanna has to want *something* that's in here," I growled. "Otherwise, why ambush me right after I left the estate? She wanted to be sure that I still had Mab's things with me, and she needed to get to them before I put everything under lock and key somewhere."

"But you said that she was at the estate earlier today and that she helped catalog everything for the auction," Owen pointed out. "She's been around Mab's things for weeks. So why didn't she just take whatever she wanted when no one was looking?"

"Probably because she couldn't get to it before now," Finn said.

Silvio frowned. "What do you mean?"

"After Clementine Barker tried to rob the Briartop museum, Mab's art was put into storage by First Trust for safekeeping," Finn said. "And after Madeline Monroe died, so were all of Mab's personal effects from her mansion.

Mosley oversaw the entire project himself to make sure there were no more screwups or robbery attempts. No one had access to anything from Mab's estate except for him, and he went through and created a master list of each and every item, down to the last paper clip. Trust me, Mosley would have known if something went missing, and he would have known that Alanna was the one who'd taken it."

I nodded. "That matches up with what Alanna told me during the auction. She said that Mosley wouldn't even let her examine some of the items."

"But what about after everything was moved to the Eaton mansion?" Owen asked. "Wouldn't Alanna have been able to take what she wanted then? During the confusion of setting everything up? Or maybe later on, during the auction itself?"

Finn shook his head. "Nope. Mosley was paranoid about security, especially after Deirdre's robbery attempt at the bank. He didn't want anything like that to ruin the auction, so he set up cameras, alarms, and sensors everywhere, and he personally vetted every single guard. He even had the security footage continuously streamed to his phone. You couldn't have tried on a necklace or swiped so much as a teaspoon without him finding out about it in a matter of minutes."

"So that's why Alanna sicced those two muggers on him. She didn't want to kill Mosley. At least, not right away. She needed him to get access to whatever auction item she wanted, since she couldn't steal it herself." I started pacing back and forth, skirting around the stacks of books on the floor. "But when I stopped those two muggers from kidnapping Mosley—"

"When *we* stopped those two muggers," Finn interjected.

I rolled my eyes. "When *we* stopped those muggers,

Alanna had to come up with a new plan. That's why she was trying so hard to outbid me for this lot of books at the auction. I thought she was just being spiteful, but that was the easiest way to get her hands on them."

Finn shot his thumb and forefinger at me. "That would be my guess too."

"And when that didn't work, Alanna decided to kill you and take whatever it is that she wants," Owen chimed in.

"Precisely," Silvio added. "Not only that, but she could also take revenge on Gin for killing her mother. Now that Alanna is mixed up with Tucker, she has to know that Gin is the Circle's number one enemy. Alanna probably thought that killing Gin would also give her bonus points with Mason, the Circle leader, whoever he really is. Two birds, one stone, and all of that. Unfortunately for you, Gin, you just happened to be one of the birds."

"You know, you three could quit being so cheerful about my being marked for death," I snarked.

Finn stabbed his finger at me. "Don't limit my emotions. Besides, it's not like your being marked for death is some new and unexpected occurrence. I'd be more surprised if people *weren't* trying to kill you." He nudged Owen with his elbow. "Am I right?"

"Totally right," Owen replied.

"Absolutely right," Silvio chimed in, agreeing with them.

I glared at them. Traitors. They all crossed their arms over their chests and stared right back at me. After a moment, I sighed and gave them a sheepish shrug. As much as I hated to admit it, they were right. My being on someone's hit list wasn't an unusual occurrence. More like a monthly lunch date with death, that dear old friend of mine.

"Well, I at least want to know *why* Alanna wants me dead," I grumbled. "What one thing Mab had that Tucker and the rest of the Circle are so desperate to get their hands on. So let's keep looking."

Owen, Silvio, Finn, and I started going through the books again, even more carefully than before, searching for anything—*anything*—that would indicate that the volumes contained some secret that was worth killing for.

After about an hour, the words and pages started swimming before my eyes, so I headed into the kitchen to make some dinner while the guys kept working.

Given the cold weather and everything that had happened today, I wanted some warm, hearty, stick-to-my-ribs comfort food, so I melted some butter in a pan, then added a package of ground beef, along with some kosher salt, black pepper, chili powder, and a generous amount of cumin. Once the meat had browned, I drained off the excess fat and added in some red kidney beans, along with a couple of jars of homegrown tomatoes that Jo-Jo had canned last summer, creating a chunky sauce. My quick and easy version of chili.

While the chili simmered away, I dropped a pound of spaghetti into some salted boiling water and tossed together a garden salad with romaine lettuce, cherry tomatoes, baby carrots, and cucumbers. I also chopped up some red onions and put them in a small ramekin, then filled two more ramekins with sour cream and shredded sharp cheddar cheese.

When the spaghetti was done, I drained it, spread it in the bottom of a large platter, and topped it with the chili. Then I put the platter on a tray with the onions, sour cream, and cheese and took it into the den.

Finn perked up. "Spaghetti chili? You must have read my mind."

He reached out to snatch a stray noodle off the platter, but I smacked his hand away.

"There's a salad in the kitchen too. Go grab it and some plates, please."

Finn gave me a sour look, but he got the salad, along with plates, napkins, and silverware. I fetched some glasses and a pitcher of sweet raspberry tea, while Owen and Silvio cleared the books off the coffee table. Then we all settled down and dug into our meal.

"Mmm-mmm-mmm!" Finn said. "Spaghetti and chili. Two great foods combined into one dish of awesomeness."

I grinned. I couldn't have said it better myself.

For dessert, I grabbed a dark chocolate pound cake topped with a decadent chocolate ganache, dried cherries, and chopped almonds that I'd baked earlier in the week.

"Pasta. Meat. Chocolate." Owen sighed. "I could die a very happy man right now."

Nobody else spoke. We were all too busy eating.

When we finished, Owen and Silvio offered to clean up, while Finn and I kept working on the books. One by one, we went through them all again.

"This is a waste of time," Finn muttered. "There's nothing here. *Nothing.* Why, this book doesn't even have anything in it."

He tossed aside a book with a royal-blue cover and silver-foil-trimmed pages, the one my parents' photo had been propped up on.

The longer I stared at the volume, the more uneasy I felt, like there was something important about it that I was missing. So I picked up the book and flipped through the pages, but they were all blank like Finn had said.

I frowned. Given the thin blue lines on each page, this seemed less like a book and more like a diary, the kind of thing a teenage girl would use to scribble down her secrets. So why had Mab had it? The Fire elemental certainly wasn't the kind of person to pour out her heart about some long-ago teenage crush or anything else. The bitch would have had to have a heart first.

I sighed and placed the book on the coffee table next to the picture of my parents. "You're right. There's nothing here. Maybe Alanna made a mistake."

Finn shook his head. "Alanna Eaton doesn't strike me as the kind of person who makes mistakes. Neither does Hugh Tucker."

"I know," I said, rubbing my aching head. "I just hope I can figure out what they're after before it's too late."

✵ 19 ✵

It was after six now, and there was nothing more that we could do this evening, so Finn and Silvio headed home. Owen started gathering up the books and packing them back into their boxes to get rid of some of the mess in the den. While he worked, I decided to check in with Bria. To my surprise, she answered on the first ring.

"Funny," she said. "I was just about to call you. Guess where I am?"

I didn't hear any sirens, but several people muttered in the background, and I heard the words *crime-scene tape*. I winced. "Um, standing outside the botanical gardens, wondering why there's a black sedan and five dead giants in middle of the road?"

"Why, it's like you read my mind," she drawled, an amused note in her voice. "You must be psychic."

I barked out a laugh. "Not even close."

"Your handiwork, I presume?"

"Partially."

I told Bria about the attack, as well as the cryptic conversation I'd had with Tucker.

"So you think there's something in one of those books you bought that Tucker and the rest of the Circle want? And they hired Alanna to get it for them?" she asked.

I watched Owen stack books into another box. "That's the theory right now. Although whatever it is, we haven't been able to find it yet."

I promised to keep Bria posted, and she did the same, saying she would let me know if she got any leads from the dead giants. But I already had a sneaking suspicion about what she would find: that they all moonlighted as housekeepers, gardeners, and the like at the Eaton Estate.

We hung up, and I helped Owen finish putting the books away. After that, I went through the house, making sure that it was locked up tight and that the silverstone front door and the bars on the windows were secure like always. If Alanna did come here tonight, she would have a tough time getting inside the house, and we could always slip out through the secret tunnel in Fletcher's office.

Once I was satisfied that we were safe, Owen and I took a shower and went to bed.

Owen fell asleep quickly, but my mind kept spinning as I thought back over everything that had happened. Try as I might, though, I couldn't figure out what was in Mab's things that Alanna and the Circle were so desperate to get their hands on.

So I curled up next to Owen and put my hand on his heart, letting the steady rise and fall of his chest soothe me. Finally, my eyes fluttered closed, and I drifted off to sleep as well, although my dreams were anything but peaceful...

I was in trouble—serious, serious trouble.

Amelia Eaton had her hands locked around my throat, slowly squeezing the life out of me. She was much stronger than I was, and I couldn't buck her off, no matter how hard

I tried. All I really did was worm my body even deeper into the sand, as though I was digging my own grave. Maybe I was. A few feet away, I could hear the water lapping at the lakeshore. The steady smacking sound reminded me of the vampire licking my blood off her claws earlier. I shuddered in disgust and redoubled my efforts to throw her off.

"I'm not going anywhere!" she snarled. "And neither are you!"

Amelia tightened her grip. She was still wearing that metal glove on her right hand, and I could feel her digging her fingers into my neck, trying to punch those razor-sharp silverstone talons through the protective shell of my Stone magic.

But she didn't have to claw me to death. Didn't have to sink her fangs into my throat. She didn't have to make me bleed at all. Despite my Stone magic, I still needed air to breathe, and if I didn't get it in the next few seconds, then I wouldn't be breathing ever again.

Given the vampire's superior strength, there was no way I could break her grip. At least, not by conventional methods.

But I was very good at being unconventional.

My Stone magic might be my stronger power, but it wasn't going to save me in this situation, so I turned to my much weaker Ice magic. I raised my hand and sent a spray of Ice daggers shooting straight into Amelia's face.

Okay, so daggers *might be an exaggeration. A small frosty cloud sputtered out of my palm, along with a few harmless needles of Ice, but it was enough to make Amelia jerk back in surprise.*

The second her grip slipped, I snapped up my fingers and jabbed them into her eyes. My fingers weren't tipped with silverstone claws like hers were, but the sharp pokes still made her yelp, and her hands dropped away from my throat. I jutted my head forward, opened my mouth wide, and sank my teeth into her left arm, the one not protected by that metal glove.

I bit down as hard as I could, and her hot, sticky blood spurted into my mouth. The coppery taste made me want to vomit, but I ignored the disgusting sensation and ground my teeth even deeper into her tender flesh.

"You bitch!" Amelia howled. "You bit me!"

I would have asked her how it felt to be bitten for a change if I hadn't been trying to rip through her muscles with my teeth.

She yelped again and finally tore her arm free of my teeth, throwing herself a bit off-balance. I spit out the blood in my mouth and shoved her off me.

Amelia landed on her right arm, and her metal glove punched through another driftwood log lying half on the shore and half in the lake. She splashed around in the sand and water, trying to get back up, but the glove must have been snagged on something inside the log, because she fell right back down again. She snarled, got up, and braced one of her feet on the log, yanking on the driftwood and trying to wrench her gloved hand free.

I staggered to my own feet, sucking down giant gulps of air.

Continued crack-crack-cracks *of gunfire sounded from the terrace above and the woods in the distance, as Amelia's guards fired on Fletcher's position and vice versa. But I wasn't worried about the old man. He had the trees to protect him, and sooner or later, he'd finish off the guards, who were more exposed on the open terrace.*

That meant it was up to me to kill Amelia. Fine by me. I just needed to get my breath back first. As I sucked down another giant gulp of air, it occurred to me that the vamp and I had one thing in common.

I needed air to breathe, and so did she.

No matter how much blood Amelia drank, no matter how quick and strong it made her, no matter how sharp all those claws on her metal glove were, she couldn't change that one simple biological fact. So I decided to use it to my advantage.

Before Amelia could work her glove out of that driftwood log, I put my shoulder down and barreled into her, knocking her legs out from under her. She flew backward and landed in the water, the weight of her body carrying the driftwood log along with her. Amelia came up sputtering, but I wasn't done yet.

Not until she was dead.

So I waded into the lake after her. Despite the summer heat, the water was shockingly cold, although the soothing wetness felt good on my cut, bruised, battered body.

Amelia lashed out at me with her free fist, but I used my Stone magic to harden my skin again and ignored her awkward blow. Then I stepped around behind her, dug my fingers into her wet hair, and dragged her deeper into the lake. My legs churned through the mud and rocks, but I didn't stop moving, not even for a second.

"Let me go! Let me go!"

She screamed and screamed, beating at me with her fist and trying to get me to loosen my grip on her hair. Her metal glove was still stuck in that driftwood log, which bobbed along with her like a fishing lure on the surface of the water.

Amelia finally managed to get her legs under her, and she dug her boots into the mud, using her strength to yank me back toward her. I slammed into her body and bounced off. By this point, we were both hip-deep in the water, but that was perfect for what I had in mind.

The vampire snarled, reached out, and wrapped her free hand around that driftwood log, clutching it like a baseball bat. Then she pulled the whole thing up and out of the water and swung it at me as hard as she could.

But the water slowed her down, and I ducked her reckless blow. She drew back the log for another swing, but I surged forward, hooked my leg around hers, and knocked her off-balance, sending her crashing down into the water.

She popped right back up again a second later. "You bitch!" she screamed. "I'll kill you for this—"

I kicked her legs out from under her again. Then I dug both of my hands into her hair and shoved her head under the water.

And this time, I didn't let her surface again.

Amelia kicked and heaved and thrashed, but the bottom of the lake was muddy and slippery, and she couldn't get enough traction with her stiletto boots to stand up and throw me off. I squished my bare feet and toes even deeper into the cold mud, bracing myself as best I could, and kept my body pressed down on top of hers.

Amelia lashed out with the driftwood log over and over again, still trying to hit me, but her blows grew slower and weaker, until she was just flailing around. Then even that stopped, and she quit struggling altogether.

I held her head under the water for another three minutes, just to be sure she was dead.

Finally, I let go, and Amelia floated up to the surface. Her black hair billowed out around her like an inky cloud, but her green eyes were frozen open in shock, panic, and fear. I let out a ragged breath, glad that she was dead instead of me.

The waves pushed us back toward the shore, and I

grabbed hold of the driftwood log and tugged Amelia along with me. I wasn't quite sure why, but I dragged her out of the water and back up onto the sand before finally letting go. The driftwood must have hit a rock buried in the sand, because the log split open, revealing the metal glove still on Amelia's right hand. The claws glinted in the moonlight, and her fingers were curved, almost like she was going to leap up, swipe out with them, and cut me again. The thought made me shiver—

"What did you do?" A soft, anguished whisper sounded.

My head snapped up. A teenage girl stood on the sand a few feet away. Even if Fletcher hadn't shown me pictures of her, I still would have known exactly who she was, since she had the same black hair, green eyes, and pretty features as her mother.

Alanna Eaton, Amelia's daughter.

She was supposed to be away at boarding school for another week, which was one of the reasons Fletcher had wanted to do the job tonight. What was she doing here? My heart dropped, and my stomach twisted. Watching me kill her mother, for starters.

Oh, no—no, no, no, no, no.

Alanna stared at me, then at her dead mother, then back at me. "What did you do?" *Her voice grew higher and sharper with every single word.* "What did you do!"

"I—I—I—" *I sputtered, but of course I didn't have an answer.*

But she didn't need one, since it was so painfully obvious *what had happened, what I'd* done. *Alanna ran past me, threw herself down onto the sand, and started shaking Amelia's shoulder.*

"Mama!" *she screamed.* "Mama! Wake up, Mama! Wake up!"

But of course, her mama was never going to wake up—and I was the reason why.

Alanna collapsed in a heap on top of Amelia's body, still screaming and sobbing and begging her mother to wake up. I just stood there, cold, numb, and frozen, knowing that there wasn't a damn thing I could do to help her.

Amelia Eaton had been an evil vampire bitch who hunted down innocent people, cut them open, and snacked on their blood and bones. She would have done the exact same thing to me if I hadn't killed her first. It had been her or me, simple as that. I didn't regret killing her.

What I did *regret was that Alanna had seen me do it.*

Every single one of the girl's screams was as sharp as a knife to my heart. I almost felt like Amelia was still alive and slicing me to ribbons with her metal claws one anguished cry at a time.

But the worst part was that I knew exactly *how Alanna was feeling. I knew those screams, those sobs, that wretched heartache, all too well. I had experienced them myself when the Fire elemental had murdered my mother.*

And now I had just inflicted that same soul-crushing pain on another girl.

Being an assassin meant hurting people, but this was the one thing I had vowed never, ever to do to anyone. I had never wanted another daughter to see her mother die the way I had seen mine. Guilt, shame, and regret churned in my stomach. Bile rose in my throat, and this time I couldn't keep it down. I staggered away and spewed up all the champagne I'd drunk earlier in the evening.

I heaved and heaved until my ribs ached and hot tears streamed down my face. I felt like I'd vomited up my heart along with everything else, but I forced myself to wipe off my mouth, straighten up, and see all the misery I'd caused.

This was my mess, my mistake, and I didn't get to slink off and pretend like nothing had happened. Like I hadn't just destroyed another girl's whole world.

Alanna was still huddled over her mama's body, although she had stopped screaming. Now she was holding Amelia's hand, the one with the metal glove, and whispering something to her dead mama, although I couldn't hear what it was.

I drew in a breath and slowly shuffled toward her, not quite sure what I was going to do. Apologize, maybe...or something. I didn't know. I just didn't know, but I needed to do something. *I needed to find some way to help her—*

"Gin," a voice called out.

My head snapped to my right. Fletcher was standing at the bottom of the terrace steps, a rifle clutched in his hands. The old man looked no worse for wear, except for a splatter of blood on his cheek. More blood gleamed on the butt of his rifle. He must have had to get up close and personal to finish off the vampire guards.

Fletcher took in my sick, guilty expression, then looked over at Alanna, who was still whispering to Amelia. Regret filled his green gaze, as sharp and bright as shards of glass, but it was quickly replaced by a coldness—one that I had never seen before, especially not directed at a teenager like Alanna.

"Let's go," he said in a low, rough voice.

"But what about her?" I whispered back.

"She'll be okay." That coldness in his face echoed in his voice now. "Lights are coming on all over the estate. The other servants heard the gunshots. They'll find the girl soon enough. We need to leave."

He turned and started walking along the shoreline, but I remained frozen in place, still wanting to comfort Alanna, even though I knew that I couldn't. Fletcher realized that I wasn't following him, and he stopped and made a sharp motion with his hand.

"We need to leave," he repeated. "Right now."

Slowly, I staggered forward, trudging through the sand. Alanna and Amelia were between Fletcher and me, and I had to walk right past them to get to him.

My shadow fell over Alanna, who looked up, hate blazing in her eyes. She snarled, her lips drawing back to reveal her fangs, and surged to her feet. Something metal glinted in the moonlight, and I instinctively threw my arm out.

Too late, I realized that Alanna had pulled the metal glove off her mother's arm and strapped it to her own.

Her claws sliced deep into my right arm, and I felt the silverstone points scraping against my bones. I screamed and staggered back. Pain shot up my arm and spread out through the rest of my body.

Alanna grinned, held up her index finger, and licked my blood off the claw, just like her mother had done. Shock spiked through me, even harsher than the pain of my wounds. It was like I was looking at a mirror image of Amelia, one I'd just helped to create.

Alanna snarled and charged at me again, but Fletcher came up and pushed her from behind, and she tripped and fell to her knees in the sand.

The old man rushed over to me. "Gin! Are you okay?"

I cradled my injured arm up against my chest, feeling my own warm blood soaking into my wet dress. But that pain was nothing compared to seeing the horror of what Alanna was—or, rather, what I'd turned her into.

"Fine..." I rasped, even though it was a lie. "I'll...be... fine..."

"Here. Let me help you." Fletcher slung the strap attached to his rifle up over his head and then down across his chest, so that he would have both hands fee. He stepped forward and put his arm around my waist, supporting me. "You're losing a lot of blood. Put pressure on the wound. You know what to do."

I did know what to do, but that didn't make it any easier. I bit my lip, wrapped my left hand around the deep, jagged wounds, and clenched tight, even though it made another wave of agony ripple through my body.

White stars exploded in my eyes, and I would have fallen if Fletcher hadn't tightened his grip on me. Alanna saw this as an opening, and she started to get to her feet, but Fletcher stabbed his finger at her in warning.

"That's enough," he snapped. "That's enough. Stay down."

For a moment, I thought Alanna was going to surge to her feet and charge at him anyway, but she finally realized that she couldn't win, and she huddled in the sand next to her mama's body again. She gave Fletcher a sullen look, then turned her gaze to me. Rage flashed in her green eyes, making them glow as brightly as two emeralds set in the pale beauty of her face, and her hand curled into a fist.

"I'll kill you for this!" Alanna screamed at me. "Do you hear me, you assassin bitch? I'll kill you for this! I'll kill you for this!"

She kept screaming those words over and over again and shaking her fist, which was still encased in that metal glove, even as Fletcher dragged me away from her.

A few minutes later, we made it to the trees, and Fletcher helped me move into the shadows. We stopped, and I swayed on my feet as he cut off the bottom of his shirt *and wrapped it around my clawed arm. He tied off the makeshift bandage as tightly as he could, making me whimper.*

"There," he said. "That will have to do until I can get you to Jo-Jo."

I blinked the latest burst of stars out of my eyes, and my gaze locked onto Alanna, who was still sitting next to her mama's body. Flashlights sparked to life on the terrace above her, and more shouts cut through the air. One of the beams fell on Alanna's face, and she snarled up into the light like a rabid animal.

Twin fists of guilt and shame crushed my heart one after another, and I would have doubled over and vomited again if I'd anything left in my stomach. Fletcher put his arm around my shoulder, hugging me tight.

"I know what you're thinking, but it's not your fault, Gin," he said in a low voice. "Amelia ruined her. That girl already had venom in the veins long before we came along."

Venom in the veins? *He made it sound like some horrible, incurable disease, something that you couldn't escape no matter how hard you tried, something that would haunt you for the rest of your life. Just like what I had done to Alanna would forever haunt me.*

"How do you know?" I whispered.

"Look at her clothes."

I forced myself to look at Alanna again. I hadn't noticed it before, but she was wearing a red jacket with gold buttons, along with black pants and boots. The same sick, twisted hunting outfit that Amelia had on.

More horror filled me, and I looked at Fletcher.

"Amelia started taking Alanna on hunts when the girl was just five years old," he said in answer to my silent question. "Alanna was going to help her mother track you

down tonight, and she would have happily torn you to pieces right alongside Amelia."

"But...I killed *her mama...right...in front of her." Tears streamed down my face, and fresh pain spiked through my body, although it had nothing to do with my wounds.*

"You couldn't help that," Fletcher said in a gentle voice. "You didn't know that Alanna was here, and Amelia didn't give you a choice about killing her."

"But...it's just like..." I started to say what happened to me, *but I couldn't get the words out over the hard knot of emotion in my throat.*

Fletcher hugged me closer. "I know it is, sweetheart. I know."

We stayed like that for several moments, with me crying and him still hugging me.

The people with the flashlights reached Alanna, and she scrambled to her feet and pointed in our direction.

"They went into the woods!" Her voice rang out across the lake. "Get out there, and chase them down! Now! I want them brought back to me! Alive!"

I shuddered at the deadly promise in her voice. Fletcher was right. She did want to tear us to pieces, but I couldn't blame her for it. Not after what I'd just done to her.

The people with the flashlights swarmed around her for a few more seconds, and then the beams swung around in this direction.

Fletcher's mouth flattened out into a thin, grim line. "C'mon, Gin. Time to go."

The old man put his arm around my waist again and led me deeper into the woods. Our feet crunched through the underbrush, but the noise wasn't nearly as loud as Alanna's screams ringing in my ears over and over again...

I woke up with my heart in my throat, my stomach tied

in knots, and tears leaking out of the corners of my eyes. Beside me, Owen murmured and threw his arm across my chest, as though he'd sensed my turbulent emotions and was trying to reach out and comfort me, even while he was asleep.

But I couldn't be comforted. Not tonight.

I lay absolutely still for several minutes until I was sure that Owen wasn't going to wake up. Then I slipped out from beneath his arm, got out of bed, and threw on a fleece robe. No way was I going back to sleep anytime soon. Not with that nightmare fresh in my head and my guilt and shame pulsing in my heart.

So I went downstairs and walked from one room to the next, peering out the windows and staring into the dark night. I'd done the same thing at Owen's mansion last night, and things were as quiet now as they had been then. Strange. I'd expected Alanna to send some more hired hands after me by now, but nothing moved or stirred, and I didn't see the telltale signs of flashlights bobbing through the woods that flanked the house.

Whatever item she wanted from Mab's estate, it didn't seem like Alanna was coming here after it tonight. But it was only a matter of time before she made another run at me. I was certain of that, and I didn't blame her for it, not one little bit.

Not after I'd killed her mama right in front of her.

Once again, it struck me how very much alike Alanna and I were, with our murdered mothers and lost family homes. But the thought that troubled me more than anything else was the fact that I was her Mab Monroe, the person responsible for destroying her family.

I grimaced. That was the thing that shamed me the most. I'd *never* wanted to be like Mab, but ironically enough, I found myself following in the Fire elemental's footsteps more often than not. Killing my enemies, becoming queen of the underworld, ruthlessly eliminating everyone who was a threat to me and my loved ones. And now I was being confronted by the daughter of the woman I'd killed, just as I'd finally confronted Mab, just as I planned to confront Mason.

Alanna wasn't the only one who suffered from venom in the veins—I did too.

Fletcher had been right when he said that Amelia had ruined her daughter and twisted Alanna into a younger version of herself, vampire cannibal and all. That had happened long before I came along. But I had added to Alanna's pain and rage, which made me partly responsible for what she'd become.

But Owen was right too. Alanna was all grown up now, and she made her own choices, especially when it involved hurting other people. And if she came after me or Mosley or anyone else I cared about, then I would take her down, despite the role I'd played in creating her.

I just wondered who would win this family feud in the end, Alanna or me.

And what the cost might be to us both.

20

When I was satisfied that no one was lurking in the woods, I went into the den and turned on the lights, fully intending to sort through Mab's things again until I found what Alanna, Tucker, Mason, and the Circle were after. But the sight of all those boxes filled with all those books depressed me, so I procrastinated and went into the kitchen instead.

I grabbed some oversize marshmallows, dark chocolate bars, and graham crackers from the cabinets, stacked them together on a cookie sheet, and baked myself some s'mores. Golden puffy marshmallows, ooey-gooey melted chocolate, crispy graham crackers. Not quite as good as making them over a campfire, but they still hit the spot.

On a night like this, I needed something warm and sweet to get me through the cold, bitter memories.

I stuffed one s'more into my mouth, put the others on a plate, and carried them into the den, along with some napkins and a glass of milk. While I nibbled on my late-night snack, I pulled a few books out of the box closest to me. I halfheartedly flipped through the pages, but they were the same as before. Just books. Words on pages, ink on paper. Nothing more, nothing less.

So I set the books aside, finished the last of my s'mores, and wiped the graham cracker crumbs off my hands. Then I leaned forward and picked up the photo of my parents, which was still lying on the coffee table.

The picture must have been taken at some society gala, since my mother was wearing a glittering blue gown and my father had on a classic black tuxedo. Eira and Tristan made quite the handsome couple, despite their tense expressions.

I traced my fingers over their faces, then studied the background, trying to tell when or at least where the photo had been taken. But all I could make out were a few round tables covered with white linens and some white twinkle lights in the distance, both of which could be found at any party at any time of the year.

So I stared at the other person in the photo, Mab Monroe.

Despite my hatred of her, even I had to admit that Mab had been stunningly beautiful, with her red hair, black eyes, and creamy skin. The Fire elemental was dressed in a white gown that set off her bright, coppery hair, and a sly smile curved her scarlet lips, as if she knew some great secret that my parents and I didn't. Smug bitch.

I had started to set the photo aside when a small bit of blue against Mab's dress caught my eye. Curious, I raised the picture back up again.

I'd been so focused on my parents that I hadn't noticed that the Fire elemental was clutching something in her hand. The object was at the very bottom left corner of the picture, almost out of sight of the lens. I frowned and squinted at the photo, trying to figure out what the flat shape was.

Was that…a book?

I reared back in surprise, then leaned forward and squinted at the photo again, but I couldn't quite make out the shape. So I got up, went into the kitchen, and rummaged through one of the drawers until I came up with Fletcher's old magnifying glass. Armed with the glass, I went back into the den, grabbed the photo, and stared at it through the lens.

It *was* a book.

I still couldn't tell when or where the photo had been taken, or even what the occasion had been, but for some reason, Mab was holding a book down by her side, almost as if she didn't want anyone to realize that she had it.

My gaze darted around the den, flitting from one cardboard box to the next. Books, books, books, everywhere I looked. That couldn't be a coincidence.

So I brought the magnifying glass up and studied the photo yet again. And I realized that Mab wasn't holding just any old book. Oh, no. She was clutching one with a royal-blue cover and pages trimmed with shiny silver foil.

The same sort of book that was sitting on the coffee table right in front of me.

I frowned, then leaned forward, grabbed the book, and compared it with the one in the photo. A slender volume with a royal-blue cover and pages trimmed with silver foil. Color, size, shape. They were exactly the same, right down to how brand-new they both looked.

I flipped through my book again, but the pages were as blank as before. This couldn't be the same book Mab was holding. That photo of her and my parents had to have been taken more than twenty-five years ago, before my dad died. Why keep a blank book for all those years? It didn't make any sense.

But it was the only lead I had, so I sat there, looking from the book in my hand to the photo on the table and back again. And once again, something about the book nagged at me, far more than the photo did. Or maybe it was something about the book and the photo together...

My frustration grew and grew. My fingers curled around the book, and I suddenly wanted to hurl it into the fireplace, douse it with lighter fluid, toss a match on it, and watch it burn. But that wouldn't help anything, so I forced myself to lean back against the couch cushions, close my eyes, and take in several slow, deep breaths.

What I needed to do was clear my mind, think things through, and go back to the beginning. Back to the auction, the Eaton Estate, and the library where I'd first seen the photo of my parents, along with the bookcase.

So I thought back to last night, mentally retracing my steps through the ballroom and down the corridor to the library. What had happened after that? I'd gone into the library, noticed the books and other furnishings, and talked to Lorelei, who was staring at the photo of Lily Rose, her mother—

My eyes snapped open.

Lily Rose's photo had been nestled in a bookcase that was identical to the one I'd bought. In fact, her picture had been sitting on the same shelf, arranged the exact same way—propped up on a book with a royal-blue cover.

Alanna didn't want the book *I'd* bought—she wanted the one *Lorelei* had.

Another chilling thought zipped through my mind. Lorelei and Mallory had picked up the book and the rest of their things at the estate earlier today, and the two women were at their mansion right now, along with Mosley.

After the attack on the road earlier today, I had thought

that Alanna would come after me again. But Tucker had said that Alanna was smart, and she must have realized how difficult it would be to break into my fortified home.

But the Parker mansion wasn't nearly as secure.

Even if Alanna didn't realize her mistake about the book yet, even if she didn't know that Lorelei had the right one, she still wanted Mosley dead, and tonight would be as good a time as any to make that happen.

The book, Mosley, her revenge. Alanna could have them all at one fell swoop.

And she could be on her way to the Parker mansion right now.

I grabbed my phone off the table and called Lorelei. But it was after eleven now, and my call went straight to voice mail. I hung up and tried again, with the exact same result. She probably had turned off the sound on her phone so she could sleep, which meant that there was no way I could warn her.

I dialed Mosley next, but he didn't answer either. Neither did Mallory. After them, I tried Finn, but he didn't pick up, and neither did Bria. Finally, I called Silvio, but for once, even he didn't answer me.

Every unanswered call only increased my worry and frustration. Sure, Lorelei, Mosley, and Mallory might be sleeping and have their phones turned off—or Alanna could be at the Parker mansion right now, killing them all.

Only one way to find out.

I tossed my phone down, leaped to my feet, and raced upstairs. "Owen!" I yelled. "Owen, get up! We have to go!"

I'd just made it to the top of the steps when the door to my bedroom burst open and Owen rushed out into the hallway. He was wearing a T-shirt and boxers, and his black hair was a rumpled mess, but he was holding a large blacksmith's hammer over his shoulder, ready to bring it crashing down on whomever got in his way.

I stopped a moment to admire the tense, tight muscles in his broad shoulders. Getting out of bed and grabbing a weapon first, even before you put your clothes on. Now, *that* was a man after my own heart.

"Gin?" he asked, his gaze darting up and down the hallway. "What is it? What's wrong?"

"Where did you get that hammer?" I asked.

"I put it under your bed a couple of weeks ago, remember?" Owen's head swiveled from side to side as he kept searching the hallway for intruders. "What's wrong? Is someone outside? Is Alanna here?"

I shook my head. "Not here, but I know where she's headed."

While we hurried to get dressed and gear up, I told Owen my suspicion that Lorelei had the blue book that Alanna really wanted and that the vampire might be on her way to the Parker mansion right now, if she wasn't already there.

Ten minutes later, we were in Owen's car and zooming down the driveway. While he drove, I called everyone again, but no one answered. I dialed Lorelei three times, but her phone went straight to voice mail each time.

I cursed and looked over at Owen. "Drive faster."

He stomped his foot down on the gas.

Given the late hour and deserted roads, it didn't take us long to reach the Parker mansion. Owen turned off his headlights and slowed down as we approached the driveway that led from the road up to the mansion. Given how late it was, the gate should have been pulled shut

across the entrance for the night, but it was standing wide
open. Even worse, several of the bars were broken, as
though someone had used their strength to peel them back
and shove the gate out of the way.

I cursed again. "Alanna's already here."

Owen's hands tightened around the steering wheel.
"You want me to go up the driveway?"

Despite my desperate need to make sure that Lorelei,
Mallory, and Mosley were okay, I shook my head. "No. I
don't want Alanna to know that we're here. The element of
surprise is the only advantage we have. Go down about a
quarter of a mile and park on the side of the road."

Owen did as I asked, pulling off the asphalt and getting
as close to the trees as he could. I grabbed a black duffel
bag full of supplies out of the backseat, while he picked up
his blacksmith's hammer from the floorboard. Then the two
of us left the car behind and hiked through the woods until
we could see the Parker mansion.

By Northtown's highfalutin standards, it was a modest
home, three sprawling stories with around thirty rooms
total. A garden, a pool, a stone patio covered with furniture.
My gaze zoomed past all the familiar features. No one
seemed to be lurking around outside the mansion, but it
was far from deserted.

Three black sedans sat at haphazard angles in the
driveway, as though they'd zoomed up the pavement and
screeched to an abrupt stop. The car doors were standing
open, and I could still smell the harsh stench of rubber from
the tires. Several sets of boot prints went from the cars,
through the snow-dusted grass, and over to one of the
doors, which had been reduced to splinters clinging to the
frame from where someone, most likely a giant, had
barreled through it.

Most of the mansion was dark, but lights blazed in the first-floor library. Through the lace curtains, I could see several man-sized shapes moving back and forth.

Owen pointed at that section. "That's the library, right?"

"Yeah," I whispered back. "Alanna must have realized that Lorelei has the right book after all. Or maybe she just wants to cover her bases and recover Lorelei's book before she comes after mine again. Either way, it looks like she's in there searching for it, along with Phelps and however many men they have. We need to get into the mansion before they find it—"

A figure appeared in the busted doorway, and Alanna strolled outside. She was dressed all in black, just like I was, which made it easy for me to spot the blue book in her hand. My chest tightened, and my heart sank like a lead weight. She'd already found it, which meant—which meant—

Lorelei, Mosley, and Mallory were already dead.

The horrible thought slammed into my brain like a sledgehammer, shattering everything inside me. For a moment, I couldn't think, couldn't blink, couldn't even *breathe*. After Fletcher had been murdered in the Pork Pit, I vowed to do whatever it took to protect the people I cared about. I had never wanted to lose someone else the way I'd lost the old man. But it had happened again, and it was all my fault.

Because I hadn't realized what Alanna was really after until it was too late. Because she hated Mosley in no small part due to my actions.

Because I was the one who'd helped turn her into a monster by murdering her mother right in front of her.

Owen spotted my guilty, miserable expression and laid a warm, comforting hand on my shoulder. I sucked in a deep, ragged breath, trying to get my emotions under control—

"What was that?" Alanna's sharp voice cut through the cold night air.

Owen and I both froze. We looked at each other for a moment, and then my gaze darted over to Alanna, who was staring at the trees where we were hiding in the shadows. I bit back a curse. With her enhanced vampiric senses, she could hear everything around her, including my sudden intake of air.

Owen realized the same thing, and his hand tightened on my shoulder in warning. Other than that, the two of us remained absolutely still, not moving a single muscle.

Alanna kept peering in our direction, her green eyes glittering in her beautiful face. After several seconds, she turned and snapped her fingers at someone still inside the house.

"Bring them," she commanded.

Alanna stepped away from the opening, and several giants streamed outside, gripping the arms of two other men and dragging them along the ground. The giants stopped and dropped the other men's arms, letting them flop to the ground. I recognized the two men as bank guards. Their faces were bruised and bloody, but their chests rose and fell in a steady rhythm, telling me that they were unconscious instead of dead.

Alanna snapped her fingers again, and Terrence Phelps stepped out of the house. He gestured with his gun, and two much shorter figures appeared—Mallory and Mosley.

All the air escaped my lungs in a loud, relieved rush, but I didn't care if Alanna heard the sound. My friends were still alive. That was all that mattered right now. And they were going to stay that way, no matter what I had to do in order to save them.

"Get them in the car," Alanna ordered.

The giants moved forward and surrounded the two dwarves. Mallory wore a light blue robe over matching pajamas and slippers. She looked fine, except for her furious expression, and she was even wearing her usual array of diamond rings. The gems sparkled and flashed as the giants pushed her along, but she ignored her captors and focused on Mosley, who had his head bowed and was shuffling along at a much slower pace beside her.

I recognized his slow, painful walk as that of a man who'd been severely beaten. Mosley stepped into a patch of light and lifted his head. I sucked in another breath. His face was a bruised, battered mess, just as I'd expected it to be, but those injuries were nothing compared to the claw marks that raked down his cheeks in deep, jagged lines.

Blood dripped out of those wounds, rolled down his neck in a steady stream, and spattered all over the front of his navy robe and pajamas. Mosley shifted on his feet, and I realized that his face wasn't the only thing that had been sliced up. His robe and pajamas hung in tatters on his frame, and more claw marks zipped down his arms and across his chest. Someone had used the dwarf like he was her own personal scratching post.

"That bitch is dead," I snarled.

The words escaped before I could stop them, and Alanna's head snapped back around in this direction. Her eyes narrowed, and I knew that she'd heard me. She held up her hand, ordering her men to stop. They did, with Mallory and Mosley still trapped in the middle.

I did a head count. Alanna had brought half a dozen giants with her, along with Phelps, who still had his gun trained on Mallory and Mosley. My mind spun around, trying to figure out a way to rescue my friends, but there wasn't one. Phelps could easily pull his trigger and shoot the two dwarves before I even took three steps out of the woods.

Then another thought popped into my mind, and I finally realized what—or, rather, who—was missing.

Lorelei.

She wasn't standing with Mallory and Mosley, so Alanna hadn't taken her prisoner. My gaze flicked over the mansion, then the yard, then the woods beyond, but I didn't see Lorelei. She had to be here somewhere, though. I was sure of it. She would never abandon her grandmother, and she wasn't dead. Otherwise, Mallory would have been inconsolable.

A hasty plan took shape in my mind, and I crouched down, unzipped the black duffel bag at my feet, and drew out the blue book that had belonged to Mab, the one that had been included with my auction items.

I straightened up. Owen spotted the book, and his face creased with worry.

"What are you going to do with that?" he whispered.

"Make a trade."

He frowned, but then his eyes widened in realization, and he shook his head. "No, Gin. No. She'll kill you. You know she will."

"I know she'll try." I grinned at him. "And I also know you won't let her succeed."

Worry, concern, love, pride. All those emotions and more flashed in Owen's gaze, as hot and fast as violet lightning. But right now, the most important emotions were the last two that filled his features: understanding and acceptance.

Understanding that I *had* to do this, that this was *what* I did, that this was *who* I was. And acceptance of that, acceptance of all the worry and fear that went along with it, acceptance of *me*, Gin Blanco, the Spider.

Owen reached out, pulled me toward him, and crushed his lips to mine. I cradled his face in my hand and returned his kiss with equal fervor, drinking in his smell, taste, and touch. Then the moment passed, and we broke apart, our hearts full of grim determination. I nodded at him, and he nodded back at me. Together we faced our enemies again.

Alanna strode out into the middle of the driveway, her black stiletto boots *clack-clack-clacking* against the asphalt like she was grinding bones to dust under her towering heels. Once again, her gaze focused on the shadows where Owen and I were still hiding.

"Come out," she ordered. "Or I'll kill the dwarves. You have ten seconds—"

My phone rang, cutting her off.

I winced. *Sloppy, sloppy, sloppy, Gin!*

I'd made so many calls on the drive over here that I'd forgotten to silence my phone when we crept into the woods. But of course someone would call me back *now*. Still, I might as well see who it was, so I pulled the device out of my pocket and stared at the name on the screen.

Lorelei Parker.

My heart lifted, and I showed the phone to Owen. He frowned, and then his eyes widened as he realized what it meant. I made a circling motion with my finger, asking him to go around and sneak up on Alanna and her men from behind. He nodded and hefted his blacksmith hammer a little higher on his shoulder. Owen cupped my face in his hand for a moment, letting me see the love shining in his eyes, then turned and vanished deeper into the woods.

I thought about answering the call, but I didn't want Alanna to hear Lorelei's voice—wherever she was—and realize that the other woman was here. So I let the phone ring and ring until it went to voice mail. I didn't need to talk to Lorelei anyway. Not really. She'd already told me everything she needed to.

I silenced my phone and started to slide it back into my pants pocket, but I thought better of it and shoved the phone inside my right boot instead. I slid the device inside my sock and pushed it all the way down past my ankle, where it would stay safe and secure and where hopefully no one would think to look for it.

"Five seconds," Alanna called out. "This is your last warning."

"All right!" I yelled. "All right! I'm coming out!"

Still holding the blue book, I raised my hands and walked out of the woods. I strode across the lawn at a slow, steady pace before stepping onto the driveway.

Mallory and Mosley both gasped at the sight of me. Mallory's blue eyes darted left and right, wondering who else I might have brought with me, while Mosley's hands curled into fists. Despite the blood, bruises, and claw marks that covered his body, he winked at me, telling me that he was still in the fight. As much as I wanted to grin back at him, I kept my face blank.

I stopped about ten feet away from Alanna and slowly lowered my hands to my sides.

Her gaze flicked over my black vest, turtleneck, cargo pants, and boots. "So this is you, Gin Blanco, the Spider, as you really are."

I shrugged. "What you see is what you get."

Alanna tilted her head to the side, making her long black hair slide over her shoulder. "You know, when I saw you battling my muggers on the street the other night, I almost didn't recognize you. Then again, I was expecting red hair and a cute little cocktail dress. That was the disguise you used to sneak onto my mother's estate. I searched for that redheaded woman for a long, long time. I had almost given up hope of ever finding her."

I shrugged again. "I've worn a lot of disguises over the years."

"But you remember that one. You remember that night." Her voice took on a harsh, accusing note.

"Of course I do. I remember everything about that night."

She blinked, as if she hadn't expected me to be so candid. For a moment, rage sparked in her green eyes, the same murderous rage she'd shown that night on the lakeshore. But it quickly vanished, replaced by cold calculation, and her gaze focused on the blue book in my hand. Alanna might want to kill me for murdering her mother, but she still had a job to do for the Circle.

"Well, how nice of you to bring me Mab's other little blue book," she replied. "I sent several people to fetch it from you earlier today, but apparently, they weren't up to the task."

She looked over at Phelps.

He grimaced, and an angry, embarrassed blush mottled his cheeks. "I told you she had help—"

Alanna snapped up her hand, and Phelps swallowed down the rest of his whiny explanation. She waited a moment, until she was sure that she'd put him back in his place, then crooked her index finger at me.

"Now, if you would be so kind as to hand over Mab's book, we can finish this."

I laughed. "Seriously? You think that I'm just going to hand it over to you? No way. We're making a trade—the book for Mallory and Mosley."

This time, Alanna laughed. "Seriously?" She mocked

me with my own word. "You think you have a chance? I have seven men with me. There's only one of you, Gin."

I shrugged for a third time. "And I've already killed some of your people today. I'm happy to add to the body count."

I looked past Alanna at Phelps and the giants, all of whom started shifting on their feet. They knew enough about the Spider to take my threat seriously.

"You really think I'm going to let Stuart go?" Alanna countered. "After everything he's done to me?"

"You mean setting up that trust fund and making sure that you were financially taken care of for life? Oh, yeah. He's been a complete and utter bastard to you."

"He took my home away from me!"

Her voice came out as a shrill screech, her hand clenched into a fist, and I got the impression that she was very close to stamping her foot like an indignant child. I had finally punched some holes in her cool façade, and now all of her pent-up emotions were leaking out for everyone to see. Good. I wanted her angry, I wanted her off-balance. Even better, Phelps and the six giants kept looking from me to their boss and back again, completely caught up in her little hissy fit.

Alanna reined in her temper and focused on me again. "Forget about Stuart. Do you really think I would ever let *you* go? I spent *years* searching for the bitch who killed my mother. Do you really think I'm going to trade my revenge on you for some lousy book?"

I spotted a gleam of metal in the woods off to my left, as well as a pale glint in the shadows directly behind the giants.

"Nah." I grinned at her. "I just needed to keep you busy until my friends could sneak up on your men."

It took half a second for my words to sink into Alanna's brain. But when she realized what I meant, she whirled around. "Watch out—"

But she was already too late.

Crack!

A single shot rang out.

❊ 21 ❊

One of the giants who'd been guarding Mallory pitched to the driveway, dead from the elemental Ice bullet that had just punched through the back of his skull.

Lorelei stepped out of the shadows, dusting the remains of her Ice gun off her hands. She too wore a blue robe over her pajamas. She must have heard Alanna and her men storming into the mansion, because she'd had time to grab something on her way outside: a black leather belt studded with elemental Ice guns.

Lorelei plucked another gun out of its slot, pointed it at the second giant guarding Mallory, and pulled the trigger. The Ice shattered in her hands, but the single bullet zipped through the air and punched into the giant's skull. His head snapped back, and he too fell to the ground dead.

Lorelei yanked out a third Ice gun, while Mallory dropped to her knees and reached for the dead giant's weapon so she could join in the fight.

With a loud yell, Owen rushed out of the woods to my left, raised his blacksmith hammer high, and brought it down on the chest of another giant, making that man scream and tumble to the ground. Owen stepped forward and whipped up his hammer for another strike.

One of the giants started to attack Owen from behind, but Mosley rammed his shoulder into that giant's stomach. The two men went down in a heap, grunting and punching and kicking each other.

Me? I only had eyes for Alanna. I was going to end this—and her—right now.

I tossed my blue book aside, palmed a knife, and rushed toward her. She saw me coming and tossed her book aside as well. Then she snarled, her lips drawing back to reveal her gleaming white fangs. Alanna raised her fists, and I expected her to charge at me. But she held her ground, letting me come to her instead. Too late, I realized why.

Just as I snapped up my knife to bury the blade in her heart, she sidestepped and then swept my legs out from under me, all in one smooth motion. I had just enough time to grab hold of my Stone magic and harden my skin before I hit the pavement.

CRACK!

I wasn't sure if that was the sound of Lorelei shooting another one of her Ice guns or my head slamming back against the asphalt. My magic absorbed most of the impact, but my brain still rattled around inside my skull, making white stars flash in front of my eyes.

I pushed the pain away and rolled over onto my side, but Alanna stepped up and slammed her boot into my ribs over and over again in a quick, staccato rhythm. She put her vampiric speed and strength into the blows, making me feel every single one, despite the protective shell of my Stone magic.

I'd thought Amelia had been fast and strong, but Alanna easily surpassed her mother in both of those categories, as well as being far more vicious. Alanna wasn't simply hitting me, she was trying to kick her way *through* me.

My elemental power was the only thing keeping her from cracking my ribs and driving the bony shards into my lungs, and her blows were coming so fast and furious that I couldn't even lift my arm to strike back at her with my knife.

"Forget the others! Get Blanco and the books!" Alanna screamed, even as she kept kicking me. "Now!"

Phelps darted away to grab the books from where they had landed, while the two remaining giants ran over to me. The giants' long legs blocked my view, so I couldn't see what was happening with my friends. I couldn't tell if they were still here or if they'd retreated to the safety of the woods. I just hoped they were okay.

Alanna finally stopped kicking me, but before I could recover, she bent down and wrested my knife out of my hand. Then the two giants stepped forward, grabbed my arms, and lifted me off the ground. I kicked and thrashed and struggled, but they easily held me in midair between them, and I felt like a spider suspended in someone else's web.

"Hold her still," Alanna snarled.

I reached for my Ice magic to send a spray of daggers shooting out at her and to freeze the two giants holding me. But once again, she was quicker than I was, and her fist cracked against my face. She put all of her strength behind the blow, and a sharp, stunning pain exploded in my mind, filling every single part of my body and overcoming everything else, including my Stone magic.

Lights out.

Sometime later, I started becoming dimly aware of things.

Rough hands digging into my upper arms. The weightless sense of being carried around before my body was twisted into an awkward shape and thrown down. The slap of my cheek against a cold leather seat. The low, throaty rumble of an engine.

I knew that I was in a car and being taken someplace where I most certainly did not want to go, but the pounding pain in my head was too great, and I couldn't focus, no matter how hard I tried. The steady rocking motion of the car made me drift off again…

Still a while later, I experienced those same sensations again. Rough hands digging into my upper arms. The weightless sense of being carried around before my body was twisted into an awkward shape and thrown down. The slap of my cheek against a cold leather seat.

But this time, instead of the rumble of a car engine, I heard a faint crackling, and a soft light flickered over my face, although I couldn't open my eyes and see what it was.

Hands roamed over my body, but I couldn't do anything to stop them. One by one, they took all my knives away, including the two tucked into the sides of my boots. I held my breath, wondering if they would find my phone stuffed inside my sock, but they didn't notice it.

The hands retreated, and then there was…warmth. This soothing, surprisingly gentle warmth on my face, and I fell down into the blackness again…

The third time I woke up, it was for good. Mainly because I couldn't ignore the steady *tink-tink-tinking*, like a fork being continuously tapped against a champagne glass. I focused on the annoying sound. That was *exactly* what it was. Someone was celebrating at my expense.

All that damn *tinking* made my head ache even worse, but I forced myself to draw in slow, deep breaths, push the pain to the bottom of my brain, lock it down tight, and freeze it over for good measure. I couldn't afford to let my injuries get the best of me.

Not if I wanted to survive this.

I opened my eyes and found myself staring up at a gold-framed painting that showed a lovely forest scene, along with a lake and a lavish mansion. I focused on the image for several seconds, letting my eyes adjust to the light, then slowly turned my head from side to side, studying the rest of my surroundings.

I was sprawled across a dark green leather sofa close to a fireplace. Flames crackled merrily behind the iron grate, providing some much-needed warmth in the large, chilly room. Floor-to-ceiling bookshelves flanked the fireplace, while thick rugs stretched across the floor.

I was back in the library at the Eaton Estate.

Tink-tink-tink.

And I wasn't alone.

I slowly pushed myself up to a seated position. More pain rippled through my skull, down my spine, and out into my arms and legs, and it took me a moment to get my breath back.

Freeze it out, Gin. Freeze it out! I ordered myself. Easier said than done, but I managed it.

When I felt steady enough, I looked at the woman perched in the overstuffed armchair in front of the fireplace. Black hair, green eyes, perfect skin. For a moment, my vision blurred, and I thought I was seeing Amelia Eaton. But then I remembered that she was dead, thanks to me, and that I was staring at her mirror image in Alanna.

Her hair had been done up into an elaborate braided bun, and she had exchanged her previous clothes for a familiar outfit: knee-high black boots, tight black pants, and a red jacket with gold buttons running down the front. I remembered those clothes from my nightmares, and I had hoped never to see them again. But here I was, confronted with them yet again, along with a vampire cannibal who was planning to hunt me down and make me her dinner.

Alanna was steadily *tink-tink-tinking* a fork against the glass of champagne in her other hand. Her black stiletto boots were propped up on the antique wooden table in front of her, and every so often, she would scrape her heels along the wood, like a cat carving up the furniture with its claws.

She didn't seem to be carrying any weapons, but she didn't need them, given the four giant guards standing behind her, along with Phelps. I glanced to my left. Two more giants were stationed a few feet away, both of them with their guns out, ready to shoot me if I did anything stupid. She must have called for reinforcements after the fight at the Parker mansion.

Alanna finally stopped that damn *tinking* and laid the fork down on a table next to her elbow. A second fork was resting on a plate littered with a few crackers, green grapes, and cheese cubes, as though she'd had a snack while she was waiting for me to wake up. An empty glass and an open bottle of champagne also sat on the table.

Instead of looking at me, Alanna held her glass up to the cheery glow coming from the fireplace, almost as if she was toasting herself on a job well done. She admired the bubbles streaking up through the golden liquid for another moment, before closing her eyes, raising the glass to her lips, and taking a delicate sip.

She let out a long, loud, satisfied sigh, apparently enjoying the taste of her champagne more than anything else, but it was just a power play. She wanted to piss me off by not immediately acknowledging my presence, even though she was the one who'd woken me up.

Well, it was working.

Alanna savored her champagne—and her seeming victory—for another moment, before draining the rest of her drink and setting her glass aside. Only then did she deign to take her feet down off the table, open her eyes, and look at me.

"Ah, Gin," she purred. "I'm so glad that you're finally awake."

✵ 22 ✵

*A*lanna stared at me, her green eyes gleaming like a cat's in the flickering glow from the fireplace. Her tongue darted out, and she slowly, deliberately licked her lips, letting me know that she was hungry for far more than champagne—and that I was on her dinner menu.

One nice, bloody Gin Blanco steak coming right up.

Once again, I felt like I'd stepped back in time to the night I'd killed Amelia, since Alanna was threatening me the same way her mother had done back then. I might have had a hand in molding Alanna into who and what she was, but Amelia had corrupted her daughter long before I came along. The hunting, the killing, the cannibalism. That was all on Amelia and Alanna. Like mother, like daughter.

Alanna crooked her finger at me, then waved her hand at the matching armchair across the low table from her. "Come. Sit. Have a drink."

And just like her mother, she wanted to play with me first before she moved in for the kill. History might be repeating itself tonight, but the outcome was going to be the same as before, and she was going to die screaming at my hand just like her mama had.

I did as she asked and slowly stood up. Not because I was afraid of or intimidated by Alanna, Phelps, or the giants and their guns, but mainly because I wanted to get closer to that table by her elbow.

My head ached at the sudden change in elevation, making me sway on my feet, and it took me a moment to blink the white stars out of my eyes. Even after my vision cleared, I still made a big show of staggering forward, as though I was more injured than I really was. I wobbled by that table next to Alanna, deliberately driving my leg into the side of it. My knee *cracked* against the wood, making me hiss with real pain and double over.

The sharp blow rattled the snack plate on the table, along with the two glasses and the bottle of champagne, although Phelps hurried forward, elbowed me out of the way, and steadied the table before anything toppled over.

Limping for real this time, I straightened up, hobbled over, and plopped down into the armchair across from Alanna. I reached down with my left hand and massaged my aching knee, rubbing the pain away. I kept my right hand down by my side, though.

All the better to hide the fork that I'd swiped off that snack plate.

Oh, the fork was a small, pitiful tool, to be sure, but I didn't see my knives anywhere, and I desperately needed some sort of weapon. Besides, anything could be lethal if you were motivated enough, and sitting here watching Alanna smirk motivated me *plenty*.

So did remembering Mosley's bruised and battered face, as well as the horrible claw marks that had crisscrossed his body like thin red ribbons. Alanna hadn't done that simply because she wanted to get information out of him. No, that was the kind of sick, twisted torture she engaged in purely for fun, just like her mother had.

I held my breath, wondering if Alanna would realize what I'd done and order the giants to shoot me, but she stared at me a moment longer, then turned to Phelps.

"Terrence," Alanna purred again. "Would you be so kind as to hand me a refill? And pour our guest a drink as well. I wouldn't want Gin to be thirsty while we have our little chat."

Chat? Please. Alanna thought she'd won, and she was going to rub her victory in my face for as long as possible. I had no doubt that she'd done this same exact spiel before. The smiling, the talking, the drinking. It was all part of her hunting ritual, and maybe even her mother's before her. Alanna was trying to lull me into a false sense of security, maybe even give me a chance to beg for my life. Then, when I was at my lowest, weakest, and most desperate point, she would lunge forward and sink her fangs into my neck.

My fingers tightened around the fork still hidden in my hand. Well, this Spider was going to bite back.

Once again, I wondered if Phelps would realize that I'd swiped one of the forks off the table, but he didn't seem to notice, so I stayed still and quiet while he poured the champagne. He handed one glass to Alanna, who accepted it with an appreciative nod, then turned and held the other glass out to me. I grabbed it with my left hand.

Alanna took a sip of her champagne, sighed with satisfaction again, and wriggled even deeper back into her chair. I rested my glass on my knee and stayed perched on the edge of my seat, digging my boots into the rug, ready to move when the time came.

Alanna sipped a bit more of her champagne, then glanced around the library, admiring the fine furnishings. Her head tilted back, and her gaze focused on the same painting of the estate on the wall that I'd been staring at earlier. After several seconds, she finally dropped her head and looked at me again.

"Isn't it beautiful?" she said. "The library was always my favorite room. Whenever I was home from school, I used to curl up in this very chair in front of the fireplace and read for hours on end. Then, when Mama was done with her business meetings for the day, we would go hunting in the forest at night. Those are some of my favorite childhood memories."

The soft, dreamy tone to her voice told me that she was being absolutely sincere. Other kids had fond memories of summer camps or ski trips, but Alanna's warm-and-fuzzies were of murdering, butchering, and eating innocent people. I held back a shudder.

"How did you get in here?" I asked. "I thought Mosley had the estate locked up."

She waved her glass around. "He did, but that was for the auction. All of Mab's things were shipped out hours ago, so the auction is officially over. Mosley and his men packed up and left earlier this afternoon."

"And what? You decided to just move on in?"

She shrugged. "It's my family's home—*my* home. I have the right to come and go as I please."

I wondered if she actually had a key or if she'd broken in. And if she had broken in, whether she'd tripped any alarms. My gaze flicked up to the security cameras mounted in the ceiling corners. I didn't see any lights blinking on the devices, so I couldn't tell whether they were on. Didn't much matter either way. No one was going to bust in and save me from her, so I'd just have to save myself.

I shook my head. "In case you've forgotten, the estate doesn't belong to you. It belongs to Mosley, right down to that champagne glass in your hand."

Alanna waved her glass around again, unconcerned by my words. "As long as he's alive, which won't be for much longer at all. I've already got men hunting down Stuart, as well as the rest of your friends who escaped with him."

Her words filled me with relief. I'd been so worried that she had captured the others and had them stashed somewhere, just waiting to trot them out and use them against me. I didn't care what happened to me. I could endure any kind of torture the vampire dished out. Well, until she started eating me. But it would break my heart—it would break *me*—if my friends were hurt.

"It's only a matter of time before my men figure out where Stuart's hiding. Once they do..." She grinned, showing off her fangs. "Well, let's just say that I'm looking forward to finishing my previous conversation with him."

Given how injured Mosley had been, Owen, Lorelei, and Mallory had probably taken the dwarf to Jo-Jo's salon so she could heal him. Good. That was good. Jo-Jo would be there, along with Sophia, and the two of them could help Owen and Lorelei keep Mallory and Mosley safe. At least, until they could call Finn, Bria, and Silvio for backup.

"Let's say that you find Mosley and you actually manage to kill him," I said. "You still won't get the estate back. It's part of First Trust's assets, which go to Mosley's heir, not you."

"True," she agreed. "But I imagine that person will be far more reasonable about selling the estate back to me, especially given how much money I plan to offer them.

And if they're not reasonable, well, they'll either see the error of their ways, or I'll be dealing with the next person in line to inherit my family's property. And so on and so forth."

I couldn't fault her methods. Killing people until you got what you wanted was a time-honored tradition, especially in Ashland.

"And where are you getting all this money from?" I asked, even though I already knew the answer. "You don't have anything but that trust fund that Mosley set up for you. I know you're rich, but you're not *that* rich."

Alanna's smirk thinned out, becoming as sharp as a razor's edge. She didn't like being reminded of everything Mosley had done for her. Ungrateful brat. She had no idea how good she'd had it, thanks to him.

Yes, her mother had been murdered, and she'd lost her home, but she'd never had to eat garbage or wrap newspapers around herself to stay warm or sleep behind trash cans so that no one would beat, rob, or otherwise hassle her during the night. I'd had to do all those things and a dozen more that were even more horrible. I would have literally killed for a guardian angel like Mosley to come and save me from the streets. In a way, I supposed I *had* killed by becoming the Spider after Fletcher took me in.

"You're right, Gin. I don't have the money to buy the estate." Alanna leaned forward, her smile turning genuine again. "But Hugh Tucker and the rest of his friends certainly do."

Silvio had already told me that Tucker and the Circle were backing her, but I wanted to know everything she knew about them, so I kept fishing for information. "And how exactly did you meet Tucker?"

She leaned back in her seat again and took another sip of

champagne. "Don't you know? My mother used to work for the Circle. Before you killed her, of course."

My fingers slid down the champagne glass still resting on my knee, and I almost lost my grip on it completely. Surprise rippled through my body, adding to the ache in my skull, but I pushed it away and studied Alanna. She arched an eyebrow, noting my shock, but she kept staring at me, her gaze steady on mine.

I thought back to the photos of the Circle members that Fletcher had left in those safety-deposit boxes at First Trust bank. I had spent days going over each and every one of those pictures, and I was absolutely certain that Amelia Eaton hadn't been in any of them, not a single one, not even in the background.

But I couldn't deny the certainty on Alanna's face and her smug delight in dropping this little bombshell on me. She was telling the truth. Her mother really had worked for the Circle.

Every time I thought that I was finally getting somewhere, that I was finally getting a clear picture of the evil group's operations and chipping away at their rotten core, something like this came along and threw me for another loop.

"And what did your mother do for the Circle?" I couldn't keep the surprise out of my voice.

Alanna let out a light, pealing laugh. "You haven't guessed already? I would have thought the answer would have been obvious. My mother did what she did best. What my family has done best for generations on this land."

She gestured up at that painting of the lake and the forest that surrounded the mansion. I frowned, not understanding her cryptic words. The only thing Amelia had ever excelled at was killing people—

I suddenly remembered Fletcher telling me about the Eaton family and all the folks they had supposedly hunted like animals through the woods. Not just one or two unfortunate souls but dozens and dozens of people over the years. Enough people that their bones littered the surrounding woods like dead leaves. If you knew that someone was a cannibalistic vampire, then why not take advantage of her proclivities and send your enemies her way? Two birds and one stone, just like Silvio had said earlier.

"Your mother was some sort of Circle assassin?" I asked.

Alanna tipped her glass at me. "Now you're catching on. Not just my mother. Her parents before her and their parents before them." Her lips puckered in thought. "Although I wouldn't call her an *assassin*, exactly. Not like you, Gin."

"Then what was it like?"

"Let's just say that Hugh Tucker brought certain people to my mother's attention, and she made them disappear—forever."

Alanna glanced up at the painting again, and her lips curved up into a genuine smile, as if the casual discussion of dozens of murders brought back more fond memories. It probably did. And I realized that this was about much more than merely killing people. It was about getting rid of them—permanently.

"So your mother let Tucker and his Circle buddies bury their bodies on the estate," I said. "The Circle members *literally* buried the bodies of their enemies out here in the woods."

I thought about what Silvio had told me about the big deposits Amelia would get in her bank account every month. Most likely Circle payments for services rendered.

Alanna turned her bright smile to me. "Exactly! Although I always thought it was *so* much more fun when they would bring us a live person instead of just a boring old dead body. Taking care of the live ones, well, that's how my mother taught me to hunt."

Cross the Circle, get tortured and eaten by cannibalistic vampires, and have your body taken so far out into the woods that no one would ever find what was left of you. Well, that was certainly an effective way to deal with your enemies and warn off anyone who might be thinking about making a move against you.

Oh, yes. I could see my dear friends hiring some little fresh-faced ingenue like you to take me out. They don't approve of my activities out here, although that certainly doesn't stop them from using my services to hide their own dirty laundry. Hypocrites. Amelia's voice whispered in my mind. I hadn't realized it back then, but she'd been talking about the Circle, and she'd thought they had sent me to kill her.

"And since the estate is private land, *my* land, there's little risk of anyone realizing what we do out here." Alanna shrugged. "Of course, every once in a while, some stupid trespassing hikers will stumble across some bones and call the police, but the Circle has connections everywhere, and those sorts of annoyances are easily taken care of. Most of the time, the cops are able to convince the hikers that they've stumbled across the bones of some wild animal."

"And if someone doesn't agree with the cops' assessment?"

She shrugged again. "Then there are other excuses that can be used."

Like the cops claiming that someone had been mauled to

death by a bear, like they'd done with Taylor Samson, the college boy Amelia had murdered.

I glanced out the library windows. The exterior security lights were on, bathing the yard beyond in a soft golden glow, but the illumination didn't come close to reaching the woods in the distance. The moonlight and starlight frosted the evergreen trees, making their spiky tops look like tombstones resting on top of a dark, solid wall, about to be sucked down into the unending black hole of the forest, never to be seen again.

It truly was a graveyard in the sickest sense of the word.

"Of course, my mother's arrangement with the Circle came to an unfortunate end with her death," Alanna continued. "She'd already started grooming me to take over when you killed her."

"Aw, so sorry to derail your family's evil legacy," I drawled. "I just hate that for you."

At my taunt, her fingers tightened around her drink, and the glass shattered in her hand an instant later. I'd hit a nerve.

All around us, the giants shifted on their feet. Alanna's temper tantrum made them nervous, but she remained in her chair, although her eyes glittered with fury. She held out her hand, and Phelps pulled a white silk handkerchief out of his jacket pocket and passed it over to her. Alanna wiped the bits of glass and drops of champagne off her fingers, then tossed the cloth onto the table beside her.

Playtime was definitely over.

She snapped her fingers, and Phelps gestured for one of the giants to step forward. I hadn't noticed it before, but the man was holding two very familiar things: the blue books that had belonged to Mab.

The giant handed the two books to Alanna, bowed his

head, and stepped back. She put one book down on her lap, then held the other one up where I could see it.

"As you know, Mab Monroe was a full-fledged member of the Circle, and she came into possession of certain records of the group's activities," Alanna said. "Of course, Mab being Mab, she leveraged the records to secure her own position within the group."

Yeah, I could totally see Mab doing that. She might have ostensibly worked for the Circle, but the Fire elemental would have hated being under anyone's thumb, and she would have done everything in her power to ensure her own safety and wrest control away from Tucker and especially the mysterious Mason. So the records had been her leverage against them, at least until I'd killed her. Then they had disappeared into Mab's estate with the rest of her things.

Tucker and Mason must have thought that the book was gone for good and would never see the light of day again. It probably wouldn't have if Jonah McAllister hadn't tried to steal Mab's will from the Briartop vault. But that had set in motion a long chain of events, including the charity auction. Now, at the end, I had wound up here with Alanna.

And only one of us would get out of this alive.

"After Mab's death, the book seemingly vanished," Alanna continued, confirming my suspicions. "Until I came across it when I was cataloging items for the auction. The book was something of a legend within the Circle, and my mother mentioned it to me several times. She even thought about stealing it from Mab, but she never got the chance."

"So you took your discovery to the Circle, and they hired you to retrieve their little blue book of secrets. Let me guess. You get the book for them, and they give you the money to buy your family's estate. Oh, and you get to kill Mosley as an added bonus."

"I saw an opportunity to make a deal, so I took it. Seemed like more than a fair trade to me," Alanna said. "But of course, Stuart kept such a tight watch over things that I didn't get the chance to actually look inside the book, much less bury it with some dusty old volumes that no one would want. Then there was the fact that there were *two* books instead of just one, like my mother had told me. Of course, I was planning to buy both books during the auction, but it quickly became apparent that you and Lorelei Parker would not be denied those photos of your parents."

"And you didn't want to tip your hand by bidding on both books." Another thought occurred to me. "Plus, you saw Lorelei and Mallory with Mosley during the auction. You knew that hurting the Parkers would be just as good as hurting him."

"Of course. I figured that I would get your book first, then go after the one the Parkers had, since they were far less likely to realize its importance than you were." Alanna waggled the book in her hand at me. "This is the book that you had, Gin. The one that I ordered my men to retrieve on the road outside the botanical gardens. I thought it was the one I wanted, but it's blank."

She flipped through the book, showing off the blank pages, and then tossed it down onto the table between us. She grabbed the second book from her lap, lifted it, and showed it off to me as well.

"And this is the book that Lorelei Parker bought." Alanna flipped through the pages. "But as you can see, it's also blank."

She flipped through the pages again, much more slowly this time, giving me a chance to focus on them. She was right. They were all shockingly, mockingly blank. Page after page sped by, and none of them contained so much as a random doodle.

Surprise spiked through me. Blank? How could it be blank? I could see Mab maybe having one blank book as a decoy, but two seemed like overkill.

Alanna tossed the second book down on top of the table right next to the first one. "There were only two blue books with the auction items, so you obviously swapped out your book—the real book—for the fake one that you were carrying around tonight. After all, you would never risk giving me the actual ledger. Well, your little switcheroo game is over. What did you do with the real book, Gin? Where is it?"

More surprise spiked through me. This whole time, I'd thought Alanna had just brought me here to gloat before she killed me. But that wasn't it. At least, not entirely. She still needed the book so that the Circle would give her the money to buy the estate.

And she thought I had it.

I quickly dropped my gaze to the glass of champagne still in my hand so that Alanna wouldn't see my surprise. These two blue books were the only ones I knew about, and I didn't have any idea where the real ledger was, if it even existed at all.

As soon as she realized that, Alanna would start carving me up like a Thanksgiving turkey. Maybe it was my aching head, but the strangest thought popped into my mind. Despite her sick, monstrous appetite, she couldn't eat me all at once, and I wondered if she would make sandwiches with my leftovers the way I always did with the holiday turkey. I shuddered. I didn't want to know.

My brain churned, trying to figure out how to turn this to my advantage and get out of the library alive. I shifted in my seat, making a few bubbles drift up through the champagne glass still in my hand. The bubbles caught my attention, and an idea popped into my mind.

I might live through this yet—if I was very good and very, very lucky.

I lifted the glass to my lips and gulped down some champagne, as though I was suddenly nervous. The bubbles fizzled in my nose the way they always did, and this time, I did nothing to hold them back.

"Achoo!"

I let out a loud, violent sneeze. Alanna's lips curled with disgust, and she jerked back in her chair, as if I was going to infect her with some deadly disease just by sneezing on her. Please. She was a fucking *cannibal*. She'd willingly eaten a lot grosser things than my snot.

But my sneeze had the desired effect of putting a few more precious inches between us.

"Sorry," I said. "Champagne always makes me sneeze—"

Another sneeze rose up in my nose, and I turned to the side and let it out.

"Achoo!"

This time, the giants to my left stepped back, not wanting to be exposed to my germs any more than Alanna did. Their movements created a little bubble of space all the way around me. Now, to take advantage of it.

Alanna opened her mouth, probably to order me to tell her where the book was again, but I held up my champagne glass, cutting her off.

"Sorry!" I chirped. "So sorry! I feel one more coming on... A-a-achoo!"

Unlike the first two, my third sneeze was just for show, although I faked like it was stronger than the others put together, so strong that I fell off the edge of my chair and landed on the floor.

As I went down, I deliberately dashed my champagne flute against the table between Alanna and me, breaking the glass and curling my fingers around the jagged stem still in my hand. My trap was set, and now all I had to do was wait for someone to take the sneezing assassin slapstick bait.

"Get her up," Alanna said in a disgusted voice. "And make sure you take that glass stem away from her before she tries to stab you with it. Really, Gin. Fake sneezing all the way out of your seat so you could break that glass against the table. Could you *be* any more obvious? I thought you had more imagination than that."

Oh, I did have more imagination than that—a whole lot more—but she swallowed my act hook, line, and sinker, which was all that mattered.

One of the giants stepped forward, reached down, and wrested the glass stem out of my hand. He tossed it into the fireplace, then grabbed my arm and hauled me to my feet.

I grabbed hold of his tie, as though I was having trouble standing up on my own. He sighed and reached out with his other arm to steady me. Perfect.

I tightened my grip, used the tie to yank his head down, and rammed the fork still hidden in my other hand straight into his throat.

✲ 23 ✲

The giant screamed.

At least, he tried to. Hard to really scream with a fork stuck in your throat.

I twisted the utensil in even deeper. One of the tines must have hit an artery, because blood started gushing out of the wound. The giant gurgled and flailed at me, trying to get me to let go of the fork, so I obliged him.

My hand darted down between us, and I plucked the gun out of the holster on his belt. Then I shoved the giant away, sending him staggering back into the armchair that I'd been sitting in. He collapsed down onto the seat hard enough to make the whole thing flip over with him it in and crash to the floor.

I whirled around again, snapped up my stolen gun, and aimed it at Alanna.

Crack! Crack! Crack!

I fired over and over again, but she was quicker, and she threw herself out of her seat. I completely missed her, although puffs of fabric floated through the air like snowflakes from where I'd mortally wounded the armchair.

Alanna rolled across the floor and came up in a low crouch next to the couch. I raised my gun to fire at her again, but Phelps and the remaining giants lifted their weapons and unloaded on me instead.

Crack!

Crack! Crack!

Crack! Crack! Crack!

I reached for my Stone magic and hardened my skin half a second before the first bullet slammed into my chest. Thanks to my magic, it didn't really hurt me, but the impact still threw me back, and I stumbled over the giant I'd forked to death. But I went with gravity and the backward motion, rolling over the giant and the chair he'd upended.

I landed on the floor on the far side of the library and snapped up my gun again. Alanna had moved so that she was crouching behind the couch, so I didn't have a clear shot at her. I turned my attention to Phelps and the giants, who scrambled to take cover even as they fired at me again.

Crack! Crack! Crack!

Bullets zinged past me and thudded into the books on the shelves behind me, making bits of paper flutter through the air, along with the fabric from Alanna's bullet-ridden chair.

"You idiots!" she screamed. "Don't kill her! We need her alive!"

Phelps and the giants listened to their boss and quit shooting at me. So I unloaded on them instead.

Crack! Crack! Crack!

I wasn't as good a shot as Finn was, especially not under this kind of pressure, but I managed to hit one of the giants in the chest. He screamed and stumbled forward, smashing a table to splinters on his way down to the ground and giving me a clear shot at Phelps. If I couldn't get Alanna, I would settle for her right-hand man, so I took aim and pulled the trigger—

Click.

But I was out of ammo.

Phelps and the giants realized that I was empty, and they got to their feet and surged toward me. I snarled and threw my stolen gun at them. It didn't do any damage, but it made them flinch and hesitate for one precious second.

I used that second to turn and run out of the library.

I careened out of the room and into the hallway. My boots slipped on the slick floor, and I had to windmill my arms to keep from falling on my ass. Even as I fought to regain my balance, I reached for even more of my Stone magic, using it to harden my skin again, knowing what was about to happen next—

Crack!

Sure enough, a bullet blasted out of the library, but it only slammed into the back of my thigh instead of my skull. Phelps and the other men must be trying to just wing me now. Either that, or their aim was as lousy as mine. Thanks to my Stone magic, the projectile rattled away and *ping-ping-pinged* down the corridor. I finally got my balance back and started running, heading for the opposite end of the hallway.

Crack!
Crack! Crack!
Crack! Crack! Crack!

Bullets chased me down the corridor, slamming into the walls and floor. One of them even hit a chandelier over my head, shattering the crystals and showering white sparks everywhere. I ignored the chaos and kept running.

I sprinted out into the grand ballroom, my gaze darting left and right, searching for something that I could take cover behind. But Alanna had been telling the truth when she said that Mosley and his men had packed up everything and left. All the auction items, the red velvet ropes, even the table where I'd set out the barbecue lunch were gone, and the ballroom was now an empty, cavernous space, which made it easy for Phelps and his men to take aim at me again.

Crack! Crack! Crack!

More bullets chased me across the ballroom. I grunted as some of the projectiles punched into my arms and legs, making me stagger from side to side, but I kept sprinting forward the whole time. I couldn't afford to slow down, not even for an instant, not until I got out of the open.

"You idiots!" Alanna screamed again from somewhere behind me. "Stop shooting before you kill her!"

This time, her men finally listened to her, and no more bullets zinged in my direction. Still running full steam ahead, I risked a quick glance over my shoulder. Phelps and the giants were racing toward me as fast as they could, not caring about anything else other than catching me—

One of my boots slipped on the marble floor, then the other one, almost causing me to lose my balance. Once again, I had to windmill my arms to stay upright, but the awkward motions made an idea pop into my mind. The next time my boots slipped, I went with the motion, throwing myself down onto the ballroom floor like a kid hopping onto a winter sled for a wild ride.

Whee!

I slid all the way over to one of the doorways. The second I stopped moving, I swung my legs around so that I was facing my pursuers, slapped both my hands down onto the floor, and let loose with my magic.

Ice crystals exploded out of my palms and rushed over

the marble like a tidal wave spreading out in every direction. I pushed my magic out as fast and as far as it would go, coating the entire floor in a solid sheet of elemental Ice.

The giants chasing me only managed to take a few more steps before the Ice surged over to where they were in the middle of the ballroom. They hurried forward, and their feet flew out from under them. All the men hit the floor hard, including Phelps.

They groaned and yelled and tried to get up, but the Ice was too slick, and every time one of them made it to his feet, he fell right back down again and took the others with him. Their frantic antics reminded me of clowns at a circus.

Now that I'd bought myself a few seconds of breathing room, I got to my feet and looked across the ballroom.

Alanna was standing on the far side of the open space, right at the edge of my Ice field. She stared at her men in disgust as they all fell back down yet again. Then she focused on me.

The vampire brought her arm up and saluted me with her right hand. At first, I didn't understand what she was doing, other than being cocky. The motion made something gleam on her hand, and she slowly spread her fingers out wide and waggled them at me.

That's when I realized that she wanted me to see what was strapped to her hand: a metal framework glove tipped with silverstone claws.

The same glove her mother had used on me all those years ago.

The last time I'd seen that terrible contraption had been on the lakeshore after I'd killed Amelia, and I certainly wished that I wasn't looking at it again right now. But of course, Alanna would have kept it. Using that glove to carve up people probably made her feel close to her mother the way studying that photo of my parents had made me feel close to mine.

Alanna must have seen the horror on my face, because she grinned and tapped each one of her fingers against her thumb, making the metal claws *clank-clank-clank-clank* together, just like her mother had done. I couldn't help but shudder. I remembered that sound from my nightmares, and I knew exactly what Alanna was telling me.

That she was going to hunt me down, slice me to shreds, and snack on my bones. Like mother, like daughter.

I shuddered again, turned, and ran away from the ballroom as fast as I could.

Despite all the weddings, parties, and other events held here, the Eaton Estate hadn't changed much over the years. I sprinted past room after room, all of them frozen in time and filled with the finest furnishings imaginable. It would have made for a great private tour.

If I hadn't been running for my life.

Alanna and her men must have had more trouble with the Iced-over ballroom than I'd expected, because their shouts quickly faded away, soaked up by the silence that permeated the rest of the mansion. I ducked into what looked like a private office and stopped, sucking down breath after breath. I also released my grip on my Stone magic and let my skin revert back to its normal texture. I'd already used up a good chunk of my power, and I needed to save what was left for when I ran into Alanna and her men again.

But right now, I needed to let my friends know where I was. I crouched down and grabbed my phone from its hiding place in my sock. Silvio had an app that let him track my phone, and for once, I was hoping that he was already doing that, but I was still going to call so that he, Owen, and the others would know exactly where I was.

My heart sank at the sight of the bullet hole in the center of my phone. My Stone magic might have protected me, but my phone hadn't been so lucky, and it was as dead as dead could be. I cursed and tossed it aside. I'd just have to finish escaping on my own.

I had started to sprint out of the room when a gleam of gold caught my eye. I glanced over and realized that a landline telephone was sitting on a table inside the doorway. My heart lifted with fresh hope. No, the estate hadn't changed much, and I was hoping that extended to the phones as well. I snatched up the receiver and held my breath.

A faint *click* sounded, and a sweet, sweet dial tone buzzed in my ear. I let out a breath and started dialing Owen's number. But this was an old-fashioned rotary phone, more for decoration than anything else, and I had to stand there and wait for each number to *click-click-click* all the way around. While I waited, I opened the table drawer and rifled through the items inside. Most of it was junk, except for a silver letter opener. I palmed that and shoved the drawer shut with my hip.

With each passing second, I knew that Alanna and her men were searching the mansion and getting closer to me, but I kept dialing, and finally—*finally*—the last number hit home.

He answered on the first ring. "Gin?"

"Owen!" I hissed. "I'm at the Eaton Estate."

"Gin!" he yelled. "I can barely hear you! Where are you?"

"I'm at the Eaton Estate. Alanna's here, along with several men—"

A shadow moved out of the corner of my eye, and I jerked back just in time to keep Alanna from raking her claws down my face.

The telephone wasn't so lucky, though. Her talons sliced neatly through the cord, leaving me holding a dead receiver. I snarled, threw it aside, and whirled around to face her. I was still holding the letter opener, and I snapped it up into a fighting position. It wasn't as sharp and balanced as one of my knives, but it would have to do.

But instead of attacking me, Alanna waggled her claws at me again. "What's the matter, Gin?" she purred. "Don't you like my shiny nails? I'm sure you remember them. After all, my mother was going to rip you to pieces with them. I'm so happy that I'm finally getting to finish what she started."

She paused a moment. "Actually, that's not quite true. Mama was going to kill you quickly. She always liked to tear into our dinner the second it was down on the ground. But me? I like to take my time. Really, fully, truly *enjoy* every single piece of my meal, blood, bones, steak, and all."

My heart clenched at the sadistic hunger rasping in her voice and gleaming in her eyes, but I forced myself to ignore her vicious, disturbing words.

"What about that precious book of Circle secrets?" I asked. "If you kill me, you'll never find it."

Alanna bared her fangs at me. "I'm not letting you get away again. Fuck Tucker and Mason and their book. I don't need them or their money. I can take back my estate myself. After I kill you and Stuart, no one will be stupid enough to stand in my way."

She was probably right about that, but I wasn't going to boost her ego and tell her so.

Alanna swiped out at me with her gloved right hand. I managed to jump back and twist most of my body out of the way, but I wasn't holding on to my Stone magic, so my skin was vulnerable. Her claws sliced across my left forearm, tearing through my shirt and breaking the skin underneath. I hissed with pain and glanced down. The wounds weren't all that deep, but they burned like a dozen little bees had just stung their way across my arm.

Even worse, the vampire lifted her claws to her lips and licked the blood—my blood—off the razor-sharp blades. A tiny spark of magic glimmered in her eyes as she absorbed my elemental power. "Mmm. Tasty. Elemental blood has always been my favorite. Yours tastes like…fresh, cold snow with a bit of granite mixed in."

My lips curled up in disgust at her wine-snob critique of my blood. I darted forward, trying to take her by surprise, but Alanna glided out of the way. So I whirled around and attacked her again.

Back and forth, we battled through the office, with her swiping out at me with her claws and me doing the same thing with my letter opener.

Alanna must have had a fresh hit of blood recently, because she was all strong, sleek grace. And she was *fast*. Not as insanely, unnaturally fast as Tucker, but she was close, and she was much, much quicker than I was. She kept attacking, slowly wearing me down, playing with me like a cat with a mouse.

I *hated* being the fucking mouse.

But the worst part was those damn claws. She wasn't even trying to kill me with them. Not yet. No, Alanna was taking great delight in simply cutting me. Shallow slices, mostly. Just enough to break my skin and make me bleed. She hadn't dug deep into my muscles and tendons yet. She didn't have to. If she opened up enough wounds, I'd eventually pass out from the blood loss, and then she could do whatever she wanted to me. Either way, it was death by a thousand cuts—and then some.

Oh, I could have used my Stone power to protect my skin or even shot a spray of Ice daggers out of my hand, although Alanna was fast enough to avoid that sort of attack. But I was running low on magic, and I needed to save what was left in my body, as well as the reserves in my spider rune ring and pendant, to do something spectacular, something that would kill her once and for all.

Too bad I had no idea what that spectacular thing was yet.

So I went on the offensive, swinging, swinging, swinging, and I landed several solid blows, driving my fist into her stomach and kidneys, as well as cracking her square in the jaw. I even managed to slash my letter opener across her shoulder and make her bleed for a change. But Alanna was still stronger and faster than me, and my blows didn't do much more than annoy her, judging from the low, angry snarls that rumbled out of her lips.

She swiped out at me with her claws again, but I was tired of being her personal scratching post, so I went on the defensive. I upended chairs and overturned tables, trying to keep the furniture between us until I could catch my breath and think of some way to kill her.

"What's the matter? Feeling a little slow, Gin? Have you started seeing double yet?" Alanna sneered. "Because I can tell you right now that you won't be getting some magical second wind."

She waggled her talons at me, then clicked each one of

her fingers against her thumb, making those strange, sickening noises ring out again. *Clack-clack-clack-clack.*

I hadn't really noticed it before, but she was right. I did feel slow—too slow and too tired, even with the blood loss—and my vision was starting to blur a little around the edges like she said. My gaze focused on her talons, and I realized what was happening.

"You bitch," I growled. "You coated your claws with some sort of poison."

Alanna smiled. "Guilty as charged. Don't worry, though. It's not poison, just a mild sedative. It's a little trick my mother taught me. It makes my prey so much easier to butcher. It cuts down on the screaming too."

So she was going to butcher and eat me while I was still somewhat alive. I'd thought that was her plan, but my stomach still roiled in disgust at hearing it out loud. The Eaton Estate wasn't just her mother's or the Circle's graveyard. It was hers too.

"Alanna!" Phelps called out, his voice echoing through the mansion. "We're coming to you!"

Footsteps sounded in the distance, growing closer and louder with every passing second. Once the men reached the office, I would be surrounded. I wondered if Phelps and the giants would stand around and watch while Alanna carved me up and snacked on my bones. My stomach roiled again. I didn't really want to know the answer to that. Either way, I had to get out of here before they arrived, or I was dead.

Alanna sidled toward me, thinking that I was distracted, and I let her creep closer and closer. Then, at the last second, just before her claws would have raked across my arm again, I sidestepped her, grabbed a crystal lamp off one of the tables that I hadn't overturned, and smashed it straight into her face.

I lashed out with my Ice magic, driving shards of my power into the lamp to do as much damage to it—and her—as possible. The crystal shattered on impact and spewed all over Alanna's face, neck, and arms, slicing her up the same way she had sliced me. She screamed and screamed, and blood welled up out of the dozens of cuts that now marred her perfect skin.

I raised my hand to shoot out a spray of Ice daggers, hoping that I could get lucky, punch one through her eye, and finally kill her, but she blindly lashed out with her claws, driving me back and spoiling my aim. The daggers slammed into the wall behind her, sticking there like cold, frozen arrows.

"Alanna!" Phelps yelled again. "Alanna!"

The footsteps grew quicker and louder. The men were almost here, and I was out of time. I threw my letter opener at Alanna, but it wasn't as balanced as one of my knives, and it only lodged in her shoulder, instead of in her heart the way I wanted it to. She screamed again, staggered away from me, and yanked the letter opener out of her shoulder.

"Alanna!" Phelps yelled.

She kept backing away from me, blindly following the sound of his voice like they were playing some weird version of Marco Polo. I growled in frustration and started across the office to attack her again, but I was too late.

Phelps rushed into the doorway, snapped up his gun, and fired at me.

Crack! Crack! Crack!

I ducked down and headed in the opposite direction, toward a set of glass double doors at the back of the room. The bullets *thunk-thunk-thunked* into the furniture all around me, sending up sprays of expensive wood, fabric, and stuffing. Phelps's gun clicked empty, and he cursed and stopped to reload.

"Get her! Now!" Alanna screamed, still blindly staggering around, trying to swipe the blood and crystal shards off her face.

Phelps slammed a new magazine into his gun. Behind him, more men appeared and started plowing through all the furniture I'd overturned.

Time to leave.

I reached one of the glass doors, shoved it open, and staggered out into the cold, snowy night.

✶ 24 ✶

I stumbled out of the office and onto the stone terrace without getting shot in the back.

The only problem was that there was no place for me to go.

The whole allure of the Eaton Estate was its picturesque—and remote—location. Sure, a road ran by the front of the estate, but I was standing on the back side of the mansion, more than a mile away from the road.

I also wasn't close to the mansion's spacious garage, much less the driveway or other parking areas out front, so I had zero chance of getting to a car before Alanna, Phelps, and the giants caught up to me. Even if by some miracle I did manage to find and hot-wire a car, they could always shoot out my tires or get into another vehicle, chase me down, and run me off the road. Then I'd probably be more injured than I already was, along with being trapped in a crumpled car.

I could head for the woods at the edge of the lawn and try to disappear into the trees, but given my many injuries and the obvious blood trail I was leaving behind, my enemies would easily be able to track me no matter how deep into the woods I went or how well I managed to hide myself. No doubt Alanna would enjoy hunting me. It would give her another sick little thrill to stalk me like I was a deer before she killed me.

Shouts and yells sounded from inside the mansion, getting louder and louder. I had maybe a minute, two tops, before Alanna and her men regrouped, reloaded their weapons, and charged outside after me—

Something moved in the shadows at the edge of the woods.

My head snapped in that direction, and my gaze locked onto the trees—the same ones that Fletcher had hidden in so long ago.

For a moment, that same eerie sense of déjà vu that I'd had at the auction swept over me, and I half expected to see the old man step out of the shadows with his rifle propped on his shoulder.

Longing filled me, clutching my heart like an icy fist, but I pushed the emotion aside. My eyes were just playing tricks on me. Fletcher was dead, and I would be too if I didn't think of some way to escape.

So I hurried across the terrace, not really sure where I was going, other than away from the mansion. All the while, I looked back and forth over the landscape, but the scene didn't change. Stone wall in front of me, grassy yard beyond that, woods off to my right, lake down the hill to my left.

A bit of hope flared to life in my chest, and I lurched over to the wall and stared down at the lake below. Maybe I didn't need a car. Maybe I could hop into a boat and zoom across the lake. That would at least put some distance between me and Alanna and her men.

But my hope quickly sputtered out, as though it were a match being doused by the cold, steady breeze blowing off the lake. No boats were tied to the wooden dock, not so much as a rickety old canoe. Of course not. Given how frigid the January weather had been, no one in their right mind would take a boat out onto the water. Even if a boat had been tied up at the dock, I couldn't have used it anyway, given the solid sheet of elemental Ice that covered the surface of the lake—

The Ice.

My gaze locked onto the Ice, which started at the sandy shore and stretched out like a smooth, shiny silver mirror as far as I could see. The elementals Alanna had hired to create the skating rink for the charity auction had done a bang-up job of it. They must have sunk a significant amount of magic into their creation for the Ice to still be intact more than twenty-four hours later.

I was going to find out just how much magic they had used.

A plan formed in my mind. Admittedly, it wasn't a very *good* plan, since it would pretty much ensure my own death, right along with Alanna's, but I'd rather go down fighting than be butchered and butterflied for her dinner.

"There she is! Get her! Get her!" Alanna's voice rang out.

I glanced back over my shoulder and saw her standing at the office doors, waving her talon-tipped hand in the air, telling Phelps and the rest of the men to hurry. In less than a minute, they would all storm outside and chase after me.

I didn't have a choice. I sprinted across the terrace and raced down the steps, heading down the hill toward the frozen lake.

Less than a minute later, I reached the bottom of the steps. Even though I'd been going down instead of up, I was still out of breath. That sedative from Alanna's claws was working its way through my system, slowing me down, so I bit my own tongue, concentrating on that sharp sting of pain instead of the lethargy that was slowly creeping up on me.

"She went down to the lake!"

"Follow her!"

"Hurry!"

Shouts echoed across the terrace above me, and footsteps smacked against the stone. Alanna and her men would be down here any second, and I had to put my plan into action before they caught up with me. So I sprinted forward, my boots crunching through the cold, frozen sand—

My boot caught on a piece of driftwood half-buried in the sand, but I wrenched it free and kept going, still heading toward the frozen lake. The driftwood made me think of the last time I'd been here. Amelia Eaton had died in this very spot.

I just hoped that I wasn't about to meet the same fate.

I plowed through the sand as fast as I could. Up ahead, the moon and stars, combined with the illumination from the mansion's exterior lights, brightened the landscape enough that I could make out the grooves in the Ice where the skaters had performed their fancy leaps, spins, loops, and twirls during the charity auction. I reached the edge of the sand, drew in a breath, stepped forward—

And almost fell flat on my ass as my boots slipped treacherously on the slick, frozen surface.

For the third time tonight, I windmilled my arms and managed to catch myself, but the sharp, jarring motions made more pain spiral out from my many cuts, bumps, and bruises. I felt like there were dozens of ice-skaters sliding every which way over my body, cutting into my skin with their sharp blades, going a little bit deeper with every pass they made. I swallowed down a snarl, pushed the pain away, and kept moving forward.

Whether it was natural or made by an elemental, ice was still ice, and this sheet was smoother and slicker than most, given its exposure to the elements, especially the wind that continually gusted through the valley. I half walked, half skidded along the elemental Ice, moving as fast as I dared. I kept my gaze glued to the surface, searching for any cracks or other telltale signs that the Ice wasn't thick enough to hold my weight. So far, I didn't see any—

Suddenly, several spotlights flared to life, bathing the shore, the lake, and me in their bright, dazzling glow. I threw my hand up against the glare and looked back over my shoulder. Alanna, Phelps, and the rest of the men had reached the bottom of the steps and turned on the lights.

Alanna stabbed her finger at me. "There she is! Get on the Ice and surround her! Now!"

So she didn't want her men to kill me. She just wanted them to run me to ground for her. She thought that I was trapped out here on the lake, and she wanted her men to drag me back to shore so she could finish cutting me to pieces with her claws.

A grim grin lifted my lips, and I bared my teeth at her. Let the bitch come—let them *all* come. Because I had a special surprise in mind for every single one of these bastards.

Since it didn't seem like Alanna or her men were going to shoot me in the back, I faced forward and kept plodding along, squinting at the Ice below my boots the whole time.

Walk, slide, walk, slide, walk, slide...

I got into a rhythm, and I was able to shuffle across the frozen surface at a steady clip, almost as if I had snowshoes strapped to my feet instead of my regular boots.

But Phelps and the other men were in much better, uninjured shape than I was, and the steady *scrape-scrape-scrape-scrape* of their boots on the Ice rang out behind me. I kept moving forward, doing my weird shuffle-skate, trying to get as far away from shore as possible, despite the sedative in my system, which was still slowing me down—

Click.

The distinctive sound of a hammer being thumbed back on a gun made me stop, especially since it was much closer than I expected. They'd already caught up with me, but that was okay. My plan would still work.

I hoped.

"Stop!" Phelps's voice boomed out. "Or I'll shoot you where you stand!"

I was exhausted, both from my injuries and from the sedative still coursing through my body. Despite the cold wind gusting over the lake, sweat ran down my face and neck, and blood dripped in steady trails from all the cuts on my arms, legs, back, and chest. Several drops ran down my fingers and plopped onto the frozen lake, staining the silvery surface a shocking scarlet.

I stared down at my own bloodstains, still searching for any telltale cracks in the Ice. I didn't see any, but I did spot something else—the dark surface of the water, shimmering below the Ice. This would have to do.

I held my hands out to my sides and slowly turned around. "All right," I said. "All right. You got me. Don't shoot."

Phelps was standing about thirty feet away from me, along with the giants. All of them had their guns drawn, and they slowly advanced on me, their boots *tap-tap-tapping* against the Ice like fingers drumming on a table. I held my breath, wondering if any of them would realize what I was really up to, but they kept coming at that same steady pace.

Phelps and his men moved forward until they were about five feet away, then spread out, forming a rough semicircle in front of me.

Clack-clack-clack-clack.

The familiar sound of Alanna tapping her talons together rang out, and the men slowly parted so that she could move forward. Thanks to the spotlights, the entire lake was illuminated, giving me a clear look at the damage I'd done to her.

Alanna was still wearing her fancy metal glove on her right hand, but she didn't look nearly as smug as she had before. She couldn't, given what a mess I'd made of her pretty face.

That crystal lamp I'd shattered had sliced up her skin every which way, and dozens of thin red lines crisscrossed her face from top to bottom. Blood oozed out of the wounds, most of which still had crystal shards embedded in them. The pieces puckered her skin, making her look like some victim from a slasher movie.

Oh, she was a victim, all right, *my* victim. She just didn't realize it yet. I had helped create this monster, and tonight I was going to end her.

Alanna looked me over the same way. Her green gaze took in my bruised, sweaty face and the blood dripping out of the cuts she'd opened up in my skin. But she wasn't quite sold that I was hers for the taking. Not yet. She was too smart for that, and she glanced around, staring out across the lake and into the forest beyond. But nothing stirred in the cold, quiet night, and I didn't see any movement in the shadows like I had before up on the terrace.

Finally, after about a minute, Alanna turned back to me, apparently satisfied that she had me right where she wanted me. She didn't realize that it was the other way around.

"Where did you think you were going?" she sneered. "Even if you made it across the lake, there's nothing out there but trees and more trees."

"I know," I said. "And I'm actually quite happy about that. There's no one around to hear you scream. I imagine that all of you will make quite a lot of noise as you die. Especially you, Alanna. You seem like a screamer to me."

She let out a low, ugly laugh. "The only one who's going to be screaming is you, Gin, darling."

I tilted my head to the side and stared at her. "You know what? Your mother said something similar to me right before she died. Do you remember how I killed her? Surely, you do. After all, you were there."

It was a cruel, heartless thing to say, but I said it anyway. Because, like it or not, my will to survive was stronger than anything, even my own guilt and shame.

Alanna's jaw clenched, but she didn't respond. Beside her, Phelps frowned, wondering what I was talking about, and the giants shifted on their feet, glancing around, nervous and wary, on the lookout for some kind of trap. But they were already snared in my web, and I was going to fucking kill them with it.

"Your mother was a strong vampire, a great fighter, just like you are," I said. "I got in a situation where I couldn't beat her. Not in a fair fight, anyway. But do you know what the good thing about being an assassin is? I don't have to fight fair."

Alanna's eyes narrowed, wondering what I was getting at. For once, someone else's curiosity was going to be the death of her.

"I realized that I couldn't beat your mama in a conventional fight, so I decided to be unconventional. I tackled her and shoved her ass into the lake. And then I drowned her." I grinned. "Just like I'm going to drown all of you right now."

I dropped my hands to my sides, so that my palms were facing down toward the surface of the lake, and reached for my Ice magic. Alanna's eyes widened as she spotted the bright, silvery flare of my power on my palms. In an instant, she realized what I was going to do with my remaining scraps of magic—and exactly how I was going to kill her, Phelps, and the giants.

"Shoot her!" she screamed. "Shoot her now—"

Too late.

I drew my hands up and reached for even more of my power. Then I snapped my hands right back down again and let loose with my magic, blasting the frozen lake with every single bit of Ice magic I had left.

✦ 25 ✦

I could do a lot of tricks with my Ice magic.

Create lockpicks, send sprays of daggers shooting out at people, even freeze someone's skin with a touch of my hand. But in the end, my power boiled down to two simple things.

I could create Ice—and I could destroy it.

And that's exactly what I did right now.

I sent wave after wave of my Ice magic shooting down at the surface of the lake. Dozens and dozens of daggers spewed out of my hands, driving themselves like spikes into the sheet of elemental Ice that we were all standing on.

One crack appeared in the Ice. Then two, then three, then half a dozen, all of them accompanied by loud, sickening *pop-pop-pops!*

The cracks zigzagged out farther and farther, like spiders drawing crazy, elaborate webs across the surface of the Ice. And of course, all that cold, cold lake water rushed in, filling in and widening those tiny, tiny gaps, until—

CRACK!

The Ice split apart with a thunderous roar.

I'd angled my hands forward, trying to shatter the Ice under Alanna's feet and take her out with that first strike. But she was quick, and she grabbed Phelps and shoved him forward. He yelped in surprise, and his feet flew out from under him. His head cracked against the edge of the Ice, and he disappeared into the water below. He didn't resurface.

The giants turned to run back toward the shore. They might have actually made it if they had spread out and taken their time picking their way back across the Ice. But they clustered together in a tight group, and their combined, heavy weight only made things worse. I whipped my hands up and sent another blast of magic in their direction.

CRACK!

Another gaping hole opened up below their feet, and the lake swallowed them as well.

A few of the giants bobbed up to the surface like oversize apples, and they screamed and flailed around, trying to pull themselves back up onto what was left of the Ice. Again, they might have made it if they had spread out and taken their time. But in their panic, all they did was crack away more and more chunks of Ice. One after another, they slipped below the surface of the water. Some of them actually resurfaced a second time, but the lake quickly swallowed them up for good.

Alanna stared at me with wide eyes, but she knew better than to try to move. At least, not as fast as the giants had. Instead, she slowly slid one of her feet back, then the other one, holding her breath the whole time. Her stiletto boots scraped across the Ice, but they didn't crack it and send her plunging down into the water.

I snapped my hands up and blasted the Ice again, but I was completely out of magic, including the reserves stored in my spider rune ring and pendant. Only a few pieces chipped off the edge of the chasm that I'd opened up between us.

Alanna grinned at me and kept backing up, one slow, smooth step at a time.

I couldn't let her get away, but I couldn't get to her either. A stream of water separated us now, one that was steadily growing wider and wider as the water kept eating away at the edges of the Ice. I could still leap over the stream, but my weight landing on the other side would definitely shatter the Ice, and I'd doom myself along with Alanna. Something she realized, judging from her smug smirk.

But I couldn't stay on my side of the chasm either. This far from shore, the elemental Ice was already weak and thin, and it was only a matter of time before the water washed it away, including the piece I was standing on.

Besides, I hadn't gone through all of this just to watch her skate away now. If Alanna escaped, she would go after Mosley again, and Mallory and Lorelei and whoever else got in her way. But I could prevent that. I could keep my friends safe. All I had to do was stop her right here and now.

In the end, it was an easy decision to make—because the Spider always caught her prey.

"Fuck it," I snarled.

I drew in a breath, then ran forward across the Ice, even though I could hear it *crack-crack-cracking* away under my feet with every step I took.

"What are you doing?" Alanna screamed. "Are you crazy? You'll kill us both! Stop! Stop!"

She quickened her pace and started backsliding away from the edge of the Ice as fast as she could, but it was too late. I reached the end of my section and leaped forward, all the way across the water and onto her side. I crashed right into Alanna, and my boots hit the Ice a second later with a loud, sickening *thud*.

The Ice shattered under my feet, and we both plunged into the dark water below.

I'd expected the lake to be, well, as cold as ice. But I wasn't prepared for how absolutely, unrelentingly, breathtakingly *frigid* it was.

The water closed over me like an icy fist, squeezing all the warmth out of my body. In an instant, I was soaked to the bone and bitterly, bitterly cold—colder than I had ever been before in my entire life. As if that wasn't bad enough, the water forced its way into my eyes, down my throat, and, worst of all, up my nose. But I kicked my arms and legs, and I broke through to the surface, coughing, sputtering, and sneezing. And I'd thought champagne always made me sneeze. This was a thousand times worse, like I was spewing tiny icicles out of my nose—

Claws raked down my cheek. I hissed and jerked my head back, blinking through the blood and water that covered my face. Suddenly, Alanna was there, bobbing along in the lake right beside me.

"You bitch!" she screamed. "You fucking bitch!"

She lashed out with her glove again, and I barely managed to turn my head in time to avoid her clawing out my left eye. Even in the water, Alanna was far more graceful than I was, and she kept swiping at me. All I could do was hold my arm up and block the worst of her blows, even though she was shredding my skin with her metal glove.

Alanna was killing me but not nearly as quickly as the cold water was.

My body grew number with every breath I took, and the wind whistling over the lake only made it that much worse. I had to kill Alanna, or I was dead, and I had to get out of the water and get warmed up, or I was dead. So I decided to focus on the first problem: the vampire bitch in front of me.

The next time Alanna took a swing at me, I wrapped my left hand around that metal glove, yanked her toward me, and slammed my right fist into her face, breaking her nose. Her head snapped back, and she screamed, although her face slipped below the surface, and the water drowned out her cries.

I grabbed hold of her hair and wrenched her to the side so that I could hook my arm around her neck. She screamed and lashed out at me again. I hissed as her claws punched into my scalp, but I tightened my grip and shoved her head below the water.

And this time, I kept it there.

Alanna thrashed and thrashed like a fish caught on a hook, twisting and turning and trying everything she could think of to make me let go of her. But I was an animal now too, and the only thing that mattered was my survival. Her claws raked into my head and face time and time again, opening up more bloody cuts. Snarls spewed out of my throat, but I didn't loosen my grip—not for one second.

Slowly, Alanna's struggles grew weaker and weaker, and her hands started slapping at the water instead of at me. Then, after another minute, even those motions slowed and finally stopped altogether. But I didn't loosen my grip. Not until her claws fell away from my body completely.

That's when I knew that she was finally dead.

I let go of her, and Alanna's body turned over and floated back up to the surface. Her eyes looked like two pieces of green glass in her face, while her mouth was frozen open in one final, waterlogged scream. Her gaze focused on the moon and the stars above, but she wasn't seeing it anymore.

Alanna Eaton was dead.

Like mother, like daughter, after all.

✳ 26 ✳

nother gust of wind whistled over the lake, slapping me in the face and reminding me how bitterly cold I was.

Alanna was dead, and I was going to be too, if I didn't find some way to get out of the water and get warmed up.

I swam over and tried to pull myself up and onto the Ice, but it was too slick and smooth, and I couldn't get a good grip on it with my numb, frozen hands. I needed something sharp, something with a point that I could dig into the Ice, something like—

Claws.

My head snapped around.

Alanna's body was still floating on the surface of the water, although the current had carried her several feet away from me. I ground my teeth to keep them from chattering and swam over to her.

My hands and fingers felt dead, like they weren't even attached to my arms anymore, but I forced them to move and bend and flex. It took me several precious seconds, but I managed to strip off Alanna's metal glove and shove my right hand inside the contraption. I didn't get it exactly into place, but it was good enough for what I had in mind.

I spun around so that I was facing the edge of the Ice again. Then I drew in a deep breath, kicked my legs hard, and propelled myself up and out of the water as far as I could.

I didn't get very far up on the Ice, given the water weighing down my boots and clothes and trying to suck me back down, but I did manage to stab the claws on the end of Alanna's glove into the Ice.

Tink.

I flopped my other arm up and onto the Ice, bracing myself with my elbow. Then I kicked my legs again, even as I stretched and reached out with Alanna's glove, digging those claws into the Ice a couple of inches higher than they had been before.

I repeated those motions over and over again, digging and pulling with my talon-tipped fingers, bracing with my elbow and kicking with my legs, trying to escape the sucking grasp of the water and squirm higher and higher onto the Ice.

Dig, pull, brace, kick. Dig, pull, brace, kick. Dig, pull, brace, kick...

The rest of the world fell away except for those four simple motions. I didn't know how long it took, but eventually, I managed to kick up out of the water one final time, drag myself forward, and roll over onto my back on the surface of the Ice.

For a moment, I lay there panting from the exertion, even though I could barely feel my own body anymore. My fingers, hands, arms, legs, feet, toes. Every single part of my body felt cold, heavy, and numb. Another gust of wind sliced across the lake, making my teeth chatter and adding to my wet, frigid misery. But it also reminded me that I wasn't done yet, that I had to keep moving, that I had to get back inside the mansion where it was warm, or I would wind up as dead and frozen as Alanna and all the men in the lake.

So I forced myself to roll over, get up on my hands and knees, and start crawling across the Ice.

I'd done a better job of cracking the Ice than I'd thought, and the entire surface creaked and groaned under my weight. If the Ice broke under me, I wouldn't be able to pull myself out of the water a second time. I had to get off it as fast as possible, but I was so cold at this point that I couldn't do much more than worm forward a few inches at a time. So I lifted my head, focused my gaze on the sandy shore in the distance, and kept crawling.

Inch by inch, foot by foot, I crept toward the shore, watching it slowly get closer and closer. Even when I reached the sand, I still wouldn't be safe, since I had no idea how I was going to climb the stone steps back up to the terrace, much less actually make it all the way back inside the mansion. But first, I had to get there, so I kept going, slithering across the Ice like the slowest snake ever.

The rest of the world fell away again, and all I was aware of was peeling my hands and knees off the ice, shoving them forward, and dragging my body after them.

Peel, shove, drag. Peel, shove, drag. Peel, shove drag...

My hands reached out, but instead of more slick Ice, they touched something gritty. I blinked and realized that I'd done it. I'd actually made it back to shore. I slid off the Ice and crawled into the sand, which was as cold as everything else. I raised my head and focused on the stone steps looming up in front of me. So close yet so agonizingly far away.

I wasn't going to make it.

By this point, I was so cold that my teeth weren't even chattering anymore. All my strength was gone, and my body felt absolutely dead. Even my brain seemed dull and slow, as though it was slowly being frozen, like the rest of me already was. Before I knew what was happening, I had pitched forward and landed face-first in the sand. The grit worked its way into my eyes, up my nose, and down my throat, choking me, but I didn't even have the energy to lift my head up out of it. I'd escaped the water only to drown in the sand. If I'd had the strength, I would have laughed at the bitter irony of it, but a tidal wave of blackness swept over me, and I couldn't push it back anymore...

A pair of hands grabbed my shoulders and rolled me over. At least, I thought they did. My body was so cold that I couldn't quite tell, but my face wasn't smushed into the sand anymore, and I could breathe much easier. A slight improvement, but I'd take what I could get.

"You've really done it this time, haven't you?" a familiar voice muttered, although I couldn't have said who it was or why the sound made my heart clench with dread.

Whoever that voice belonged to lifted my arms up over my head and started dragging me along the shore. All I could do was stare down at my boots, watching them leave deep grooves in the sand. For some reason, the sight amused me, and I tried to laugh, but all I really did was croak up sand...

The next thing I felt was...warmth.

Welcome, welcome warmth. My eyes cracked open, and I realized that I was lying on the floor in front of the library fireplace. Red-hot flames danced and crackled behind the grate, much higher than they had the last time I'd been in here fighting Alanna and her men. Someone had stoked the fire.

And that same someone was in here with me right now.

Fingers moved over my body, peeling off my frozen boots and socks and unzipping my silverstone vest and tossing it aside. But my entire body was still so cold and numb that I couldn't even turn my head to look and see who was helping me...

After that, I had the sensation of being lifted up and then set back down. Something deliciously warm and soothing flowed around me, all the way up to my chin, as though I were taking a luxurious bubble bath. The warm wetness soaked through my cold clothes, bringing some much-needed heat back to my body. I thought I let out a soft, happy sigh, although I couldn't tell what was real and what wasn't right now...

"Drink this," a voice commanded.

Someone pressed a mug to my lips, and I obediently swallowed, too out of it to try to resist. Something hot scalded my mouth, and I tried to pull away, but that person shoved the mug up to my lips again and kept it there, making me swallow the liquid inside until it was all gone. Eventually, I realized that it was hot chocolate with a ton of sugar in it, as if someone was force-feeding me dessert. The drink was far too sweet, although Silvio would have loved it. The thought made me giggle, and I drifted off again...

The next time I woke up, it was for good. It took me several seconds to blink the world into focus. When I finally did, I realized that I was still in the library, and I hadn't been imagining that warm, soothing bubble bath after all.

I was lying in a claw-foot tub that was filled to the brim. I was still wearing my black turtleneck and cargo pants, only now they were soaked through with warm water instead of the frigid lake water. A few feet away, the flames still crackled merrily in the fireplace, and the tub was turned so that I could bask in as much of the fire's heat as possible.

I frowned. Okay, I wasn't that out of it. At least, not anymore. This tub had not been here before. Someone had dragged it—and me—into the library. But who? Sophia was the only person I could think of who had that kind of strength. My friends must have found and rescued me after all.

A soft creak sounded, and I glanced to my right, finally realizing that someone was in the room with me, but it wasn't Sophia, Silvio, Owen, or any of my other friends.

Hugh Tucker was sitting in a chair by the fireplace.

✶ 27 ✶

I jerked back in surprise, making water slosh up and over the rim of the tub. The drops spattered against the floor like a sheet of rain. My whole body tensed, but I forced myself to sit still. Tucker could easily kill me before I managed to get to my feet, much less actually climb out of the tub.

I didn't think he was going to do that, though. If he'd wanted me dead, he could have left me lying down by the lake. I probably would have frozen to death by now. But instead, he'd brought me up to the mansion, shoved me in warm water, and force-fed me hot chocolate.

He'd saved me. But why?

"You're awake," Tucker murmured. "It's about time."

He raised a delicate china cup to his lips and took a sip of the steaming liquid inside. Probably more hot chocolate, since that's what he'd made me drink. I could still feel the warmth of it swirling around in my stomach.

I let out a breath and made myself relax, as though I wasn't concerned by the fact that my nemesis was sitting less than ten feet away. But down in the water, below his line of sight, my hands clenched into tight fists. I didn't know what game he was playing, but I was going to be ready for any move he made.

I slowly sat up a little higher in the tub, my gaze sweeping around, searching for a weapon that I could use against the vampire if he changed his mind and attacked me after all. An empty mug sat within reach on a tall table that stood next to my tub. It would have to do.

But that wasn't the only thing resting on the table. So was Alanna's metal glove.

Tucker must have stripped it off my hand after he'd brought me in here. I didn't know why he'd just left it sitting there, but I focused on him again. I didn't want to look at the horrible contraption right now.

The vampire slurped down the rest of his hot chocolate and set his cup on a low table by his elbow. I hadn't noticed them before, but my knives were lined up on the table. Tucker must have found where Alanna had stashed them. But he ignored the blades and picked up two other familiar items from the wooden surface: the blue books that had belonged to Mab Monroe.

Tucker flipped through one book, staring at the blank pages, then set it back down on the table and did the same thing with the other volume.

"All this fuss for nothing." He shook his head and laid the second book down on top of the first. "I told the others that Mab was bluffing. That she never had anything on us. But, as usual, no one listened to me. Still, I suppose it was better to be safe than sorry."

Tucker started tapping his index finger on top of the books. I looked at the two volumes a moment, then focused on him again. Those books couldn't kill me, but he still could.

"So you brought me in here and warmed me up," I said. "Let me guess. You were that weird shadow that I spotted in the woods earlier. Watching from a safe distance to see who would win, Alanna or me. That's certainly your style. Well, I hope you enjoyed the show."

He shrugged, not even bothering to deny it. "I told you on the road outside the botanical gardens that I had a personal interest in this matter."

My eyes narrowed. "What interest? Alanna taking your spot as the Circle's enforcer? As your buddy Mason's right-hand hit man? Why would you care about that? From what I've seen, from what you've told me, it wasn't exactly your choice to work for the Circle, and you grew tired of it long ago."

"True—very, very true." His face hardened, and his finger stilled on top of the books. "But it's *my* job, and no one is going to take it away from me. Especially not some spoiled little princess who wasn't nearly as tough and clever as she thought she was."

"So you just stood by and let me kill your competition? Even though it only hurts Mason and your precious Circle in the end?" I snorted. "That's some seriously twisted logic you've got going on there, Tuck."

He shrugged again. "My logic is my own business. I don't expect you to understand."

Well, he was right about that. The more I learned about Hugh Tucker, the less I understood about his motivations. First he tried to get me to work for the Circle. Then, when I refused, he tried to kill me multiple times. Now he had saved me from freezing to death—but only *after* I'd eliminated his enemy.

It seemed like the vampire's kindness was based solely on how it benefited him. I wondered what he expected to get from tonight's generosity. Part of me didn't want to know, but I couldn't help asking the many questions that crowded into my brain.

"If you wanted Alanna dead for however she slighted or threatened you, then why didn't you just kill her yourself?" I asked. "You wouldn't have even had to leave the woods to do it. You could have easily shot her the second she stepped outside the mansion, just like you killed her men on the road earlier today."

"Certainly." A mocking smile curved his lips, and his black eyes glittered with amusement. "But it was so much more fun to watch you run around and do it instead."

White-hot rage erupted like a volcano in my chest, and I didn't even think about what I was doing. I lifted my hand out of the water, snatched the empty mug off the tall table, and tossed it straight at his smug face, even though it was my only weapon.

But Tucker was faster than my speeding mug. His hand snapped up, and he easily caught the mug and set it back down on the low table next to him. The spider rune scars in my palms itched, and I burned to grab the mug and hurl it at him again, but the result would be the same. As much as it pained me, even I knew when to quit.

Tucker arched an eyebrow, waiting to see if I would continue my temper tantrum, but when he realized that I was done—for now—he leaned back in his chair again.

"Although I have to admit that I thought you had lost your mind when you went out onto the lake. I didn't realize you were going to try to kill yourself, along with Alanna and her men. I'm starting to think that you have a death wish, Gin."

He shook his head, as though the thought greatly pained him. If only I could have reached one of my knives, I would have shown the bastard what *real* pain felt like.

"And why didn't you leave me out there to freeze to death?" I asked. "That certainly would have solved a lot of problems for you."

He sighed and stared into the crackling flames, instead of looking at me. "Call me a sentimental fool."

That volcano of rage exploded in my chest again. "My hair is brown, not blond. I don't look like Eira this time," I snapped.

A couple of weeks ago, Bruce Porter, the Dollmaker serial killer, had dyed my hair blond in an attempt to turn me into his dream woman and fulfill his sick, twisted fantasy. Tucker had seemed haunted by how much the dye job made me resemble my mother, the woman he still loved despite all the years she'd been dead. He hadn't helped me defeat Porter, not really, but he hadn't killed me when he'd had the chance either.

Tucker finally looked at me, his black gaze sweeping over my features. I didn't have my mother's blond hair and blue eyes, not like Bria did, but I did have her cheekbones, nose, and lips.

"You will always look like Eira to me, little Genevieve. Whether you like it or not." His face creased into another smile, although this one was more sad than mocking. "Besides, it's been rather fun watching you bulldoze your way through the Circle ranks. You, my dear, are certainly not boring."

"You ain't seen nothing yet."

He arched his eyebrow a little higher at the venom in my voice. "No, I imagine not. But keep this in mind: neither have you. Not when it comes to the *real* power within the Circle. Damian Rivera and Alanna Eaton were pretenders, wannabes who thought their money and gruesome appetites made them stronger than they truly were. A lesson that you would do well to remember."

His warning delivered, Tucker got to his feet. For the first time, I noticed that he was wearing the same sort of anonymous black clothes as mine, along with a thick black parka. I wondered how long he'd been lurking in the woods, waiting and watching. It must have been quite a while, given how warmly he was dressed.

But the worst part was that I couldn't stop him from leaving. Not when I was still thawing out, I didn't have a knife in my hand, and my magic was severely depleted. And especially not when he'd gone to so much trouble to save me, whatever his motives might have been.

Like it or not, Hugh Tucker would live to see another day—and so would I.

"I've already called your friends. They should be here within the half hour," he said. "You should be happy to know that your loyal assistant, Mr. Sanchez, threatened certain parts of my masculinity if I laid so much as a finger on you. So did Mr. Grayson."

"Silvio's a good friend that way. And Owen loves me."

"Yes, yes, Grayson does love you," Tucker murmured. "You should treasure that, Genevieve. You don't know how lucky you are."

He stared into the fire again, but I could tell that he was looking at something far beyond the flickering flames. I wondered what memory of my mother was playing in his mind. Part of me didn't want to know.

Tucker shook his head, coming back to himself. Then he reached over and grabbed the two blue books from the low table, although he left my knives behind.

He saw my sudden interest and gave me another amused

smile. "Did you really think I was just going to leave these here?"

"I had my hopes," I muttered. "Although why take them if they're just filled with blank pages?"

He shrugged. "For proof, of course. That this unfortunate incident is finally settled once and for all. I told Mason that Alanna wasn't up to the task of recovering the books, but he didn't believe me. So I think a firm, visual reminder is in order."

"So you're going to rub it in his face how wrong he was?" I shook my head. "That seems like a dangerous thing to do, if Mason is really as powerful as you say he is."

Tucker's lips drew back, revealing his fangs. "I can handle Mason. I've been doing it for a long time now. Although your concern for my welfare is quite touching."

I snorted. The motion made more water splash over the side of the tub. "Not concern. I'd just like to know where to find your body after he finally kills you."

"Going to drive a stake in my heart and burn me to ashes to make sure that I'm really dead?"

"Something like that."

"You say the sweetest things."

Tucker slid the two books inside his black parka and zipped the whole thing up. Then he started slowly backing away from me, never taking his black gaze off my gray one. "Think about what I said about the real power of the Circle. Because next time, it just might be the death of you, Genevieve."

He gave me a mocking salute with his hand, then turned and left the library.

✢ 28 ✢

I stayed where I was in the tub, listening, but the soft sound of Tucker's footsteps quickly faded away. Two minutes later, I heard an engine roar to life somewhere outside the mansion and then a car driving away. The vampire was gone, and I knew that he wouldn't be back.

Not tonight, anyway.

The water in the tub was still pleasantly warm, and the chill of the frigid lake hadn't quite left my bones yet, so I stayed where I was, staring into the fire and thinking about everything that had happened over the past few days. Eventually, I leaned back in the tub, rested my head on the edge, and looked up at the painting on the wall.

Most people would have found the scene of the lake, the woods, and the mansion to be quite lovely, but the sight made me shudder and slide a little deeper down into the tub, as if the warm water would protect me from my memories of almost dying here twice now. My head tilted back, my gaze climbed higher, and I found myself focusing on the security cameras that Mosley had strung up to keep watch over the auction items.

My head tilted back a little more, and my gaze darted from one camera to the next. *Hmm.* A thought popped into my mind, one that was far more tantalizing than the warm water, and I sat up and heaved myself to my feet. Even though I was barefoot and dripping wet, I climbed out of the tub, left the library, and went to the office where Alanna and I had fought.

The large antique desk in the back of the room was just about the only piece of furniture that hadn't been overturned during our vicious struggle. I picked my way through the debris, went around the desk, and sat down in the leather chair. I had started to open the center drawer when my gaze fell on a photo on the corner of the desk, one of Amelia and Alanna.

Just like the painting in the library, the sight of the photo made me shudder, since both women had nearly killed me. But I was a glutton for punishment, so I grabbed the picture and took a closer look at it.

The two of them were smiling and standing by the stone wall out on the terrace, staring down at the lake below. Alanna looked to be around fifteen in the picture, which meant that it had probably been taken shortly before I killed Amelia.

Both of them were dressed in the exact same green sundress, with their hair braided the same way and the exact same shades of makeup on their faces, right down to their red lips. They looked more like twins than mother and daughter. I supposed that in a way, they had been twins, especially when it came to their evil appetites.

Still, I couldn't help but wonder if Alanna might have turned out differently if her mother hadn't worked for the Circle and hadn't raised her daughter to be a cannibal like she was. But most of all, I wondered what might have happened to Alanna if I hadn't killed her mother right in front of her.

Maybe Alanna would have found a way to move past her mother's death. Maybe she would have left Ashland and never looked back. Maybe she wouldn't have targeted Mosley. Maybe she wouldn't have been consumed by vengeance the same way I was.

Maybe I wouldn't have had to kill her tonight.

That familiar mix of guilt and shame churned in my stomach. I still felt responsible for the pain I'd inflicted on Alanna when she was a girl, and I could sit here all night and wonder how things might have turned out differently. But Alanna was dead, along with her mother. There was no bringing either one of them back, and I was going to have to live with the consequences of my actions the way I always did.

Still, I wondered if Mab Monroe had ever felt this way. If she ever thought about how many people had suffered because of her actions, if she ever felt any guilt or shame or regret for any of the horrible things she'd done, if she ever thought about how deeply she had hurt me and my family. Probably not. As far as I knew, the Fire elemental had never been much for reflection.

But I was chock full of it, and I couldn't help but admit that I had once again followed in Mab's footsteps by eliminating a dangerous enemy. And I couldn't help but wonder what other terrible things I would do before my war with the Circle was finished, one way or another. I'd never wanted to be Mab, but tonight I felt more like the Fire elemental than I felt like myself.

At what point did fighting against monsters turn you into one yourself? At what point did the venom in your veins drown out everything else? I didn't know, but I had the sickening sensation that I was going to find out before this was all said and done.

I stared at the picture of Alanna and Amelia a moment longer, then set it back in its original spot on the corner of the desk. I didn't need to look at it anymore.

Their ghosts would haunt me all on their own.

I grabbed a pen and a notepad from the desk, then left the office. I roamed around the mansion, moving from room to room, drawing a crude map, and marking where the security cameras were. I even opened one of the doors and stuck my head out onto the terrace to check the cameras out there, although the cold wind quickly chased me back inside.

Finn hadn't been exaggerating when he told me that Mosley had covered every single inch of the mansion with cameras, and I was going to use the dwarf's thoroughness to my advantage. I stared down at all the little Xs on my notepad, and my face split into a wide grin.

Tucker was wrong. This thing wasn't over yet. Not by a long shot.

It was just getting started.

When I finished with my map, I went back to the library to dry out by the fire and wait for my friends to arrive.

A few minutes later, loud voices rang out through the mansion.

"Gin! Gin! Where are you?"

"Here!" I yelled back. "In the library!"

Footsteps pounded in this direction, and my friends appeared in the doorway and raced into the library, skidding to a stop in front of me. Owen, Finn, Bria, Silvio,

Lorelei. They were all armed, and so was the final person with them, Mosley.

I got to my feet and studied the dwarf, but Jo-Jo must have healed him, because his face and body were whole once more and free of Alanna's ugly claw marks. Mosley stared right back at me. When he realized that I was okay, he let out a soft sigh, and some of the tension drained out of his body.

"Gin!" Bria cried out, stepping forward and swooping me up into a tight hug. "You're alive!"

I laughed and hugged her back. "Of course I'm alive. I'm fine, guys. Really."

One by one, I hugged the others, including Mosley, who hung on to me far longer than I expected. I started to pull back, but he hugged me again, squeezing my ribs tight. I winced and patted his back, telling him that I was truly okay, and he finally let me go. He cleared his throat and turned away, but not before I saw him wipe a tear out of the corner of his eye. His concern touched me.

Finn stared at Tucker's chair by the fireplace, which was where I'd been sitting when they burst into the library. His green gaze focused on the pen, the notepad, my knives, and the empty hot chocolate mugs on the low table next to the chair, then finally on the tub of water. He holstered his gun and slapped his hands on his hips in indignation.

"What is all of *this*?" he sniped. "We thought Tucker was in here torturing you. Killing you dead. Not letting you take a freaking bubble bath."

"Oh, that wasn't the only bath I took tonight."

I told them everything that had happened, including my drowning Alanna and her men in the lake and Tucker saving me from freezing to death.

Owen frowned. "Why do you think he saved you?"

I shook my head. "Honestly? I have no idea. There's no telling what goes on in that man's mind."

I didn't say anything about Tucker telling me how I would always remind him of my mother. No one else needed to hear that, and I wished that I hadn't heard it myself. It almost made him seem...*human*.

I didn't *want* Hugh Tucker to be human. No, I wanted—*needed*—him to be an unfeeling, uncaring monster, a horrible, twisted, evil *thing* that I could kill with no hesitation, no mercy, and especially no regrets.

But I wasn't sure that I could do that now, which bothered me more than I cared to admit.

Silvio placed his hand on my shoulder. "Well, I'm just glad that you're okay."

"How's Mallory?"

"She's fine," Lorelei said. "A little shaken up by everything that happened. She wanted to come with us, but I made her stay at Jo-Jo's house and rest."

I nodded. That was probably for the best, especially since our night was far from over.

I looked at Mosley, who was staring out over the mess in the library. "I was wondering if you could help me with something."

"Anything," he replied in a gruff tone.

I pointed up at the security cameras in the corners of the ceiling. "Are those still hooked up?"

"Yes. I turned them off earlier this afternoon after all the auction items had been shipped out, but they still work." Mosley's eyebrows drew together in confusion. "Why do you ask?"

"I want to be sure that I can see every square inch of the mansion, inside and out."

"Why?" Silvio asked. "You just told us that Alanna and her men are dead and Tucker is long gone. There's no one left here to spy on."

I grinned at my friends. "Not yet, but I'm betting that there will be."

✸ 29 ✸

"Why do your grand, elaborate plans always end up with me out in the middle of the woods, freezing my ass off?" Finn whined.

I rolled my eyes. "Now you sound like Phillip Kincaid. You're whining even worse than he did when the two of us staked out Jonah McAllister's mansion a while back."

"At least he got to do his stakeout in a van," my brother muttered. "Where there was always the option of turning on the engine and having a little blast of heat every once in a while. He wasn't stuck out here in the great outdoors like I am."

Finn yanked his black toboggan even farther down on his head and stuck his gloved hands under his armpits, as if he were about to freeze to death right this very second. He should go jump in the lake. Then he'd know what it *really* felt like to be cold.

"Oh, quit being such a crybaby," Owen rumbled. "You've only been here an hour. Gin and I are the ones who stayed out here all night."

Silvio pointedly cleared his throat.

"And Silvio," Owen amended.

Finn, Owen, Silvio, and I were sitting in a row of camping chairs inside the tree line at the Eaton Estate. We'd picked this spot so that we would have a clear view of the terrace on the back side of the mansion, as well as the lake in the valley below.

Owen, Silvio, and I were wearing our usual winter hats, coats, gloves, and scarves, but Finn had gone the extra step of wrapping himself up in a sleeping bag, like it was his own personal blankie.

I glanced over at Silvio. "Anything?"

He took off his gloves and hit some buttons on the laptop perched on his legs. Several images popped up on the screen, each one showing a different view in and around the mansion. He studied them for several seconds before shaking his head. "Nothing yet."

Last night, I had told my friends about Tucker taking the two blue books as proof that he'd recovered them and that the Circle's secrets were still safe. After Tucker had left the estate, he probably expected me to do the same and never return. Normally, that's exactly what I would have done, since Alanna and her men were dead. Besides, assassins never stuck around at the scenes of their crimes.

But it had occurred to me that Tucker might have called my friends to come get me because he wanted us to leave, because he was planning to come back to the estate himself at some point. If I was a Circle higher-up, if I was Mason, the leader, I would want to come to the estate myself and make sure that things were finally taken care of once and for all.

So I'd decided to stake out the place, with the help of Mosley's security system.

Mosley had turned the system back on last night, and Silvio had downloaded the necessary software to view and record the camera feeds on his laptop, which he'd had in his van since he never went anywhere without his electronics. The two of them, along with Finn, had stayed at the estate last night to set everything up, while Bria and Owen had driven me over to Jo-Jo's house so she could heal my wounds and make sure I wasn't suffering any lingering effects from my polar bear swim.

Once Jo-Jo had given me a clean bill of health, I'd gone home, showered, changed, gathered up some supplies, and come back out to the estate. Owen had helped me pitch a tent and set up my spy camp in the woods, and he'd insisted on staying out here with me, along with Silvio, but the night had passed quietly. Now here we were, at nine o'clock in the morning, waiting to see if Tucker, Mason, or some other Circle members might show up.

"I knew I should have gotten some of those chemical hand warmers from that box Jo-Jo had in the salon and put them in my boots," Finn muttered, stomping his feet. "I can't even feel my toes anymore."

I opened my mouth to snipe back at him, but my phone buzzed in my pocket. I pulled it out, stared at the name on the screen, and straightened up in my chair. The guys leaned forward, and I turned the phone around so they could see that Bria was calling me. They too snapped to attention.

Bria and Xavier were sitting in her sedan, which she'd parked in one of the paved lots on the front side of the estate next to the vehicles that Alanna and her men had driven last night. It had been Bria's idea to hide her car in plain sight with all the others.

I peeled off my glove and swiped my finger across the screen to answer her. "You got something?"

"Three cars just parked in the estate driveway," Bria

replied. "I'm looking at them through my binoculars right now. All black SUVs. Xavier's writing down the license plates so he can run them. Lots of giant bodyguards getting out of the vehicles. I see Tucker too."

My fingers tightened around the phone. "Is anyone else with them? A man who looks like he might be the leader?"

"I can't tell from this angle. Sorry, Gin."

"That's all right. I can see them for myself on the security cameras when they step inside the mansion. So sit tight. And if anyone spots you, you guys peel out of there."

"Got it."

I hung up with Bria and looked over at Silvio. "We finally have some action."

He nodded and hit some more buttons on his laptop, pulling up the security feeds from inside the mansion again. Finn and Owen pulled their chairs closer to his so they could see the images. I grabbed the binoculars that were hanging around my neck and peered through them at the mansion, but I didn't see anyone through the windows. So I lowered the binoculars, got up out of my chair, and stood behind Silvio, staring down at his laptop.

And then we waited.

One minute ticked by, then two, then three, and no one appeared on any of the security feeds.

"How long does it take to get out of a car and walk inside?" Finn muttered. "You would think they would hurry up already, as cold as it is."

Owen, Silvio, and I all shushed him. Finn grumbled something under his breath and pulled his sleeping bag a little higher up on his chest.

Another minute ticked by. Then two, then three.

Finally—*finally*—a giant stepped inside the mansion, and he wasn't the only one. A dozen men appeared on the security feeds, their guns out, roaming from room to room with swift, military precision, making sure that the mansion was empty. These men didn't just glance into the rooms and move on. They did a thorough search, checking behind the desks, peering under the beds, and even moving the curtains from side to side so they could be sure that no one was hiding behind the fabric.

Owen let out a low whistle. "That's an awful lot of muscle to bring with you just to search an empty house."

The four of us kept watching the security feeds. The giants moved through the mansion for ten more minutes before they were finally satisfied that it was empty. At that point, I thought Tucker and whoever was with him might finally come inside, but the giants weren't done searching yet.

One of the men opened a glass door on the back of the mansion, and they all streamed out onto the terrace, checking it like they had checked everything else. I palmed a knife, moved to the edge of the trees, and crouched down, watching them. I didn't think the giants would search the woods, but I was ready for them if they did.

Finn and Owen got to their feet and joined me, both holding guns. Silvio stayed seated, still watching the security feeds.

The giants spread out across the terrace. From there, they split up, with some of the men heading down the steps to the lake, while others scanned the lawn. But none of the men approached the trees where we were hidden, probably because no one in their right mind would be out in the woods on such a cold winter's day. Then again, I was very rarely in my right mind, according to Finn.

"Hey!" one of the giants called out. "I see a body in the lake!"

They all rushed down the steps to the water. The giants knew better than to step out onto the Ice, and a couple of them split off from the main group and disappeared. They returned several minutes later, carrying a large canoe.

"Where did they get that from?" Owen asked.

"There's a boat shed on the east side of the estate," Silvio whispered back. "I can see it on the security feeds."

We kept watching them. A couple of the giants cracked through the Ice at the shoreline so they could put the canoe in the water and paddle out to where the body was. I peered at them through my binoculars. One of them reached down and grabbed something…red.

It took me a moment to realize that it was Alanna's red hunting jacket. Of course, her body would be the one they would find.

I didn't know how she was still floating in the water after so long, but the giant fished out her body and dumped it in the bottom of the canoe. Then the two giants paddled back to shore, hauled Alanna's body up to the terrace, and set her down on the stone about a hundred feet away from where we were still hiding in the woods.

"Gin," Silvio whispered. "Tucker has finally stepped inside the mansion—and he's not alone."

I got up and crept over to him so that I could see the security feeds on his laptop. Tucker strode through the mansion, moving from room to room, along with another man. My heart started pounding. Could this be the mysterious Mason?

I bent forward, peering at the various feeds, trying to get a good look at his face, but the cameras looked down from their high vantage points, so all I could really tell about the mystery man was that he had dark hair.

Tucker led the other man into the library, where the tub

and the rest of the mess was still sitting, except for Alanna's glove, which I'd taken back to my house for safekeeping. Tucker gestured at various things, as though he was explaining everything that had happened last night. There was no sound, so I couldn't hear what he was saying, but I guessed that he was leaving out the part about him saving me from death by hypothermia. He wouldn't want his Circle buddy to realize that he'd gone soft by not letting me die.

The other man crossed his arms over his chest, and his head swiveled from side to side as he took in the destruction in the library.

"Come on," I whispered. "Forget about the library. Come outside. You know you want to. Come outside where I can see your face."

And for once—for once in my life—I actually got lucky.

The two men left the library and headed in this direction. I crept back over to the edge of the woods. A minute later, Tucker opened one of the doors and stepped outside, followed by the mystery man. The two of them strode out into the middle of the terrace and stopped, looking over at the giants who were still clustered around Alanna's body.

My heart pounded in my chest like a jackhammer. Hands shaking, I grabbed the binoculars from around my neck, raised them up to my eyes, and peered through them at the mystery man, getting my first good look at him.

And finally—*finally*—putting a face to the mysterious Mason.

He was a tall, handsome man with dark brown hair and light eyes. Even now, in the dead of winter, his skin had a tan, sun-kissed look, as though he spent a lot of time outdoors. I would put him somewhere in his mid-fifties, and he had the kind of high cheekbones, straight nose, and strong jaw that would let him continue to age well. A long black overcoat was draped over his broad shoulders, hiding most of his black suit underneath, and his black wing tips were polished to a high gloss.

I didn't know exactly what I had been expecting, but it wasn't this anonymous person. Despite the expensive clothes, he could have been any businessman in Ashland, and I wouldn't have given him a second look if I'd passed him on the street outside the Pork Pit.

This was Mason? This was the evil mastermind behind the Circle and my mother's murder? Really? This was *him*?

Disgust and more than a little disappointment filled me—until I realized that I could feel his magic.

Even though I was a hundred feet away from him, I could still tell that he was an elemental—a very, very powerful one. Even though he wasn't actively using his power, magic continuously rippled off him in cold, hard waves, like he was a pebble that had been thrown into the center of a pond, disturbing all the water around him. He shifted on his feet, and another blast of his power hit me.

No, not a pebble, more like a cement block.

I'd never felt so much raw magic before, not even when I'd battled Mab. This man…he was even *stronger* than she had been.

No wonder she'd been afraid of him. It felt like he had enough power to crush anyone who dared to stand against him with a mere wave of his hand.

Including me.

But the worst part was that his magic felt as familiar as my own power did. Unless I missed my guess, he was a Stone elemental, although I couldn't tell if he might be gifted in another area, like Ice or metal. Didn't much matter, given how much magic he already had. I shivered and had to fight the urge to wrap my arms around myself and turn away from him.

Finn holstered his gun and picked up a video camera from our supplies. He zoomed in with the lens and started filming the man, along with Tucker. Meanwhile, Silvio got up from his chair, grabbed a directional microphone, and crept up to the tree line with the rest of us.

"Do you think that's Mason?" Owen whispered.

"It has to be," I whispered back.

I kept staring at Mason through my binoculars. Dark brown hair, light eyes, handsome features, expensive clothes, tons of magic. Nothing about him had changed, but the longer I looked at him, the more familiar he seemed, like I had seen him somewhere before, sometime very recently.

I thought back to the charity auction two nights ago. Had he been at the estate for that? Hiding in plain sight with the other rich folks? Had I seen him across the terrace or sitting with everyone else in the ballroom, waiting to bid on the items?

No, I didn't think so. Mason was all about maintaining his anonymity, right down to his understated suit. He wouldn't have risked coming to an event that he knew I was likely to be attending, in case I somehow recognized him. That was why he had sent Tucker to the auction instead of attending himself.

Still, something about him bothered me, even more than his incredibly powerful magic, and for the third time in as many days, a strong sense of déjà vu swept over me. This should have been my moment of triumph, finally putting a face to the name that had haunted me for weeks now, but instead, I felt sick to my stomach.

"Is it just me, or does this guy look vaguely familiar?" Silvio whispered.

"It's not just you," I whispered back. "I know him from somewhere. I *know* I do."

Owen gave me a sympathetic look and squeezed my shoulder. "You'll figure it out, Gin."

I forced myself to smile and nod back at him. He was right. I would figure it out. But I also had the sinking feeling that it was only going to cause me more pain in the end.

Owen and I focused on the two men again, while Finn stopped his video recording long enough to snap off a few photos of them. He gave me a thumbs-up, telling me that he had a good, clear shot of Mason's face. Silvio turned on his directional microphone and pointed it at them, and we finally got some sound to go along with the view.

Mason and Tucker strode forward, their wing tips tapping against the terrace like low, steady drumbeats. The giants nodded their heads respectfully and stepped back so that the two men could examine Alanna's body.

"Well, you were right. Alanna wasn't up to the task after all. Disappointing but not surprising." Mason's voice was a rich, deep baritone with just a hint of a Southern drawl, the kind of smooth, seductive voice that you could listen to for hours on end, even if all he was doing was reading the phone book. And just like his face, the sound of it made more cold dread pool in the bottom of my stomach.

Because I'd heard his voice before.

I didn't know from when or where, but I *knew* Mason's voice, just like I knew his face. My heart clenched with worry, but I forced the emotion aside. All I could do right now was watch and pick up as many clues as possible.

I thought that Tucker might pipe up and snidely say *I*

told you so, but he didn't respond to the obvious opening. The vampire's face remained a blank, remote mask, but I could have sworn I saw a glimmer of satisfaction in his black eyes. Like he'd told me last night, he might not enjoy working for the Circle, but no one was going to take his place in it. Even I had to admire his twisted determination to hold on to his position and what little power and prestige he had within the group.

"Well, at least we recovered the books," Tucker said. "And finally determined that Mab was bluffing all along about having them."

Mason tilted his head to the side, studying the other man. "And you're sure that those were the only ledgers in Mab's possession?"

Ledgers? He made it sound like there were more than just the two empty ones that had belonged to Mab. How many books of Circle secrets were floating around Ashland? And how could I get my hands on one of them?

Tucker nodded. "I'm sure. Alanna gave me a list of the auction items, and I double-checked it myself. I also visually confirmed it by studying all the items during the auction itself."

So that was why he'd really come to the event, to make sure that Alanna was telling him the truth about there being two blue books.

Mason kept studying him, and Tucker stared right back. Neither man showed a flicker of emotion, but I could see and feel the tension between them. All around them, the giants carefully, quietly backed up a few more steps. Couldn't blame them for that.

"I wouldn't want to be in the middle of that macho sandwich," Finn muttered.

"You're not the only one," Owen whispered back.

Finally, Mason tipped his head at Tucker, almost as if to say *Good job*. The vampire nodded back at him, and the tension between them lessened. More than one of the giants exhaled in relief.

"What do you want to do about Alanna?" Tucker asked.

Mason gave a dismissive wave of his hand. The motion caused a silver signet ring to glint on his hand, although I couldn't make out what rune or initial might be engraved on it. "Throw her back into the lake, then call in an anonymous tip to the police. Let them come, investigate, and draw whatever conclusions they want about what happened. Most likely, they'll declare it an accidental drowning."

"There was nothing accidental about it," Tucker said. "There never is when Gin Blanco is involved."

Mason shrugged. "Either way, we didn't kill her, and there's nothing here that connects us to her."

Tucker nodded. "And what about Stuart Mosley? It was Alanna's idea to kidnap him to get the books in the first place. Do you want me to have him taken care of once and for all?"

Finn sucked in a worried breath. Yeah, me too. I'd thought that Mosley would be safe now that Alanna was dead.

Mason crossed his arms over his chest and tapped his right index finger against his left elbow, casually weighing the dwarf's fate. "No. Leave him be—for now. The only reason the ledgers were exposed in the first place was Alanna's foolish kidnapping ploy. If she had just left Mosley alone, no one would have been any the wiser about the ledgers, and you could have quietly bought them at the auction like you wanted to all along."

Tucker nodded again, and Finn and I both let out the collective breath we'd been holding.

"And what about Gin Blanco?" Tucker swept his hand out toward the water. "She could be out there in the lake too. Do you want the men to start searching for her?"

I frowned. Tucker knew good and well that I wasn't floating in the lake, since he was the one who'd saved me. But he didn't want Mason to realize that he'd been here last night, much less that he'd rescued me. Once again, he was playing both sides against the middle. A very dangerous game, especially with me on one side and Mason on the other. Then again, I had the feeling that Tucker wasn't on any side other than his own.

Mason stared out over the lake, his gaze even colder than the water. "It would be better if she were down in that lake, along with the rest of Alanna's men, but Blanco has an uncanny habit of surviving such things." He shrugged. "Besides, she doesn't have any of the ledgers. She doesn't have anything now."

My hands curled around my binoculars tightly enough to make the plastic creak in protest. I didn't need anything else now that I'd seen his face. I'd get his real name soon enough, and then I'd start plotting the best way to kill him.

Mason looked at Tucker again. "If Blanco is still alive, then I want you to keep tabs on her like you've been doing all along. I want to know exactly how much she knows about us and what her next move might be."

Tucker tipped his head, acknowledging the order. "Of course."

He turned away from Mason and gestured at Alanna's body. A couple of the giants stepped forward and picked her up, and Tucker went over and spoke to them. A few seconds later, he followed the men while they carried her body back down the terrace steps to the lake.

Mason stayed where he was, all alone on the terrace, like a king in a castle, watching his servants work down below. Once again, that eerie, sickening feeling of déjà vu swept over me. I knew this man. I was certain of it. I just couldn't remember from where or when at the moment.

It would come to me eventually, though.

The nightmares always did.

✲ 30 ✲

It took another half hour for Mason, Tucker, and the giants to finally clear out and leave the estate.

My friends and I stayed in the woods another half hour after that, just to make sure that they weren't going to double back. Then we packed up our gear and left, heading off to our regularly scheduled lives.

Now that we had seen Mason, we had to be more careful than ever before. I didn't want him or Tucker to realize that we finally had the advantage, so that meant going on with our daily routines as though everything was normal.

Luckily, Tucker and Mason had shown up at the estate early enough for me to make it back downtown and open up the Pork Pit on schedule. Silvio came with me, and he perched on his stool, already firing up his laptop again and going through the security camera footage, along with the photos and videos Finn had shot.

"I'll go ahead and send you a photo of Mason so you can study it and see where you might know him from," Silvio said.

My phone chimed a few seconds later with said photo.

"It will take me a few days to go through and identify the giants, but maybe I can trace one of them back to Mason himself." My assistant actually sounded happy about the mountain of work he was facing, and he started humming to himself as he clicked through image after image.

I left him to it and got busy with my own work. Now that I had seen Mason's face, now that we had a real chance of identifying him, I half expected Tucker and a dozen giants to storm into the restaurant to try to kill me. But nothing suspicious happened, and the lunch rush came and went like usual. I kept a lookout for anyone I thought might be working for Tucker and eating here just so they could spy on me, but the restaurant was so busy that it was hard for me to pick anyone out of the crowd.

But two familiar faces did show up around two o'clock: Mallory and Mosley.

The two dwarves stepped into the restaurant, hung their coats on the rack by the front door, and headed over to the counter. For some reason, Mosley was carrying a small white box tied with a royal-blue ribbon, like he'd brought me a present. I studied both him and Mallory, but they looked no worse for wear, despite the ordeal they'd been through last night.

I did notice one telling thing about the couple. Instead of her usual array of diamonds, Mallory sported only a single one on her finger. She caught me eyeing it and held out her left hand so I could get a better look at the ring. Even by Ashland standards, it was an impressive diamond, and I could hear each one of the lovely carats singing about its own sparkling beauty, along with Mallory's happiness.

"Stuey and I are engaged," she said in a proud voice.

Mosley smiled and laid his hand on top of hers. "We had been talking about it for a while, but after everything that's happened over the past few days, we thought there was no time like the present."

"Congratulations! I'm so happy for you!"

I stepped around the counter and hugged both of them. Silvio shook Mosley's hand and offered his congratulations as well.

Mallory beamed at me. "Thank you, Gin. We've just started planning things, but I wanted to ask you to be one of my bridesmaids. Bria, too."

Her request touched me, and I reached out and hugged her again. "I would be honored."

She hugged me back.

Mosley cleared his throat and looked around the restaurant for a moment. Then he put the white box with the blue ribbon down on the counter and pushed it over to me. "I wanted to bring you a gift, Gin. To thank you for everything you've done for me over the past few days."

I reached for the box to open it and see what was inside, but Mosley waved his hand, stopping me.

"Open it later," he said. "Tonight. When you're alone and can really…look at it."

The serious tone in his voice made me wonder what was inside the box that he didn't want anyone else to see, but I trusted his judgment, so I slid the box under the counter and out of sight.

"Okay. Thanks."

Mosley nodded at me, but a strange, almost pitying look filled his face, as if he'd just handed me a live grenade and was waiting for it to explode and blow me to pieces.

Mallory and Mosley sat down on the stools next to Silvio

and started chatting about their wedding plans, deliberately lightening the mood. I'd never been big on weddings, but I wholeheartedly joined in the conversation. I needed some lightness, some happiness, after everything that had happened.

The happy couple lingered over their lunch for more than an hour before leaving to meet with a wedding planner. I watched them go with a smile on my face. I had a feeling that theirs was going to be a romance and a wedding to remember.

The rest of the day passed quietly. I closed the restaurant a little after seven, grabbed Mosley's mysterious gift, and headed home for the night.

As much as I wanted to open the box right away, the chill from the lake still lingered in my bones. Or maybe that was just the uneasy feeling of realizing that I would be dead right now if not for Hugh Tucker. Either way, I went upstairs and took a long, hot shower. Then I put on my pajamas, along with a thick robe, and headed back downstairs.

I went into the den, sat down on the sofa, and grabbed Mosley's gift from the coffee table. I shook it, but it was so well packaged that I didn't have any idea what might be inside. So I undid the ribbon, popped the top off, and pushed aside the white tissue paper to reveal...a book.

But not just any book—one with a royal-blue cover and silver-foil-trimmed pages.

I was so surprised that I almost dropped the box and the book onto the floor, but I tightened my grip and managed to hang on to them. I set the box down, then grabbed the book out of it and started turning it over and over in my hands.

I examined it from all angles, but it was exactly the same as the two blue books that had been with Mab's things, the ones that Mason and Tucker had been so desperate to get their hands on. But where had Mosley gotten *this* book? According to Tucker, only two blue books had been part of the auction.

Then I remembered our dinner conversation at Underwood's the night this whole thing had started. Mosley had said that Fletcher had given him some book, one that Mosley had kept safe for all these years. He must have finally found the book buried in one of those boxes at his mansion.

I frowned. But where would Fletcher have gotten this book from? The answer came to me a moment later. Mab— he must have stolen it from Mab Monroe.

Fletcher must have figured out that Mab had the book and that she was using it as leverage against the Circle. So he'd decided to steal it from her. After all, it wasn't like Mab could tell anyone that she didn't have the book anymore. So the old man had swiped the book and given it to Mosley for safekeeping.

If my theory was right, then that meant this was the *real* book, the one with all those damning Circle secrets in it.

Hands trembling, I held my breath and opened the book, half expecting the pages to be blank…

But they *weren't.*

Rows of numbers, dates, times, places, and names filled the pages from top to bottom and front to back. I flipped through page after page, and each one had just as much information as the last. It was some sort of ledger just like Mason had said. But that wasn't the biggest shock. No, the biggest shock was that I recognized the elegant handwriting that flowed across the pages.

My mother had written this book.

I was so surprised that I almost dropped the book again,

but I managed to hang on to it, although I sagged back against the couch cushions. I slowly flipped through the pages, but they were all the same. Numbers, dates, times, places, and names, all in my mother's handwriting. I scanned a few pages, but they seemed to be written in code, so I couldn't make sense of them right away.

Emotion surged through me. I couldn't sit still, so I got up and started pacing back and forth through the den, clutching the book to my chest and trying to figure out what this meant.

I knew that my mother had been part of the Circle, although I'd never known exactly what she had done for the group. But this made it look like she'd been some sort of...bookkeeper for them. Not just of money but of other things too.

Like where some of the Circle's many bodies were buried.

If Eira had been the group's bookkeeper, then she would have had access to all sorts of damning information. Maybe she'd been getting ready to go public with the Circle's sins. Maybe that was why Mason had ordered Mab to murder her.

Mab had been all too happy to kill my mother, but she must have realized that the same thing could happen to her someday, so the Fire elemental had taken my mother's book. But when? The night that photo of her and my parents was taken? Or sometime later? Maybe Mab had even taken the book from Eira's office the night she killed my mother. No way to know for sure.

But no matter when she had gotten the book, Mab had used it to keep herself safe from Mason and the rest of the Circle, at least until Fletcher had come along sometime later and stolen it from her. That's when Mab must have gotten those other two blue books, just to keep up appearances that she still had the real one.

I didn't know if I was right about everything, but I was betting that I'd guessed the rough outlines of how everything had gone down.

I kept pacing back and forth, and my steps took me over to the fireplace mantel. I stopped and stared at my mother's snowflake rune pendant resting on top of the matching, framed drawing. Eira's snowflake was the symbol for icy calm, but I felt anything but calm right now.

"Were you planning to expose the Circle?" I whispered. "Is that why they killed you?"

But of course, my mother didn't answer me. She couldn't, thanks to Mason, Tucker, and Mab. I had started to turn away and continue my pacing when I felt a wave of magic. I froze and looked at the fireplace again.

That sapphire paperweight, the one that had been with Mab's things, glinted at me from the mantel. I reached out, picked it up, and hefted it in my hand. A second later, I realized why it was bothering me so much.

Because the magic emanating off the jewel felt *exactly* the same as the magic that had rippled off Mason at the Eaton Estate earlier today.

I frowned and curled my fingers around the sapphire, concentrating on the feel of the magic. Cold and hard like my own Stone power. Unless I was mistaken, Mason had coated this jewel with his magic and then given it to Mab as...what? A warning? A reminder of his power and how easily he could crush her with it?

More and more questions crowded into my mind, but I didn't have answers to any of them. Frustrated, I set the jewel back down on the mantel. This time, I did turn away from it, although my gaze landed on something else: the photo of my parents that was lying on the coffee table. I stared at my mother for a moment before my gaze moved over to my father's face—

Shock stabbed through my heart, as sharp as one of my silverstone knives.

The blue ledger slipped from my grasp and thumped to the floor, but I didn't care. I bolted over to the table, snatched up the photo, and held it up to the lights where I could really see it. My father looked the same as all the other times I'd stared at this photo in the past few days. Dark brown hair, gray eyes, handsome features, tall, strong body.

But my father also looked exactly like *Mason*.

The photo slipped from my fingers and sailed through the air before gliding to the floor, but I didn't care. This time, I lunged over to the couch and snatched my phone up off one of the cushions.

My heart was pounding, and my hands were shaking so badly that it took me a couple of tries to enter my password, pull up my email, and open the photo of Mason that Silvio had sent me. I grabbed the picture from the floor, sat down on the couch, and held it up next to my phone, comparing the two images, the two men.

Same dark brown hair, same light gray eyes, same handsome features. They even had the same tall, strong bodies.

Mason and my father could have been twins.

For a moment, I had the mad, crazy, insane thought that *Mason was my father*. But as soon as the thought occurred to me, I rejected it. Mason wasn't my father. He *couldn't* be.

My father's name was Tristan, and he had been dead for years. Besides, the man I had seen at the Eaton Estate was nothing like the kind, caring man I dimly remembered from my childhood, the man my mother had always told me about.

No, Mason wasn't my father. He just looked exactly like him. Eerily so.

Mason isn't my father… Mason isn't my father… Mason isn't my father…

I kept repeating the words to myself over and over again, but it still took me quite a while to slow my racing heart and get my thoughts under control.

When I was calm again, I leaned forward and studied the two photos even more closely. Tristan's and Mason's features remained the same as before, but I realized that they *weren't* the same man. My father had a small dimple in his right cheek that Mason didn't have, while Mason had a mole on his neck that my father didn't have.

But the two of them were most definitely related, probably brothers, given how much they looked alike.

All this time, I'd thought that my mother had been the one involved with the Circle. I hadn't even considered the idea that *my father* might have been a member too—or that he was related to the group's evil leader.

That *I* was related to Mason, the man who'd ordered my mother's murder.

I racked my brain, thinking back, trying to remember every single thing my mother had ever said about my father's family. But I couldn't recall anything. No awkward holiday visits, no phone calls from Grandma and Grandpa, no cousins coming by our house to play, nothing like that at all. As far as I knew, Tristan hadn't had any family.

But Mason was proof otherwise.

So I studied the photos yet again. If I had to guess, I would say that Mason was the older brother, given how young my father looked in that photo of him and my mother with Mab, but I had no way of knowing for sure.

I thought about calling Bria to see if she might remember something that I didn't, even though she'd just been a baby when our father died. Maybe Eira had said something to her that she hadn't said to me. I looked at the clock on the wall, but it was late, so I blew out a breath and put my phone back down on the table.

I'd let my sister sleep tonight. But I would call her first thing tomorrow morning and tell her what I'd found out. Bria deserved to hear it from me first before I told the rest of our friends. And I knew that it was going to rock her world just as soundly as it had mine.

All along, I had wondered what was so special about Mason that Fletcher hadn't given me a photo of him along with photos of the other Circle members. Well, now I knew. And just like I'd expected, it was only going to cause me more heartache in the end.

I'd always thought that I was the worst person in my family. The coldest, the cruelest, the most ruthless and heartless. But it seemed as though my entire family had venom in the veins, just like Amelia and Alanna Eaton, and I was beginning to think that I couldn't hold a candle to Uncle Mason.

Uncle Mason. I still couldn't quite believe it.

But the practical side of me took over, and I called up the photo of Mason on my phone again and put it on the coffee table right next to the picture of my father. Then I grabbed a pen and a notepad out of the drawer and started scribbling down every little thing that I could remember about my father and my mother and anything anyone had ever said about my father's family.

I didn't know what, if anything, I might remember, but one thing was for sure. It was time to dig into the old family tree and see what skeletons might be hanging from the branches. And when I figured out exactly who Mason was and what had happened to my parents, well, then I would cut the tree down and burn the bastard with the wood.

It was time for some family feuding—Spider-style.

✹ GIN BLANCO WILL RETURN ✹

About the Author

Jennifer Estep is a *New York Times*, *USA Today*, and international bestselling author, prowling the streets of her imagination in search of her next fantasy idea. She is the author of the following series:

The Elemental Assassin series: The books focus on Gin Blanco, an assassin codenamed the Spider who can control the elements of Ice and Stone. When she's not busy battling bad guys and righting wrongs, Gin runs a barbecue restaurant called the Pork Pit in the fictional Southern metropolis of Ashland. The city is also home to giants, dwarves, vampires, and elementals—Air, Fire, Ice, and Stone.

The Crown of Shards series: The books focus on Everleigh Blair, who is 17th in line for the throne of Bellona, a kingdom steeped in gladiator tradition. But when the unthinkable happens, Evie finds herself fighting for her life—both inside and outside the gladiator arena.

The Mythos Academy spinoff series: The books focus on Rory Forseti, a 17-year-old Spartan girl who attends the Colorado branch of Mythos Academy. Rory's parents were Reapers, which makes her the most hated girl at school. But with a new group of Reapers and mythological monsters on the rise, Rory is the only one who can save her academy.

The Mythos Academy original series: The books focus on Gwen Frost, a 17-year-old Gypsy girl who has the gift of psychometry, or the ability to know an object's history just by touching it. After a serious freak-out with her magic, Gwen is shipped off to Mythos Academy, a school for the descendants of ancient warriors like Spartans, Valkyries, Amazons, and more.

The Black Blade series: The books focus on Lila Merriweather, a 17-year-old thief who lives in Cloudburst Falls, West Virginia, a town dubbed "the most magical place in America." Lila does her best to stay off the grid and avoid the Families—or mobs—who control much of the town. But when she saves a member of the Sinclair Family during an attack, Lila finds herself caught in the middle of a brewing war between the Sinclairs and the Draconis, the two most powerful Families in town.

The Bigtime series: The books take place in Bigtime, New York, a city that's full of heroic superheroes, evil ubervillains, and other fun, zany, larger-than-life characters. Each book focuses on a different heroine as she navigates through the city's heroes and villains and their various battles.

For more information on Jennifer and her books, visit her website at www.JenniferEstep.com. You can also follow her on Facebook, Goodreads, and Twitter, and sign up for her newsletter on her website.

Happy reading, everyone! ☺

Other Books by Jennifer Estep

THE MYTHOS ACADEMY SPINOFF SERIES
FEATURING RORY FORSETI

Spartan Heart

THE MYTHOS ACADEMY SERIES
FEATURING GWEN FROST

Books

Touch of Frost
Kiss of Frost
Dark Frost
Crimson Frost
Midnight Frost
Killer Frost

E-novellas and short stories

First Frost
Halloween Frost
Spartan Frost